GL

THE CASSEROLE *Courtship*

Recipes for Romance in the Time of Contagion

by Elizabeth Guider

Foundations Book Publishing
4902 Lakeland Drive, #398, Flowood, MS 39232
www.FoundationsBooks.net

**The Casserole Courtship:
Recipes for Romance in
the Time of Contagion**
Elizabeth Guider

ISBN: 978-1-64583-098-6

Edited by: Steve Soderquist
Formatted by: Keri Ranger

In Memoriam

Walter Francis Collins

For always being there, and now — forever in my heart.

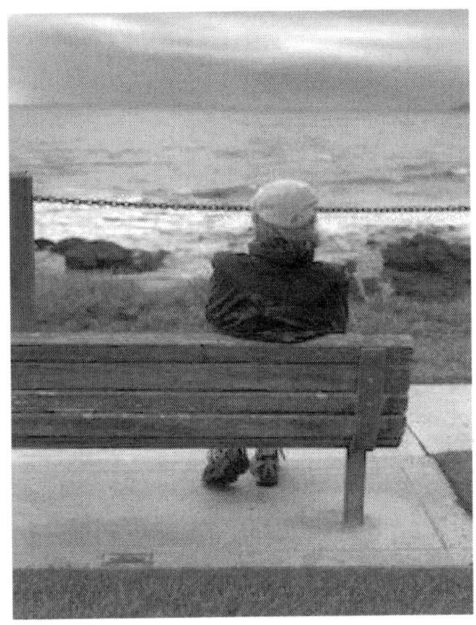

Walter at Shell Beach, CA in 2019

Table of Contents

The Casserole Courtship

CHAPTER ONE

Eliot

Que Sera, Sera

The Pyrex dishes posed a problem. One was round, one oblong, and one square. Eliot Etheridge had scrubbed them thoroughly before tackling a basic recipe for chicken Tetrazzini. His wife, so proper in her relations with others, would have frowned upon his returning a container empty.

He did not want to disappoint her, even now, seven months since…

After meticulously filling and covering each with aluminum foil, he was stumped, unable to recall which of the three ladies had brought over which dish. Exasperated, Eliot closed his eyes, trying to summons in which cookware had been Daphne's spicy jambalaya, in which Kathleen's beef bourguignon, and in which the vegetable medley that Serena had concocted.

None of the ladies had bothered with a label, each presumably persuaded that at this point—the summer solstice being the latest pretext for celebration with a casserole—she alone was ministering to his culinary cravings and, by extension, to his re-entry into the circle of life.

Or so Eliot had intuited. He had not disabused any of them of his state of mind, at least not so far. To be blunt about it, he wasn't certain what his state of mind actually was.

As a Harvard-trained lawyer, rational, unflappable, he assumed he'd be able to compartmentalize, placing the feelings that related to his spouse in a bottom drawer and by turning the key of the file cabinet, as it were, lock thoughts of her away.

He had failed.

Weeks after Silda's funeral, when all the condolences had been acknowledged and friends, neighbors and assorted relatives had dispersed, including his two adult children, Eleanor and Jared, he still trundled around in a fog. He walked through the rambling Sorenson home in Shell Beach, oblivious to the time of day, when to eat, when to take the dog out, when to sleep.

It had required several phone calls from his long-time assistant at Bryson & Tillotson to coax him back to Santa Barbara, stressing that there were clients to advise and issues to resolve that only he could handle. In-person. Caroline Morris's insistence was something of an exaggeration, but the repetitive force of it shook him enough that he put on a business suit and, as best he could, his game face.

The gestures of normality fooled no one.

"Unfortunately, Eliot's still floundering. We're going to allow him to set up shop from Shell Beach, if that's what he wants to do. You can drive up twice a week to check on him, Ms. Morris, update his calendar, connect his calls, get him back into things," he had overheard old Tillotson instruct Caroline.

Scurrying down the hall to his own office, he buried himself in documents related to a real estate dispute. He hated to be talked about as though he were coming apart.

That weekend in March of 2019 Eliot decided to rent out the house in Santa Barbara and retreat to his wife's family home eighty miles up the coast. From the upstairs bedroom windows, he could see the ocean and hear the waves break on the rocky beach. They had been wise to hold onto the place through the years, especially now that prices for the town's older homes had skyrocketed.

At first baffled by their father's decision, Jared and Eleanor eventually came round. "Sorenson House could be a refuge, and perhaps a new beginning," the one told the other.

Once relocated to Shell Beach, Eliot made efforts to busy himself, repainting the downstairs parlor and setting up a proper office, and not succumb to the desolation that overwhelmed him at inopportune moments.

In the late spring, he replanted the garden—bougainvillea and roses along the back fence, azaleas surrounding the gazebo—and sat outside to read through the law journals that had accumulated on his desk, and which Caroline in discrete batches would bring over.

Likewise, Eliot culled his social activities, eager to avoid people and places that brought back memories too closely tied to his marriage. In his meticulous way, he ticked the items off a checklist: renew annual membership in the Central Coast wine club; agree to substitute now and again at the bridge club, he having been the more enthusiastic attendee and better player. He allowed himself to be recruited to teach a seminar on legal ethics at UC-Santa Barbara, a gig, unbeknownst to him, that one of the firm's partners had recommended him for.

Encouraged though he was by various acquaintances, he could not, however, handle the *soirées* at the ballroom that he and Silda had graced. To do the foxtrot to *their* song — "Dancing in the Dark" was invariably on the playlist—so saddened him on the one occasion he had ventured to do so, he had to retreat to the foyer to regain his composure. Not wanting to be rude, he mumbled excuses when the flustered partner tried to entice him back to the floor: his feet ached, it was late, and he had an early morning consult.

Nor could he summons the requisite enthusiasm to attend the book club of which Silda was a leading light and which, to please her, he put in an appearance if she urged him deftly enough.

"How blessed I am to have a husband who both rhumbas and reads!" she had more than once mused aloud. Like most spouses, he was susceptible to flattery, even if he suspected that his wife was being half-facetious when she so importuned him.

On paper at least, Eliot designed his widowhood in reaction to the fact that he missed his wife more than he had bargained on. But he could not control everything.

Scenes from those final weeks of Silda's battle with pancreatic cancer would inadvertently obtrude, leaving him newly bereft or benumbed.

One instance in particular.

"That old Italian song has been flitting through my head. Doris Day sang it, remember?"

His wife had roused herself, humming the tune, one afternoon toward the end. He had nodded, if only to humor her. She persisted. "You have so much to live for, for both of us. So many lovely women in the world. You mustn't close yourself off," she had gone on, patting his arm with her paper-thin hand.

"Don't be ridiculous," he had snapped, his eyes filling up. "I'm married to you."

To get a hold of himself, he had turned to the window and the sea beyond. A winter storm was brewing. Dark clouds scudded across the sky; whitecaps dotted the waves. He closed the shutters and lit the lamp on the nightstand.

"Mariella should be along shortly to see to things," he said matter-of-factly, eyeing his Rolex. "I'll be headed out now. Got a deposition at 7:30 tomorrow but I should get back Friday afternoon. If the weather clears, we'll dine on the balcony."

"I should like that enormously," she had replied, her breath shallow.

The weather did improve but the chance to eat *al fresco* did not come. By the time Eliot returned for the weekend, Silda had slipped into semi-consciousness, murmuring names he didn't recognize, other than those of the children and their golden retriever, Keats. She passed away on a Sunday morning in January, wind rattling the shutters. She was sixty-two.

Since her death, Eliot had often thought of what she meant about not closing himself off. Many long-married men needed a nudge from their spouses to forge relationships, he had read or been told. He just didn't want to be pushed. Whatever will be, will be.

The Pyrex predicament had not resolved itself. He pulled open a drawer and rustled around for a magic marker to identify the three dishes: *Chicken Tetrazzini, July 2019, with thanks for your dish, and your thoughtfulness. Eliot*

It was Caroline, ever practical, who had pointed out the importance of a date on covered dishes in case the recipient did not wish to partake immediately. She had not pressed him as to how well he knew these women who cooked, or whether he planned to know them better. Rather, she advised him simply to scribble his first name on each note.

"I doubt anyone around here is expecting to receive more than one casserole from a man named Eliot," she had drily observed. "Your last name would be superfluous."

As usual, he followed his assistant's instructions. She could be relied on for discretion, never prying into his personal affairs, as he did not inquire after hers.

The thing was, he liked each of the three ladies who cooked and did not wish to offend any of them. Each was helping him navigate the rough waters of his widowhood; he was pleased to be diverted and had begun to be interested in them, in one way or another.

None of the lawyers at the firm had an inkling as to the reason the cloud over their colleague began to lift during the summer. Caroline, however, considered it part of her job to zero in on the ladies of the casseroles. One by one, they had entered her boss's life, each leaving a different calling card, as it were. Just doing her due diligence, she told herself.

Kathleen Calhoun Pavonine had presented herself at the visitation as an old acquaintance of the Sorensons, bringing along a dish of baked scallops, one of the few Eliot had savored that awful day. Efficient even in trying circumstances, Caroline had jotted down the names of all visitors: who brought flowers, who made charitable donations, and who came bearing platters of food or bottles of wine.

"I had the pleasure of running into your wife a few months ago," the lady of the scallops had murmured as she squeezed his hand in sympathy. "She was dining at the restaurant I now manage, the Lantana. After so many years, we recognized each other and planned to get together. A shame that it didn't happen."

Eliot had smiled politely, not registering what local restaurant this Ms. Pavonine was talking about but soothed by her poise. He would have continued the exchange, but other well-wishers had come up to offer their condolences.

Ms. Pavonine lingered in the parlor for only a few minutes to study the photos of Silda displayed on the sideboard.

"The one who brought the scallops, she makes a nice impression," Caroline had commented as she finished labeling and refrigerating the dishes that were left at the house that afternoon of the visitation.

Eliot was seated at the kitchen table going over paperwork from the funeral home. He looked up, not certain to whom his assistant was referring.

"That Ms. Pavonine," Caroline added, "apparently knew your wife as a child."

"Silda mumbled some strange names toward the end. But I don't remember a Kathleen being one of them."

"Not unusual that people from the past get dredged up, especially when..." Caroline shut the refrigerator but did not finish her thought. "Not to worry. Take all the time you need, Eliot, and call when you want me back up here. And please tell Jared and Eleanor goodbye for me. You should try to do something fun with them before they head back East."

Shortly before their return flight to New York City, Eliot did, in fact, take the children out for a proper meal, ending up in what Jared had googled to be one of the fancier locales in the Five Cities area, a place called the Lantana Grill.

This time it was Kathleen who recognized the three Etheridges dining out on the glassed-in balcony overlooking the ocean. The son had a scowl on his face, the daughter was scrolling through her phone, and their father looked disconsolate. She instructed the waiter to roll the dessert trolley over to their table, with compliments of the house.

As the three were leaving, she re-introduced herself, promising the children she'd be glad to check on their dad "now and again." And quickly going out on a limb, that she'd heard through the grapevine that he enjoyed opera. From time to time, tickets to performances in San Francisco were thrust upon her. Eliot had stammered his thanks and shook her hand perfunctorily.

Several weeks after the encounter at the restaurant, Kathleen had tracked down and rung the law firm in Santa Barbara, explaining to the lawyer's assistant that she happened to have last-minute tickets to *Tosca* for that upcoming weekend. She wondered if "Mr. Etheridge" might like to join her; they could fly up to San Francisco together.

The invitation was soon relayed, Caroline encouraging her boss to accept. "You love music. The lady seems pleasant enough. You might enjoy yourself."

Thus prodded, Eliot accepted.

He soon discovered that Kathleen Pavonine had a discrete circle of well-heeled acquaintances in the Bay Area, which she did not make a fuss about but into which she appeared happy to introduce him. That she was charming in company rubbed off on him, so much so that he gladly accepted another invitation to a gallery opening in the flower district followed by a dinner on Nob Hill. Once or twice, he took Ms. Pavonine's arm, helping her in or out of a cab or a dining chair, but so far that was the extent of their intimacy.

If she sometimes flashed her eyes at him, he did not take the hint, if it were one.

A bridge too far, he told himself.

As for Eliot's acquaintance with another of the casserole contingent, Serena Samuels, their first encounter took place thanks to the ever-sociable Keats. The Etheridges' retriever had kept Silda company in Shell Beach during her sojourns there before and then throughout her illness. In so doing, the canine and his mistress became a fixture along Ocean Boulevard.

After her death, Eliot found himself at first a resigned pet owner, though as the months passed, he began to enjoy the bracing salt air and the casual nods from other residents along the promenade. On a brilliant day in April, Keats all of a sudden lit out down the stretch toward a dog lollygagging in front of one of the newer mansions.

It took Eliot a couple of minutes to catch up and try to separate his charge from what looked to be a basset hound.

“They're already acquainted, though we haven’t seen Keats in a while,” a woman called out from her front porch. Startled, he looked up in the direction of the voice. She was wearing a floppy hat and reading a book. He inclined his head but remained on the sidewalk. Within a minute she closed her book, donned a pair of sunglasses and approached. By that time, and ignoring Eliot, the dogs were rolling around in the grass, nipping at each other's ears.

“Opposites attract, I guess. My name's Serena,” she volunteered, holding out her hand. Eliot took it, mumbled his name, and then squatted to re-attach the leash on Keats.

“A lovely lady walked him. I used to see her, along with another neighbor a few houses further up,” she offered, matter of fact. Eliot looked unconvinced. “Hard to forget a name like Keats. However, a strange name, hers. It escapes me,” she went on.

“That would have been my wife,” Eliot muttered, straightening up, blood having suffused his cheeks. “She passed away months ago. Silda was her name.”

“Oh, I'm so sorry,” Serena burbled, flustered. Regrouping, she asked, "Do you live around here now, or still?"

“My wife and I resided in Santa Barbara but her parents, the Sorensons, owned the old two-story two blocks up,” he explained, canting his head to indicate the top end of the promenade.

"Well, I find it enchanting here. Such a well-kept secret, this stretch of the coast—at least to us ex-Angelenos."

"Yes, I suppose," Eliot rejoined, not sure that he wanted to become familiar with this person, assuming, given her big-city provenance, she would be too brash for his taste. He preferred things understated.

Still, as he observed her more closely, he was taken by her intelligent face. Not an especially beautiful face but appealing in an uncluttered way. Her eyes were eager, restless. *How often,* he asked himself, *does a woman sit on her porch reading a book rather than fiddling with an iPhone?* He should give her credit. He managed the hint of a smile.

"Keats and I should be moving on. But I suspect they'll get together again somehow."

"Fondly to be wished," Serena returned, something bemused or suggestive in her voice, he couldn't be sure which, or whether it mattered.

"As for names, I didn't get your dog's."

Serena laughed. "Actually, you did. It's Dog." Eliot looked confused. "Like Colombo's." He still looked confused. "Peter Falk's basset hound in the TV show was called Dog."

"I see," Eliot replied tentatively.

"Anyhow, they'd doubtless like each other whatever their names," she quipped.

"Doubtless." With that, Eliot gave a short tug to Keats' leash. "Until next time," he heard himself add.

Several weeks later, while poring over a contentious real estate transaction on Ocean Boulevard and eyeing the comps, he came across Serena Samuels' name. She was listed as "a single woman" who had acquired the house barely a year earlier. For a whopping $2.5 million. He wondered if Miss Samuels might have been an actress—she had been wearing a hat and sunglasses, attire which he associated with movie stars. As for Peter Falk, he had only the foggiest notion.

"Don't ever delude yourself that you could be an asset on a Trivial Pursuit team," Caroline had deadpanned when asked to shed light on the TV series. "Everyone watched *Colombo*, Eliot.

The dog, like his beat-up car, was a fixture. Anyway, this woman likely worked in show business—most everyone in Los Angeles does. They're all overpaid."

"I don't follow. Whom are you talking about?"

"The dog owner you ran into. Serena something-or-other. Isn't that why you asked about *Colombo*?"

Not wishing to be quizzed, Eliot gathered up the legal papers he had worked on during the week and sent Caroline back to Santa Barbara with a thick folder and steaming hot coffee in her thermos.

"Have a good weekend, Eliot. The weather is supposed to be brilliant. You might want to take Keats down to the beach at Pismo and let him run about. Looks to me like you're overfeeding him."

And he had done just that, letting the golden retriever cavort along the sandy half-mile expanse unimpeded, after which he had utilized for the first time since the funeral his membership at the sports club overlooking the beach.

On his way out after a quick swim and an even quicker sauna, he caught a glimpse of a woman playing racquetball. Against a male opponent. She was more than holding her own.

While his card was being stamped at the desk, the player appeared, rosy-cheeked and sweated, to fill her water bottle. She also squirted something from an inhaler into her mouth. It was Serena Samuels.

"Fancy seeing you here, Eliot," she called out. "Are you coming in or going out?"

Turning his head, it occurred to him that his neighbor, whom he took to be about fifty, had exceptionally toned limbs, thanks arguably to exertions at the gym. For an instant, he wondered if he should engage in something more rigorous than lazy laps in the pool. Perhaps Keats was not alone in being overfed. At sixty-eight and working from home, he had become more sedentary and less active than when employed full-time at the firm, and when he and Silda still— "Just leaving. Keats is in the Escalade, so I limited myself to a dip in the pool."

"Until next time then—Saturday mornings I never miss—I'll bring Dog. He and Keats could romp on the beach and then wait for us while we..." Serena hesitated, something extraneous seemingly flitting through her mind. "Racquetball, I can attest, makes you forget all your troubles. I promise to go easy on you—at least the first time!"

Eliot smiled, wondering if her banter were purposefully suggestive or merely a reflection of a bemused take on life. Either way, he didn't mind. She might be brash, but living so close by, she was convenient company. If she made walking the dog less of a chore or challenged him to get back in shape, so much the better.

Meet new people, do new things, people had advised. Why not with Serena Samuels as well?

One Friday afternoon in September as they wrapped up business, Caroline had delicately inquired if Eliot needed help disposing of Silda's clothes. She had noticed cardboard boxes stacked in the hallway, several already with labels: dresses, shoes, purses.

Blushing, Eliot had stammered a response.

"Actually, one of the neighbors has volunteered to sort through her closet." Caroline's eyebrows went up. "That Serena person I've told you about. Says there's a thrift shop in San Luis Obispo ideal for fancy attire."

"Ah," Caroline had responded, irritated or disappointed. Her boss had apparently forgotten she helped out at a battered women's shelter in Santa Barbara. The organizers were constantly in need of clothes and shoes for their clients, some of whom showed up empty-handed and were afraid to venture back home.

To regain her composure, she glanced around the makeshift office Eliot had set up, her eyes settling on the Singer in the corner.

“Oh, that thing,” Eliot interposed, relieved to change the subject. “Belonged to Silda’s mother. Back then women made a lot of their own frocks. Even Silda put together a few ball gowns on the thing.” For an instant, he appeared lost in thought.

“You might want to take more time to part with certain items. There is no deadline,” Caroline responded, a note of sympathy seeping back into her voice.

She did not mention the women's center nor comment on the nosy neighbor who would be rifling through the closet of a dead woman she had never met. Whereas *she*—

Shortly thereafter, declining the offer of decaf for her drive back to Santa Barbara, Caroline took her leave. She would inquire as to the shelter’s needs that weekend, including whether any of the staffers could use a sewing machine.

Eliot drank two cups of coffee out on the veranda, wondering why Caroline had out of nowhere become short with him. It occurred to him that she might have wanted a few of Silda's skirts or blouses for herself—or for her child. She did, if memory served, have a daughter, but then again, perhaps not. Silda had been what was called willowy, and Caroline was, well, more like oak, solidly built. As for the purported daughter, he had no inkling.

Presumably, neither mother nor daughter knew what to do with a sewing machine.

Before he finished off the chocolate chip cookies that his assistant had baked and downed the last of the decaf, Eliot made a mental note to check with Daphne Dupree as well. The lady of the creole concoctions, as Caroline had dubbed her, might be in need of something from the house, if not a sewing machine, then something, though he couldn't put his finger on anything. This particular lady lived in a trailer—likely too cramped for a bulky Singer console—and likely did not know how to sew.

From what he had pieced together, she spent most of her time outside in front of her easel, either in a bathing suit or, when chilly, in paint-splattered overalls. That is, when she wasn't busy in an apron emblazoned with the *Cafe du Monde* logo, stirring some spicy dish, ostensibly for him.

He would ring Daphne in the morning, and were she amenable, drive down to the trailer park on Sunday. Take her for an outing. Provided Saturday's racquetball game with Serena didn't do him in.

CHAPTER TWO

Caroline

Reading the Tea Leaves

On the drive back home to Santa Barbara, Caroline switched on the radio to dispel her sour mood. A glance in the rearview mirror revealed frown lines she had not noticed before. Letting out an annoyed sigh, she tuned in to the university's music station and turned up the volume. "I've Got You Under My Skin" was playing, Frank Sinatra singing.

Apt enough, she thought.

Increasingly, she had found herself irked—with the firm for not reimbursing her for gas to and from Shell Beach twice a week, with her daughter Chloe, whose friends were questionable, and with Eliot, who, she had assumed, would remain in mourning longer and more touchingly. Or, if not, that he would have become more aware of the needs of people around him—those who had supported him through his ordeal—and demonstrate more empathy.

In short, she had come away from Shell Beach that September evening with her nose out of joint. It bothered her that Eliot hadn't inquired as to whether she might want, as a token of her esteem for the deceased, one of his wife's evening jackets or beaded handbags. However much his spouse's elegant wardrobe might be unsuitable for her.

The image of Silda gliding through life in Chanel or Valentino flitted across her mind. She didn't begrudge the woman her attire—she possessed the figure and the confidence to pull off any look. And why not? Her husband was a successful lawyer, in demand for his legal acumen, while she taught music off and on in the Santa Barbara school system, and dispensed private lessons to select students.

A couple of years ago, Caroline had toyed with the idea of having Chloe take from her, until she learned what Silda charged.

In any case, the Etheridges had both money and taste and cut an impressive figure in social and business circles throughout the Central Valley. For the last decade, Caroline had dutifully penciled in charity balls, fun runs, school outings, political action groups, sporting events, and assorted dinner parties into her boss's desk calendar, making sure he consulted it every morning before the partners convened.

"Don't know what we'd do without you, Caroline," Silda had confided whenever she rang up to remind her husband of one or another function to which he was obliged to accompany her.

And from Caroline's vantage point, he seemed to do so willingly, and only rarely, if other attendees were considered boring or boorish, resignedly. Eliot Etheridge was not a man who openly griped.

Yet now?

Things were changing in ways she had not foreseen. She had heard the old adage: "Women grieve but men replace," but she had not imagined that would be the case for her bereaved boss, as it arguably wouldn't have been for his spouse, had he been the one to succumb to cancer.

Still, Caroline told herself, it was not for her to decide the proper way to wear one's widowhood.

She drove on. But her mind raced faster. Those ubiquitous Pyrex dishes in his kitchen said it all: Eliot was, consciously or not, allowing himself to be caught up in new arrangements, if not entanglements, with three different women. None of whom could hold a candle to his dead wife.

"Men," she harumphed, decelerating for the traffic around the bustling town of Santa Maria. Of course, few husbands were as execrable as her ex, who early on had devolved into a lazy do-nothing and even now remained a pest. At the thought of Mickey, she vowed to renew that old restraining order as soon as she could carve out time to pin down his latest whereabouts.

Given that it was a shambles, Caroline didn't readily talk about her personal life with anyone at the firm, professional aplomb being a prerequisite for the job, one she prided herself on exemplifying.

For his part, Eliot behaved toward her with exemplary rectitude, the two vying to maintain the most cordial but impersonal of relationships. As he appeared to do with all women in his professional orbit, except perhaps for that former college friend with whom he chatted off and on, his voice dropping a register whenever she rang. What *was* her name? She couldn't summons it, though she instantly recognized the New England twang whenever the woman rang up, identifying herself as "his old chum from Harvard Law."

Which was just often enough to leave an impression.

Even so, Eliot had been, to Caroline's mind, what could be called "very married," and given her own disastrous go at the institution, she was in awe of the couple. Never more so than the last time she had seen them together, at the firm's Christmas Party in 2017, one she had helped organize at a swank banquet hall in nearby Montecito. She herself had considered bringing along one of the young men from her night school law class, but none jumped out as sufficiently suitable.

Among the well-heeled clients from that tony enclave as well as the firm's own partners, the Etheridges had stood out as the most handsome, and in her view, most enviable, twosome. Especially when they took to the dance floor, putting everyone else to shame with their Fred and Ginger routines. As she applauded their foxtrot along with other guests, Eliot had escorted his wife back to their table. Mumbling something in her ear, he then crossed the room, to ask *her*, of all people, to honor him with a waltz. Sensitive about her bulk, she demurred but he persisted, leading her as adroitly as possible through "This Nearly was Mine."

Afterward, Caroline resolved to add lessons at the local Arthur Murray studio to her list of things-to-do in the coming year. Three quarters through 2018, she had not gotten around to anything on said list, including the items designed to help her lose weight. She did, however, re-up her daughter for ballet class. Chloe was pretty enough, and definitely thin enough, but at seventeen she lacked poise. Soccer was fine in its way, but from what Caroline had observed, success in the business world required more finesse than kicking a ball.

Caroline Morris was more of a snob than either her boss or his dead wife.

As the sun turned purple and began to sink into the Pacific, Caroline pulled over at the only rest area between the Five Cities and Santa Barbara. She stretched her legs in the adjacent park, used the public bathroom, and took a few swallows of the burnt coffee on offer.

Why had she rejected Eliot's offer to fill her thermos? As he had remarked, and not for the first time, it was Silda's belief that coffee was like wine: it should be of good quality or not drunk at all. He had seemed disconcerted when she declined, as though she were refusing something of his dead wife's urging.

Browsing the travel brochures next to the sugar and the creamer, Caroline suddenly recalled that same befuddled expression on his face when she had intercepted that awful phone call at the office. More than a year ago. A man's anxious voice, saying Silda had fainted in Eldwayen Park—he had seen her from his front window and rushed out. He was driving her to the ER in Arroyo Grande. Mr. Etheridge would find her there. "I will keep the dog as long as needed," the man had closed with, and hung up before she could get his name. He had an accent.

"What was that about, Caroline?" Eliot had inquired, a stack of documents in hand for her to scan. "Your wife. She fell or something. A neighbor is taking her to the hospital. He hung up before—"

Blood draining from his cheeks, Eliot let the papers flutter to the floor and bounded out. She had never seen him so undone.

Caroline pitched the half-full paper cup in the bin and hurried back out to the Camry. With Friday night's traffic, it could mean another hour until she reached home. Being newly caffeinated would help her focus.

Back out on the freeway, she determined to phone her boss during the weekend and apologize for her bad mood, attributing it to something vague, not meriting discussion. To care for a loved one with cancer had to have been challenging; Eliot deserved whatever diversions might come his way.

As for the three ladies who were competing to divert him, Caroline kept circling back to the same conclusion: either they were after sex, money or contacts. She wasn't certain as to which one wanted what.

Nonetheless, not being a mean-spirited person, she tried to summons sympathy for them. Their relationships with men heretofore may have been as fraught as her own. Were a good man to come into their sights, why shouldn't they target him?

That Ms. Pavonine, for example, had struck the perfect tone at the visitation, which was in Caroline's estimation, not the sort of gathering to put anyone at ease. Dressed in an understated charcoal-gray suit, the woman had zeroed in on the widower but did not—as some other guests thoughtlessly did—monopolize him or overdo her commiseration. That duty completed, the visitor had turned to mingle with others, speaking briefly to Silda's two children before taking her leave. Unobtrusive but unerring.

What if she had a pointy nose, and not a figure to call attention to? Here was a woman who moved through the world unruffled, Caroline had deduced.

In her first phone call to the office a month later, Ms. Pavonine had been gracious, apologizing for intruding upon the firm's time—and reminding Caroline they had met at that sad event at the Sorenson home. Then a deft segue to her purpose: to invite Eliot to the opera, sounding as though he might be first on her list of potential dates but hardly the only one in her little black book.

A woman who might, Caroline had gleaned from reading a few French novels, be referred to as *d'un certain âge*. In other words, the lady of the scallops came across as one who, albeit no longer young, still had options open to her.

After fifteen years in her position at the law firm, and three years of night courses toward a law degree, Caroline prided herself on her ability to pinpoint people's motives.

Regarding the neighbor with the big house on Ocean Boulevard, she was no spring chicken either, Caroline surmised from her online search. Per the Internet, Serena Samuels boasted three thousand connections on LinkedIn; her Facebook status was listed as complicated. She had risen through the ranks at Universal Studios, shepherding numerous movies and TV shows. Eventually, she had become something called an EVP, but had "resigned" in the wake of a takeover, though that verb, Caroline had come to understand from her work at the firm, covered several different departure scenarios.

In any case, Serena's Hollywood exit purportedly was cushioned by what *Variety* referred to as "a golden parachute," though the trade paper did not hazard a monetary figure. Said cushion did likely explain how she could afford the mansion Caroline had driven by one afternoon after her stint at Eliot's home office. She had spotted a tall blonde woman out front, dressed in leggings and a t-shirt, tending to shrubbery. As Caroline slowed to a crawl, Serena wrested a cumbersome palm from out of a pot and plopped it into a hole. A sleepy looking dog sat curled up nearby, not bothering to assist.

About the third owner of a Pyrex dish, all Caroline had ascertained when this Daphne person rang the office was a southern accent, which made her sound younger and more clueless than she might be. That, and the fact that Eliot had let slip that the woman lived "for the interim" on a cordoned-off section of Grover Beach. Meaning, in a trailer!

So he had revealed when she had queried him about a gift for the woman in thanks for a dish she brought over. Jambalaya, if she remembered rightly. "Not sure about an actual address," he had sputtered, brushing off the idea of a note. "I'll pick up flowers next time I visit her." He had reddened and changed the subject.

"In extremis, some men go off the deep end," Caroline muttered, "and there is little to be done about it."

Switching stations to check traffic reports, she noted the time on the Camry's dashboard, 7:45, it having taken a good ninety minutes to make it from Shell Beach to the outskirts of Goleta, the suburb north of Santa Barbara. Because it was home to the local college and a balmy Friday night, students would be out and about. She should have left Eliot's sooner if she wanted to catch her daughter. Here was someone she needed to obsess about—not her boss—and in whose life she needed to intervene. Forcefully.

For reasons that eluded her, Chloe had recently become troublesome, holing up in her room and, given her recent grades, not hitting the books. At the drop of a hat, she'd dash out of the house without a convincing explanation, running around, so it appeared, with an older crowd: kids with their own cars, and money in their pockets, judging from the red convertible she noticed pulling up now and again.

The two had argued about it.

"If I'm not around, text me where you'll be and with whom. Your curfew hasn't changed. It's 11 p.m. sharp." Chloe had rolled her eyes.

The first time the girl "forgot" to do as told, she was grounded for the following weekend, however loudly she slammed the door to her room and however adamantly she refused to come out for meals.

Still, Caroline figured she had the upper hand. Sole grip on the purse strings and no husband to counter her decisions...except when Mickey decided to show up and undermine her by putting unrealistic ideas into the girl's head, like how come *our daughter* doesn't have her own car?

"Because I know best when it comes to what Chloe needs," she had retorted a few months ago when her ex had brought his daughter home from a soccer match. "Of course, if you wish to buy her a car, be my guest," she had added sarcastically. Mickey had cursed under his breath but let the subject drop.

Later that weekend, Caroline had suggested that Chloe might want to look around for a part-time job. "That way, you can hasten the day when we can afford to buy you a decent used car. People at the office will know where to send us for a good deal."

As far as Caroline knew, Chloe had made only tentative stabs at finding work of any kind. Perhaps it wouldn't hurt to impress upon her daughter that she herself had held summer jobs throughout high school. Come to think of it, she wondered whether any of Chloe's schoolmates had part-time jobs; indeed, she wondered who her daughter's friends *were* at this stage, her senior year at Central Coast High. A meeting with the high school guidance counselor wouldn't be a bad idea. Chloe's grades had slipped from *B*s to *C*s during the semester, even though her course load had not become more onerous.

"I've not been paying enough attention," she murmured aloud. "At her age, I—"

Just then her iPhone beeped. She waited a minute until she hit the Pike Street exit ramp off the 101 before glancing at the text.

Couldn't wait for you any longer, Mom. A concert in town. Going with Ian, Gloria et alii. See, I know some Latin too! Back around 11.

Chloe was not a bad kid, she told herself, a little off-balance but most girls were nowadays. She vowed to look into financing some kind of vehicle for her. For the first time, a year-end bonus had been written into her latest contract with Bryson & Tillotson.

Once home, Caroline dumped the Etheridge folder on her desk and headed to the kitchen to warm the vegetable soup made the night before. Apparently, Chloe had not helped herself to it or anything else in the fridge before she left with her friends.

Teenagers, she thought*, are often oblivious to food*. Still, it would be prudent to find out more about the crowd her daughter was running with: who was this Ian, and exactly how much older was he, or Gloria, or any of the others? She couldn't put a face to any of them. That's what she got for working all day, taking night classes, and spending her Saturdays counseling at the women's center, persevering through a Pilates class, and running errands.

At least that's how her friend Ella described it when last they had coffee in one of those fancy places along State Street. Truth be told, Caroline made a better brew at home, but Ella enjoyed people-watching, and spending her dermatologist husband's money on whatever caught her eye.

"I shouldn't say it, but you risk becoming a stick in the mud, Caroline," her friend had ventured, cutting a large slice of carrot cake in two and sliding the extra plate toward her. Picking up her fork, Caroline pursed her lips in exasperation but made no effort to defend herself. "Those lawyers you work for take advantage. I hope they're paying you extra to trudge up to Shell Beach. Hope the guy at least buys you lunch or something."

Caroline took a bite of the cake and sipped her cappuccino. "I don't mind the trek. Eliot Etheridge's been through a lot, what with his wife dying and the kids being—aloof, distant, whatever. Besides." She looked out over the busy street, where lines of college kids and tourists were forming for the trendier restaurants or bars.

"Besides what?" Ella persisted. "Don't tell me you have designs on the widower. How old is he anyway?"

"Absolutely not. Mr. Etheridge is in his sixties, and if you must know, he has several lady friends who look in on him. You know, taking him casseroles."

"How quaint," Ella returned, eyeing her friend more curiously. "Nonetheless, it might do for Chloe to have a strong male presence in her life. You did say she's become a handful."

"Yes, someone, anyone, other than Mickey would be an improvement. It's just that right now I have so much going on. Once I finish the night courses and take the bar, it'll be different."

"I didn't realize your ex was still in the picture."

"He's not, as far as I'm concerned. He drops by sporadically, always unannounced, to take Chloe out. I guess I shouldn't complain. They get on, though he does put exalted ideas into her head."

"You need a proper partner, Caroline. That's all there is to it," Ella wound up, motioning for the bill. "Plus, your mood might improve with Botox. You know, on those stress lines," she added, running her fingers over her smooth forehead. "Call David. He'll squeeze you in."

Ella was the kind of person that dispensed advice whether solicited or not, but Caroline had nurtured few friendships since her divorce. Besides, her friend sometimes hit the nail on the head, as it were. About Chloe's needing a stronger hand, it would have been hard to disagree. Or about the lines etched on her forehead.

Only on Sundays did Caroline have a chance to connect with Chloe, and even then, the girl usually pussyfooted, claiming she had places to go and people to see.

Not this time, however. Caroline had scoured the Internet for something fun the two of them could do that particular day in late September, settling on a folk music festival at a vineyard in the hills. She tossed out the idea at the breakfast table, having made blueberry pancakes as a treat.

Although Chloe instantly rolled her eyes, the girl acquiesced when she saw the disappointed look on her mother's face. “Okay, okay. Believe it or not, I had planned to study today, before going out with—never mind—but if you really...” she gabbled, before mopping up the last pancake.

“Agreed then,” Caroline responded. She finished her coffee before ratcheting up the ante. “I get that you have your own friends now, Chloe, but you and I need to catch up with things. Not to mention it's a beautiful day to be outside.”

“Got it. Can I bring Asta?”

“If you'll be in charge of him.”

During the drive into the interior of the Central Valley, Caroline again broached the subject of job-hunting. Her daughter stiffened, but she plowed ahead.

“It’s not that we are hurting, Chloe, but I know you want certain things, and I want them for you. Some of them cost money. Certainly a car does. Were you to contribute to the purchase of one, you'd feel a sense of accomplishment. It would be yours, not just something your mother bought you.”

Chloe's face constricted. She reached around to the back seat to pet the terrier, who took the gesture as a cue to jump into the front seat.

“Stay put, Asta,” Caroline called out in a tone that the canine, if not the girl, recognized as authoritative. After a pause, she added, “So, what do you think, Chloe: does that make sense?”

“Actually, Mom, I don’t need a car, or anything,” she retorted. “Ian has one, a Maserati no less.”

Exasperated by the inanity of such a remark, Caroline strained to keep her equanimity. “Surely, you can't expect to depend on this Ian, or anyone else, forever. To pick you up and take you places. At some point—”

“You don’t get it,” Chloe broke in. “I’m pregnant, Mom, and Ian and I plan to get married. He’s rich, and I won’t need a car or a job or anything else," she wound up, her voice more shrill with each word.

Caroline had to swerve to avoid crossing the median and crashing into an oncoming Dodge Ram.

Thoroughly jostled, her thoughts came tumbling out: first, that her daughter must be joking; second, that however worldly and well-fixed this Ian person might be, her daughter was a clueless teenager. And finally, self-centered though it might be, that this was the last thing she needed right now in her own life.

Ergo, how could she in good conscience allow Chloe to do something so stupid, something that would ruin her life, and likely derail her own.

Slowing to a crawl, Caroline turned toward the youngster. (Chloe's face had flushed; she was biting her lip, but no tears were falling.) She took a deep breath, knowing that to berate her daughter would be counter-productive, and dangerous while on the road. "We can talk about all this later at home, sweetheart. Figure it all out. We've come this far, so let's try to enjoy the afternoon together."

CHAPTER THREE

Eliot and Daphne

Nice is Not Enough

Eliot could not have been more startled that Sunday afternoon to come across his assistant at an obscure folk festival. In all the years they had worked together, they had never run into each other by chance, either in Santa Barbara or anywhere else in the Central Valley.

With Daphne by his side, he had been meandering in the crisp air from booth to booth. At one, he pulled out his wallet and overpaid for an intricately designed wicker basket for the young woman to do her shopping. "The Chumash have been making them for hundreds of years, miss," the vendor explained, though Daphne looked bewildered as to what he was talking about. At another stand, Eliot encouraged her to pick a shawl from a rack of hand-knit items. She objected to his generosity, but not vigorously.

"See, already it's cooler," he said, draping the green and yellow wrap around her bare shoulders. It brought out the aquamarine of her eyes, but he decided not to say so. "And why pay for a bag at Trader Joe's when you can bring your own? Besides, we'll need to fill it with a couple of bottles of wine before we're done," he added, pleased with himself for having done something he considered useful for her.

From a previous look-about inside her house-on-wheels, it did not appear she owned many clothes, few winter garments and definitely no ball gowns. He was relieved not to have brought along anything from Silda's wardrobe when he picked her up earlier. His wife had been tall and slender; Daphne was anything but. And yet, appealing in her tattered shorts and halter-top, no bra in sight. He was stunned by his body's reaction. At noon no less.

Before they left the trailer park, he had diplomatically suggested she might want to cover up, since they'd be heading up into the hills. Without a word, she had switched into a pair of capri pants but did not change her sandals or her top.

Eventually, the two finished traversing the length of the fairgrounds, Daphne having spent a good thirty minutes casing the rows of paintings on sale, pausing here and there to observe a piece close up or to chat briefly with the artist. Eliot kept his own counsel, having always left it to his wife in matters of art, and not wanting to disparage anything on offer, however inept or garish he found them.

Although he hadn't heretofore thought much about Daphne's canvases, they compared favorably with these. Hers were oddly arresting. He would make a point of observing them more closely.

As a crowd of young people began to coalesce around a makeshift stage to hear the performers, none of whom Eliot had heard of, he took Daphne's arm. Slowly they weaved their way toward the vineyard's wine-tasting bar and gift shop.

Inside, they briefly browsed around and then headed for the bar. Several other customers slid over to accommodate the newcomers.

Out of the corner of his eye, Eliot spotted someone who looked familiar toward the far end of the counter. A teenager was fidgeting next to her. Assuming that the woman had not seen him, he shifted his body back toward his companion and raised his hand to get a barista's attention.

Before long, one of the servers made his way down to them.

“Any particular wine you'd like to try?” Eliot asked Daphne. "I believe they're known for pinot grigio,” he added, glancing at the barista for further guidance.

“Not really,” Daphne replied, “other than I like white more than red.”

The barista exchanged a look with Eliot but swiftly went to work pouring one of the company's varietals into tiny cups and replenishing a plate of crackers.

“This is one of our more popular vintages. It's light, with hints of apricot. Buttery too but not overmuch. After that, you might want to savor a drier, crisper varietal. Just let me know, and we'll give it a shot,” the barista said to Daphne. The timbre of his voice, if not the subtle lift of his eyebrows, made Eliot think he was flirting with his companion.

Not the first time he had noticed her effect on those of the male persuasion.

Without hesitating, Daphne downed the chardonnay in one go; Eliot swirled the liquid in his cup and sipped it extra slowly.

If he were setting an example for her to emulate, she did not appear to notice. She picked up a couple of crackers and one by one put them in her mouth.

Perhaps it was her very ignorance of things—the ritual of wine-tasting, the right clothes to wear—that made her so attractive to men. Certainly, Eliot had never known or socialized with any female so naïve, not even during his college days at Harvard. Fleetingly, he thought of his first love, Isabel Frankel, the brightest of the bright among the girls at Radcliffe. Her verbal pyrotechnics were legendary—able to summons at will the apt word, the pertinent precedent, and never giving ground on anything. No wonder she had made partner at Evans Gump by age thirty!

“Yet absolutely draining she was,” he muttered softly.

“Did you say something?” Daphne asked, turning her eyes toward him.

“Wonder if you want to taste something more daring?” Eliot regrouped, tilting his head in the direction of the barista.

"Sure, why not?"

While Daphne drank a few more glasses and casually flirted with the barista, Eliot let his thoughts drift again, a habit that had crept up on him of late.

After law school too, he reckoned, his circle of female acquaintances widened but did not veer from the norm: be they the women in Silda's book club, fellow lawyers, ballroom dancers or Central Valley do-gooders. All could be described as safely middle-class, if not privileged, safely educated, if not brainy, and safely well-bred, if not necessarily well-behaved.

He wondered if the women in what Caroline in her droll way called his casserole coterie could be said to fit that same mold.

As a restaurateur and sometime San Francisco socialite, Kathleen doubtless knew the difference between a chardonnay and a pinot blindfolded; Serena, who had worked her way up through the ranks of a Hollywood studio, doubtless possessed business acumen as well as a top-of-the-line wardrobe.

Each in her own way knew how to make an impression. Very different from the one that Daphne made.

Stultifying, Eliot suddenly thought. That's what his friendships, if not his entire life, might be argued to have been.

And yet, he also knew himself to be an impatient sort, one who did not suffer fools gladly. He did not think that a bad thing.

He downed the pinot grigio in front of him and motioned the barista for a refill for the two of them.

At this moment, he did not know if Daphne would end up irking more than enticing him. She was still munching crackers when the next round of wine arrived.

"Something special for the little lady," the barista confided, "our 2018 sauvignon blanc, which, between you and me, is our most delicious varietal." She batted her eyes at the youngish man and then gulped the liquid, again in one go. Then, without missing a beat, she whispered she would be seeking out what she called "the powder room."

Perhaps that's how they term it in New Orleans, Eliot reckoned. Nodding politely, he began to study the price list. The sauvignon blanc was, not surprisingly, the most expensive.

Right about then voices, one of which sounded familiar, caught Eliot's attention. He swiveled his head toward the end of the counter. The woman in question was his assistant, and she was remonstrating with the youngster next to her. Could that have been the reputed daughter? Silda would have known.

With Daphne nowhere in sight, he ambled over, vaguely self-conscious. And tipsy.

"Fancy running into you here," he began, holding out his hand to her, and immediately feeling ridiculous for having done so. "I'm with a friend, but she seems to have disappeared," he added, casting his eyes about. Caroline's eyes followed his around the crowded shop. Several customers were studying the labels on jam jars, while a couple were filling shopping baskets with ceramic plates. Several others were flipping through postcards on a revolving rack. Daphne was nowhere in sight.

Eliot shrugged and turned back toward the two. Asta sniffed at his pants leg, but he ignored the nuzzle.

"Anyway, the wines are drinkable, wouldn't you agree?"

It was Caroline's turn to feel awkward, wondering if her daughter's querulous responses to her had drawn the attention. She had been stressing to the youngster that her "situation," as she termed it, should be discussed with their doctor.

Chloe had objected, her voice high-pitched: "You can't control everything. Just don't tell anyone, not Dad, or anyone else. You have to promise."

"And this young lady?" Eliot continued, not wanting to conjecture wrongly.

"Oh, I assumed you two had met. This is my daughter Chloe. She's a senior at Central Coast High," Caroline managed, then added more pointedly to her daughter. "This is Mr. Etheridge, dear, one of the partners I work for at the firm." Chloe made a tentative effort to relax the muscles in her face.

"I should have surmised. She looks like you. Very pretty, I mean," Eliot babbled, his face reddening. Perhaps, he reckoned, sipping so many wines on an empty stomach was not a good idea. For an instant, he wondered if Daphne had been sidelined in the bathroom by an upset stomach.

Another barista, this one an older woman, cleared her throat to gain Caroline's attention. "I understood you'd like two bottles of the pinot grigio, madame. Will that be all today?"

"Yes, that's it—unless, sweetheart, you'd like to look around for postcards or something?" she asked her daughter.

Receiving only a bored shrug of the shoulders, Caroline began to rummage in her handbag for her wallet.

"No, no. Allow me," Eliot quickly interposed, pulling out a credit card and reaching over the counter to the barista. "Add on a bottle of the chardonnay, the 2019 vintage, and the sauvignon blanc as well. In a separate bag, please." he further instructed.

"You really shouldn't, Eliot, but thank you," Caroline responded.

While he signed off on the order, Caroline scanned the shop again, wondering if her boss had brought along Madame Pavonine or the neighbor from Ocean Boulevard. Probably not the former, she calculated, since she had a restaurant to run. Perhaps not the other either, since she appeared to spend her weekends potting and un-potting plants in her garden.

A completely different woman—younger, noticeably buxom and oddly dressed—sidled up to Eliot's elbow.

"I got side-tracked, looking at cookbooks," Daphne said, indicating a rack on the far side of the store.

"Of all things, I ran into, uh, my assistant actually, and her daughter: Caroline and Chloe," he gabbled, stepping away from the counter so that the women could shake hands…or not.

"This is Daphne Dupree. She's a painter, lives at Grover Beach—." He smacked his lips shut, wishing he hadn't alluded to her living arrangements but wishing that she had changed out of her halter top. Silda, so silky and sophisticated, would have never—

"Nice to meet you, Daphne. We spoke on the phone not long ago," Caroline reminded her, raking the young woman's ample body head to toe and coming back to her face, notably to the aquamarine eyes.

"You sound different," Chloe chimed in. "Your accent."

"I'm from New Orleans. Been out here less than a year. Love the ocean."

"I never think about it. The water, that is. Mom either," Chloe rejoined, in what Eliot imagined was something of a put-down, though he had never been good at assessing the comments, or the motives, of teenagers, his children included.

"So, what exactly do you paint, if you don't mind my asking?" Caroline interjected.

"Seascapes. As I said, the ocean here has so many moods. No day is ever like another."

"Indeed," Caroline managed, looking nonplussed by what she was hearing.

Sensing awkwardness in the air, Eliot resisted making any comment about the canvases he had seen strewn about Daphne's trailer. Besides, he wasn't sure how to describe them, what artistic tradition they could be ascribed to, or how they were to be interpreted. Sort of like how Daphne herself came across: captivating but hard to categorize.

As he stood uncertainly, shifting his weight from one foot to the other, the barista passed him a receipt for the wine purchases and gestured toward the cashier near the entrance. "Pick-up's over there, with a complementary jar of tapenade in each bag."

"Well, now that we've done what we came in for, why don't we take one last stroll around the grounds, grab something on a stick if you're hungry, and then head on back," Eliot suggested, turning his attention back to his companion.

Nodding in compliance, Daphne pulled the shawl from the wicker basket and swung it around her shoulders.

"Very becoming," Caroline said, noting how the green shade accentuated the young woman's eyes.

"Eliot picked it out—from one of the vendors. It's colder up here than it is at the beach."

"Nice to have met you, Daphne," Caroline then said, shifting her gaze toward her daughter.

"Me too," Chloe added on cue. "I like that basket."

"That too he chose," she explained, tilting her head toward Eliot. "Made by Indians."

Mother and daughter exchanged a glance but said nothing. Embarrassed, Eliot tried again to take his leave.

"Glad we ran into you two. And I'll see you, Caroline, on Tuesday around 3:00. Remind me to give you the bottles then. You know how distracted I get."

On the way back to Grover Beach, they drove in silence, Daphne with her bare feet up on the dashboard, her face turned toward the window, Eliot focused on the winding road.

Finally, she piped up: "Your secretary seems nice. What was her name again?"

It was an adjective that never failed to irritate Eliot. *Nice* meant nothing; that people couldn't come up with anything more pertinent or imaginative irked him, especially when the speaker was someone he had decided to cultivate. The muscles in his face tightened in disapproval of her lazy effort. His companion apparently didn't notice.

"Her name's Caroline, her daughter's Chloe. And she is a highly competent, admirably discreet, and indefatigable executive assistant," he replied curtly. He had routinely said so in personnel reviews and signed off on raises on several different occasions. Doubly glad now that he had done so, having seen with his own eyes that she did in fact have a daughter to raise.

"Whatever that long word means," Daphne muttered under her breath. She flipped open the igloo lodged between them, pulled out a can of Ginger Ale, and took a swig—without offering him any. For a minute or two, neither spoke.

Eliot hadn't expected that Daphne would register his rebuke, though arguably his description of his assistant was intended as such. He was at a loss as to how to dial his behavior back.

"Anyhow, they didn't seem to be having a nice time together, mother and daughter."

Eliot's eyebrows arched in surprise. He hadn't noticed anything off between the two, only that he himself had been ill-at-ease.

"Why do you think that?" he asked, this time attempting a warmer tone.

"So stiff they were, angled away from each other. The mother drumming her fingers, the girl fiddling with her hair."

Eliot had to give Daphne credit: she might not be adept with adjectives, but she had been observant. He liked this woman despite noticeable limitations, including her unconventional address.

Once back at Paradise RV Park—he would henceforth abandon the word *trailer* to refer to her abode—he carried the bottles of wine into her *home* and set them on the only uncluttered surface. Various canvases were propped against stool legs or cabinets. The smell of turpentine made his nose twitch.

Daphne unlatched a couple of locked windows. "Nothing is as nice as hearing the waves," she declared, kicking off her sandals. Eliot nodded, determined not to comment on her word choice. "Anyhow, I'll be right back," she added, before ducking into the tiny bathroom at the rear of the vehicle. From inside, she called out, "You can put the wine in the icebox and help yourself to whatever."

Now that was a word Eliot hadn't heard in a while. He wondered if calling the refrigerator an icebox was a southern thing or if she had an amused taste for the anachronistic. Glancing around, he spotted the aforesaid appliance tucked in the corner, opposite the stove and sink. It was battered; a chipped ceramic bowl overflowing with tomatoes and avocados sat precariously atop. Three boxes of different crackers sat open on the adjacent counter.

Carefully, he pried the refrigerator's stubborn door open to find it chock-a-block with dips and salsa, several half-wrapped cheeses, olives, jams and peanut butter. No "real" food in sight. He slipped one of the two bottles into the freezer between cartons of sorbet and frozen shrimp to chill it quickly, and the other he wedged in the fridge between jars of peaches.

Everything his friend ate or drank, he deduced from the labels, likely had been purchased from the Trader Joe's a couple of miles away.

Not that he was surprised.

He had first encountered Daphne in that very store one sultry afternoon back in July. Or did he now remember the day as sultry because it was she who had struck him as such—sultry being the word that came to mind when she had addressed him, a knowing look in her eyes.

He and Silda discussed the usage of words all the time, riffing on their meanings, entertaining each other with preposterous usages. It was not a diversion he ever expected to do with anyone else—certainly not with Daphne. He threw off the thought.

Still, he had been affected by the young woman's aura that day. Despite himself. Not a regular shopper while his wife was alive, he had gone to that grocery to get into the habit, and not have to rely on Mariella to run the errands. He felt proud of himself for making the effort and had been determined not to feel sorry for himself for having to make the effort.

While he could hear water running in the bathroom and the humming of some pop song over it, he allowed himself to dwell on that first meet-up. He was scouring the shelf of coffees—Silda enjoyed trying new flavors, but he had never paid the names much heed—bewildered by the choices. That's when he glanced around at a young woman munching the freebie snack on offer. She held out her hand, the one with an extra cracker cradled in a napkin.

"They're really good, with cheese and apple slices atop, if you want to try one," she had volunteered.

Unlike most of the other young women in the store, and for that matter in the state, this one, he noted, was Rubens-like. Something abundant about her.

"I'm having enough trouble settling on what coffee to choose, but thanks," he replied, waving his hand palm-up to decline her offer.

She had smiled quizzically—her lips were full, her skin tawny—and fixed her eyes on him. They were aquamarine and he had looked into them.

Checking out at adjacent registers, he had volunteered to carry one of her two bags of groceries. It was weighed down with jars and topped up with apples and bananas. He had placed it on the passenger seat of her dusty pick-up.

"Louisiana plates. You're far from home."

"Not anymore. I live in Paradise now, literally and figuratively," she replied.

He looked flummoxed.

"Paradise Park, not far from the butterfly sanctuary and the sand dunes. I paint."

"So, where would I find you, when you're not at Trader Joe's?" he had inquired half-joking, not realizing that he was bent on befriending a woman not half his age.

She wriggled her nose to weigh a response. "I'm not hard to find. I'm usually outside on Grover Beach, in front of my easel."

Eliot had nodded, figuring it would be easy enough to find a gated community called Paradise Park, if ever he were of a mind.

Right about then, he heard the wrench of a faucet and the groan of pipes. Within a few seconds, Daphne emerged from the bathroom, wrapped now in a lime-green cotton robe and slippers. She had gathered her copper-colored locks on her head and fastened them with clips. Her face appeared scrubbed clean. It was flawless except for freckles dotting her nose.

His insides quickened at the sight of her. Outside, the wind had picked up; he could hear the sound of waves far out to sea.

"You could open the wine," she suggested, "and we'll toast the arrival of fall. Soon, I'll have new colors to put on my canvases, and there'll be more fish to choose from." Eliot looked befuddled. "In the grocery, silly, the fish. So, I can make another seafood casserole for you!"

"Oh, I see. That would be nice," he said, his least favorite adjective slipping out. He took the chardonnay from the freezer and turned back toward her, holding the bottle aloft.

"The corkscrew should be somewhere in the drawer to your left," she said. "Glasses are in the cabinet."

While he poured the wine, she pulled out the plate of cheeses from the fridge and then grabbed up a box of soda crackers. When she turned back to face him, her arms laden, her robe fell open, exposing a breast.

Eliot averted his eyes, color rising to his cheeks nonetheless.

It had been longer than he cared to recall since he had been so unsettled by the sight of someone's body. Even if only a sliver thereof. At sixty-eight, and now regularly bested by a woman at racquetball, Eliot wasn't convinced he'd be up to performing anything more athletic, however voluptuous the woman standing mere feet from him was.

From that distance, Daphne tilted her head as if beckoning him to make a move. Letting the opportunity pass, he busied himself by sliding disparate papers and a sketchbook to the far end of the table and then pulling out the bench for her.

Once seated across from each other, they sipped their drinks and nibbled on the cheese and crackers.

A garrulous enough lawyer when required, Eliot could think of nothing to say. If he desired Daphne's body, it was clear, to him at least, that he was not diverted by her mind.

He wasn't certain the disconnect mattered, but reckoned it was too soon to decide if it did.

CHAPTER FOUR

Serena

Games People Play

Serena Samuels was nothing if not singularly dedicated to the things she took on, and not one to shy away from a challenge. As a teenager she took up several surprising sports, as a film executive, she gravitated toward anemic movie scripts that needed doctoring, and at this point in her life, she set her sights on one particular man, a finicky, hard-to-read man. Fortunately, over the decades, she had become less noticeably avid in her pursuit of things, and more adept at making her endeavors appear effortless.

To try too hard would spoil the fun.

So her parents had impressed upon her at an early age, they being Chicago-based pulp fiction writers who earned a lot when their stories were made into movies, and otherwise scraped by as editors for hire when they didn't.

For her part, Serena developed what seemed to her less fickle pursuits than writing fiction. To the dismay of her parents, who only ever pounded away at their typewriters, correcting each other's mistakes and drinking themselves silly, she showed no interest in following in their precarious footsteps. Nonetheless, she grew up as hard-boiled as any of the *film noir* characters that her parents created on the page, which she never bothered to read. During the long midwestern winters, she dedicated herself to ice hockey; during the short, hot summers she practiced badminton.

A reserved, if not suspicious person, Serena had avoided discussing her background with anyone, and couldn't conceive of doing so with Eliot Etheridge. In her view, he was one of those successful men little interested in a woman's past, unless it dovetailed with his own. What she wanted from or expected of him was not yet clear to her after the five months of their acquaintance.

After a few random meet-ups on Ocean Boulevard in which they chatted about local dog groomers, vets, and parks that don't require leashes, Serena offhandedly invited Eliot to the house she had bought from one of the region's top developers.

"Since you're sorting through all these real estate transactions, it might be amusing for you to see how one of these mansions turned out. So far at least mine is still standing!" she had wryly remarked when making the overture. She wouldn't have dreamt of mentioning how much she had paid for it, in cash no less, but he already knew the figure.

They were standing in Eldwayen Park looking out to sea, the two dogs doggedly tugging on their leashes. "Oh, and bring Keats. He can play with Dog in the back yard. It's fenced."

And so, Eliot had come over to lunch on a jasmine-scented day in June, the sky blue, sharp as a razor.

Ringing the doorbell at precisely noon, he shoved a bouquet of delphiniums into her unsuspecting hands, not having hitherto registered her expansive garden, which he later saw wrapped around the entire house. It featured abundant delphiniums as well as roses, azaleas, snapdragons, peonies, marigolds and birds of paradise as well as exotic aloes and cacti positioned around the veranda. A pink-blossomed mimosa filled in the corner at the far back; clumps of blue lilac broke up the fencing.

Despite high-polished furnishings in the parlor and an ambitious menu of minestrone, broiled salmon and summer squash, Serena did not appear to have a housekeeper or a cook. Not that Sunday at any rate.

"The soup is excellent," he said. "Nothing like what one gets used to from cans."

"Home-grown heirloom tomatoes and bell peppers help," she replied. "And since I as usual made too much, I've put aside a bowl for you to take home. It actually tastes better the second or third day."

Beyond his appreciation for her cooking, she liked that Eliot was *not* inquisitive about her childhood or her Hollywood career. In fact, he asked few questions, concentrating on his description of the historic changes along the Central Coast—from the influx of migrant labor, to the takeover of land by vintners, to the arrival of the rich and famous to enclaves like Montecito. She listened attentively, interjecting an observation or two when he paused to sip his wine or cast his eyes about the room.

"Fortunately," she observed at one juncture, "not everyone around here is nouveau riche like *moi*. I've met a few who've been here for decades—interesting people in their own right. A few stockbrokers naturally but also a former Broadway producer and a Russian musician who lives a few houses down." She gestured with her arm toward the north-facing window of her dining room.

Eliot nodded politely, ostensibly unaware of the persons she referenced. Serena blinked a few times before recalling something more precise. "That's right. Your wife knew the Russian. Maks something-or-other. They walked their dogs together."

When she caught the disconcerted look on her guest's face, Serena could have kicked herself. Bringing up the memory of his wife apparently still disturbed him. She searched around for something else to alight on. "Why don't I show you the back yard? I'd love your opinion as to where to put a fishpond."

A few weeks later, the two had drinks in the parlor and then traversed several rooms to her library. Huge French windows gave onto the back yard; the other three walls were covered with floor-to-ceiling bookcases. Eliot wandered over to take in the titles, mostly novels and cookbooks but also several shelves of assorted DVDs. He didn't recognize any of the movie names.

On the other side of the room, he lingered in front of several trophies and a framed diploma on one of the upper shelves.

"I hadn't realized you went to Duke. We always thought students there worked harder and learned more than we ever did at Harvard," he said.

"That was a myth," she answered, "but we certainly outshone the Ivy League when it came to sports, lacrosse included."

He inclined his head to indicate agreement with her appraisal.

She did not supply the fact that she had landed a four-year sports scholarship to the university, where she captained the women's lacrosse team, leading it to regional championships three years in a row. Nor did she mention that her parents did not live to see her graduate. The memory of their car crash on an icy road outside Chicago was something she took pains to tamp down.

Still, he lingered in the room, perplexed perhaps by the disparate pieces of her past on display.

"Such a hodgepodge," she commented. "Lugubrious even for me. Why don't we go outside and enjoy the sunset?"

"By all means. But first: how ever did a lacrosse champion and honors graduate from Duke end up in Hollywood?" he asked, having fixed on several plaques atop the bookcases, including one for best drama series in 2008.

"To be honest, it was a fluke," she let herself confide, and went on to explain that a former teammate had invited her to attend the Los Angeles Olympics in 1984. "Like so many young people, I fell in love with the sunshine and the palm trees. You know how it is, I met people."

Eliot stopped browsing the shelves and trained his eyes on her.

She swallowed hard. "Anyway, one of them was my friend's uncle, who turned out to be a studio bigwig."

"I see," he replied. (Eliot's tone suggested that the uncle being a bigwig and her, a small fry, explained everything. *Perhaps to a man it did,* she suddenly thought.)

"Things went from there," she wrapped up, waving her arm in the air.

Eliot arched his eyebrows, expecting more, but she did not elaborate.

Even if her guest had not been a person whose interest in others, especially women, was circumscribed, Serena was not in the habit of regaling anyone with the story of her rise in showbiz. By nature private and not given to self-promotion, she kept her trials as well as her triumphs in Tinseltown to herself, shrugging them off as par for the course. Throughout her career, she had only rarely confided them to friends or, when necessary, reported them to the powers-that-be.

Beginning with her college friend's uncle.

A distinguished-looking man, in an immaculately tailored suit, had sidled up to her one evening that first summer as she stood by herself, sipping an Arnold Palmer and staring off at the city lights. Like so many parties in the Hollywood Hills she went to in the years that followed, this one was studded with starlets and awash in champagne. At twenty-six and with no prospects to speak of, she was not yet of the place.

"Quite a view from up here on Mulholland Drive. Never fails to impress," the man had ventured, puffing on a cigarette, which he soon tossed onto the gravel path and scrunched with his shoe. She had smiled, not knowing how to reply and not adept at small talk. The shoe though she noticed—expensive-looking, like his suit.

"Samuels, Samuels," he had mused a few minutes later as he queried her about where she was from and how she knew his niece. "From Chicago no less. You wouldn't be related to David and Sarah Samuels, by any chance?" She was stunned; he elaborated. As a script supervisor at RKO in its heyday, Barry Burstein had shepherded several of her parents' books to screen in the fifties. "Sad about that horrific accident. They were talented."

Now based at Paramount, he ended their chat by inviting her to visit the studio. "With a degree from Duke and your family connection, there might be a few jobs you could apply for. I might be able to help..."

Ten days later he raped her in his office suite. She could still recall the poster of *Sunset Boulevard* on the wall behind his desk.

If Burstein surmised wrongly about how familiar his latest hire was with film noir, Serena made it her purpose to learn all she could about that and every other movie genre. By the time she switched from Paramount to Universal five years later, she was reckoned one of the town's most knowledgeable film mavens, and one who could whip a script into shape in no time flat.

"You're being way too modest, Serena. Looks like you landed several awards for scripts you oversaw. Nothing lugubrious about that," Eliot said, turning back her way. It was the first compliment he had given her. "It must have been rewarding, doing what you did, all those years." If not precisely a question, it did invite a response.

"Largely true. In any case, I prefer to dwell on the positive side of my years there, and shrug off the negative bits," she replied cryptically.

After that conversation, Serena made certain to steer far from touchy subjects like non-disclosure agreements—she had signed one years ago—or how rampant sexual misconduct still was in Tinseltown. Leaving aside her own experience, she had seen enough over the years of female colleagues ousted or marginalized when they spoke up against male abusers, and more recently, impugned for *not* sticking up for themselves in the face of harassment. Serena believed in nuances, relishing them, in both her male and female friendships. She liked to think of herself as liberated in that regard.

Now and again over the next few months, Serena did, however, regal Eliot with a few light-hearted anecdotes from her studio days, mostly with the idea of piquing his interest in classic movies or award-winners. One Saturday after racquetball, they drove to San Luis Obispo to catch a recent picture which she claimed ought to have won the Oscar the year before. "It's both a tongue-in-cheek take on Tinseltown and a love letter to it."

Eliot had seemed intrigued by the premise of *La-La Land.*

"Not to mention that there's music and dancing, which, if I understand rightly, you do a lot of."

He looked flummoxed by the remark. "Of the ballroom type, yes. We did a lot of that," he confirmed, but with finality.

Serena did not point out that she had taken a semester's worth of so-called smooth dancing at Duke, the year she twisted her ankle and had to forego lacrosse. Nor did she mention that San Luis Obispo boasted its own contingent of ballroom dancers, who happened to gather for monthly sessions.

All in due course, she told herself.

CHAPTER FIVE

Eliot

Aches, Pains and Plans

acquetball was something Eliot had never expected to play with a woman. And to be bested at it, never.

Like most men, he enjoyed games, especially ones he could win.

He had competed against other Harvard classmates at tennis and on the fencing team, cheered on by fellow law student and erstwhile girlfriend, Isabel Frankel, and latterly by his future wife, Silda Sorenson. Neither young woman cared for games nor practiced any sport themselves, that he could remember. Isabel, who boasted several prominent judges in her family, was enamored of the law, the only exercise she indulged in was verbal jousting; Silda, a liberal arts major who played the piano and spouted a little Russian, was too limp-wristed or disinterested to handle a racquet or toss a ball.

If he had to bet, neither woman he dated, as different one from the other as they were, owned a pair of sneakers.

Mostly, as he soaked his own aching feet that Monday morning after the game against Serena on Saturday and the jaunt with Daphne on Sunday, he remembered those college digs.

Isabel's lodgings off-campus were cluttered with books and papers and post-it notes, clothes tossed on the floor, a leaky toilet in the bathroom, and a mirror partially obscured with messages scribbled in lipstick. There were more red smears on the glass than ever on her lips: *buy more No-doze, call father about that 1920 precedent, don't skip the seminar on tax reform.*

His first serious girlfriend was the least self-conscious person Eliot had ever met; everything about her was unrehearsed and unfiltered. She did not dress up or act up.

What he remembered most about Silda's Radcliffe dorm room—she was only a freshman when he was in his third year of law school—was the closet. The image of her neatly arrayed outfits, all on identical wooden hangers, had stayed with him through the years.

"Ouch," he winced, as he rubbed his right insole. Traipsing around the fairgrounds with Daphne hadn't helped his feet, but it was the exertion in the gym the day before that had triggered the pain. Letting the hot water work a little longer, he closed his eyes and returned to his Harvard days.

If Issie, as he called her, could be described as unaffected, and unbothered by the impression she made on others, Silda was scrupulously put together, her every move meticulously arranged—from her carefully constructed coiffeur to her carefully assembled coterie of friends.

Where Eliot had been bowled over by Issie's smarts and invigorated by having to compete against her, he was outclassed by Silda's more calculated game. When he threw over the former for the latter, he, like most men in similar circumstances, had no idea what he was getting himself into. Married less than a year after meeting and albeit six years his junior, Silda figured him to a *T*, yet made him believe they were playing by his rules, and that he was winning.

So Issie eventually summarized the situation, round about the time the two began to meet up again, at this or that law conference.

"Silda has you wrapped around her little finger, Eliot. I bet there's not a thing you do in life that she has not figured on before you do it," she had further opined during one of their trysts. "Including this," she had capped the thought, literally seconds before giving him a blow job.

Yes, Issie was nothing if not unabashedly spontaneous.

Sitting now with his legs bare and his feet rosy in the hot water, Eliot wondered why his mind kept wandering back to those extracurricular activities. While he still refused to acknowledge that screwing Issie was tantamount to adultery—to him their encounters were simply a token of their enduring friendship—he did feel out of sorts comparing her to his now-dead wife.

"*Basta*," he uttered aloud, tossing his head to throw off the thought of his old chum and refocus on what he had been advised to do: make a concerted effort to rejoin the circle of life.

To join women like Daphne, Serena and Kathleen in such a circle required, however, more stamina and imagination than Eliot had mustered in some time. Not that he begrudged the effort—anything was better than wallowing in self-pity—but he would need to dedicate more energy to the effort. And get to know these ladies better. In their different ways, they had much to recommend them. And they all could cook!

As Caroline had counseled him, "Women aren't that dissimilar from men. They want to be appreciated for who they are, not for whom men want them to be." He had looked at her skeptically. "Playing games is what kids do," she had added to drive home her point.

Her gloss on relationships had struck Eliot as a warning of how much women's expectations might have evolved over the last few decades. Decades during which, as a married man, he was oblivious to these changes, she might be implying.

What he did not confess to Caroline was how hesitant he was to open himself up for scrutiny. Not only did he still struggle with bouts of depression, but he didn't like being prodded or his assumptions questioned.

Should he explicitly let these ladies know—his version of scribbling a note on a mirror or handing them a post-it note? He wondered if any of them would pick up such hints on their own, or if he would pick up on what might irritate *them*!

It probably takes a marriage, he reckoned. Only then do two people let down their defenses, inviting entry into the recesses of their minds as well as of their bodies.

So, it had been with Silda, he staunchly believed, at least during the early years, when, arguably, she had revealed more of herself than he had of his. Eliot had long believed he had many interesting things going on in his life, Issie among them; Silda, however charming, had revealed herself to be a less complex person, with fewer things to hide.

Unlike him, his wife had by and by, (he could not pinpoint the year), lost her taste for sex. His desires had never flagged. Besides, there was the added titillation of screwing the very woman he had thrown over for Silda and who still, year after year, apparently—nay, certainly—hankered after his body.

So he told himself as he massaged his swollen ankles and then dried each foot gingerly. He considered his aches and pains a genetic condition, unconnected to his age or the lack of regular exercise.

"Whatever, you do, don't grow old, son," his father used to joke, as he would grimace upon rising from a chair. The old man, no-nonsense New Englander that he was, had held on until he reached ninety-nine, as clear-headed and opinionated as ever.

At this point, Eliot dearly hoped to be and do the same. Preferably with a woman to cheer him on.

CHAPTER SIX

Kathleen

From Basil to Bouillabaisse

Neither inordinately bright nor beautiful, Kathleen Pavonine was considered a handsome woman, with a sensible head on her shoulders and an air of self-possession. Without undue effort, she put others at ease rather than on edge.

Such were the qualities that Eliot came to appreciate as their friendship grew. The evening at the opera in San Francisco was a case in point, an opportunity to experience not only an exquisite performance of *Tosca* but to benefit from the aplomb with which his companion had drawn him into her circle. She had a gift, he concluded, for promoting the people she was interested in without embarrassing them or making others feel diminished by comparison.

That summer night in the city by the bay he decided Kathleen was a person worth cultivating.

What he didn't pick up on so readily was how clear-eyed Kathleen was, unflinching in the assessment of her limitations, and unwavering in efforts to improve upon her strengths.

One of those strengths was putting congenial people together and keeping ill-suited ones apart. She had learned the trick as a child, given that her own large family was plagued with squabbling parents, unpleasant in-laws, and antagonistic siblings. Without axes to grind of her own, she honed her skills as a peacemaker.

As time passed, she also learned how to gauge the distances between people, and how to shorten or lengthen them—depending.

Others noticed, one acquaintance remarking that Kathleen Calhoun could have been a diplomat had she been blessed with the right privileges and connections. She had neither but she made do.

After working her way through college at San Jose State—she did well enough to earn a master's in Business Administration—she headed to the big city, fingering a couple of recommendations in her pocket. They didn't help. Jobs in the late seventies were scarcer than she had anticipated. To make ends meet, she tended bar around Fisherman's Wharf or waited tables in Haight Ashbury, crashing at the apartments of friends and eating largely from food trucks.

At one such window, as she pulled out her wallet to pay the $3.75 for her lunch order, she looked up into the eyes of an exotic-looking young man with big brown eyes. He had just served her up a toasted tomato and avocado sandwich, with trimmings.

"Believe it or not, this is the tastiest meal I've eaten all week—at least from a truck," she commented, smiling at the young man.

"*Naturellement*," he replied pleasantly. "I put…how do you say? Extra *bazile* on it. Gives it the flavor."

"Ah, basil, you mean," she returned, correcting his accent while nodding approvingly. It was another of her strengths, recognizing and encouraging talent.

In any case, the modest sandwich was the beginning of her thirty-year partnership with François Pavonine in the San Francisco restaurant business. He knew how to cook—and learned to do so with more than just herbs—and she knew how to do things on a shoestring and get the word out.

Together, the two had moved from eighteen-hour days managing a fleet of food trucks to running a popular establishment on Nob Hill—and eventually buying out the owner.

However hard-earned Kathleen's self-assurance and fearlessness, they stood her in excellent stead. She turned them into an art form, beating the bushes to make sure François was featured in news stories and introduced to potential backers. Eventually, reasoning that the restaurant business, however good at it they were as a team, was too precarious on its own, she steered her husband into business extensions—a line of soups for local supermarkets and an online blog about cooking with spices, which she wrote but he put his name to.

Friends thought of their relationship as a marriage made in heaven. "What cheese is to an omelet, Kathleen is to François," one of their long-time customers quipped.

If sex had never been central to their life together, she rationalized the lack of interest in their single-minded pursuit of culinary perfection, and the enjoyment of perks that accrued to it. The idea of having children, they never got around to discussing.

Her equal in the endeavor to make it was her husband, whom she still referred to in speaking to strangers as "the well-known French chef François Pavonine." If she exaggerated his Parisian resumé, she did so with such conviction and affection for him that patrons, including the well-heeled ones who frequented their Nob Hill eatery, *La Chanson*, (where indeed song added an additional spice), took the couple under their wings.

To extricate themselves from the kitchen and the counting-house even faster, the couple took to sending their best clients personalized, hand-drawn recipes to their most popular dishes at Christmas, and when pressed at parties they catered, could run through a medley of Charles Aznavour standards as energetically as anyone. She could tickle the ivories well enough; he could carry a tune better than most.

Together, they were undaunted, in-demand, and openly amused by their success.

As a result, the duo began to put aside the pots and pans and account ledgers, devolving them to sous-chefs and assistant managers, and to take up the opera and the theater. Like everything they set their minds to, they absorbed quickly, he becoming an aficionado of Bizet's *oeuvre*, she of Verdi's canon. Within a couple of years, they were gifted a box at the San Francisco Opera by one of their Silicon Valley patrons and season tickets to the San Francisco Playhouse by a Marin County real estate magnate and his wife.

Their dream of making it big and enjoying the fruits thereof were in sight and would arguably have continued to unfold.

But on a foggy night in 2014, while switching stations on the radio, François lost control of his Land Rover on his way to cater a wedding reception in Palo Alto. The car plunged over an embankment; both victims were pronounced dead at the scene.

Kathleen—herself at home that evening, singing along to a Johnny Halliday tape while penning a blog about the delights of tarragon—got the call on her cell.

"Mrs. Pavonine? Your husband has been in an accident. Unfortunately, neither he nor his passenger made it. You'll see a roadblock and rescue trucks ten miles north of Palo Alto, past the exit for Redwood City. The police will assist you there."

Like many spouses in middle age, Kathleen had taken the marriage for granted—not François *per se*, whom she never once in their shared life considered an optional ingredient—but the idea that their bond might abruptly and irrevocably be severed had never troubled her mind.

Moreover, and not unlike the tragic denouements on the opera stage, she was ill-equipped for any such real-life turn-of-events. Had medical personnel not held her back, she might in her initial despair have leapt from the cliff herself.

"Like Floria Tosca about to launch herself from the parapet, our poor friend," one among their clientele had regaled their coterie back in San Francisco.

Only later did Kathleen snag on the other passenger. She had not been apprised that one Sophie Moreau, a French-born chef at a place near the Wharf, had accompanied her husband that ill-fated evening. So adamant François had been that he could handle the wedding event on his own. "No need to trouble yourself, *ma chère*. Get some rest. I'll be home by noon tomorrow."

That he might have found a paramour—Mademoiselle Moreau's picture in the *Chronicle* revealed her to be young and pretty—gnawed at Kathleen for longer than she might have wished.

As if she didn't have enough on her plate. It took well-nigh two years to right herself sufficiently to dig out from debts accumulated under the less-than-stellar management the couple had put in charge of their operations. Nor had the two ever gotten around to anything so mundane as life insurance policies. But she plowed her way through, untangling the legal wrangles and settling the regulatory issues that had dogged the couple's business holdings, relieved, after a fashion, to have something to focus on. If it hadn't been for her stepson, Pierre, she might not have managed through the worst of that period. She retained her interest in *La Chanson*; her stepson returned to Paris to finish his apprenticeship but with a promise to return to the States. Anon.

Eventually, after selling off the condo on Nob Hill, she retreated, well-fixed enough, to the Central Coast "to reconnect with her past," as she vaguely explained to the dwindling circle that remained steadfast in their friendship.

Ever inventive, it didn't take Kathleen long to find new footing in the enclave of her childhood. The Calhoun family home with a partial ocean view had long been razed and a mansion erected on the site, her parents dead, her unpleasant siblings dispersed far and wide. She lucked into a charming, if modest, hilltop home in Pismo proper, joined a network of Central Coast restaurateurs, and followed up on a few job leads with local vintners. One or two San Francisco-based big shots who had kept in touch made calls on her behalf. Within a few months, she got the call from an establishment overlooking the Pacific Ocean between Pismo and Shell Beach.

Although busy enough now managing the Lantana and making improvements to the menu, the staff and the marketing, she kept up as best she could with the cultural calendar and remaining friendships from her San Francisco days. Still, trying to keep a toehold in the city was an effort, and an expense, now that the Pavonine box had been reassigned and the season tickets had dried up.

More crucially, she no longer had a companion with whom to share her interests and expand her tastes: someone with whom to laugh at the world, to sing their hearts out—or to cook up something special together.

One early October evening after the Lantana closed and she drove home, Kathleen sat alone looking out the window toward the sea, sometimes humming one or another aria while desultorily flipping through old recipes. The 3x5 cards were all in François' neat hand, many with remarks in French for dishes, a few with dates and places the concoctions were first introduced. Perhaps a cookbook in his memory would be "piquant," she mused, plucking one of his favorite adjectives out of the air.

She took a deep breath, determined not to allow herself to dwell on the past on such a beautiful evening.

Instead, she pulled out one of the index cards, one with fingerprint smudges of butter or oil, and looked it over. Why not prepare a pork tenderloin, with roasted russet potatoes and a potpourri of vegetables—and why not invite Eliot Etheridge over for dinner?

She had not seen him properly since that Nob Hill dinner party in July, though he had shown up at her door not long ago to return a Pyrex dish. He had appeared distracted, and declined to come in. Holding the round dish, which she did not recall as hers, he went on about not being a good cook and hence having fallen back on what he hoped most anyone could enjoy.

That out of the way, he shifted gears. "Perhaps we can catch a play, in Santa Barbara, say, next month, or whatever else you might like to do there. It's not San Francisco by any stretch, but there are things to do..." He had trailed off.

She had nodded but did not want to appear overly eager.

"Restaurants, I imagine, you may have had your fill of," he rattled on, before correcting himself to say he didn't mean that the Lantana hadn't been a delicious discovery.

"Very sweet of you, Eliot, and yes, Santa Barbara would be fun." She took the covered dish from his hands. He had labeled and dated it. "To get together again. Let's be in touch."

If something had cooled between the two of them over the summer, Kathleen couldn't pinpoint it. She had not thought overmuch about it in the past six weeks—once or twice perhaps, but then let it go. If a gentleman did not enjoy her company or continue to seek it out, it was futile to persist. Especially if the gentleman in question had been recently widowed.

She knew something about such an ordeal: the way through it was winding and treacherous.

Still, Eliot Etheridge was charming and intelligent, and seemingly at loose ends. Worth the effort, in short. She made a quick calculation: her next night off would be Friday. After dining on the pork, they could listen to Verdi, sit outside on the terrace—she had acquired two space heaters for the approaching season—and toast the arrival of fall.

And, were he so inclined, they could talk about what it was like for him.

Perhaps she could encourage him to unburden himself. She might explain how, purely by chance, she had read about Silda's death in the Five Cities paper, and how, having grown up literally around the corner from the Sorensons, though in a less grand house, she had made a point of taking a casserole over to the house.

Perhaps she would not say that leaving the dish would have been the extent of it, had she not spotted the widower (whose hand she had held a little longer than necessary at the visitation) a week later dining at the Lantana. Leaning forward, he had appeared solicitous toward the two younger people whom she remembered as his children. Something about how he gestured with his hand in making a point to his son and reached over to pour his daughter more wine had resonated with her.

Eliot Etheridge appeared to be *très civilisé*, as François might have put it.

She had reintroduced herself, and an exquisite dessert, on the house, arrived on the table before the bill. She made a mental note—duly transferred to her iPhone reminders app later that evening—to ring his office the coming week.

Things had gone from there, including the weekend in San Francisco, but then rather fell off.

A tenderloin might be just the thing, she told herself.

CHAPTER SEVEN

Eliot

The Lives of Others

Life was not fair, Eliot had long ago discovered—but as he now understood, it was particularly unfair for women. His wife had rarely harped on such a subject, she being blessed with beauty, brains and sufficient money of her own, but she didn't demur when the discussions on the subject at the Santa Barbara Book Club became heated.

Mostly, those in attendance at these *soirées*—even the few men who were regulars—had concurred that the battle between the sexes was rigged. Whether they were re-reading classics by George Eliot or Thomas Hardy, it was always the heroines who paid the price for being uppity.

"Surely, things have improved in the last thirty-odd years, wouldn't you all agree, ladies, even in fiction?" he had once ventured. Silda, who rarely betrayed her emotions in public, looked bemused.

"For some, arguably," one of the women had opined, keeping her equanimity, "but for those who are no longer—how can I politely put this in mixed company—bed-able, their lot is, at best, to become invisible. Society has decided they no longer matter."

Some murmurings followed this provocative contention, although Eliot couldn't recall what Silda had chimed in with, if anything. He did remember the pall that descended over the usually polite, and only rarely disagreeable, proceedings. Most of the dozen regulars in the club, two of which were wives of other lawyers in the firm, were well past fifty, and as such, could be said to be no longer—well, he didn't wish to put a more vulgar word to it.

If he hadn't much thought about the injustice of it all back then, he now believed that older women had to work harder at practically everything: if not how to make a casserole, finding the appropriate male to whom to take it.

In his case, not one, not two, but three ladies were catering to him in such a fashion, though what they had in mind as a *quid pro quo* he wasn't prepared to articulate.

All he would allow when queried, chirpily, by Caroline or on the phone, pointedly, by his children, was that he had enjoyed "a pleasant-enough get-together" with one or another of these women during the waning weeks of the long California summer. To himself, he did also admit that he enjoyed their company in different ways and marveled at how they managed to interest him in things he had never much thought about or undertaken to do.

With Serena, he had, after those initial months of wandering around the house in a fog and sleeping ten hours a night, not only acquired more energy playing racquetball, racing her up and down the lap pool or walking the beach at Pismo, but she had turned him into an admirer of movie directors like Billy Wilder and William Wyler. Not only did she come up with amusing anecdotes about the filmmakers, but she brought along tasty dishes, from vegetarian chile to mushroom risotto, to go with their viewing sessions.

With Daphne, Eliot took a different tack, making an effort, with Caroline's help, to interest a couple of gallery owners in her paintings. That entailed his assistant's coming along to the trailer park to sift through canvases and settle on a few to take to the Ocean View Gallery right off State Street. The owner, an older gentleman who presumably favored paintings of the sea, had been represented by the firm in a suit brought by one of his artist clients, and as Caroline suspected he would, found it hard not to return the favor.

Eliot himself browsed through Silda's art history books, determining that Daphne's seascapes most closely resembled those of Scandinavian painters, including a few by Edvard Munch. When he pointed this out, she appeared flummoxed, while ferociously stirring the gumbo she had prepared for the two of them.

At that moment, Eliot's heart went out to her, thinking she was the closest thing to an innocent he had ever come across. He had already vowed that sex would be out of the question with Daphne, and to steel himself in his decision, engaged Caroline to pick out a few "more acceptable" tops for his young friend.

With Kathleen, Eliot found that he could, if subtly prompted, begin to unburden himself of matters that still troubled him. Unlike what he had at first assumed about Madame Pavonine, she was not so much a social butterfly as an excellent listener.

He might have missed discovering this had he not returned a Pyrex dish around the end of September, and on the spur of the moment, invited her to a play. While at UC-Santa Barbara to teach his course on legal ethics, he had noticed a flyer for a series of classic French plays to be performed at the college.

"It'll be nothing as grand as *Tosca but* seeing *Tartuffe* might allow you to revel in the language, and me to bone up on my lackadaisical acquaintance with it. Plus, it's supposed to be funny," he had gone on in his convoluted way, standing there with the dish in hand. For whatever reason, Kathleen had accepted, postponing her home-cooked meal for another time.

When, almost a month later, the two did get together for dinner at her home on the hill, the autumn wind had picked up, making the veranda out of the question. They ate in the dining room, by candlelight, a CD of French *chanteuses* playing softly in the background. For an instant, Eliot wondered if the candles and the voice of Edith Piaf were supposed to encourage a romantic reading of the occasion. Unlikely, he concluded: his hostess was dressed in her usual elegant but conservative style and chattered away animatedly about the play.

"The performers were excellent—except for Tartuffe's wife when she forgot her lines and gesticulated so frantically toward the prompter's box. It was hard not to crack up. Anyway, I'm glad you chose Molière rather than some dreary thing by Racine."

To keep the focus on her, and not let things take too intimate a turn, he shifted the conversation toward her culinary past.

"The pork is excellent, Kathleen. A recipe learned at your mother's knee or a secret your husband swore by?"

Before responding, she wiped her lips with her linen napkin and took a sip of the Sancerre he had brought.

"My mother had her hands full with us kids. I ended up in charge of keeping the others from squabbling. As for François, he believed in slow roasting and rosemary, so I suppose you could say I follow that advice for most meat dishes."

"Well, you outdid yourself," he replied diplomatically. "That aromatic spice I couldn't identify?"

"Straight from the pot of rosemary on the veranda," she said, gesturing with her arm. "And this may sound crazy or presumptuous, but I'm toying with the idea of putting together a cookbook—in François' memory. He had such eclectic tastes and conveniently jotted everything down on index cards." Eliot's eyebrows went up. "Something to keep me busy, and, however it sells, to give as gifts to his friends and former clientele."

"An excellent pursuit," he replied. After a pause and another shift in tone, he added: "You two must have been a formidable pair. You no doubt still miss him."

On the CD player, the sultry *chanteuses* had given way to the feisty Jacques Brel.

She inclined her head, accepting the observation, though a quiver briefly distended her mouth. At the next lull in the music, she repeated the title of the song they had just heard: "*Ne me quitte pas,*" she said, pronouncing each word distinctly, "was also the name of one of our restaurants." He nodded again, not knowing what to say. "But people do leave us, don't they?" He looked disconcerted by the question, however rhetorical. "And there are things we never get to ask."

Eliot raised his gaze enough to catch the faraway look in her eyes. Slowly he gathered his thoughts.

"The suddenness must have been devastating, but I can assure you it is also anguishing to watch the slow decline of someone you love," he replied softly. This time she closed her eyes in seeming commiseration. "No escape either way."

Without speaking again, they finished off the bottle of Sancerre, he straining to follow Charles Aznavour's fervent rendition of "*Emmenez-moi.*" The song had been a favorite of Silda's—her French still fluent despite few chances to practice it. *Why had they never traveled together to France?* he asked himself.

Seeing her guest so absorbed, Kathleen quietly rose from the table and brought from the kitchen a bowl of fresh pears sprinkled with blue cheese, golden raisins and walnuts.

"Those are wonderful CDs. I only wish I could follow along better than I do. Molière's play was easier."

"You'll be amused—François and I used to sometimes sing for our supper. He put personality into his performances. I accompanied him on the piano, decently enough, all things considered." Her face had lost its pained expression.

"Then I must cajole you to play at the house sometime."

"He was the main attraction, not I," she laughed, "but it was fun. People seemed to like it."

Eliot nodded; Kathleen put her hand to her chin in thought. "Did you and your wife—I seem to remember them, at the Lantana, pouring over a musical score—play anything together?"

He looked perplexed.

"The occasion when I recognized Silda and we spoke. She was with a friend or a relative of some sort."

Eliot made a skeptical face as if to suggest he had no idea of what or whom she spoke.

"Anyway, it looked as though one or the other was composing something. They had pencils, marking things up. François did a little of that too, though it would have been hard to improve upon the songs Aznavour or Brel wrote."

Eliot finished up his pear salad and sipped the cognac she had poured. Whom could Kathleen be talking about, he wondered. Silda did have an uncle, a solitary sort living nearby in Oceano, but he had been a sailor and then a civil engineer, not likely musically inclined. Nor could he imagine Seth Sorenson dining at the upscale Lantana Grill.

"The closest she and I came to something like that," he eventually allowed, "would have been ballroom dancing. Our foxtrot won us trophies."

"That must have been exciting."

"Not that we cared so much for the competitions, but we loved dancing to Big Band music. And she to dress up...gorgeous gowns, golden slippers."

Kathleen eyed her guest closely. "You must miss her—terribly. She looked lovely that day I glimpsed her."

"Yes, she was. Lovely, that is."

They both took another sip of the tawny liqueur. Eliot re-arranged his face to erase whatever residue of regret might have lingered. Still, he was glad to have had their exchange, to have established where the common ground, and the boundaries between them, stood.

Looking intently across the table at him, Kathleen spoke in a low voice. "All I can say, Eliot, is that things get easier, with time. And with other distractions..."

CHAPTER EIGHT

Eleanor and Jared

Sibling Suppositions

ad? Fancy catching you at home," Eleanor began, the veiled complaint masked by the alcohol she had consumed and the noise in the Upper East Side restaurant where she and Jared had just finished their main course. She looked over at her brother and nodded her head in the affirmative.

Proceeding to pour the rest of the chianti into their glasses, he made a face as if to say better you than me: to inquire, that is, into how their father was getting on and to submit to his turning the tables on them, when he would inevitably, and insistently, pry into—and if they weren't prepared for it, critique—their lives.

While Eleanor did her duty, pressing Eliot on how the office in Shell Beach was working out and what else he was doing, eliciting only the most generic of responses, Jared ordered a cognac for himself and a tiramisu for the two of them to share.

However rarely they got together and how little they saw eye-to-eye on anything, they did respect each other's food and drink preferences. As usual, too, Eleanor would be picking up the tab, she already on track to become a partner at Carlyle, Messerschmidt and Perkins and *ergo*, expected to expense any meal during which she offered legal advice.

In the case of Jared, there was always something to advise about.

To what he called his "utter astonishment," he had recently been accused of "harassing" one of the interns at the magazine where, as a junior editor he had labored for the last four years. Pushing thirty-five, he had never received assurance that he might be in line to move up. And now this setback.

Over the pasta primavera, Eleanor had grilled her sibling over his relations with this Miss Fitzhugh, ascertaining that he had raised his voice to her when she had fiddled with the punctuation in a piece he had painstakingly edited. In short, he had, within the hearing of others, called her "a fucking moron" for turning his semicolons into dashes and his colons into ellipses.

"You should not have gotten so riled up about punctuation, dear brother, but if that's the worst of it, I doubt she'll actually file suit," she had opined.

"Conceivably, but others might have misinterpreted the outburst. I can't afford to lose this job."

Eleanor had bit her lip, declining to say that in her opinion the job might not be so important to hold onto. Rather, she nodded in acknowledgment of his concern and suggested they should ring their father.

"We might catch him before he goes out. It's only 7 p.m. on the West Coast."

The landline in the Sorenson home, rang several times before Eliot picked up.

"I tried you several times recently, Dad, including last Saturday." At his response she rolled her eyes. "You were where? At a dinner party up on the hill. Lawyers or what?"

Eleanor was trying to make sense of his account of the evening he was out, raising her voice over the din in the trattoria. For an instant, she regretted they chose Italian: her favorite French places in the neighborhood would have been quieter. She stuck a finger in one ear and pressed the iPhone against the other. “A lady friend, huh? And she’s writing a cookbook. Do we know her?”

Her eyebrows arched in curiosity, Eleanor glanced across the table, exchanging a look with Jared. He rolled his eyes.

“No, no. Everything’s fine here. We got together for dinner, that’s all,” she explained, exasperation slipping into her voice. “And yes, he’s still at the magazine and still working on—I’ll let him fill you in.”

Thrusting the phone in her brother’s direction, she gave him her big sister look. Sighing in resignation, Jared put down his drink and took the cell. “Don’t forget to tell him,” she stage-whispered.

“Hey, Dad, how’s it going there with that dog?”

Eleanor pursed her lips in mild rebuke, (the dog, really?) but then quickly occupied herself with the last bites of the dessert her brother had ordered. *Men*, she thought. However much company or solace Keats had brought her mother, she for one was glad not to have a pet, or, for that matter, a man, in her life.

She did wonder about the women now in her father’s. The one on the hill overlooking Pismo Beach, the one who lived around the corner in Shell Beach, and apparently another one too, from what the Sorenson housekeeper had let slip on the phone several weeks ago, prattling on about Pyrex dishes and chicken Tetrazzini.

There could come a time, Eleanor mused, when some financial considerations might come into play.

“This is New York, Dad. Not enough time for a pet. And dog walkers cost an arm and a leg here,” Jared replied, parrying his parent’s thrusts.

Like her mother, Eleanor squirmed at any hint of penny-pinching, even when penury was not, strictly speaking, the case. However, in her estimation and she had said so, more than once, to his face, hence the infrequent get-togethers, her brother would do well to finish his literary epic—and get a real job. That she could recall, her younger sibling—only eleven months her junior and furnished with a respectable education—had never paid for a meal with her in the seven years he'd been in Manhattan.

Not that she minded, but Jesus.

"Yes, I'm making progress," Jared hissed through his teeth, his face clouding over. "No, I can't sit down every day to write. I have a job, remember? I have to carve out time and be in the right frame."

As usual, he had begun to react testily to the cross-examination about his coming-of-age novel. What was it he called it? A *Bildungsroman* or some such. Jesus.

He had turned his body away as he talked so that Eleanor now saw him only in profile. From her perspective, his jawline appeared hardened in resentment. For an instant, she felt dismay that he had grown up, involuntarily or not, imprinted to his mother as she had, quite consciously, emulated her father.

For a woman to be willowy was plausible; for a man, the trait shaded off into effete, if not ineffectual.

While Eleanor was trying to keep her disapprobation from rising at what she considered both her parents' obliviousness with respect to their children, the bill arrived. For $154, without a tip. How her brother—or anyone else—could enjoy Manhattan without an expense account was beyond her. She pulled the firm's platinum card from her wallet and slipped it into the pouch.

"Not really, Dad. I know she's the daughter of one of your partners, and a poet of sorts, but I haven't had the time to call her," Jared stated, color having suffused his cheeks. His dark good looks were now even darker. Why hadn't he found a proper girlfriend? Eleanor wondered. There had been one girl, a translator of some sort, but it seemed the thing had petered out. "And besides, Dad, writers typically don't hang out with other writers. If they have extra time, they sit down and write. It's a solitary occupation."

Eleanor debated whether to let the conversation deteriorate further or to intervene. She cleared her throat audibly. "Tell him we're planning to come for Thanksgiving—for an entire week. Go on, do it."

Jared shifted his weight in the chair to regain his composure. "Actually, we called for a reason. We're coming home for Thanksgiving. Flying to LAX on Tuesday."

Eleanor had intended to ask if coming out was okay, but it had always been convenient enough when they visited.

"We'll look forward to it too, Dad," Jared replied, this time more warmly.

Retrieving the phone, Eleanor told her father she would text details as soon as they had tickets in hand. "Oh, and before we hang up, I ran into an old schoolmate of yours. The Southern District of New York was sponsoring a conference and she was on a panel. Said you called her Issie. You'd know who I meant."

Walking his sister back to her condo on East 67th Street, Jared rattled on about how maddeningly intrusive their father was. "Such irritating queries. You'd think he could be more subtle and not put us on the defensive, like criminals or something."

Eleanor gave him a sideways glance. "He's a lawyer. Plus, he's now trying to fill Mom's shoes as well."

He swallowed hard, as he did whenever reference to his mother was made. "All I can say is, Mom was light-footed; he treads heavily, to complete the synecdoche."

"So literate you are, dear brother. Finish the damn book though, so others will know too," she chided him, retrieving the door keys from her shoulder bag. She smiled at him, aware that he suffered their mother's loss acutely, even now, ten months on. They were standing in front of her building, the doorman preoccupied with helping two old ladies out of a cab.

"Humph," he murmured in reply. "Working on it as best I can."

She nodded noncommittally, not wanting to further put her sibling on the defensive.

All of a sudden, he shifted gears. “What was that Dad went on about—a woman with a casserole or something.”

“Oh, that. That’s what they do, silly. Unattached women—with widowers. They take them covered dishes, highly caloric ones, not only to funerals but sometimes when they least expect it.”

“How weird.”

“No, quaint, but not weird.”

“Maybe. I guess we’ll find out in a couple of weeks.”

CHAPTER NINE

Caroline

The Trouble with Teens

It's not a good idea to dilly-dally over an unwanted pregnancy.

That was Ella's droll retort when Caroline reached out for help. Whether or not Chloe's pregnancy was unwanted, or by whom, was still an open, and touchy question.

Several weeks had elapsed since that Sunday outing in the hills, mother and daughter at an intractable stand-off. Chloe crept out early for school and follow-up study sessions at friends' houses, re-entering only at supper time, declaring herself not hungry and closeting herself in her room; Caroline had scrambled to line up an appointment with her doctor and with the pastor of the church they intermittently attended. She resorted to leaving post-it notes for her daughter on the fridge.

She also kept telling herself to give the child time and space to think things through, but Ella was right: the clock was ticking. The sooner the issue was resolved, the better, and the safer.

Naturally too, Caroline fretted over the young man in question. Where was he and what were his intentions, if any? Chloe had not uttered his name since her outburst in the car.

That piece of the puzzle, however, Ella had managed to shed light on, thanks to her own daughter. The girls weren't precisely best friends, but they did suffer through the same math class and took ballet together.

"Natalie is in the dark about Chloe's, well, condition, saying only that this Ian person used to come around in a red Maserati, but she hadn't noticed him, or the car, of late," Ella had further ascertained.

Caroline pondered this tidbit but said nothing. Ella jumped back into the void: "Turns out he's a Worthington." Still no visible reaction from Caroline; the surname only vaguely registered with her. "Father's that construction magnate. You know the one: bulldozing his way to billions up and down the coast, the wife spending the money as fast as he can make it."

Ella waited to see how that news was received.

"Would explain the Maserati, I guess," Caroline deadpanned.

They were splitting some fancy, overpriced appetizer and sipping a sauvignon blanc at yet another trendy eatery on State Street. For Caroline, it was the end of a long work week at the law firm and several sleepless nights. Ella's blasé tone, as well as the choice of bistros, irritated her but she had no other obvious friend in whom to confide. Mickey was out of the question, and in fact needed to be kept in the dark; Eliot she had already phoned to say she couldn't get up to Shell Beach due to "family issues."

"I'll have to thrash it out with her this weekend," Caroline said. "It can't go on any longer."

"Of course not. Plus, you look strung out. Why don't you take sick leave to handle this thing? Get Mickey involved, if necessary, or that nice boss of yours, the widower. A man might have more sway with her."

Caroline tried not to look put out. She did not bother to let her friend know that Eliot had rung up the day before to ask how things were at home and to offer his help, but she had been too stymied to let him in on the crisis. She had skipped her night school classes and now risked having to forego the final exams on tax law and legal ethics.

She said nothing about that either.

As for the ethics involved in the abortion option, Caroline was nominally pro-choice and the procedure, however newly under threat from pro-lifers, was still the law of the land. Not that she had ever discussed it with anyone, but she had herself considered terminating a pregnancy when it became clear that her marriage was failing. However little her choice did to salvage things with Mickey, having a daughter had given her own life new meaning.

Still. This pregnancy was different. Chloe was a clueless teenager, with limited resources and prospects, and this Ian Worthington was, if nothing else, a privileged prick.

"It's really down to me, Ella. But yes, I'm involving Dr. Kendricks and the pastor over at Methodist. For starters."

Ella nodded. "Santa Barbara is a small town. David will know of a decent 'practitioner,' if need be." She patted Caroline's arm, checked her cell phone, and stood up to leave. "Got to pick up Natalie from piano. She's due for a fitting for her homecoming gown. Maid of honor. Thought she would be queen." She turned her gaze skywards. "Never a dull moment with daughters, right?"

Caroline smiled wanly in agreement, albeit she thought the comment didn't do the subject-at-hand justice. "Go ahead. My turn to treat," she said. "And thanks for the advice."

For another half hour, Caroline sat sipping a second glass of the wine and rehearsing the speech she planned for her daughter. Although startled by the $82 charge, she left a hundred-dollar bill on the table and hurried around the corner to her car. It being a Friday evening, traffic crawled on the 101 North. It took her twenty minutes to exit onto Pike Street and turn onto Sunflower Lane. As she did so, a flash of red streaked by in the other direction, almost side-swiping her Camry.

But only when she pulled into the driveway did it dawn on her: a Maserati. She took a deep breath and went inside the house. Chloe was pacing the living room, wringing her hands, fuming. A table lamp lay smashed on the floor, cushions flung helter-skelter.

"He's a bastard, Mom. Said he doesn't love me—never did—and I need to grow up." Bursting into tears, she crumbled into her mother's arms. "I hate him, hate him, hate him," she sobbed.

Three weeks later, mother and daughter drove to a nondescript building in Goleta recommended by Dr. Kendricks where Chloe underwent a routine procedure to end her pregnancy. Even so, the girl returned home stricken and taciturn, taking a sick leave through Thanksgiving weekend and missing out on homecoming festivities.

For her part, Caroline felt relieved but emptied out. When Mickey showed up unexpectedly a few days later, she refused to let him in, claiming both she and Chloe were "highly contagious."

CHAPTER TEN

Eliot

Silda's Shadow

The holidays are fraught in the best of times, but for those who have recently lost a loved one they can be veritable trials.

Not excluding Eliot.

The long Thanksgiving weekend had traditionally been a festive family affair for the Etheridges, anchored by a candlelight turkey dinner (albeit catered) on the Thursday followed by a couple of social engagements—a lavish affair hosted by the firm and a Saturday night dance—and on Sunday afternoon parlor games and a croquet match in the back yard. All these were interspersed with phone calls to distant relatives and shut-in friends and fortified with an over-abundant buffet.

For thirty years Silda had choreographed every element to perfection.

But now panic set in. *How is it*, Eliot asked himself, *that his wife had so managed things during the holidays that he never even knew she was having to manage? If I lifted a finger, it was only to carve a bird.*

Without a convincing answer, he toyed with the idea of skipping town altogether, hopping a plane to, say, Talinn or Vilnius, exotic destinations he had always yearned to see. Silda had humored him in this fantasy: "The Baltics? They sound so, so bracing." But neither ever went so far as to purchase tickets. And now? He might have done so, but the crestfallen or nonplussed faces of his two children at the door, reading his message: *Spending a few days in the Baltic capitols. The house is yours*, deterred him from such action.

Perhaps as importantly, there were those three expectant ladies, who might call up, or come over, or leave a casserole on the porch.

Talinn and Vilnius would have to wait.

That decided, Eliot focused on getting through the four days with the right mix of company, and without any serious missteps. For all of those reasons, and despite not having laid eyes on her for several weeks, he called upon Caroline for help.

To adhere to tradition, he would order up a turkey for the Thursday and host an enlarged gathering for the Sunday afternoon. He would accept the invitation to the firm's annual post-Thanksgiving bash Friday evening. He had not yet determined which, in any, of his lady friends to bring along. The ballroom dance was out of the question.

On the tenth of November, he rang Caroline at home, having been told by the firm's receptionist that she was "recuperating apace."

"So glad you're better, but I wanted to catch you before, hopefully, you make alternative plans," he said, prefacing his invitation to come to dinner on the Thursday afternoon, and naturally to bring along her charming daughter.

Having not had the time or energy to make her own plans, Caroline jumped at the chance to get herself, and Chloe, out of the house. Since her marriage ended, she had had no in-laws to visit for the holidays. The dinner spent at Ella and David's home the year before had been full of doctors with trophy wives and spoiled teenagers. Even Natalie was on her way to becoming insufferable. She was relieved to have an excuse not to make a repeat appearance.

"Sounds delightful, Eliot. Let me know what dishes you'll need as we get closer," she had volunteered.

Having locked down his assistant to help out, and assuming Eleanor would pitch in as well, he rang up Silda's favorite and sole surviving uncle in nearby Oceano. He hadn't spoken to Seth since the funeral service. The crotchety old man hemmed and hawed but agreed to make the effort on both occasions "for Sil's sake," which made Eliot wonder if the octogenarian had forgotten his niece was dead.

Later the same evening, wine glass in hand and music in the background, Eliot considered what would be the adverse repercussions, if any, of having Daphne, Serena and Kathleen in the same room at the same time. "Shouldn't matter," he finally concluded, his friendship with each solid and innocuous enough, none likely to impinge adversely on the others. However, he was still not sure if any of them had undue expectations in his regard. Did any of the casseroles provide hints? Might chocolate mousse or hearty meatloaf signal something he was not picking up on? Could homemade soup have a subtext?

It was all too much to puzzle over, so he redoubled his efforts not to fret. As Silda would have counseled, the crucial question is which of these ladies would otherwise be at loose ends, and hence grateful for such a haven as the Sorenson home at holiday time.

For once, think of others, he scolded himself, suddenly overwrought. He decided not to put Mozart on the CD player ever again in the evening, especially after a glass of wine.

To his surprise, Kathleen declined the Thanksgiving dinner invitation. She would be flying to San Francisco to be with friends—and her stepson Pierre. Taken aback, Eliot could not remember ever being told about the latter.

"However," she was quick to add, "he has promised to return with me here for a few days. Perhaps..."

"Of course. We're having a few folks over Sunday afternoon. Come then and bring Pierre."

After they hung up, Eliot sat for a moment, trying to remember if his friend had ever mentioned her relation or what the young man did. Had he been so self-absorbed not to have registered any such allusion?

Plausible, he concluded, and, shrugging it off, proceeded to scroll through his phone for Serena's number. When last the two of them had met up, it was to walk the dogs along the boulevard. She had prattled on about some structural problems with the house, things not detailed in the inspection. He had enough such issues at the law firm; he tuned her out.

As it happened, Serena too would be otherwise engaged on the holiday itself, driving to Los Angeles for dinner with friends "in the biz." However, on the Sunday she'd be free—and would bring Dog, a casserole, and "an amusing enough neighbor."

For Daphne, Eliot left a message on her cell, figuring she was outside painting in one of her inevitable halter tops. Several hours later she texted back: *Sure. I'll bring a dish—and something special just for you—not eatable! But on the Sunday. Can't make Thanksgiving Day.*

At first relieved, Eliot was, upon reflection, disappointed that none of the three ladies would be coming on the Thursday. It would be left to Caroline to pick up the slack—or his children, were they in the mood.

These are the things I need you for, he murmured to himself, as he tidied up the parlor, polishing the antique dining room table to a high gloss. It was one of the few chores Silda enjoyed doing, never allowing Mariella to take it on.

The dinner came off just well enough—the turkey was tasty, Jared and Eleanor's version of dressing moist but crunchy, a congealed cranberry salad that Kathleen had sent over, refreshingly tart, and Caroline's pound cake made no one pine for pumpkin pie. Conversation did occasionally flag—: Chloe could barely be drawn out, not even by an inquisitive lawyer like Eleanor; Jared cut Caroline short when she queried him about the novel; Seth dozed off right after the dessert and snored loudly. Still, Eliot did his best to keep things on track, engaging Chloe one-on-one after the meal, but it was harder than it should have been.

To improve upon things for the Sunday gathering, Eliot ran through his count on Friday, concluding that more men, preferably younger ones, would help.

He phoned Caroline. “Bring someone, like a date.”

The request irked her, but she did owe Kevin, her acquaintance from night school. He had come over several times to catch her up with missed classes. He was, she had to admit, not as much of a klutz as she had presumed.

As luck would have it, one of those autumn storms off the Pacific brought strong gusts and intermittent downpours with it in the morning. There would be no buffet table or croquet match in the backyard and no newly picked gladiolas or camellias for Silda’s antique vases in the parlor.

However, there was a potpourri of dishes to savor, an assortment of indoor games, improvised music, a surprise painting, and an enjoyable enough movie—courtesy of the women in Eliot’s new life, and with assists from the men they brought along.

Caroline arrived early, two dozen homemade biscuits in hand and dragging behind her, a determined-looking Kevin, whom she introduced as “my fellow partner in crime.” To his credit, the young man had boned up on the history of the law firm, including its battles on behalf of the Indian tribes in the region—something Caroline knew nothing about. Before others arrived, Eliot took the young man into the library to see the now-faded daguerreotypes featuring founders of the firm and chieftains of the Chumash tribe.

While host and guest were ensconced in the study, Kathleen arrived with her stepson, two shopping bags dangling from his arms. He had, she explained, recently returned from Paris to take over as sous-chef at a bistro in San Francisco. One that was still “*en famille*,” as she put it.

After the requisite introductions, Pierre rolled up his sleeves and set about finalizing his father's salsa verde pollo creation in the Sorenson kitchen. Eleanor, the only one who had greeted him in French, and whom he immediately complimented for her accent, joined him in the effort, chattering away vivaciously while chopping scallions and simmering wild rice. He meantime shredded the meat from the chicken thighs, deftly using two forks, and she had time to admire his expressive hands.

Serena arrived minutes later, depositing Dog on the back porch to consort with Keats. She then handed a covered dish to Mariella—"It's basically spinach," she explained self-deprecatingly, "but panko crumbs and crushed pine nuts enliven it"—and dangled a Ziploc bag with two DVDs inside in front of Jared.

"One's arguably dated but a classic of its genre—and the other is a later, but little seen, masterpiece by the same director," she told him. She placed the bag with the films next to the TV screen. "We'll have a vote as to which to watch, if and when. If not, they'll be just for your father."

"Marvelous," Eliot broke in, "but what about…? I thought you were bringing one of our neighbors."

"Funny, that," she replied. "He was primed to come along, but when I rang him with details this morning, he begged off. Something about having to finish a composition. He's Russian, a composer of some sort. Unpredictable."

Some fuzzy memory stirred in Eliot, but he couldn't fix on it. "For another time," he replied.

"He's the neighbor whose dog used to play with Keats," Serena reminded him.

Eliot shook off his consternation. The doorbell had rung again.

Daphne, blushing, her damp hair corkscrewed into unruly curls from the rain, stood on the doorstep, her disarray in sharp contrast to her attire. She was wearing a powder-blue blouse with a Pierrot collar buttoned to the neck and a dark skirt of the same silky material falling below the knee. Likely things that Caroline had purchased on his behalf.

Eliot half-opened his mouth to compliment her before realizing she was not alone. Behind her stood an older gentleman in a three-piece suit, gold pocket watch on a fob. In his left hand, he was holding a dripping wet umbrella. He held out his other hand to Eliot.

"Braunstein's the name. Arthur. Pleased to meet you," he volunteered, Daphne having not yet uttered a word. She was holding a Pyrex dish covered with aluminum foil. Awkwardly.

Eliot took it out of her hands. "So glad you could both make it. Do come in," he responded, wondering who on earth this Arthur could be. *Old enough to be her father*, he thought, *but then...*

"I'll be right along. Something else in the car I need to fetch for Daphne," Arthur demurred, and gesturing the two inside, carefully made his way down the slippery front steps toward the car. Glancing over Daphne's head, Eliot saw a shiny black Mercedes parked at the curb.

Inside, Caroline soon approached the newly arrived guest to re-introduce herself. "I'm so glad you and Mr. Braunstein connected. Have you managed to visit the gallery?" she asked, handing Daphne a goblet of white wine from the tray she was carrying.

"Yes, I have. He—they—may show a few of my works. I brought something over to properly thank Eliot—for the introduction, that is," she added, turning away from Caroline. "Arthur is bringing it in. It's wrapped." Ill-at-ease in company, she raked the room for a haven.

At that point, Jared wandered over. No longer needed in the circumstances, Caroline crossed the room to help Mariella arrange things on the buffet table.

Not long after, Arthur returned with the gift for Eliot and propped it against the wall.

"I didn't have much time to cook, Eliot, so I tossed some shrimp in a bowl of cheese grits. But this is the reason why,"

Daphne blurted breathlessly, as she knelt to untie the string and lift the cloth wrapping from around her gift. Arthur held the backing in place and then hoisted the painting.

His face flushed in embarrassment. Eliot took the canvas in his arms. "Why it's lovely. You really needn't have but—"

"As you can see, Daphne adopts a very distinctive palette for her seascapes. They remind, though only indirectly, of the Nordic Expressionists—Munch and so on," Arthur interjected, accustomed as he was to being the art authority in the room. "The notes of purple in the water, the subtle shades of mist." He made motions in the air with his right arm to conjure the different hues.

Several guests nodded politely. "Tell us more about it, Daphne," Jared encouraged her.

"It's the first time since being in California I've included a human figure, along with the butterflies and birds," she obliged. Timidly. "If you look closely, you can spot a person near the shoreline." She pointed. "It's Eliot."

Her tone made her host blush further; Jared stifled an expression of amused bewilderment. Serena caught Kathleen's eye, but neither betrayed an overt reaction.

"Naturally, you will want to have it framed, Eliot—the gallery can assist if you like—and then find a space where it doesn't compete with others," Arthur instructed, seemingly without any irony.

After guests had a chance to admire the painting, Pierre made his entrance with his *pièce de résistance.* Eleanor helped ladle the stew into her mother's china tureens. "I've tasted it: it can only be described as *superbe*," she enthused in her best French, her face overheated.

"*Merci, et bon appetit*," Pierre replied, visibly pleased, his face rosy as well.

Kathleen beamed. "Before long, my stepson will run the place in San Francisco. You all must come up when that happens."

Once seated at the table, the guests attacked the stew along with Daphne's shrimp grits, Serena's spinach quiche,

Caroline's biscuits and eventually Kathleen's black bottom pie. "The secret may be the ounce of rum I added," she confided to Caroline when asked. "My husband always believed a thimble-full of liquor enhanced the flavor of most everything."

Afterward, as conversation began to lag, Uncle Seth hurled himself into the breach, regaling the assembled with tales from his ocean-going days. Were the assorted medals on his tattered vest from Korea or Vietnam, Eliot couldn't tell but thought better of asking. The old man might not recall. It was left to Daphne to be particularly charmed, and, having imbibed too much wine, to accompany the ancient mariner in a disjointed medley of sea chanties. Halfway through the spectacle, Eleanor and Jared exchanged a look as if to say, yes, we too have a crazy uncle in the family.

When it came time for charades, Caroline stepped in to suggest they choose a specific category, like movies or songs or historic characters. At first, they decided to impersonate film titles, until it became clear that Eliot, for one, would be at a total loss, and Serena at a decided advantage.

The group soon settled on books as the category. Of all people, Kevin proved himself the most adept at pantomime. He contorted himself mercilessly to conjure *The Hunchback of Notre Dame* and came up with an equally convincing recreation of *A Tale of Two Cities.*

"I knew you had talent but never would have guessed this particular one," Caroline complimented him afterward.

"Before I screwed my head back on, I had dreamed of making it in Hollywood," he replied. "Now, if you and I can get through night school, we can perform all we want as real-life Perry Masons!"

As for Serena's movies, they were both by Alfred Hitchcock, and, as with charades, they took a vote on which one to watch together.

Eliot encouraged her to do an intro— "like those guys on AMC do," Jared chimed in—and she obliged with a short rundown of the director's early silents in Britain and then his transfer to the U.S., namely to "her" studio, Universal, where he made his more famous films. In the end, the assembled group opted for *The Lady Vanishes*, which only Jared had ever seen. *The Paradine Case*, a courtroom whodunit with Gregory Peck, which only Kevin knew anything about, would be left at Eliot's.

"For another evening, that one," Serena said, confidentially enough that Eliot turned away to fiddle with the DVD player.

Despite a few touchy moments, things that Sunday went well enough that some indefinable weight lifted for Eliot, leaving him less burdened, and less tethered to the past.

CHAPTER ELEVEN

Eleanor and Jared

Unexpected Encounters

"Do you think he's serious about the girl?"

The two siblings were sipping acrid coffee toward the end of their flight back to New York City. Up until that moment, Eleanor had slept with her head propped against the window, despite the intermittently lit seat belt sign. Jared had read an entire paperback which he brought along as hopeful inspiration for his own opus.

It took Eleanor a minute to register what he was referring to.

"You mean Dad and the painter, Daphne something or other? A very New Orleans name, if memory serves."

"Dupree," he obliged, wedging his crumpled cup in the seat flap in front of him.

She paused to finish up what remained in her cup. "No idea. But *you* seemed taken enough with her. Exotic-looking, that's for sure, though it's unclear what she has going on upstairs."

Jared ignored her put-down by fumbling with his carry-on tucked under the seat. Despite the heat under his collar, he soon straightened up, and came right back at her. "What about you? Flirting, in French no less, with Kathleen's step-*fils*."

"At least Pierre is charming and can cook," she shot back, not waiting for her brother to agree. "Anyway, I showed him around Santa Barbara yesterday. He'd never been there."

"*Touché*. And I went over to Grover Beach on Monday after the rain stopped. I'm no connoisseur but Daphne's paintings are surprisingly good."

Eleanor scrunched her forehead. "I can't figure her—any of those women actually. They're all three presentable, leaving aside the trailer thing, and they're each accomplished." Jared tilted his head back and forth, noncommittal. "But of course, they're not Mom," she declared with finality.

"*Ça va sans dire* would be appropriate, right?" Jared rejoined, an unexpected note of solemnity in the joshing he usually adopted with his sister.

Right about then a tired-looking stewardess passed through the cabin to collect their cups and candy wrappers. The two siblings checked their cells: another hour until touchdown at LaGuardia. Headwinds had been unusually strong.

Still, they had done well to delay their return until Wednesday afternoon, having avoided the worst of the post-Thanksgiving air traffic—and having allowed themselves a chance to firm up their new friendships.

"Do you think we should have spent the day with Dad yesterday instead of with—"

"Don't start in," Jared snipped. "Mariella cleaned up the entire downstairs while he walked the dog. Likely together with Serena and that sleepy mutt of hers. Later, when Caroline came over, the two huddled in his office all afternoon. He was busy enough without our intervention."

"But he is lonely, wouldn't you say?"

"Likely," Jared allowed. "Mom was always the one steering the ship, filling it with passengers, and now it has no ballast and he's adrift."

"A metaphor for every season," Eleanor sighed, though without criticism. Jared gestured with his arms as though to indicate he couldn't help himself. She continued with her thread.

"Clearly, Dad's still reeling from it all, and these three ladies may provide much-needed diversion." Eleanor paused for her brother to expand on her assessment, but he didn't. "I mean, a movie buff living around the corner and a culture vulture with tickets to the opera." She paused. "Not to mention Daphne, however much she counts."

At this last comment, vaguely derogatory, Jared's face twitched. Eleanor wondered what was bothering him but knew better than to ask. Instead, she wound up, trying to sound conciliatory, and judicious. "Anyway, it's none of our business what Dad does, or with whom."

A longer pause while Jared let out his breath. "Unless he decides to tie the knot again." Eleanor looked at him askance. "You're the lawyer, Sis. Our inheritance—swoosh." Jared gestured with his fingers to indicate out the window.

Eleanor tried not to look peeved, such comments about money from her brother never failing to irritate her and make her want to pick up a pen and finish the damn novel for him.

"As I said, he has to live his own life as we do ours."

"Whatever you say," Jared responded, unconvinced but not energized enough to argue further.

"In any case, it can't hurt for us to check in on him more often. You know, fly out or have him come visit us."

"When each of us can. My fortune teller says 2020 should be a very good year for adventures of all sorts."

"You believe such nonsense?"

"Madame Futura was part of my research—for the book. Read my palm and said I'd soon be dazzled by someone. Her very words."

"And has that happened, dear brother?"

"Not sure yet."

Out of nowhere Eleanor piped up: "He still hasn't gone through the boxes."

They were sharing a cab back to their apartments, Jared's a third-floor walk-up on the Upper West Side, hers a swank two-bedroom on East 67th Street, walking distance of her law firm, weather permitting.

"What are you talking about?"

"You know, Mom's things in the closet in the room she—not the master bedroom."

"Dad said her things had been parceled out to friends or charity—you know, a tax deduction. Serena even mentioned she had come over to help him."

"Those were her clothes and such—not letters or documents or old photos."

Jared shrugged, not wanting to dwell any longer on the subject and needing to get his head back focused on his New York City life. "This may sound callous, but he might do well to toss all that stuff. Likely to be receipts of things she bought, or our school report cards, or old newspaper clippings—remember the year I had that story published in *The New Yorker* and you became valedictorian—or worse, funeral notices for relatives we barely knew."

"Hmmm," Eleanor responded, not entirely of the same opinion.

"Anyway, whatever's inside, what good would it do to pour over it all—at this point?"

Eleanor looked out over the lights of the city as the cab edged its way onto the upper deck of the 59th St. bridge. *Perhaps, for once, my scatter-brained brother is right.*

Still, she regretted not having volunteered to go through things for her father while there: how was it that on the Wednesday the turkey dressing and the cranberry sauce had been so all-consuming? Or that on the Friday, the day after the festivities, when she could have kept her dad company doing such an unenviable task, she had worked on a case she was trying back East?

In short, she had limited her time with her father to commenting Trump's latest shenanigans on the evening news. "No need to get riled up about the president," Eliot had advised her. "He's hopelessly out of his depth, and your blood pressure will go up."

That was the extent of their one-on-one exchanges the entire weekend.

There was worse to chide herself about. Practically all of Monday and Tuesday she spent out with Pierre Pavonine, showing him the sights, holding hands, eating seafood sliders, and...

In the semi-darkness of the cab, Eleanor blushed at the memory, however justifiable her behavior. Three years had elapsed since her divorce—three years in which she had never allowed herself to indulge in romance, whirlwind or otherwise.

Still, she felt bothered for not being more attentive of a daughter. Especially now that her father was—casseroles notwithstanding—on his own.

"In every marriage, however unimpeachable, there's something to be upturned when the other spouse departs." So one of her colleagues had opined not that long ago about a contested will they were handling. At the time, Eleanor's mind had not reverted to her parents, but seeing all those boxes at Thanksgiving, some labeled in her mother's flowery hand, had perturbed her.

Not that she had specifically planned to sift through her mother's past, which would likely have pained her as well. She had merely gone upstairs to find a bathrobe, having forgotten to pack one. Only a few ball gowns, still shimmering, and matching dance shoes, barely broken in, remained in the walk-in closet, along with several robes and bed jackets.

She had pulled a pink one from its hanger, which was the moment she noticed the boxes atop the overhang. For an instant, she had hesitated, then reached up and touched the nearest. It was a tiny Tiffany box, dusty. But then, taking a deep breath, she pulled back, folding the robe over her arm and closing the door to the closet.

"Sis? *Sis*?" Jared called out, then nudged her. "Who first? You tell him."

Eleanor leaned forward and spoke through the transom. "The Upper West Side. Go through the park. Ninety-third, between Broadway and West End." She turned back to her brother. "This way we have more time to talk."

"What else is on your mind, El?" he asked more brusquely than he meant. Already the city was starting to weigh on him. He needed to focus on what he needed to focus on.

"I was wondering—you had gone out there a couple of times during, you know, that period. Did Mom seem different once she ensconced herself at Shell Beach?"

"Really, El. You know how she was: enigmatic, keeping us, Dad too, at arm's length."

Eleanor thought her brother could be described similarly, but she let the irony of that pass.

"But yeah," Jared went on, calling up the memory of his visit out West in the spring of 2018, shortly before his mother's diagnosis. "She seemed happier. We strolled along the seaside with Keats, even sat on the rocks in the sunshine. She was positively gay. Played the piano one evening for me. Picked flowers for the table. Prattled on about this and that—people she had met along the boulevard. Never mentioned Dad, not once."

Eleanor absorbed this account as they wound their way through Central Park, a few joggers and couples out and about even at that hour. She tried to remember if she had picked up on anything remotely similar, but by the time she had flown out on her own, three months into her mother's cancer treatment, there was little for anyone to be gay about.

CHAPTER TWELVE

Daphne

The Point of the Picture

For several weeks thereafter, Daphne found herself circling back over the Thanksgiving holiday weekend. All those polite, privileged people and what to make of them. Playing charades and watching obscure foreign films and going on about books and operas she had never heard of.

She had come away keenly aware of her considerable limitations and that most people, possibly even Eliot, did not know what to make of her.

Since her visit to the Sorenson home, she had not heard from him except for a note to thank her for the painting. *I do plan to give it pride of place, perhaps on the landing where it would be visible to all & sundry*, he had written. Nothing since.

She wondered who *all & sundry* referred to.

As for Jared Etheridge, he had made a beeline for her at the party, before the evening was done, inviting himself to visit her at Paradise Park the very next afternoon. When she acquiesced, he had appeared elated, chatting animatedly as he accompanied her to the parked Mercedes, Arthur still engaged on the porch handing around his business cards.

They had settled on 5 p.m., no mention of a shared meal nor the length of the proposed visit, so when Eliot's son hadn't arrived by 6 that Monday evening, Daphne breathed a sigh of relief.

"So much the better," she mumbled as she set about scrubbing paintbrushes and feeding the cat, a stray that had recently adopted her. She had planned to settle in and flip through a huge tome that Arthur had recently presented her with, *Five Centuries of Western Art*. ("One can never know enough about painting—other things too," he had said upon the occasion.) Then, to her dismay, a car engine sputtered, and shortly came a tap on the metal door of the RV.

When she opened it, Jared appeared fidgety, clutching a bouquet of flowers. If flabbergasted by the disarray in which she lived—her undies hung from a makeshift clothesline outside; an ashtray full of butts sat on a counter inside—he pretended not to notice.

Without a word, she rummaged around for a mason jar for the roses; he broke the silence by pronouncing her abode "splendidly bohemian," which only served to irk her.

Hell, she had grown up in a not dissimilar shack on the edge of the ninth ward, and no one in that part of New Orleans thought of their dwelling as bohemian. "The dirt-poor live dispiriting lives in dilapidated places," she had thought of responding—a direct quote from her long-dead mother—but she resisted. Instead, she forced a faint smile and plunged a corkscrew into a bottle of wine. It was the more sophisticated vintage that Eliot had bought her months ago up in the hills.

As she struggled with that task, Jared scoured the canvases stacked against the wall, making vague noises about how "arresting" or "haunting" they were. "You shouldn't let that gallery owner take advantage. He's the lucky one, not you."

She nodded, without saying anything. The last painting she had sold on her own was back in August. A couple of tourists roaming the dunes paid $65. Meeting Arthur Braunstein had been a lucky break, though she thought better of saying so.

Over the wine and crackers, Jared plowed on, suggesting that the human figure—as in the painting she gave his father—added something decidedly "piquant" to her seascapes.

"Something your eye comes to rest on, and admire," he elaborated, his voice husky. Having polished off two glasses, he fleetingly raised his eyes to gaze at her, and, despite himself, at her tank top. She met his gaze: his face was shiny, heat coming off the skin; hers, bemused, disabused.

Since childhood, Daphne had been looked upon as an exotic flower, like her creole mother before her. "But when the bloom is off, honey child, the fade is fast," Mrs. Dupree used to lament when in her chops. "And then men flee like the plague."

About the young man now wedged on a bench across from her, his stomach against the table's edge, Daphne reckoned he was older but less experienced than she was. Regardless of his privileges, or his big city life, or the allure of being a novelist—if being such a thing was in fact alluring.

She took another sip of the wine. It was tart. Eliot had declared it "subtle, with hints of lemon that linger on the tongue...." He had said she might find it more appealing than the oh-so-ordinary chardonnay. Something like that. But never did he utter anything more suggestive than that to her. Perhaps it was the age gap or a lingering ache for his dead wife.

Part of her wished the father were the one here now, but the other part of her…well, why not?

Across the table, Jared was going on about Frida Kahlo. "What," he wondered aloud, "do you make of that painter's style and the influence of Diego Rivera?" Silence. "To be frank, you remind me of her—I mean *you* do, not your paintings so much."

Daphne sighed, weary. Crayons and drawing paper had been thrust at her since childhood, anything to keep her occupied and out of trouble. By age twelve, she had become adept at draftsmanship; in a rough-and-tumble high school, a sympathetic teacher had encouraged her to take up oils. But she hadn't a clue who this Kahlo person was.

She wished her guest—did Eliot know that his son had finagled to pay her a visit in Paradise Park? —would clam up and do what he came to do, even if he didn't know what he had come to do. She *did* know, however, and she had obliged many different men, and as long as the bloom was on, would keep doing so. When it suited her.

With Eliot too, whom she reckoned she liked more than most men and regretted that he hadn't kissed her that time they drank the chardonnay, or perhaps with Arthur Braunstein, if it ever were to come to that. The book he had given her rested on the table to Jared's left. He glanced over at the cover. It featured stick-like sketches of animals, bison or something, on an ochre wall. She had planned to read the inside cover that evening to know what they were all about.

"Went there a couple of years ago," Jared tossed out matter-of-factly. "Altamira was a revelation. Really cold inside those caves though," he added, imitating a shiver.

Daphne squirmed but said nothing.

However un-encouraged, Jared gibbered vacantly about museums in New York, and how she might profit from visiting the Metropolitan and the Frick and MoMA (whatever that was).

At that point, she lost patience with his prattle. Wriggling her foot out of her slip-on sandal, she slid it up his leg. Like a practiced brush stroke on canvas. That's all it took. He was aroused but also embarrassed. He started to hiccup. Uncontrollably, interminably.

Most days, Daphne would have dabbed at her easel until around 5 p.m., when she would pause, light up, and watch the sun drop into the ocean, blowing smoke rings as the orb descended.

Today, however, was different. She had an appointment at the gallery in Santa Barbara at 4 p.m. and was advised by Arthur Braunstein's officious assistant not to be late.

While the cat watched her warily, she scrubbed paint from her hands and stepped out of her stained overalls, tossing them and her t-shirt into the kitchen sink. "Sooner or later a washing machine will be in order, Kahlo," she told the cat. She had looked the artist up online, on her phone, but Frida Kahlo's paintings were nothing like her own. Still, she liked the name—it fit the calico.

Then, after shampooing her hair in the cramped shower stall, she shook out her ringlets, ran a comb through the tangles and gathered the longest strands into a French twist, securing them with tortoise-shell barrettes. Keeping to theme, she put on the other skirt and blouse that Caroline had brought over, on behalf of, she had emphasized more than once, "my boss at the firm, Mr. Etheridge." This skirt too was dark, and woolen, the blouse moss-green and long-sleeved. Suitably conservative. Perhaps the gallery assistant would not eye her so dismissively this time. Not that she cared. Arthur clearly liked her, and he made the decisions.

After going through all the canvases she hadn't either trashed or given away, Daphne had assembled a batch of paintings to be exhibited—four that Arthur had concurred with, and two larger works she had recently completed, which no one other than a few nosy camp residents had laid eyes on.

One featured three children cavorting along the shoreline, and a few gulls swooping overhead. They were modeled on a ragtag threesome who, with their parents, had been lodging nearby for the last few months. In the other, two lovers lay entwined on the beach in the pale light of dawn. She had thought of Eliot while she worked on it; however, it had been with Jared that she had lain in the dunes that early Tuesday morning, after a night of helping him get rid of the hiccups and a raging headache.

A strong cup of coffee at first light finally did the trick.

"Tastes similar to what Dad drinks at Shell Beach—strong and aromatic," the younger Etheridge had commented, upending his mug. He had then suggested they watch the sun come up at the water's edge.

Lying there on her beach blanket, he had chattered on about his novel and how he hadn't yet figured how to end it;

she meanwhile tried to imagine what, if anything, she'd ever say to Eliot about this unusual night spent with his son.

Nothing is usually best, she had concluded but disentangled her legs from her companion nonetheless.

"I do find you amazing, Daphne, so, if it works out, I'll fly back in a few months, after the holidays. Or, you could come visit New York," he had blurted out, heedless.

She had further withdrawn her body while Jared babbled on—he was more loquacious than his father—pulling her knees up and wrapping her arms around them. She looked out at a distant ship passing by, willing herself aboard.

Eventually, his outpouring of gratitude for her ministrations during the night subsided. As neutrally as she could, she mused aloud that, if she traveled at all during the holidays, it would be to New Orleans. "To be clear," she wound up more forcefully, "cooking food and coloring pictures is all I was ever cut out for, Jared. My mother's very words. No point getting any big ideas about me."

"Whatever you say," Jared had responded, deflated. "But you under-estimate yourself." Since Daphne said nothing, he busied himself by burying his bare legs in the sand and then slowly brushing them off. "I suspect we'll be back out here soon enough—Eleanor and I—to see about our father. He has taken our mother's loss very hard."

Turning that last comment over in her mind, Daphne decided that it rang true. Jared might not be someone she sparked to—but if he were a dutiful son, he was to be commended: just not encouraged to upstage his parent by putting moves on her.

She turned back toward him to pat his arm. "This is the best time of day to paint—and this morning I feel inspired. We should head on back."

In silence they crossed the sandy beach, dodging the puddles and occasional driftwood deposited by the outgoing tide. A few butterflies flitted by. As he proceeded to get into the rented Volvo, Jared paused, reached into his slacks and handed her a business card. Then he lowered himself inside and revved the motor.

"So," he said, looking out the open window at her, his hands atop the steering wheel. She raised her eyebrows. "It's been, needless to say, unforgettable." She kept herself from concurring. "Like the song says: until we meet again."

"Right. And I'm sure your father would be pleased with more of your company." Jared looked crestfallen. "Your dad's a fine person, and it's been altogether a nice holiday."

Working feverishly, it had taken Daphne fewer than four days to complete the painting of the two lovers on the beach. She entitled the work (archly enough), *It dawned on them,* and scribbled her name underneath.

If all terms and conditions were met, and a financial arrangement agreed, she'd receive an advance on prospective sales and have enough cash to settle arrears on her Paradise Park rental space.

She applied a light shade of lipstick, powdered her freckled nose, and latched the buckles of her only pair of dress sandals. If all went well at Ocean View Gallery, and Arthur invited her to have dinner thereafter, she would not say no.

CHAPTER THIRTEEN

Serena

An Immoveable Object

With Christmas approaching, Serena wanted to do something special for—and *with*—Eliot.

To her mind, it had to be difficult for him to get through the first year-end holiday season without his wife. Having never been married, she considered the wedded state a sacred bond that, if broken, for whatever reason, left the parties untethered. It was part of Eliot's appeal that he came across as unmoored but also in want of a port.

Thus, as the December sun was about to set over the ocean, she put down her gardening tools, buttoned up her sweater, and retired to the porch glider where she could turn over various possibilities. Whatever she came up with would need to be upbeat and distracting—and involve participants of her choosing as opposed to the other lady friends now in her neighbor's orbit, circling, circling...

At fifty-nine, Serena felt acutely that were she ever to enjoy an essentially exclusive relationship with a man—a ring did not matter; time spent together did—she would have to move beyond casseroles and cassettes. *The Paradine Case* they had watched together while eating muffulettas she had tossed together with overpriced prosciutto and Greek olives from Trader Joe's. He had seemingly enjoyed the picture, the legal aspects if nothing else, making her think to add *Anatomy of a Murder* and *Absence of Malice* to her list of films to share.

In months to come.

But she had been stumped as to how to celebrate the arrival of 2020, a year that heralded even more prosperous times for the country, an erratic president notwithstanding.

Since it was impossible to converse properly while playing racquetball or tossing the frisbee to the dogs on Pismo Beach, she had waited for a more opportune moment. But none came. So, on a Saturday in mid-December after a walk along the beach, the dogs now recuperating in the back of her Highlander, she suggested lunch at Flagship, a popular locale atop the cliff, steps away from the sports club.

After seafood sliders and a salad, she casually broached the idea of a jaunt to Los Angeles—friends had reached out with invites to a couple of film premieres and after-parties, not to mention the two tickets bought online for an evening of Christmas cantatas at Disney Hall.

"We could stay at a friend's place in the Hollywood hills—she's flying back East—or in a hotel. Whichever you prefer." She tried not to sound as though she had already arranged the whole thing.

Picking intently at his salad, Eliot mumbled something about needing to remain close to home. "The kids are threatening to show up. Their timing is notoriously hard to predict."

She nodded and tried to disguise her disappointment by consulting the back of the menu. "After all that exercise, a dessert might not be amiss."

"Splendid. Whatever you fancy," he replied.

"Then a key lime pie it shall be, coffee too," she declared, chirpy.

While they waited, tensely, for the order, she debated whether to persist or to desist with her plan. Serena was not someone who gave up easily, and Eliot had become a challenge. But since he was so closed-off, it might make sense, she considered, for *her* to open up, letting him know explicitly how much he meant to her. *If not now, when*? she asked herself.

In preparation, she brushed her blond bangs off her forehead and took a deep breath.

But then, out of the corner of her eye, she noticed a man, beret on his head, matching scarf around his neck. Somehow familiar he was and headed in their direction. Within seconds he paused at their booth, twisting his head, his eyes wide in surprise. She and Eliot both looked up.

"So odd to see *you* here, Serena," the man burbled. "I mean, well, anywhere other than along the boulevard." His voice was modulated, musical.

"Unexpected indeed," she replied, jolted. The man inclined his head at Eliot, something old-school about the gesture. "It's the beret. The reason I didn't recognize—"

"Not a problem. I didn't mean to interrupt," he rushed to add, shifting his eyes from one to the other of the two diners.

"You haven't. Really," she countered, recovering. "Oh, and this is another neighbor: Eliot Etheridge. Maks lives a few houses from us."

In the seconds that followed, Maks' lip appeared to tremble, though Serena couldn't be sure. "Would you care to join us? We've ordered coffee and a dessert to share. Another fork is easy enough."

"No, no. I must be going. Just—." He readjusted the beret on his head and straightened his back. "Nice to have met you, sir. I will see you again, Serena, with Dog, I hope, in not long time." With that awkwardly constructed sentence, he hurried off.

Serena gulped the last of her mineral water, trying to dredge up the little that her neighbor had mentioned about Silda Sorenson. Eliot's eyes in the meantime had narrowed. His lips were a thin slit.

Was he rattled by the intrusion or still upset about her holiday plan? Or both. Eliot was not easy to read. "Funny how easily you can be taken aback by someone out of context," she hazarded lamely. He appeared not to have heard her.

"He's the one, right? At the last minute declined to come over at Thanksgiving," Eliot declared, the pleat between his brows prominent.

"He was busy, remember? You know, an artist on deadline."

Eliot shook his head, dismissing her explanation out of hand. "That's not it. It was because of my last name. He had been the one to find Silda in the park."

Having never heard about that episode, from either man, she gave him a look to suggest he was on the wrong track. "No, it was the dogs. Maks has a Great Dane. Pushkin, like the poet. He and Keats were friends," she rushed to explain, as though nothing could be more natural than two canines with poetic names who bond with each other.

The waiter plopped two coffees down and scooted away. Eliot drank his in silence, his brow still furrowed. Serena sipped hers, trying to pretend nothing unusual had transpired and to circle back to the upcoming holidays. She did not wish to sound pushy, or desperate, but she was beginning to feel exasperated.

Finally, while he handled the bill, she made a last stab.

"I was thinking..." she began as gaily as she could, "why don't I—*we*—throw a New Year's Eve dinner party? We could do it at my place, out on the veranda, with music and dancing. We could hire a combo. How does that sound?"

Eliot kept his head lowered over the bill. He never liked it when people, to placate him, suggested dancing. Unless they frequented ballrooms, few knew the difference between a waltz and a foxtrot. About that, he and Silda had been in sync. He sighed audibly, not knowing how to reject his friend's proposal without offending.

"Or," Serena picked back up, registering his dismay, "we could arrange for a quiet dinner, just us chickens." (She instantly regretted such a silly phrase.) "Or, I don't know, hatch a plan to do something adventurous in 2020. Like a trip—somewhere neither of us has ever been. We could draw the destination from a hat—the Balkans, the Baltic, even Bali!"

This last idea came off the top of her head, but leaving aside the alliterative element, it wasn't absurd. They both had the money and their health. What was not to like?

Eliot squirmed on the leather cushion as she enthused, and kept his head lowered until she finished. Then he slowly downed the remaining water in his glass, wiped his chin with a paper napkin, and raised his eyes to his companion.

"Racquetball," he said. She looked rattled; beads of sweat appeared on her forehead. "You have more stamina than I do, Serena." She shook her head as though the observation were neither here nor there. "I'm much older, becoming something of a homebody, and no longer able to—"

Stopping in mid-sentence, he reached to retrieve the invoice and credit card from the returning waiter, calculated a tip and a total and affixed his signature. Then he opened his wallet and slipped his card back inside. The operation appeared to take an inordinate amount of time.

While Serena waited, recent images of Daphne and Kathleen, both younger than she, floated to the front of her mind. She could not help but wonder what Eliot did with either of them, or whether he invented excuses not to spend time with them as well. That assistant of his—Caroline something or other—was, she reckoned, the only one who probably had his number and would not so demean herself.

As she, Serena Samuels—so confident, so sought-after in her day by people of all persuasions—was on the point of doing. Unless she erred (and she believed she did not), she was being rebuffed—after countless casseroles, carefully curated cassettes, and calls on her time.

Surely, she was worth more than a game of racquetball.

On the other hand, she wanted to be charitable. Eliot was older and widowed, and only now beginning to right himself. Cliché or not, good companions *were* hard to find. Why push him?

CHAPTER FOURTEEN

Kathleen

Entanglements Anew

Ironically but also serendipitously, it was only after François' death that Kathleen had bonded with her stepson. She had been forced to ring him in Paris the morning after the car crash, catching him at the noisy bistro in the *huitième arrondissement* where he worked.

Up until the tragedy, she and Pierre had spoken only intermittently and gotten together only during the few times she accompanied her husband on his trips to Paris. Their encounters had been pleasant enough but formal, restrained. As befitted those between step-relatives, she assumed.

It took an effort to get the terrible news about his dad across—*pas possible*, the young man had gasped, over and over—but, despite being overcome, he managed to fly over to attend the funeral.

And to stay in San Francisco for six months, consoling his stepmother and getting the two restaurants she and his father owned back up and running again after a discrete closure. Pierre was only thirty at the time, handsome like his father, refined in manner, and an up-and-coming chef in his own right. He had recently come off a disastrous affair in Paris, and was ready for new adventures, if not yet romantic attachments.

For Kathleen, Pierre was a godsend, encouraging her to pick up the pieces so that she could, if she wished, take the reins of the business again. That also meant dealing with several outstanding bills and accumulated debts that she had been unaware of. She kept those problems to herself.

During that interim in the States, Pierre solidified his contacts in the restaurant world, some of which were his father's past associates, others of which from the younger set whose culinary tastes were more eclectic. He also strove to perfect his English, having grown up in France until his mother died and he bummed around the continent for several years.

"The life is not over—not *terminée*—for you. You must not only survive; you must—how do you say?—thrive," he had reiterated whenever he found his stepmother despondent.

Kathleen would smile wanly in an effort to throw off her mood and engage him in conversation. So much did she come to trust him that she did allow herself on one occasion to ask if he'd ever come across Sophie Moreau. As off-handedly as possible, while she spread a delicious brie on crackers and arranged crudités to accompany them: "*Peut-être* you would have come across her in Paris. She was, I believe, an up-and-comer. So unfortunate to be traveling with your father that evening. Both, you'll recall, were hired to cook that evening."

Standing on the other side of the parlor, Pierre had paused, a corkscrew in one hand, a bottle of burgundy in the other. He raised one shoulder and tilted his head, a movement that reminded her of her dead husband.

"Near the *Place des Vosges*—a popular place. Sophie ran the kitchen. I believe Papà met her there during one of his visits. You weren't able to come across if I recall rightly. Must have been a year or so later she left France for the States."

The words wafted across the room. Kathleen let them settle undisturbed. "Ah, I see. Interesting," she replied, loud enough to encourage him to say more, if there were more.

Pierre lowered the arms of the corkscrew and ejected the cork in one expert motion. He set the bottle on a lacquered tray alongside two wine glasses and brought it across the room. She looked his way expectantly.

"*Tartes au citron*," he volunteered. She looked puzzled. "Sophie. Desserts were her specialty."

Kathleen left this unexpected tidbit untouched. Instead, she gestured for him to pour the wine and talked that evening about the difference between life in Paris and San Francisco, one of those topics they could ramble on endlessly about. Often they did, peppering their conversations with observations about the food, the entertainment and the assortment of people to be encountered in each city.

As the months passed and Kathleen regained her equilibrium, she brought her stepson along to meet her friends or to take in a show. Other times—and these she came to prefer—the two strolled the city, talking about this or that.

"In Paris, you have the Seine, but here we have the bay—ceaselessly changing. I never tire of it," she said on one of their promenades. Pierre had nodded in agreement and taken her arm in the European fashion. He was, she decided, almost as charming and arguably more companionable than her deceased husband. Whoever the young lady was who had broken things off with him would come to regret it, she concluded.

By the time Pierre decided it was time to finish his culinary apprenticeship in Paris, Kathleen had made up her mind to sell everything except her interest in *La Chanson* and begin a new chapter further south, where she had grown up. If the young man were ever so inclined, the restaurant on Nob Hill would be waiting.

She did not have to wait long.

As ambitious as his father before him, the young man soon seized the opportunity, returning to America with a green card in hand and taking up a position as sous chef at the establishment his father and stepmother had turned into a three-star attraction.

Having not heard a peep from Eliot since the Thanksgiving weekend other than a note to say what a triumph Pierre's dish had been, Kathleen debated what, if anything, to propose for the year-end holiday. It would be his first since he lost his wife—what that felt like, she knew, and that it was wise to spend it with others. Not without options, he might already have made plans—perhaps with Serena, dragged along to movie premier after movie premier or to party after party in the Hollywood hills; or perhaps with the enigmatic Daphne, who, brush in hand, might cajole him to pose for her, differently this time, in the nude, say...

She shook off both conjectures—how uncharitable she was of a sudden—and returned to practicalities.

Rifling through her desk drawer, she pulled out the three-week-old note Eliot had mailed her. Perhaps he had embedded a hint of what he might like to do at year's end. Men needed to be led by the nose, as it were, especially those as skittish as Eliot Etheridge.

But no, nothing that she could deduce, other than that he had found her stepson "the epitome of Gallic charm," as indeed had his children. *Odd, that last phrase,* she thought. Otherwise, the note was polite and unrevealing.

On her iPhone Kathleen consulted her calendar for days off from the Lantana: Dec 30, 2019 through Jan 6, 2020. Time enough to drive up to San Francisco, leisurely, stopping in Napa Valley, then liaising with her stepson at *La Chanson*, dining at the restaurant, hearing some good jazz (something Pierre had introduced to the place), staying in her favorite little hotel. A view of the bay, very discreet service.

While so lost in thought, she was jolted by the phone, a call, from Pierre, asking after her—and what she planned to do during the holidays. Offhandedly, as though it were the first time the idea had struck her, she suggested it might be time to revisit the city— "catch up with a few friends."

During the silence that followed, she could hear a saxophone tuning up. Pierre must be at the restaurant, overseeing operations, like François in the old days.

In a different key, he riffed on her idea. Yes, he'd be delighted if she came up for New Year's. If she did, she'd have a chance to see Eleanor Etheridge again. He rushed through this revelation, explaining that the two had hit it off so well—"That is the proper expression, *n'est-ce pas*?"—and thus the young woman had been convinced to fly out, and afterward would drop in on her father down at Shell Beach. Unless, that is, her father had already finalized plans to be elsewhere.

Kathleen took a deep breath, wondering to what extent her stepson and Eleanor had an inkling of the relationship she believed existed between Eliot and herself. She lowered the top of the roll-top desk, stood up, and moved toward the picture window. Looking out at the blackness where the sea would be, only a few lights from boats bobbing near the shore, she asked: "Is Eliot Etheridge aware that Eleanor is coming out? We were thinking, he and I, of getting together, sometime during the holidays."

"No idea. She may have it in her head to surprise him."

"I see," she replied. Noncommittal. Not leading him where she wanted him to go.

"Now that I think about it, wouldn't it be amusing if he and you came up together—and then Eleanor and her dad would both be surprised!"

For the next few days, Kathleen struggled with her dilemma, a dilemma made worse because she had no idea what Eliot might know or not know about his daughter's year-end plans. If she invited him to spend New Year's in San Francisco and failed to mention that his daughter would be there, visiting, of all people, Pierre Pavonine, it would appear mother and stepson might have colluded.

Enough to cause a headache.

Leaving aside that quandary, extending an invitation to Eliot was not something she was clamoring to do. However self-confident in her widowhood she believed herself to be, Kathleen still preferred men to do the pursuing.

The middle of the month came and went; she heard nothing from him. The only hint of a rationale for his silence, his having alluded at the party to a property scam his firm was investigating. One on which he would need to focus for the coming weeks. Or had he said months? She had failed to zero in on the details, chatting as they were so pleasantly. Out of the corner of her eye, she had noticed the final stragglers retrieve their wraps and umbrellas that rainy post-Thanksgiving Sunday.

Daphne and the gallery owner departed first; not long after, Serena scurried home during a lull in the storm; even the young man who excelled at charades, Kevin somebody, had interrupted their chat to say his goodbyes, shaking his host's hand, vigorously, before comically bowing his way out. Only Eliot's assistant, Caroline, had seemed determined to outstay her, helping the maid scrape dishes and then taking Keats outside to do his business. As for the children, Jared had retired upstairs shortly after Daphne left, and Eleanor had retreated to the library with Pierre in tow.

Point was, Eliot had not bothered to call in the three weeks since, and there was no excuse for her, like a Pyrex dish to retrieve. Caroline had made sure the containers for Pierre's stew and her own dessert were washed, dried, and put in a Trader Joe's sack for her to take home. Plausibly, she could come up with another casserole—scalloped potatoes to celebrate the season or a cold pasta salad to offset traditional holiday fare. Eliot's tastes appeared to have expanded, and his appetite was healthy—but the effort might come across as overly-ardent.

Should she even be fretting over all this, Kathleen asked herself, before ripping a sheet of paper off her writing tablet. She did not picture herself as a woman to waste time worrying over why a man acted the way he did. In fact, she had summoned enough will-power (and swallowed enough Ambien) to no longer lie in bed mulling what her dead husband had been up to with the Parisian pastry chef. So why should she angst over Eliot Etheridge?

Things are what they are.

That settled, Kathleen straightened her spine in the wooden chair, downed the last sip of now lukewarm chamomile, and jotted down final items on her Christmas to-do list. Under *Gifts Outstanding*, she scribbled a new name: Eleanor Etheridge. Whether she traveled alone to San Francisco or with a companion, a gift for the young woman would be in order. Nothing too elaborate or personal but distinctive nonetheless. Perhaps one of those high-tech instant pots. Hadn't the younger woman complained how cramped NYC apartment kitchens were, and how little time she had to prepare anything complicated? Might be just the thing.

CHAPTER FIFTEEN

Caroline and Chloe

To Find Footing, Take a Step

For Chloe, having an abortion at seventeen was upsetting enough. That everyone at school was aware of it—and that the guy responsible had high-tailed it in his red Maserati—was downright galling.

"Been treated like a punching bag, your daughter has. David can recommend a therapist if you like," Ella had soon rung up to suggest. Breathless, conspiratorial.

Caroline declined the offer of a psychologist, but her friend couldn't resist a knock-out blow.

"Natalie tells me everyone at Central Coast is in the know—and most soon fingered, rightly so, that Worthington boy. But now, word is he has taken up with the prom queen. Which crown, rightly so, should have been my daughter's." No response from Caroline. Ella sighed. "We're all aghast but what can we do?"

Thinking that her friend overused the expression "rightly so"—irritatingly at that—Caroline had replaced the receiver and taken a dish of strawberry ice cream upstairs to her daughter. When knocking didn't work, she cracked the door. Chloe was perched on the floor, legs crossed, her cell cradled against her ear, a textbook in her lap, pencil in hand.

"Gotta go, Gloria. Thanks for the solution. Talk to you tomorrow."

For an instant, Caroline froze: *solution*—to what, life itself? Like an automaton, she held out the bowl, her eyes coming to rest on the book splayed open on the floor. Perhaps Ella was right, a therapist might be in order. But then she blinked. At the top of the page was the title, *Calculus II: Advanced Equations,* and below were swirls of numbers and Greek symbols, notes scribbled in the margin. *My daughter is actually studying, with a friend, on the phone.*

Seizing the moment and sensing some semblance of a return to normalcy, she asked Chloe to come with her to her boss's Thanksgiving gatherings. "I'd hate to go alone—and he had specifically requested I bring you along."

To her astonishment, Chloe had looked up, fleetingly puzzled, and then said, "If I can bring Asta, then yes, I'll come."

The outings to Eliot's on Thanksgiving weekend turned out better than Caroline could have expected. No one whispered behind Chloe's back; no one put her on the spot. She ate her first substantial meal in ten days, conversed, albeit minimally, when accosted at the table, and only after dessert absconded to the porch to play with the dogs.

Later, while guests mingled in the parlor, Chloe reappeared. It was Eliot, who, unsolicited, made a special effort to draw her out.

Without hovering, Caroline overheard snatches of their exchange, Eliot inquiring as to what the girl liked studying at school, and her daughter, rather than replying "nothing in particular" pointed to history and philosophy, "stuff like that."

"That's what my son, Jared, gravitated toward," he said, offering her a flute of champagne. "I don't think your mother will mind. You are a high school senior, after all, and it's Thanksgiving," he added *sotto voce*, conspiratorial. Chloe accepted the drink and took a sip.

"Have you thought about where you might want to go, for college, I mean?" he plowed on, holding out a plate of cheeses.

She picked up a cube of cheddar on a green toothpick and held it in her free hand.

"My grades haven't been great but if I get them up, maybe UC-Davis would take me. One of my friends has been accepted. Gloria's brainy. At least in math."

Eliot nodded, adding something about Jared having gone there and eventually becoming an editor, of sorts. "You could ask him what he made of the place," Caroline heard him add, then turn his head to see where his son was. Nowhere to be seen. At that interval, she made her way over to relieve Eliot or retrieve her daughter, but he remained in place, chatting about colleges, how some were over-rated and some under-appreciated.

"But you went to Harvard, right?" Chloe asked, downing the rest of her champagne. "You have to study all the time there, everyone says."

Eliot chuckled. "Not in my case. Fortunately, I found time to have fun—including tennis and fencing, of all things." The girl looked impressed. After a pause and in a quieter tone, "and to meet my future wife."

To stop Chloe from asking something awkward, (would the teenager recall that Silda had passed away?), Caroline stepped in to suggest the two help Mariella stack the dishes in the kitchen. Without a whimper, the youngster obeyed.

Some kind of awakening? Whatever it was, it was to be encouraged.

At the Sunday gathering, Chloe was more relaxed. While Asta, Dog and Keats romped on the back porch, she joined in to play charades, watch an old movie, and participate in a sing-along that Eleanor and Pierre orchestrated—belting out "Climb Every Mountain" in full throat.

After the musical interlude, Eliot once again sidled up to her. "Do you play as well as sing, Chloe?"

She reddened. "We have an upright at home. But it's been a while."

"It may not mean much now but it's something one can do throughout life. My wife played beautifully. She taught a number of young people around here."

Chloe smiled politely. Caroline nodded in recognition, remembering the only time she had been invited to the Etheridge home in Santa Barbara, some milestone of the firm's to celebrate. Silda had sat down and banged out a medley of show tunes. Even Tillotson had hobbled over to the Steinway, raising his voice in the chorus to "Try to Remember."

"Which reminds me," Eliot recommenced, brightly. "I have yet to go through my wife's sheet music—much of it graded courses for her students. Perhaps Chloe would be inspired to continue, you know..." he hazarded, glancing from mother to daughter.

"That's terribly kind but you have so much else—"

"I'd like that," Chloe burst out.

Eliot clucked his tongue. "Then it's settled. I'll get around to the boxes over the holidays. If you can already play '*Für Elise*,' you'll be able to work your way through most of them. With practice, mind you."

"That's what Mom says, about everything."

"Your mother's a smart lady," he had added, a bemused glance toward his assistant.

Caroline had traveled back to Shell Beach several times in December to help Eliot finish up the evidence file he had amassed on the property scam, but they had not spoken further about anything other than work. He had seemed focused and energized, often ringing one or another of the partners to go over technicalities, leaving Caroline to make the coffee and a light lunch or simply wander about the place.

On one occasion, a chilly but cloudless Friday shortly before Christmas, she took Keats for a walk while her boss returned client calls. On their way back, they ran into, not Serena and the basset hound, but a handsome man sporting a beret. It sat at a jaunty angle, a becoming one, Caroline observed. He was walking a Great Dane, who suddenly tugged at his leash. The two dogs appeared to be acquainted; they checked each other out, entangling the leashes.

The man eyed her curiously.

“Keats is looking well. Are you the dog walker?”

“Not *per se*. But I am for the moment walking the dog. There is a difference, right?”

The man appeared to turn the query over in his mind, uncertain of the distinction she was making. Caroline had time to note the unusual way he held himself—slightly forward, expectant. Something arresting about the posture—the voice too. It was melodious, the words musically fashioned.

The two dogs proceeded to nuzzle each other, a low gurgling sound emanating from the Great Dane.

“Is he alright? Should I pull Keats away?”

“They're playing—like old times,” he said. Wistful.

Something clicked in her mind.

“Now I remember: you're the person who rang up when—when Mrs. Etheridge stumbled, across the way.” Caroline swiveled her head to indicate the park ten or fifteen yards down the boulevard.

“Silda, yes. Mrs. Etheridge,” he murmured, barely audible. He too glanced toward the park. Several people, jacketed, with scarves about their necks, were seated on benches, soaking up the last rays of the sun. A couple of tourists were taking turns looking through the mounted telescope at cliff's edge. “Silda didn't fall down. She fainted.”

He mumbled something else, but Caroline couldn't make it out. She did glimpse his eyes, sky-blue but liquid. She paused before she spoke again.

“You two were acquainted...like your dogs,” she stated. Not an insinuation, a confirmation rather. He nodded, his face still averted toward the sea. “They do seem very fond...of each other.” She swallowed and turned her gaze toward the water as though in shared solace. Then, more brightly, “So that I know: what is *your* dog’s name?”

“Pushkin,” he replied, pronouncing the name with his native accent.

Russian, she guessed, but likely someone who has lived Stateside for many years. And just as likely, she deduced, he had known Silda, but not Eliot.

“Such a coincidence that they are both named after poets—a lovely coincidence, I must say.”

“Yes, it was. You people have a word for it: *serendipitous*.” He pronounced the adjective gently, caressing the syllables.

She felt a tinkling in her chest, and disconcerted by it, lowered her eyes to the dogs. “And what is your name, may I ask?”

“Maksim Mirovich, Maks for short. I live several houses further along. And you?”

“Caroline. I work for Eliot Etheridge—at his law firm. I had answered the phone that day...” she trailed off, letting the memory of that call drift out to sea.

The winter wind had started to pick up, whipping up whitecaps close to shore. Neither spoke for a time.

Finally, Maks checked his wristwatch and pulled at Pushkin’s leash. “We need to be getting back, but I’m glad to know Keats is well and has such a dedicated walker.”

“That took a while. Did you enjoy the walk?” Eliot inquired when Caroline re-entered. He was sealing up a cardboard box with scotch tape, a magic marker on the table in front of him.

“Yes, we both did. Keats ran into an old friend, a Great Dane who lives along the promenade.”

As he finished marking up the top of the box, he paused his movements, as he often did whenever an unexpected reference to Silda came up.

“Seems she made a number of new acquaintances around here,” he offered up. Caroline nodded but did not elaborate on her encounter. “Dogs are a help in that respect.” He put the marker down and turned to face her.

"That something I need to take back to the office?" she asked. Business-like.

"Home, actually. For Chloe."

She looked flummoxed.

"Your daughter plays, at least a little, and Silda had amassed reams of sheet music. I thought Chloe might be encouraged to practice." He raised his eyebrows in a question.

Dumbfounded, Caroline blushed. When had her boss become interested enough in others to bestow such a pertinent gift? That she knew, her child had not touched the upright in the parlor for ages. Perhaps if she'd forked out for lessons when Silda was alive...

"Chloe will be thrilled. Very thoughtful on your part."

"High time I got to grips with things that are serving no purpose here. Silda would have wanted that," he wound up, his voice wobbling at the end.

"Indeed. Holidays are a good time to take stock—you know, to discard some things and repurpose others. You will have set an example," Caroline returned, trying to steer the exchange back to neutral ground. She wondered again what other plans—something more amusing than rifling through boxes—he might have made for the year-end. And with whom.

"Alright then," Eliot said, enticed out of his reverie. He gathered up the tape, scissors and magic marker, all of which he slid back in the top drawer of the sideboard. At that moment, the antique clock on the wall chimed six times.

"Unless there's something else, I should be on my way," Caroline said.

"As usual, I've detained you longer than I should have. But do fill your thermos. The coffee is extra strong, Jamaican this time, and will help on the drive. Some people are already out celebrating, so take special care," he advised. "I believe the firm won't be open again until after the sixth."

Without waiting for a response, Eliot picked up the box and proceeded to lug it out to the Camry.

From the kitchen window, Caroline watched him open the back door of the car and slide the box onto the passenger seat. As he shut the car door and straightened up, his hand automatically went to the small of his back.

The gesture disarmed her. Eliot Etheridge was no longer young. Nor without troubles of his own.

CHAPTER SIXTEEN

Eliot

To His Unbeknownst

gainst his better judgment, Eliot put up a fir tree, not a tall one as in decades past, but a short, full one which he bought on sale in Oceano three days before Christmas. He had driven down that way to take several of his old but barely worn jackets to Silda's uncle, along with one of the casseroles that had languished in the freezer. He was uncertain as to which lady had brought the dish over, months earlier, which made it easier to pass it on.

Uncle Seth appeared at the door disheveled, but Eliot declined to go in. The door itself seemed to be on a precarious hinge.

"Just a few things to get you through the winter. And a casserole you can thaw. You have a good holiday, Seth, and be in touch," he had hurried to say, placing the box of clothes on the front stoop and putting the dish directly into the old man's hands.

"What on earth, what on earth," Seth had muttered, whiskey coming off his breath, but he took the offerings nonetheless. And regrouped: "And the same to you and Sil. Merry Christmas."

You never knew with the elderly, Eliot thought. Still, he had done a good deed for the old man. Silda would have approved.

It was on his way back to the entrance of the 101-N that he saw the nursery with the hand-written sign: "Last chance: Xmas trees. All varieties." He slammed on the brakes, pulled in, spotted one of the few remaining Douglas firs that wasn't scraggly, and forked out $25 in cash. The attendant obliged by hoisting the tree and its stand into the back of the Escalade.

Once hauled into the house and secured in the front alcove, it dawned on Eliot: he had no inkling where Silda stored her family's Christmas ornaments—in the attic or the basement? Or upstairs, but in which closet, which boxes?

Leaving the tree unadorned would be worse than not having one at all. Mariella would know about decorations, but she had already left for her daughter's home in San Diego until after *la Noche de Reyes,* she had told him. He assumed that meant Epiphany.

What to do? Choose simple ornaments but ones that make a statement—like the clear, concise closings he was known for making to juries, and which Silda had often said was the secret to most things in life—clear, concise lines, those uttered, those found in art, and those in nature. He stared at the tree. It was not large, it wouldn't take much to make of it what she would have approved.

Closing his eyes, he conjured Christmases past. What about, he soon asked, those hand-painted songbirds made of Murano glass, which the Sorensons had acquired on a trip to Venice? Silda had strung them atop their trees in Santa Barbara with special care, chattering on every year about the family visit to the tiny island where she watched the glassblowers. Entranced. She was around twelve at the time, he reckoned.

And why hadn't the two of them ever gone back to Italy together or anywhere else as enchanting in all their married years together?

It being already 9:30 at night, Eliot opened a bottle of Glenfiddich and poured himself a shot. But it being already the 23rd, he needed to take a stab at finding the ornaments before going to bed. He discounted the dreary basement as being an unlikely repository; venturing up to the attic with a flashlight, he scoured the area, mostly old furniture, a wooden rocking horse, tattered dolls, even a sword in a scabbard. He returned to the upstairs closet in the room Silda had died in, and in which he had barely set foot since.

Opening the sliding closet doors, he pulled out the footstool to survey the shelves above. Several boxes were labeled in his wife's florid hand: gloves and scarves, hats, family papers, and so forth. Then he noticed a Tiffany box tied with string and the oddest thing: lettering in her hand, but in what looked like Cyrillic. One short word and it was easy enough to make out the first letter: *M*.

The songbirds could wait.

He took the box downstairs, untied the bow, and retrieved a slim packet of letters. He poured himself another shot, took a deep breath and sifted through them. They appeared to be arranged in chronological order. Clear and concise the handwriting. Everything in bold black ink, salutations and signatures in Cyrillic.

He started with the first, dated May 2016. The first was an invitation, humorous yet deadly serious: *Pushkin requests the company of Keats on Saturday afternoon. And I have received a package from St Petersburg of caviar and the finest Russian vodka. Do come!*

The second, dated July of the same year, with Silda's name spelled in Cyrillic as well as the sender's, the rest in English: *Dearest Silda, Please come again. I could not bear it if you do not. Yours, Maks*

His hands trembling, Eliot flipped through the rest, one more dated in winter of 2016 and three or four in 2017 and 2018, most of their contents all in Russian, with a few scribbled words in English—*me inside you, your moans, our ecstasy*—indicative if not probative, he tried to tell himself. And failed.

There were also a few lines of musical notes in one letter, with the proviso: *Next time we'll try this earlier version of the piece, found a decade ago among Scriabin's papers.*

Eliot took another swig of the Scotch and held his head in his hands to slow his pounding heart and shut out what he had stumbled across.

It did neither. Anger flooded him from inside in a burning-hot wave.

Setting the letters aside, he peered into the bottom of the box and retrieved two photos. One was of Maks, in profile, seated at the piano, one hand aloft ready to strike a note. The other, taken in a mirror, was of the two of them, on a large bed, sheets snarled, Silda's breast exposed, the camera against Maks' bare chest. The lighting was low but sufficient to suggest satiety. On the back was scribbled: *"I Loved You" (that Pushkin poem, 1832, remember?) and you and I now (September 2018).*

Finally, a sole sheet of cream-colored stationery looked to be tear-stained and consisted of a single phrase printed in bold letters, as though for someone who did not have the strength to read more than that: *Waking or sleeping you are in my heart. Eternally. M.* It was dated Christmas 2018.

It didn't take Eliot long to realize this last was written less than a month before Silda died.

Nor did it take him long to realize that there were many things—important things—that he did not know about the woman he had been married to for forty years. Those, to him, minor fault lines in his marriage had at some point cracked open. He had never noticed their widening.

From now on, Eliot told himself, everything about the past would be colored differently.

Christmas Day came and went. He walked around in a daze, the Venetian songbirds still languishing in a box on the floor, the fir tree still bare.

On Dec. 29, he took Keats for an outing through the side streets of the town and did his best to throw off his funk. And as Silda had urged, think of others.

Daphne had accepted an invitation from Arthur Braunstein to fly to NYC, Serena had driven down to Los Angeles, and Caroline had taken Chloe to visit her grandparents. He would ring Kathleen and were she still favorably disposed, accept her invitation to spend New Year's in San Francisco.

When he got back home the phone was ringing off the hook. Of all people it was Issie.

"Guess what? I'm in Denver. Memorial service for Dad. State Supremo, remember? More legal minds gathered in one place than I've seen since you and I went to Hugo Black's visitation down in Maryland."

"I'm sorry. I didn't know."

"He was ninety-two, cantankerous to the end, but people said nice things. Plus, he did get me into Harvard, which, well, you be the judge..."

Motor-mouth though she was, Isabel Frankel had a way of dispelling anyone's bad mood.

"Denver you said? Then hop on a plane. Can't provide anything exciting but we can usher in 2020 on the terrace. It's supposed to be a propitious year. And more immediately, you can see the ocean and not freeze to death!"

"In your company, I have never done that," she lobbed back. "Frozen to death."

Even on the phone she made him blush.

Later that evening, Eliot hung all twenty-four songbirds on the fir tree, tacked an old but still presentable wreath on the front door, and transferred a couple of casseroles from the freezer to the fridge. Issie arrived the next afternoon with several gifts in hand and tales of life as a prosecutor for the Southern District of New York.

Eventually, they got around to life post-Silda. If Eliot were to unburden himself to anyone, to whom better than to his oldest friend. Sharing a Barolo and finishing a mincemeat pie on the terrace, Issie cut to the chase. "Okay, since men rarely concoct casseroles or bake pies, and never edible ones, I deduce there is a lady friend in the picture."

"Always knew you'd make a great lawyer," he lobbed back.

She smiled conspiratorially. He wondered for an instant if they'd end up in bed to celebrate the coming year.

"So, let's hear it." He looked disconcerted. "You know, the casserole coven or pie princesses or whatever they are."

"I suppose one could argue there are—or were—three," he began. She shot him a quizzical look. "I've rather bungled it, with each of them."

"Go on," she said, pouring them both another glass. It was only 10:30, no sound of firecrackers as yet, just waves crashing against the rocks.

"As you wish. Daphne, who baked that creole thing we had yesterday, is way too young, a budding painter though, if something of a naïve herself." He paused, deciding not to mention her breasts or his former interest therein. "Anyway, she's in NYC right now—her first ever visit. Didn't even know what MoMA was."

"That is troubling. Not her youth, I suspect, but her being uncouth, or uncultured," she tossed out.

"To Serena you would relate. Worked in Hollywood, seen every movie ever made, and plays a ferocious game of racquetball." Issie nodded, seemingly in approval. "Even has a basset hound, named Dog."

"An homage to '*Colombo.*' Witty, I guess, if one lives on the West Side—of Hollywood, that is."

"Well, you'd like her. Not so young now but then neither are we, right?"

"Thanks for reminding me," she deadpanned.

"The problem is, Serena tries too hard, which makes her brittle, and I'm well…" Here he hesitated, blinked, and tried to pull down an apt appraisal.

"Still fishing?"

"Something like that." His words, uttered with half-hearted conviction, brought a moment of silence. "Anyway, she invited me down to L.A., but I invented some excuse about the children coming for the holidays. She didn't believe me." He shrugged and took another sip of the wine. "You do know your vineyards, Issie."

"Learned the hard way. Remember how we used to drink that awful chianti in the straw-covered bottles? Amazing how we survived." He nodded in recognition of the long-ago time. " '*Wild nights, wild nights*,' as Dickinson put it, though I wager, strait-laced New Englander that she was, our poetess didn't have any such times as we did."

In shadow, Eliot appeared to wince but said nothing about the poetic reference. Issie did talk too much, her ex-husband had always said so, relieving himself of her company after six years of marriage.

For a few more minutes, the two sat listening to the wind and the waves. Keats had curled up at Eliot's feet, every so often being handed a dog treat.

"There is a third lady, right?" Issie eventually asked. Leading but subtle, as in a cross-examination.

Eliot fondled the dog's ears while he composed a description. "Yes, Kathleen Pavonine, *née* Calhoun—she too widowed. Her husband was a prominent chef in San Francisco. Not surprisingly, she's an excellent cook. I had been thinking of accompanying her there for New Year's until I came across—"

Issie gestured with her hand for him to proceed. He put down his drink, straightened his back and stared into the darkness.

"Came across what, Eliot?" she persevered.

He rushed through the telling, abbreviating, eliding. Silda in the throes of a passionate love affair, with a Russian musician, almost up until her death. (Letters he found days ago.) Even has a dog—Pushkin, like the poet. "All to my unbeknownst," he climaxed.

Bitter the recitation, he still not entirely believing the words he uttered.

Issie forced herself to wait a beat. "It's often to the unbeknownst of the other partner, Eliot. That's how these things work," she said. Philosophical, non-judgmental.

"But I never cheated on *her*, in all those years," he retorted.

Dumbfounded, Issie took a breath and slowly let it out. "Then what is it, Eliot," she asked, her voice tight, "that you would call what we have done, albeit intermittently, for all these years?"

"That doesn't count," he snapped.

They dropped the subject, took Keats out for a walk, watched the ball drop in Times Square—and retired to separate bedrooms.

Before falling asleep, Issie lay under a down comforter stewing over the only cutting remark her lover had ever made to her.

Before falling asleep, Eliot lay atop his cashmere blanket, puzzling over his friend's sudden moodiness.

Things, he concluded as he drifted off, will certainly get better in the new year of 2020. He liked how the date rolled off the tongue.

CHAPTER SEVENTEEN

Issie

The Writing on the Wall

The first time Issie saw Silda Sorenson she knew the thing she herself had with Eliot would never be the same. The couple was crossing Harvard Yard arm-in-arm, arguing about the article they were jointly writing for the law review.

As their friends could attest, arguing was what the two of them did best, which was understandable, even encouraged, given that they were rising stars in the firmament of the university's law school. Their arguments were dazzling constructs, full of wit and wisdom—she, citing abstruse precedents from memory, he, bringing unassailable logic to bear—never pompous, often self-deprecating. By all accounts, Eliot and Issie were popular and admired, their fellow students placing bets as to which firm, in Boston or in New York, would eventually snag them. The two of them as a team. Once married and all that.

Of a sudden, on that glorious spring morning in 1973, Eliot had stopped dead in his tracks, his eyes snagged on a gaggle of girls—pretty ones, especially the tall blonde who was gesturing as the group laughed their way across the grounds. Presumably toward some class or other, since they cradled their textbooks purposefully, which, even so, did not obscure their carefree youthfulness or undercut their air of privileged insouciance.

"What?" Issie had asked, also pulling up short, trying to locate what had so diverted the attention of her boyfriend that he failed to register her objection to the high-handedness of Washington politicians. Surely, he wouldn't insist on coming to the defense of the Nixon administration in what was shaping up to be scandalous disregard for the rule of law. Citing national security as grounds for its actions was one of the oldest ruses of autocrats, she had been arguing. Convincingly, even while moving at a clip.

Annoyed, she squinted into the glare and, despite her near-sightedness, saw the future.

Within two weeks of that first sighting, Eliot got to know the "Cliffie" from California, a liberal arts major who was studying both music and Russian. On the evening he and Issie had agreed to iron out their different approaches and finalize their piece, deadline looming, Eliot was a no-show. She re-vamped the article on her own but left the joint byline intact.

To no avail.

Her boyfriend had squired the Radcliffe freshman to a concert in town that evening—all Russian composers—and spent the night with her thereafter. He geared himself up to tell Issie a few days later; she already suspected.

"We absolutely have to remain friends, Issie," he had insisted, babbling on non-stop, extolling her exceptional qualities, trying to let her down gently. He had paced the room, gesticulating wildly, unable to look her in the eye. "We have so much in common."

"Shostakovich is not one of them," she had remarked drily. "I didn't think you liked him either. So derivative."

Eliot had blushed, but he was besotted now. With someone else. There was no going back.

When all had been said (and for once there was no point for the two to argue different sides), Issie walked out of his off-campus apartment for the last time. Within a year after her *summa cum laude* degree, she landed at one of New York City's top law firms. Although he too received an offer or two from firms in Manhattan, Eliot, who had lost his focus and failed to pull off "the *summa*," settled into practice at a respectable, if somewhat sleepy, firm in downtown Boston.

Eliot and Silda married the day after she graduated with a double major in Russian literature and classical music. He was by then twenty-eight, she not yet twenty-two. Eventually she convinced him to relocate to the West Coast, his New England parents having passed away, hers on the Central Coast of California not getting any younger.

About their marriage and the move out West, Issie heard nothing for several years.

But now, lying in bed in the Sorenson family home that New Year's Day of 2020, she tried to retrace the paths that the three had taken after Harvard. How had it come to this: that, with Silda dead, after having conducted a clandestine love affair her last three years on earth, here *she* was, having carried on an intense, if infrequent, liaison with the dead woman's husband for almost four decades?

Then there was the more immediate question of why the two people now in this charming but to her NYC eye for space, pointlessly large, and to her sense of order, too casually ramshackle a house had fallen so out-of-sync in their last conversation. So much so that they had gone to bed in separate rooms when they could have—

Throwing back the comforter and tossing aside the too-plush pillows, Issie stretched her limbs and took a few deep breaths. Her Upper East Side yoga instructor had advised never to go to sleep or wake up with a negative thought top of mind. She had failed the test last night; she would try to pass it this morning.

But it would be hard.

The man for whom she had carried a torch her entire adult life—and required so little of him—had been obtuse. Offhandedly he had diminished, if not symbolically deleted, the fact that the two former "chums" had been screwing each other off and on for eons. To her mind, they had done so avidly, with no demands made.

She would need a cup of that strong coffee Eliot was so proud of—Ethiopian or Jamaican, she couldn't recall, except that it was Silda who had steered him toward such esoteric brands; she herself generally settled for Folgers.

Not this morning.

At this juncture in their relationship, it was time to parse the past and signpost the future, whether he liked it or not. Mainly, that she relished sex with Eliot: he was a thoughtful lover, if less adventurous than early on, and he had never let on that he didn't reciprocate.

This was all delicate territory, however, and would require her much-vaunted logic, and whatever diplomacy she could summons.

Issie threw off her nightgown, took a hot shower, carefully made up her face, a hint of mascara included, and put on her only Max-Mara outfit: a sheath of silk-wool, with a keyhole neckline and an eye-catching belt. With all the walking she did in Manhattan, her figure was firmer than it had been in college, her hair expertly styled, her eyes better served by contact lens than those tortoise-shelled glasses she depended on back when.

Albeit she was no longer young *per se, she* had learned to enhance what she could, downplay what she could not.

Having glimpsed an entire stack of foil-wrapped and labeled dishes in Eliot's freezer, she wondered about the ladies of the casseroles—what they were like, how old, and how persistent. He had made them sound pleasant enough, but he had not gone overboard. In any case, Issie considered herself beyond jealousy, *per se*, so she decided that to be curious about them was acceptable; to fret over them, however, would be unwarranted.

From what she had observed in less than twenty-four hours, Eliot hadn't gotten over Silda's death. And yet, it was possible the discovery of his wife's affair might, ironically, assuage his grief, and diminish his guilt.

Once, that is, he got over his indignation at having been left in the dark for three years about her "betrayal."

She tiptoed downstairs.

Eliot was already in the kitchen fussing with the coffee, a brand with an unpronounceable name. He was chirpy; she took up the refrain, chirpier still. They talked about this and that, drank a couple of cups apiece and ate slices of a pound cake, which he unwrapped from its tin foil.

"My assistant, Caroline, has a knack for baking," he explained. "At Thanksgiving, she brought over homemade biscuits, which went over, well, like hotcakes."

"Seems all the women in your circle know how to cook, among other talents," she replied, her tone unimpeachable. "I'm more a *devotée* of delicatessens. I can even say 'hold the mayo' in Korean, would you believe!"

Her quip, mildly self-mocking, made Eliot smile. They munched in silence for a minute or two.

"Since I've been working from home, Caroline's been assiduous, not only with the baking but with keeping me on top of cases. "You know how it is in a firm. Lots of sharp elbows, lots of maneuvering."

"Yes, I've heard that," she replied wryly, thinking of the politics which beset the Southern District of New York but of which she tried to steer clear. She seized upon his opening. "How long do you plan to toil away at Bryson & Tillotson?" Issie asked, having recently had her contract extended for another three years.

"Hadn't thought about it until recently. A part-time arrangement might be in the offing. I'd like to do some serious traveling, to places Sil and I never..." he confided, his voice trailing off as though to some faraway destination. He cut another slice of cake and dipped the corner of it into his coffee.

Issie nodded. Noncommittal. She took another sip of the brew—it was beyond bracing—and wondered what places intrigued him, and if he had a travel companion in mind. But she didn't inquire. Instead, she looked toward the window over the sink, the slats tilted open, sunshine pouring in.

Eliot's eyes followed hers. "Speaking of travel, I know what you're thinking," he said. "Why sit here when we could take a drive up the Pacific Coast Highway. There's a lovely spot where we can rent a boat, have a meal, drink more champagne—whatever else," he wound up.

The throwaway line took her aback. Had he forgotten his insult? *Men were incorrigible*, she thought. But indignation being unbecoming, she swallowed hard and smiled in agreement.

"A drive along the coast sounds lovely."

Ribbons of clouds had drifted onshore by the time they wound down a road shaded by eucalyptus to an inlet called Avila Beach. It was 2 p.m. and the winter sun was only visible intermittently. The town, such as it was, consisted of a dozen weathered structures arranged to face the water in a gentle arc. They included a souvenir shop, a bookstore, a bank, an ice cream parlor, a bar, a couple of eateries, and one small hotel.

Issie found it enchanting—and said so.

"Good. Later, we'll look around," Eliot replied, before driving around to the other side of the inlet where several dozen boats were docked. They hired a small one, bought a couple of sandwiches and soft drinks, and paddled out toward open water. Seagulls swirled overhead, darting sporadically at the sailboats further out to sea. They soon attacked their sandwiches and drank the Ginger Ale, letting the boat drift.

During that interval, they spotted dolphins cavorting off to the northwest. With binoculars, they were able to distinguish four or five. But they did not paddle closer. The wind had picked up and they couldn't risk being stranded far offshore.

"I can't remember the last time I did something like this or expended so much energy doing it!" Issie called out as they finally came within sight of the dock.

"Well, I can," he returned.

"Pray tell," she yelled back, challenging his recollection.

"Some celebration or other on the Charles, remember? It started to rain cats and dogs. Everyone got drenched, the cake was ruined, but somehow, we finished off the beer and had a jolly ole time. Except for the birthday boy, Phil somebody. I think he had a crush on you."

She gave him a blank look. Then, slowly, she recalled that ill-fated bash on the river, which ended with the two of them in the cramped boathouse, tearing at each other's sodden clothes, desperate to get inside each other. Friends had waited for them outside, hearing them, snickering good-naturedly.

Only a couple of months later, Issie now calculated, Eliot upped and left her for Silda.

She paddled more vigorously.

By the time they returned to Avila Beach proper, a few people were scattered about on the sandy shore, ostensibly locals, with their dogs or children in tow. Fast-scudding clouds, however, had amassed overhead and the wind began to gust.

"I reserved a table for early dinner at the hotel," Eliot tossed out, turning his head toward the façade of the Avila Arms. "I figured there might be a crowd, it being a holiday."

"Splendid," she said. "I'm famished. Must be all the paddling!"

They ordered the local delicacies, a lemony soup of mussels, followed by sand dabs, which the *maitre d'* insisted were collected from the beach in front of them. By the time dessert and cognac arrived, the heavens had let loose.

"Quite a way to usher in the new year," Issie remarked. "And all the pundits say 2020 is supposed to bring only good things."

"Fondly to be wished, whatever the weather," he concurred. They clinked glasses.

When the bill arrived, Eliot quietly said, "Just put it on my room."

Issie canted her head.

"I took the liberty," he explained, his color high, "to make up for—besides, driving back in all this might not be wise."

She gave him a slightly crooked smile, as if to suggest she knew he was incapable of articulating an actual apology.

Through the night, the two longtime lovers pleasured each other, tenderly, taking time to rest, much more time now than decades ago. If there were moans to be heard through the thin walls, they were muffled by the storm.

After a leisurely breakfast the next morning, they detoured inland to a couple of wineries. A reluctant sun was pasted sullen in the sky. Eliot bought a few bottles of the local vintages while Issie picked out a few tapenades, fancy cheeses, olives, and crackers.

"We can make a meal of all this if we ever do eat again," she said.

"I suspect we'll be hungry again, at some juncture," Eliot replied. "That's always been the way with us."

She wasn't sure what, if anything, to read into that comment. It had never been their habit to analyze their relationship, and there didn't seem to be reason enough to do so now. Besides, she had a flight back to Denver to catch in the evening and then another to New York after tying up loose ends of her father's estate.

While Eliot navigated the slick roads, she gazed out the car window to admire the scenery. Everything—the cows, the horses, the birds, the occasional farmer out in his field, the perfectly aligned rows of grapevines along the hillsides, looked happy to be in California. For the first time, she, a fiercely partisan New Yorker, understood the appeal of the place.

As they pulled into the Sorenson driveway at about 4 p.m., Eliot jerked his head around. Another car, a silver Porsche, was parked at the curb.

"What on earth!" he mumbled, looking, Issie thought, both bewildered and embarrassed.

Craning her neck, she scoured the porch and spotted two women fumbling with the front door. When Eliot shut off the motor, one of the two scrambled down the steps toward them. Something about her was oddly familiar.

Eliot lowered the driver's seat window: "Eleanor! I had no idea." He turned crimson, both hands grasping onto the steering wheel.

The young woman bent forward and poked her head inside the Escalade. "I wanted to surprise you, Dad. Didn't bargain on your being away at New Year's. Kathleen had said—"

"Kathleen? What has she got to do with it?"

Eleanor ignored the query, peering further in to get a better look at the passenger.

"I know you. From that panel last year—and you obviously do know my dad."

Meanwhile, the other woman on the porch, somewhat older, shouldering an elegant leather bag and wearing matching heels, made her way toward the car. She had a determinedly composed look on her face as if to signal it wasn't her idea to have barged over uninvited.

"Of course I remember. I'm Isabel Frankel. Your father and I—we just spent a lovely day looking around the area. It's my first trip to California."

Eleanor looked bemused, her eyes shifting from one to the other.

Once they were all inside, Eliot hurried to open one of the bottles he had bought, and Issie busied herself in the kitchen unwrapping appetizers. Eleanor, unusually ebullient, did most of the talking, explaining how, "on the spur of the moment," she had accepted an invitation to visit Pierre, and how much fun, and great food, and camaraderie they had enjoyed at his restaurant. And there they had run into a couple of Kathleen's old friends—and what a shame that he, her father, hadn't managed to join them. Especially since he had already met these charming people and dined at *La Chanson* last summer. But then she caught herself to note how equally fabulous that Isabel—one of her dad's oldest friends from back East, she stressed—had made a last-minute decision to visit Shell Beach.

"It was—did you say, Isabel?—that you had business there in Denver, and decided that it was only a short hop, especially since..."

Sideways glances were exchanged during Eleanor's recitation but the wine, liberally poured, eventually mellowed the mood. Besides, the two older women, for different reasons, decided not to outstay their welcome. Father and daughter should be allowed this rare chance to catch up.

Once that was cleared up, Kathleen insisted upon driving Isabel to the airport in Santa Barbara—no traffic to speak of on a holiday—and then double back to be home in little more than an hour.

Quickly assenting, Isabel collected her things upstairs and was ready to depart at 6:30 p.m., her flight to Denver scheduled for 8:55 p.m. In front of the Porsche, Eliot shook hands with Kathleen, thanking her profusely for doing the chauffeuring and asserting that he'd "come up for air" in a few days.

"Whatever works for you, Eliot," she answered in a tone that left little doubt she had taken stock of his recent choices. She smiled politely and pulled the car keys from her shoulder bag.

Issie stood apart, not wanting to intrude. Instead, she rooted around in her purse for a business card. "When you're back and settled in, Eleanor, let's grab coffee. We're both on the Upper East Side, if I heard you rightly."

"By all means," Eleanor had responded. "That would be lovely."

As Issie prepared to get in on the passenger side, Eliot's fingers grazed her arm. She turned and he embraced her. The gesture, although public and awkward, lasted a second longer than necessary. She wondered if either of the other women noticed.

CHAPTER EIGHTEEN

Maks

The End of the Affair

The date did not escape him. On the morning of January 20, Maks decided to make the trip early to avoid any awkward encounters. He clipped a dozen birds of paradise from his front yard, trimmed the stalks, and wrapped them in a damp cloth. She had once admired those plants in his garden, saying how she had missed their colorful heads all those years spent in Boston. After a second cup of coffee, he grabbed up Pushkin's leash, enticed the Great Dane into the car and drove the few miles south to Arroyo Grande.

Maks had not set foot in the cemetery since the funeral exactly a year ago and, even then, he had shown up only after the family had departed, leaving only the gravedigger and a straggler, an old man who appeared disoriented or inconsolable, mumbling under his breath, brushing debris off the older stones. Maks had kept his distance, not wanting to intrude.

As he intuited, the rusted iron gate was not locked, so he clanged it open and drove in. The gravesite was not far, as the cemetery was circumscribed by roads and a creek, with little room for expansion. After turning the car to head out quickly in case other mourners arrived, he got out, the dog making an instant beeline for the Sorenson plot, as though he remembered the scent of grief.

A weeping willow stood at either end of the lot's back boundary, with the older, moss-covered tombstones aligned in two rows toward the rear and the most recent one, hers, to the front, in a row by itself. So far.

The inscription read:

Silda Anemone Sorenson Etheridge

(Sept 3, 1956-Jan 20, 2019)

Beloved daughter, wife and mother

And below that in a more florid script: "*That flights of angels sing thee to thy rest*," which Maks imagined was from Shakespeare, though he couldn't identify the play.

He teared up. He had not known that his lover had a middle name or that it was so musical. He stared off at the branches of the nearby trees swaying in the wintry air. Bowing his head, he strained to picture her, playing the piano, petting the dogs, laughing at his English, reveling in the revival of her Russian, moaning in ecstasy in his arms. Gone too soon. Leaving him, others too of course, alone and bereft.

"Willowy," he said aloud, pronouncing all three syllables. He smiled at the sound of the word, stroked the back of Pushkin's neck, and knelt to place the birds of paradise in the urns on either side of the grave. He stuck the stalks in one by one—the marble receptacles were deep and unobstructed—and poured water on them from a bucket he brought along.

Whoever else might show up to pay their respects could think whatever they wished. As he placed his bucket in the trunk of the car, he did notice another vehicle, an old Mercury parked nearby, no driver visible. He shrugged, got in, and drove off.

For the rest of the month, Maks buckled down to finish scores he owed different clients, one being particularly tricky. For a documentary series about climate change, it required a range of musical moods as well as leitmotifs to evoke specific animal and plant forms facing extinction. "Also, Maks, my man," the producer had instructed him, "you'll want to accentuate horns and brass: remember, it's meant as a wake-up call for a world that continues to sleep through the crisis—especially here in the U. S. of A. *Capisci*?"

He had received the rough cut of the first three episodes but had only watched bits and pieces. On his own. That seemed to him the operative word for everything he did nowadays. He had grown depressed about it. Silda was gone, and he knew he had to move on. As he had, at a much younger age, when his Italian-born wife, Tatiana, had died in childbirth. But back in 1986 things were easier for him, especially the ability to change.

As for their daughter Oksana, she was brought up, successively, by her grandparents in the Russian enclave of Far Rockaway and by her Italian grandparents in Brooklyn and was now an interpreter at the United Nations. Parent and child had not seen each other in a decade, speaking sporadically in a polite but stilted way. Ambitious himself, Maks was gratified that her Russian and Italian were flawless and impressed that her English was exquisite. Not that he had contributed to her accomplishments. He needed to do better by her.

A trip to New York City might be just the thing. As soon as the worst of the winter had passed. He could attend a few concerts, catch up with old friends, firm up a few business contacts. Without vacillating further, he purchased a ticket online on the 31st and wrote his daughter a letter, brief but chatty. They could have dinner somewhere she liked, take in a play, go to the opera, or do whatever else appealed to her. A good month's notice should be sufficient for her to accommodate the idea.

Regarding Pushkin, there was always the kennel in Pismo Beach but perhaps Serena Samuels wouldn't mind taking him out on the leash twice a day. He scribbled a reminder to himself to invite her to dinner that first Saturday in February.

Having made these decisions, Maks returned to the Bösendorfer to work on his commissions. But first: wedged among the framed pictures of his parents, his dead wife, and Oksana as a child was that photo of Silda—at the piano, looking languid. Had they just made love, on the couch or the carpet in the parlor, their two dogs whimpering nearby?

He couldn't settle on the precise circumstance, but he did remember he had used his Leica to take the shot. She was caressing the keys, a Chopin nocturne perhaps, oblivious to what he was doing, or too absorbed in the music to care. The image he captured spoke volumes: her face in the afterglow.

But a year had passed since her death. He did not want to have to explain the photo to anyone. Like to his neighbor, who not only was casually acquainted with Silda but was on, as she had put it, "quite friendly" terms with the husband. Like many people he had encountered in Hollywood, Serena was quick-witted.

He picked up the photo in its silver frame and slipped it inside the piano bench between albums of Schubert and Liszt.

"Ah, it's you, Maks," Serena said, surprise in her voice when he eventually rang. "Haven't run into you in ages. Hope you're well. Pushkin too."

"We were thinking the same thing. And hoping that you—Dog too—could come over for dinner on Saturday." Fleetingly, he feared he sounded too forward but quickly dismissed the idea. Serena came from Los Angeles: everyone was forward there.

"That would be lovely. What might I bring?"

"Not a thing, unless Dog has a special diet he follows—or, if you do, for that matter."

She laughed. "One thing about Los Angeles that didn't rub off on either of us. We eat most anything. But how about I toss a salad. Save you the trouble."

Which she did, and, to Maks' surprise, it was delicious without being overly elaborate. She also brought along a bottle of sauvignon blanc and a sirah, not having any idea what he had prepared. The latter complemented the Moldovan stew, which had been, he announced proudly, his mother's recipe.

Having drunk a fair amount but neither wanting to get too personal too quickly, they spent an hour critiquing films that had come out in the last few years. His favorite: *The Shape of Water*; hers: *Hotel Budapest*, each admiring the taste of the other.

Beyond movies, Serena had something to say on several other topics, never insistently, never exhaustively, but enough to make conversation flow. Trump, they concurred, was a global embarrassment, but fortunately, no major crisis had arisen to accentuate his incompetence. They left politics at that.

Maks found himself wondering why this handsome woman was not married, and after they finished off the wine, what she looked like beneath that black dress. He lowered his eyes to her legs, noting how shapely they were. Shifting her position, she recrossed them, more tightly.

At the ensuing pause in the conversation, he rose to retrieve the tiramisu he had bought at the bakery on Shell Beach Road. They each had a slice with black tea to wash it down. And yes, she would be glad to look after Pushkin during the time he was in New York. His twice-weekly housekeeper would see to cleaning up and bringing in the mail.

After he rummaged around for an extra set of keys to the house, Serena retrieved Dog from the garden and gave Maks a friendly hug. He needn't trouble himself: she lived four houses down. He watched her progress from his front porch, not unhappy to have such a companionable neighbor. And one easy enough on the eye.

CHAPTER NINETEEN

Kathleen and Issie

Comparing Notes

efusing to count the days since Eliot had promised to call her, Kathleen shrugged, got a new haircut, and made herself indispensable at work.

During the first weeks of 2020, the Lantana did brisk business, her hire of a new chef, recommended by Pierre and eager to please, had started to pay dividends. Several dishes were added to the menu and a couple of mainstays, including the baked sea bass and the broiled salmon, were spiced up and enhanced with unusual sides.

Further, her promotional efforts on behalf of the restaurant began to kick in. A local TV station filmed a segment on the Central Coast's latest hot spot, with Kathleen front and center on camera. Rave reviews in a couple of the regional newspapers followed.

From what she observed from behind the reservations desk, both locals and tourists were flush with cash, the job market being tight, the economy firing on all cylinders. However dysfunctional the government in Washington, it was far away. People in central California did worry about fire season but that challenge, inevitable but seasonal, was many months off.

Almost all customers appeared to have something to celebrate—and almost always with someone else. If nothing else, the arrival of a new decade merited a toast. Food and drink—good food and drink—were *de rigueur* for these rituals.

Without asking, Kathleen got a raise and put the extra cash aside for that long-delayed trip to, well, she hadn't determined where, or with whom. The idea of China, however, had grown on her as it bore no associations with François. Hypothetically, it might be equally appealing to Eliot, unencumbered by memories from his marriage and a fascinating destination in its own right.

Admittedly, she could have picked up the phone and invited him to dine with her—they could occupy the prized corner table with a breathtaking view of the ocean, seagulls clinging to the cliff mere feet out the window—but any such invitation should rightfully be up to him.

Her drive back to the airport to drop Isabel Frankel off in early January had only confirmed her in such a view. Eliot had not moved on in any substantial sense, at least not in her direction, comforting casseroles notwithstanding.

The two women had started off the trip from Shell Beach to the airport, each polite but stiff, Isabel offering to pay for the gas or share the driving. Her overtures were rejected. An awkward silence fell over the Porsche as they made their way south on the 101 freeway.

Kathleen switched on the radio. The news was of Trump's latest tweets deriding Democrats, and a mysterious ailment plaguing some place in China.

"Amazing how a city can be that large and we've never heard of it," Issie commented to lessen the tension. "No clue where this Wuhan is on a map."

"You're right. Beijing, Shanghai and Hong Kong are all we ever think about, though the Chinese are probably the same: New York, Los Angeles and Chicago are likely all they could identify here."

The ice broken, they chatted about the pleasures of the Central Coast and the different delights of New York City—: sunshine vs snowfall, packed theaters vs deserted beaches, anonymity vs gossipy neighbors. Innocuous enough.

When those topics petered out, Isabel checked her cell phone, hastily typing a text in one instance. Slipping the device back in her purse, she turned her head to focus anew on the scenery.

Kathleen suspected that Isabel might be more than a college chum who, on a whim, had dropped in on her former classmate. And she suspected that Isabel might be equally curious about *her* relationship with Eliot.

One of them would need to reveal her hand, or at least a card or two. What did either stand to lose? Sharing intelligence might benefit them both.

Forty miles into their trip, with the sun sinking to the West, curiosity got the better of them. As they passed through to the far side of Santa Maria, the holiday traffic began to thin out. Kathleen put the Porsche on cruise control, stretched out her legs and took a deep breath. And with less to see in the fading light, Isabel rearranged her position and cleared her throat.

"So," they each began, which made both of them chuckle.

"Go ahead," Isabel said, her palm upturned.

"I was wondering. You've known Eliot a long time, so now that you've seen him again, what do you make of his—what to call it—his well-being and, you know, his next phase?"

She did not mean to be intrusive, but this other woman might be amenable to shedding light on the man she herself was in the dark about. And although it needn't be verbalized, no one was getting any younger in this affair. She was about to turn fifty; crinkles around Isabel's eyes suggested that she was even older.

In a nutshell, Kathleen did not wish to waste time if there were to be no committed relationship with this man. Surely, she did not need to spell that out for the woman seated across from her, Harvard-trained lawyer that she was.

Slowly, Isabel fumbled in her shoulder bag and pulled out a pack of Virginia Slims and a silver lighter. She offered a cigarette to Kathleen, who shook her head.

"Do you mind? It always helps with difficult cases," she deadpanned.

“Whatever works,” Kathleen replied, switching on the car’s ventilator.

After a few remarks about the expectations of her Jewish parents, both federal court judges, Isabel launched into an abbreviated version of her early love affair with Eliot, including his leaving her for Silda—abruptly.

Kathleen scrunched her brow. “Why ever would he do so in that fashion?”

Isabel shrugged in explanation.

After a pause, Kathleen came at the subject differently. “So what was she like in her college days—Silda?”

“Blond, beautiful: more Nicole Kidman than Reese Witherspoon, if you know what I mean.”

Kathleen didn’t know but didn’t want Isabel to go off on a tangent: she wanted her to fast-forward. “And you and Eliot thereafter? All these years...”

Isabel blew a few smoke rings. “We saw each other when we saw each other—on business trips,” she rejoined. Determinedly neutral the word *saw*. To be construed however.

Kathleen knew how. “And now?”

“Hard to say. I believe something shifted for each of us this weekend.”

That line of questioning appeared to have reached a dead-end, Kathleen intuited.

They drove on, catching a glimpse of the purple sun as it slipped into the Pacific around the scenic overlook of Gaviota. “I’d pull over but don’t want you to miss your flight. We’ll need to be there in thirty minutes.”

Isabel snuffed out her cigarette in the ashtray on the dashboard. Eventually, she turned toward Kathleen.

“I’m a prosecutor, as Eliot mentioned. Sometimes we’re compelled to be mercilessly direct.”

“I can always plead the Fifth.”

“*Ergo*: the two of you,” she began, pausing long enough for the idea to flesh itself out. “Is yours a friendship between opera buffs—he says you're quite the *aficionado*—or something more?"

Kathleen compressed her lips as she formulated a response. "Like you, hard to say..." She sighed deeply and took the car out of cruise control.

Isabel interrupted her. "Forgive me. I phrased the question badly. The real issue is what *you* want the relationship to be." Kathleen looked dubious. "In my case," Isabel plowed on, "I let things trundle along. Men generally go along with that approach. But if we women want more, we need to say so; and if such things can't be accommodated by the person we're interested in, then perhaps they can be by someone, or something, else. In my case, I landed a dream job: loved it, still do. It's not everything, but it's enough."

Kathleen smiled, an almost rueful smile. "Imminently sensible. In my case, everything revolved around my husband François, and that was fine until—" A catch in her voice made her falter. Issie noticed but did not step in. "And now I'm having to reinvent life without him, or perhaps without any man—any man in particular, that is."

"Unless you come across one who makes your heart leap up."

Kathleen tilted her head to assess that possibility. She then jiggled with the radio buttons to get the latest weather report. Rain was in the forecast, but so far all they had been treated to were lightning strikes in the distant hills.

"Back to your point, Isabel," she eventually replied. "Men like Eliot have more options than we do, but rest assured, I don't intend to become a nuisance to him—or an embarrassment to myself."

Isabel nodded her head in solidarity. "I suspect you have plenty of options yourself. Not to mention a charming and successful son. Eleanor certainly thinks so."

"Yes, he's splendid, my stepson. A tricky life though, the restaurant business. Work rarely lets up." She paused while maneuvering around a truck hauling livestock. "Anyway," she continued, "to tie up the past, as it were, I'm putting together a cookbook, memorializing my husband's recipes. And toying with travel plans."

Isabel looked impressed.

"Plans, by the way, which may or may not include our mutual friend."

CHAPTER TWENTY

Eliot

Fault Lines

Those cracks in his marriage. Through the month of January, they kept Eliot awake nights. Half-smoked cigarettes accumulated in the ashtray on the night table. (Mariella, who came to clean twice a week, noted the disarray but said nothing.)

Like all married couples, Eliot and Silda had talked about myriad subjects, but as time passed, sex rarely came up. In fact, he had prided himself on not needing to belabor the issue. He was virile, he was practiced enough—and by definition he loved his wife. He had assumed she felt the same way though, naturally, with less amorous experience under her belt, and less of an appetite for lovemaking than he.

Thusly, the years had flown by, un-examined. The children had grown up and departed; his career had taken hold. He could not be accused of having neglected her when it was she who had become so busy with things to do, events to attend, letters to write, pupils to teach, a house to run, pets and people to see about.

Indubitably, their lovemaking had faded, if not fizzled. Indubitably, too, he would never know if that had bothered Silda. Arguably, a person might be struck by a so-called *coup de foudre*—the French knew a lot about the mysteries of attraction apparently—which might explain what had made his wife veer off-course. And fall into the arms of a man who still lived literally down the street.

During one fretful night, Eliot arose and grabbed up the illicit letters from his desk with the idea of burning them but couldn't bring himself to strike the match. Instead, he retied the black velvet ribbon around them and stuffed the packet back into the Tiffany box. Standing on a stool, he lodged it at the back of the closet shelf, behind the songbirds from Venice.

"Over and done with," he muttered to himself.

He plunged back into work, interviewing several homeowners up and down the coastal drive who had complained about the shoddy workmanship on their homes—foundations misaligned, walls cracked, pipes broken. By the beginning of February, he had compiled a dozen such instances, including three in Shell Beach, two in Pismo, and one in Grover Beach.

As for his own extra-marital behavior, Eliot was loath to consider it in any but the most plausible of lights. Despite the fact that his comment—blasé, was it? —had offended Issie, all he meant by it being "different" was that their liaison was imminently excusable. They had known each other forever before he met his eventual wife; and after he was married, they never connived to meet up. In every instance he could recall, they had simply been thrown together at one or another business conference—in Chicago, or St Louis, or Houston, or wherever. To his mind, it was natural that they should hit the default button: screwing like crazy over an intense weekend and never betraying a word about it afterward.

The only tell-tale sign that their encounters might be construed as an affair was the postcards he would receive in the aftermath. They arrived like clockwork, invariably to the Santa Barbara firm's address, each postmarked from the city of their latest rendezvous. Scrawled in Issie's barely legible hand, they rang variations on the same inside joke: *Eliot, Good seeing you at the confab, and thanks for the expert input! Yours, I.F.*

The notes tickled him, no one at the firm any the wiser, not even Caroline.

As for Silda, she appeared oblivious. Except when, to surprise him, she did show up unexpectedly, a decade or so ago, at a bar association gathering in New Orleans. On the last night, he and Issie were drinking daiquiris on the rooftop of the Royal Orleans, his arm, if he remembered rightly, around her midriff as they looked out over the lights on the river.

The clearing of a throat behind him: Silda's. Then: "You weren't in your room, darling, so the front desk suggested I check up here, poolside. *Et voilà*."

Flabbergasted, the two lovers quickly disentangled. Eliot motioned for the waiter, (a knowing smirk on the young man's face) and ordered another round for the three of them.

"Of all people, can you believe I ran into Isabel. We've been catching up."

At this bald-faced lie, Silda's lips curled into something other than a smile, her eyes fixed on him. Unflinching. Eventually, her gaze shifted to Issie, who had meantime tied her hotel robe about her swimsuit. Eliot had no memory of any further drinks arriving to help them through the encounter.

The next day he flew back to California alone, Silda deciding to visit a couple of old friends—: "You gave me the idea to search out old schoolmates, darling, so why not?" Her version of a *touché*.

As for the mortified Issie, she had checked out at dawn for the first flight back to New York. There was no subsequent postcard from her to memorialize that conference.

Into his pillow that night, Eliot shed an unaccustomed tear. If nothing else, he had been a cad toward the two most important women in his life, one no longer on this earth, the other now on the other side of the country, and probably content to be so. If resolutions were still in order—it was, he sleepily reckoned, the last day of January—he would make a few. All to do with the well-being of others in his orbit. Compiling his list, it lengthened: Isabel naturally, but also Eleanor and Jared, Kathleen, Serena, Daphne, even Uncle Seth—and he finally fell asleep.

When he awoke at 9:15 the next morning, the phone was ringing. It was Caroline, all-business, with a rundown of calls, appointments and depositions for the month of February. But his list? She too needed to be on it.

"I have an idea, Caroline, which you might warm to and which might profit us both."

It had occurred to him, while she was rattling off his agenda, that his assistant—herself about to be certified a lawyer—might benefit by coming along on his fact-finding missions. Show her how painstakingly a case must be built and what leg work is all about. He doubted that any such on-the-job training came up in night school.

"We could start this week. Wednesday would be ideal if you can swing it with Tillotson and the others."

There had been a short silence at the other end of the phone. And then: "I don't know what to say, Eliot, but I'll make it work."

"You have reservations?"

"No, no. Not me. Chloe still has ups and downs. I'm trying to keep tabs."

"Her grades?"

"Much improved. It's her moods. From sensible to sullen in a heartbeat."

"I believe it's called being a teenager," he had deadpanned.

CHAPTER TWENTY-ONE

Serena

In the Mood

og was just asking about Keats—how is he, and you?" Serena inquired, Eliot's name popping up on the caller screen. Out of breath she sounded but droll enough for those who knew her.

"You sound busy," he began.

Serena had heard the ringing from outside where she had been clipping roses, their pale lavender blooms having benefited from the generous winter rain.

Despite her asthma, Serena refused to let her condition impede the things she enjoyed—sports and cooking foremost, but gardening was now bringing her added pleasure. The salt air along the coast had also helped keep her ailment under control.

Hastily she lay the roses on the kitchen table and picked up the phone on its fifth ring. Dog, who was curled up under a chair, had looked up sleepily but not bothered to intrude.

"No, no, this is fine. I was outside—gathering rosebuds while I may," she quipped, which elicited an uncertain chuckle.

"Since you asked, Keats is fine, though with all the rain we haven't walked as much—down your way, that is," Eliot explained, a tad defensive. "Or been to the gym."

"I noticed our schedules haven't overlapped. And in the offing, Dog has taken up with, of all things, a Great Dane," she said blithely, but pointedly too.

"Humph," Eliot replied, trying to emulate her tone. "I trust his attachment is nothing serious—nothing that Keats should worry about."

Her turn to wonder if there were a subtext to the exchange. "Just dogs being dogs, I suppose," she replied to end the banter.

In the interval that followed, she forced herself not to ask what Eliot had been up to since Christmas. He had phoned; he must have a purpose. While awaiting his move, she located her inhaler and sprayed a puff into her mouth.

"I was wondering," he eventually returned, "about something you mentioned, which I'd like to follow up on. If you would allow..."

Serena sat down in one of the kitchen chairs. "By all means. But you'll have to spell it out. We have chatted about so much I can't zero in on anything—" Her voice had modulated, a tremulous note in it.

"No, nothing like that," he cut her off. "It's your house. Something about the foundations being not right."

It took a minute for Serena to wrap her mind around this statement.

"Am I mistaken?" he persevered. "I may have been distracted at the time, but I've now put two and two together. It appears it's not just you."

If Serena had forgotten her complaint about the place to Eliot, she had indeed noticed cracks in the masonry where she had dug up shrubbery close to the house. A fissure was visible, and the ground was wet where pipes were buried.

"As it turned out, Eliot, no actual survey was done when I bought the property. Several buyers were circling, and I was in a hurry. I have been meaning to call someone who deals with such things. If that's what you're asking. The house is barely sixteen years old."

"Before you do that, you might want to consider a lawyer. In fact, we're trying to put together a case against a couple of contractors. They may have cut corners, perhaps in concert with a surveyor."

"What do I need to do?"

"The first thing would be for us to take a look at any defects in your place. Caroline and I are making the rounds in the Five Cities if one day or another would be convenient."

"I see," she replied, calculating her activities for the upcoming week. "Next Tuesday, the 14th, would be preferable, but I'll get back to you with a precise time."

"Fine," he said. "If we find malfeasance, there might be a suit to file. You might want to hold off on repairs."

"Whatever you think," she said, feeling both deflated and reassured at the same time.

"Meantime," Eliot added, abandoning his lawyerly voice, "I will make a point of being in Pismo Saturday morning, with Keats. If not for racquetball, for a walk on the beach."

"Sounds good. And thanks for the call," she returned and clicked off.

For a long minute Serena sat befuddled, berating herself for having harbored any romantic illusions (however vague) about Eliot. She picked up one of the roses and inhaled its fragrance. Whether the flowers lasted until Tuesday or not, she would invite guests for dinner that evening. Valentine's Day, after all. "Company for the two of us," she murmured, stroking Dog's back with her foot.

If by now she had a general idea what pleased the palate of Eliot Etheridge, she had not a clue what might whet that of Maks Mirovich. He had served her caviar and his own mother's version of goulash; she had no intention of competing with him on anything that esoteric. Not movies, nor European destinations—she was not even sure where his native Moldova was—and definitely not blintzes.

She spent a couple of hours going through cookbooks, hoping to be inspired by something hearty that wasn't heavy. She settled on a medley of broccoli florets, cauliflower and red peppers—colorful enough a concoction—seasoned with her homegrown spices and baked in light sour cream.

One thing could be universally counted on however: all men enjoy being in charge of a barbecue. She would present him with a tray of pre-cut veggies and cubes of fresh ahi tuna. That way he could skewer them any which way for his version of shish kabob. From what she had read, it was a staple from Istanbul to Vladivostok, (surely Moldova lay along the way), and to boot, it had been Americanized to perfection.

Thanks to her heat lamps, they could dine outside, the dogs could frolic nearby, and music—not the obvious Tchaikovsky but the more complex Shostakovich—would carry from the parlor. Perhaps a movie thereafter, fresh pears with stilton and black coffee to accompany his doubtless sophisticated cinematic choice.

And after that?

It was getting late, on yet another rainy Friday night. She would place a call Saturday morning before heading to the gym. She knew enough never to disturb a man on a weekend evening.

When the doorbell rang around 4:30 on the 14th, Serena had just arranged the top layer of vegetables in a glass dish and dribbled melted butter and breadcrumbs over the top. She rinsed her hands in the sink and hurried to the front door. How could Maks have gotten the time so wrong?

To her surprise, Eliot and Caroline stood there, both in business attire. She was clutching a loose-leaf folder, he an outsized camera.

"We were in the neighborhood and thought...but I can see you're busy," he burbled, noticing the apron.

"No, no. Do come in. I have to heat the oven but then I'm all yours," she responded, ushering them in.

Eliot and Caroline waited awkwardly in the foyer, the smells from the kitchen making it clear that they had intruded. Caroline cast her eyes about, taking in the high ceilings and spacious parlor off to her right, a terrace with fan palms in huge pots beyond.

"If she supplies us with the floor plan, we can do a walkabout on our own," she whispered.

Before Eliot could respond, Serena returned, *sans* apron and with a folder of her own—documents related to her purchase of the house. "Why don't I show you the cracks outside. You can check the basement yourselves for anything additional."

She led them through the parlor where the lavender roses had held up well and out onto the terrace. At the far edge a barbecue grill stood with its hood up. Fancy skewers lay across a metal tray, waiting to be threaded.

Out in the yard, Serena pointed to the side wall where oleander bushes alternated with mock orange. Stepping between two shrubs, she stooped to reveal a portion of the wall that had chipped off, exposing a beam.

"What worries me most is how damp the soil is, as though there's a leaky pipe undermining the foundation." She moved aside to allow the two to take photos and notes.

On the way back inside, Serena stopped to pick up something from the table, something that looked to Caroline like a nasal spray.

Pausing at the entrance to the kitchen, Serena said: "I should have offered you something to drink. Water, or fresh lemonade. The fruit trees in the back never stop producing. Or there's a Sancerre in the fridge. I think it's one you like, Eliot. If memory serves."

Color rose in his cheeks, but Eliot ignored the reference. "Lemonade sounds lovely, but after we take a look below."

"Down this other hallway," she replied, gesturing toward the back of the house. "Door's not locked and a light switch is right inside." She turned to place a lid on the Pyrex dish and slid it into the oven.

In the basement, which was spotless, Eliot and Caroline checked the walls but found nothing unusual. And from what they could tell of the pipes, nothing was amiss.

"Are we sure the same contractor worked on this house as on the others?" Caroline asked.

"Not necessarily," he replied.

She moved toward the light hanging from the ceiling to consult the folder. "What is the name we're interested in?"

"The most prominent recurring name is Worthington," Eliot responded. "Worthington & Sons, if I'm not mistaken."

Caroline's jaw dropped. "Yes," she replied slowly, scanning the documents Serena had handed them. "It does seem they were involved in the construction here." Her face had turned ashen, but in the dim light Eliot did not notice.

After they took a few more notes, the two rejoined Serena. She had poured three glasses of lemonade and laid out a platter of crackers with cream cheese and black olives.

While they sipped their drinks, Dog wandered in, looking down in the mouth.

"He looks chagrined, or perhaps it's just the breed," Caroline said. Serena stiffened at the comment.

"But a sweetheart of a pet," Eliot rushed to add.

"Well, he'll soon have company to cheer him up. Maks is bringing Pushkin over and they'll get a kabob to fight over," Serena said. Unthinkingly. It had slipped her mind how awkward the encounter with their neighbor at the restaurant in Pismo Beach had been.

Putting his glass down, Eliot consulted his watch. "We should let Serena get back to her cooking. Plus, we have another appointment to get to," he announced, his tone newly business-like.

Neither woman objected. Once out on the porch, Caroline asked if he were not feeling well. Closing the front door, Serena did not hear Eliot's reply.

Ninety minutes later, Maks arrived with Pushkin in tow, two bottles of Georgian wine in an ornate carrying case, and a DVD.

"Something different, if we get around to it, and provided it's not one you've already seen," he said, laying the disc on the sideboard.

"As long as it's one you'd enjoy, it'll be fine with me," she replied.

While she poured them both a glass, he took off his beret and lay it next to the movie. He had, she noticed, had his gray-speckled hair trimmed, which somehow enhanced his classic Slavic profile—high cheekbones, broad forehead, strong jaw. All told, he appeared to take up more space than his size would account for. "I took the chance that you might be willing to fire up the grill for shish kabob. We can dine on the veranda thanks to L.A.'s greatest invention: outdoor space heaters."

"Excellent," he said, smiling at her remark. They raised their glasses and then ambled out to the terrace, where Pushkin and Dog were already sniffing each other out.

"I would not have guessed they'd be so companionable but there's no—I only know it in Latin: *de gustibus non est disputandem*."

"Indeed, no accounting for tastes," Serena rejoined, briefly searching out his eyes. They were a deeper blue than she remembered and etched by a few fine lines. Not unbecoming.

Maks removed the top from the tray of vegetables she had arranged. "I hope I can do this justice. You went to a lot of trouble."

"Not at all," she said. "If you burn them, I've thrown together a casserole for back-up."

After they wandered around the garden, the dogs crisscrossing in their wake, they chatted on the terrace until the sun set.

"As you know, I had planned to head to New York for a couple of weeks, but the weather is so much more inviting here in winter, don't you find?"

"I do, as do most people who discover Southern California. Still, New York in the spring or fall, so much to see and do—"

"My daughter says it might be wise to wait. (Serena's eyebrows went up.) Something about this virus in China, which has made its way to Italy. She works for the United Nations, knows all these international officials. That it could reach the east coast..." He looked perturbed for an instant and then shrugged. "Likely, they over-dramatize."

"I didn't realize you had a daughter. Do you see her often?"

"Too seldom," he said, regret in his voice. "But she's very bright, beautiful too, as was her mother. Good with languages, which accounts for the job at the U.N."

"You must be proud," Serena said, though seeing how troubled his face had become, did not press further. She topped off his glass and rose to return to the kitchen. "You can start whenever. I imagine a low flame will work fine. I'll heat the casserole and bring out a salad in a bit."

"This should be fun. Haven't grilled anything in quite a while. With Sil—" He stopped himself and turned his attention to the skewers.

Inside, Serena put on a CD of Shostakovich's so-called Leningrad symphony, barely loud enough to carry outside. Back in the kitchen, she paused, tilting her head in thought. Silda Sorenson Etheridge had led a more complicated life than she had imagined. And now here she was ministering to a second man who had been in the dead woman's thrall.

After dinner, during which her guest talked about his family migration to the U.S., they did watch the movie—a Russian picture called *A Slave of Love*.

"I didn't know whether you liked political films or melodrama or comedy, so I chose one that has all three," Maks said, taking the DVD out of its jacket. The director had been a friend of his back in the day, he added, when they had both studied in Moscow. The film was one Serena had never heard of.

Toward the end, after the heroine's lover has been shot by soldiers and she escapes on, of all things, a tram, Serena sensed her guest edge closer to her. At first, she tensed, but when his fingers caressed the back of her neck, she willed herself to relax. As the credits rolled, they remained on the sofa, his other hand sliding under her skirt and up her thigh.

Getting hold of herself, Serena whispered, “There might be a better way to proceed. Over there near the fire.”

After the usual awkwardness with hooks and zippers, they switched to the rug in front of the hearth. An hour passed. Prokofiev succeeded Shostakovich on the stereo. Only embers remained in the grate when Serena and Maks rolled away from each other to get their bearings. Only then did they notice the dogs curled up with each other on the nearby sofa.

CHAPTER TWENTY-TWO

Eleanor and Jared

Masked and Unmasked

On her walk home from the office mid-March, clumps of dirty snow stubbornly clinging to the curb on Park Avenue, Eleanor ducked into a wine shop for a bottle and then paused at the corner kiosk on 64th Street for a dozen red roses. Her brother could not be counted on to bring anything on his own, never had been, likely never would be.

Everything was supposed to come Jared's way, though it did not always do so. As the only daughter, she, on the other hand, had worked hard to get where she was, graduating *cum laude* from Harvard Law, then putting in the hours to eventually make partner. Emulating her father, besting him in some respects. Her achievement was closer to that of Isabel Frankel, who—well, she, as the younger one, ought to place the call, suggest coffee somewhere, *al fresco* even, if it were ever to warm up again in the city.

There were days Eleanor missed sunny California, pulling her cashmere muffler up against her exposed neck.

Thinking of home reminded her: she needed to make sure they rang their father at Shell Beach before they separated. Other than a few perfunctory text messages, she had not communicated with him since the surprise get-together at New Year's. Happy enough to see her he had been, she reckoned, but somehow in a fog, not wanting to talk much about the family's past good times, animated only when it came to going over the legal case he was spearheading.

However, on her last day there at Sorenson House, father and daughter had cooked something together: a bouillabaisse, which recipe Kathleen had jotted down for them before she left with Isabel in tow.

"This was fun, sweetheart," Eliot had said, once they had finished cutting up shallots and adding bacon bits to the broth. "Your mother rarely allowed me in the kitchen; for that matter, she didn't relish cooking herself. So much was catered or ordered in, it seemed like the natural state of things," he had added, giving the soup one final stir. They had made enough for six but ended up eating the entire pot themselves, with a loaf of the homemade sourdough bread Caroline had brought over and a jar of a buttery sage spread Pierre had thrust upon her when she left San Francisco.

With him, Eleanor had spoken several times by phone during the first couple of months of the year, often with the sounds of a restaurant in the background—laughter, the rattling of plates, occasional shouts. It sounded lively; so did he.

As for his stepmother, Eleanor was determined to tread lightly, both because of her own "thing" with Pierre and because of her father's "thing" with Kathleen. Nonetheless, she eventually rang the home number in Pismo Beach to let her know (if Eliot hadn't already?) how much they enjoyed adopting her recipe for the fish soup and to thank her, again, for the "foodie" machine.

The gift had in fact been a godsend. That very morning Eleanor had thrown together all the ingredients for Jared's favorite dish—pot roast with potatoes, carrots, corn and green beans—and set the timer to go on at 5 p.m., with the idea that all would be ready a couple of hours later.

With that out of the way, there was nothing much else to bother with in the kitchen; brother and sister could relax and catch up.

As she approached her building on 67th Street, she vowed not to bring up his novel nor his problems at that flailing magazine whose name she could never recall. They would have plenty else to go over, including her visit out west and what to make of their father's longtime association with this Ms. Frankel.

Plus, on her list of issues to address, they needed to alert their parent to something that might not be on his radar—however much it might reconfirm his belief that his children were alarmists. From what Pierre had told her, courtesy of his foreign-born colleagues in the culinary world, this out-of-the-blue viral contagion was not to be taken lightly.

"It's coming here, Eleanor, especially to cities on the coasts. Like ours."

She had never heard of either of the places he had gone on about, Wuhan and Bergamo, yet now reports about beleaguered hospitals abroad were popping up on the evening news.

Regarding the affair with Pierre, Eleanor had not made up her mind as to its seriousness nor to what she was prepared to say to her brother about it. She had made one mistake with a man—that her ex-husband Malcolm was a gifted lawyer, who possessed a flair for courtroom dramatics, was all to the good; that other women threw themselves at him, and he responded, was not. She did not intend to make another mistake like that.

And she had been alerted. As charming and successful in his sphere as Pierre was, his stepmother had had occasion, however breezily, to describe him as "so very French." Which Eleanor took to mean flirtatious both by nature and by design.

That they lived on opposite sides of the Continent might make the whole thing fizzle. *Unless Jared decides to quiz me, I'll give the thing short shrift*, she told herself as the doorman swung wide the heavy entrance for her.

Once changed into comfortable wool slacks and sweater, Eleanor checked on the instant pot. Things were bubbling inside, sending reassuring smells throughout the apartment. Kathleen was nothing if not astute, she thought, having selected a perfect gift, pertinent without being presumptuous.

Come the summer she would reciprocate, asking Pierre for an appropriate occasion to celebrate. Perhaps they could all rendezvous in New York, her father included.

The intercom buzzed punctually at 7:15, and Jared reached her 17th-floor apartment in three minutes. Of all things, he was wearing a black mask and carrying a bottle of bubbly. She wasn't sure which of the oddities was more surprising.

"Hey, Sis," he said, giving her a perfunctory hug and handing off the bottle while he dispensed with jacket and scarf. He hung them on separate pegs on her hat rack. "In case you're curious, the mask isn't for the cold. It's to fend off this virus thing." He removed the straps gingerly from behind his ears and hung it next to his jacket.

"I never knew you to be so health-conscious, or civic-minded," she remarked, regarding him from head to toe. He looked well-groomed, even with marks across his cheeks that the covering had left.

He followed her into the kitchen where she placed the Veuve Cliquot in a silver ice bucket and retrieved two Lalique flutes from a corner cabinet. It had been a while since Eleanor had formally entertained—friends and colleagues were beginning to hunker down at home as reports of infections grew worrisome. Her brother would now count as a distinguished guest and call for her good china.

"First off, something smells fantastic. What exactly is in this contraption?" he asked, eyeing the cooker.

"One of your favorites, especially on a winter's night."

"Looks high-tech," he added, eyeing the settings.

"A gift, from Kathleen Pavonine. Remember, I spent New Year's in San Francisco, visiting Pierre," she tossed out. He raised his eyebrows but said nothing, instead extending his glass to clink hers.

"Seems like we both made an impression while at Shell Beach," he commented, his tone suggestive.

"You'll tell me more, but first, you toss the salad and I'll bake the biscuits. We can listen to the news while we get things ready.

"Deal," he said.

Later, at the oak dining table, Jared dropped his news: he had re-connected with Daphne Dupree, who had— "against considerable odds," he stressed—become a sensation. Her paintings were selling like hotcakes at some swank Madison Avenue gallery.

And, he went on, she had stayed on longer than she had intended, after wearing out her welcome at the gallery owner's place. "Remember him, Sis? He of the three-piece suit. Put the moves on her but she wriggled out of it."

Winding up his account, he explained that Daphne spent almost two months getting to know the city. "With a vengeance" is how he put it.

Eleanor passed him another biscuit. He buttered it heavily and popped it in his mouth.

"So, how did you two manage to run into each other? I didn't take you for a gallery hopper."

"Out of the blue, she phoned me. Started by saying she finally discovered what MoMA stood for. Threw me for a loop."

"I'll bet," she returned.

"Say what you will, but I have never met anyone so appallingly naive and oddly knowing at the same time. Deprived of a lot of things in childhood and dumped on by a lot of unsavory people."

"In other words, not well-adjusted enough to be boring but complicated enough to be intriguing."

"Something like that. Daphne is almost thirty but acts more like a keyed-up teenager. I'd bet she hasn't slept more than six hours a night, carrying around a sketch pad everywhere she goes. Even took the Staten Island ferry one icy afternoon to draw the passengers." Eleanor looked bemused. "And no, I did not tag along on that outing. Too cold and all that."

"So, dear brother, what *did* you do with her?" she fired off. "Or, continue to do, if she's still around?"

Jared studied his nearly empty plate before responding.

"Something like what you've been doing with your *chef du jour*," he shot back. He sang a line or two of "Getting to Know You" to reinforce his point.

Eleanor took another sip of the pinot noir she had selected earlier at the shop. Jared began to work his way through the salad.

"Funny, isn't it?" she mused. He looked up. "What these relationships have in common. Pierre and Daphne live clear across the country from us and..." Eleanor wrinkled her brow in an effort to complete her thought.

"And?" Jared prompted her.

"And we would have never met either had it not been for Dad."

"True enough. And since you brought him up, no further hint necessary. I've come girded to speak if you want to call."

"Later. Make yourself at home in the other room. I'll bring cheese and crackers. Cointreau too."

"No argument from me," he said, taking his and his sister's plate to the kitchen and placing them in the sink.

While preparing the cheeses, Eleanor could hear one of the anchors on CNN reel off the latest statistics. As of mid-March, verified cases in and around the metro area had surpassed a thousand; hospitalizations and deaths were ticking up. President Trump, he went on, had insisted that the country had the virus under control and that it would soon disappear. (She shook her head in disbelief.) Things on the West Coast had begun to deteriorate too, especially in San Francisco. (She made a mental note to ring Pierre in the next few days.)

The siblings watched the news until 10:30 p.m., Jared making only occasional reference to the mixed signals on the virus. "We're the greatest country on earth, right, El? But looks like we don't have our act together on this. Asians don masks every time they get on a plane; I'm getting weird stares on the subway for mine."

"Don't get me started. Trump may be making it worse, not better. Still, it only afflicts the elderly."

"So far. We should call Dad. Make sure he's paying attention."

To their surprise when they did ring, a woman's voice came on the line, with muffled ones in the background.

"Is everything okay there? This is Eliot's daughter Eleanor—and my brother Jared—calling," a note of anxiety in her own voice.

"We're fine here. It's Serena, from Thanksgiving. Your father and I were watching a movie. I'll pause it. He'll jump right on."

Before Eleanor could object, Eliot was summoned and took the receiver in hand.

"Sweetheart? Are you two together—at a restaurant?"

"No, no. Jared came over and I cooked. But we don't want to interrupt."

"DVD players are useful, I'm finding. Serena brought over a marvelous old movie, with Ronald Colman and Greer Garson. She's a walking encyclopedia—Serena, I mean." Eleanor and Jared exchanged an amused look. Their father sounded elated, or tipsy. "Not to mention the vegetable lasagna she put together earlier."

It sounded like Serena interrupted to object to the compliments. Her voice too sounded gay.

"We've been watching the news, Dad. We want to make sure you're being careful," Jared shouted over the distance.

"Careful?"

"About this virus," he persevered. "It's not the flu. It's a national emergency."

"The W.H.O. is calling it a pandemic," Eleanor added.

"Quite a coincidence," Eliot returned, unruffled. "This film we're watching takes place on the heels of the Great War, at the time the Spanish flu struck. A worldwide disaster. Millions died."

The two siblings exchanged another look, this one of frustration.

"Just stay safe, Dad, and we'll be in touch again soon. You can come visit us when all this is over," Jared pressed on.

Eleanor could hear the two in Shell Beach exchange words but couldn't make them out. Instead, she gestured toward her brother, inviting him to mention whatever else was on his mind: Daphne, his job, his book, whatever. He waved her off.

"And tell Serena goodbye. Enjoy the rest of your movie," Eleanor added.

When they hung up, they both looked flustered.

"So much for that," Jared said.

"But that's what we wanted, right? For Dad to stay busy and so forth."

"I suppose."

"But you're not convinced."

"I guess it's the 'so forth.' Serena seems like a fine person. But I'm finding it hard to imagine Daphne as a candidate for—(here Jared waved his hand in the air)—any serious attention."

Eleanor hesitated an instant before replying. "Daphne will likely say whatever needs to be said. She's not that naïve."

"No, I reckon not."

Having agreed on something with her brother, Eleanor retrieved the Cointreau from the liquor cabinet and poured them each a thimble-full in tiny silver goblets.

"You used to entertain a lot, if memory serves," Jared eventually hazarded, swirling the pale liquid and admiring the engraving on the goblet, an entwined *E* and *M*. "Back in the day, that is."

"They were a wedding gift. Don't use them much anymore," she answered, and took a sip herself, which made her eyes smart. "However," she picked up again, "I did use them last month when Isabel Frankel came over. You know, Dad's old friend from Harvard. Big-time prosecutor with the southern district." That description seemed to go over Jared's head. "Anyway, I bumped into her at Shell Beach. And, well, she and Dad…"

"She and Dad, what?" he asked.

To gain a beat, she passed her brother a platter of paper-thin lemon wafers. "They go nicely with the liqueur. Isabel sent them over as a thank-you for the supper I made."

"Hmmm," he replied. "You two hit it off I take it. Legal Eagles in flight," he quipped. Eleanor let the lame joke flap around in the air. "But what about Dad? Is she officially a member of his casserole klatch?" He sounded amused by the idea.

"Don't think so. But she did say that she plans to sign up for a cooking class: 'classics from the great cuisines of the world,' or something like that."

"You're kidding."

"Said she had survived too long on deli takeout and dinner invitations from friends without being able to reciprocate. And that, if I'm patient…"

"At least she is droll," Jared opined. "And the cookies are delicious."

Brother and sister savored the rest of their cordials in silence, with only the faint sound of traffic below.

After she wrapped a slab of cheese for Jared to take home, he retrieved his wrap but stuck the mask in his pocket. "Don't want to be mistaken for a burglar," he sighed.

As he turned the knob to leave, he placed a kiss on his sister's cheek. "Oh, I almost forgot. I did finish the book. Sent it off to my publisher weeks ago. Daphne had encouraged me to be done with it."

CHAPTER TWENTY-THREE

Daphne

A Change in Fortune

The first thing Daphne did when the surprised chauffeur from the airport dropped her in front of her dusty trailer was walk over to the Paradise Park office to retrieve Kahlo and pay for one more month's occupancy. She had to knock several times on the padlocked door. The manager eyed her suspiciously as she wrote out a check.

"You look different, Dupree. Your hair and all."

"Yes, well, had it cut, in New York," she replied, not raising her eyes, and not wanting to indulge the woman, whose own straggly hair was the color of mayonnaise. The less the old biddy knew about her transformation into a minor media darling the better. Being civil though she could afford. "And thank you," she added, handing her the check, "for looking after my cat. I assume the cash I gave you in December covered her food?"

"I suppose," the woman replied, as though more would not be unjustified. "Haven't seen the creature for a spell. Might turn up again now you're back."

Daphne's mouth fell open. She had specifically told the manager to ring her cell if anything was amiss with the calico. Two hundred fifty dollars had seemed fair enough to compensate for feeding the feline for two months. "When did she disappear?"

"Days ago. Figured you'd get back soon enough."

"Let me know if she returns here to the office. And I'll take any leftover pet food in case she comes back to the trailer," she declared, no longer polite.

Looking put out, the woman waddled back inside and soon returned with a bag of dry cat chow.

Back in the trailer, Daphne flicked on the lights, put a bottle of wine in the fridge, and filled a plastic container with cat food. She placed it right outside the trailer door.

This was not the homecoming she had hoped for. Cramped and close-smelling, the trailer seemed forlorn, emptied of her artwork and the only other animate creature beside herself. Fleetingly, she thought of ringing Jared, who had been more supportive than most people who flitted through her life. But what would she say, and what could he possibly do?

Stepping outside, the chill wind brought goosebumps to her arms. Quickly, she called out, "Kitty, kitty," circling the trailer and bending to look underneath it. Nothing visible except a discarded paintbrush and a rusty can of spray paint.

Back inside, she locked the door but threw open a couple of windows to clear the air. Then, after a quick shower, she poured herself a glass of the chardonnay and sat down to take stock.

However serendipitous her recent good fortune, she was still discombobulated by things she hadn't bargained on—: that so many people had demanded to know so much about her had been flattering but also unnerving. Worse were the unwanted attentions of her chief benefactor, which she had struggled to fend off without causing an irreparable rupture.

From her perspective, Arthur Braunstein had been out of line, but he had not been vindictive. When she repulsed him that New Year's Eve in his Soho loft, he desisted, his usual air of correctitude quickly reasserting itself. To demonstrate he harbored no lasting ill-will, the very next day he instructed the gallery in Santa Barbara to box up and ship to Madison Avenue all of Daphne's canvases that remained stacked in her trailer.

Although he soon returned to the West Coast, he had allowed her to remain as a guest in his loft.

No idiot, Arthur knew a good thing when he saw it—and Daphne, he calculated, could be more important as a client than as a reluctant lover.

His hunch was right. Most of her seascapes had sold by mid-February; a second check had been handed her, this one for $150,000 to cover her cut of the proceeds.

Exorbitant the sum her first reaction, but she had been too stunned to inquire about any mistake. Arthur's partner, one Darius Dravidian, whom she insisted upon calling by his last name, had grasped her hand warmly, telling her what a pleasure it had been having her around for the opening, and thereafter. "We're counting on your being back—with more of your canvases—within the year, my dear. I'm sure I speak for Arthur as well. Anything you need out there on the West Coast, let the Santa Barbara gallery know and they'll accommodate. And henceforth please call me Darius."

On the flight back to LAX, Daphne had flipped through her sketchbooks and drawn up "an action plan," an expression Jared had used in talking about his writing routine. She was now under contract to produce upwards of a dozen more oils in the year to come. Not a minute to be wasted, she told herself and determined that finding proper lodging where she could paint, and not be disturbed by transients on the beach, was not only essential but now affordable. She would give herself a month to find such accommodations for herself and, if found, for Kahlo.

Shaking herself out of her reverie, Daphne opened a box of crackers that had languished on the table in her absence. No longer crisp but they would do. Another sip of the wine, and she screwed up her courage to call the only other person she felt could be a comfort.

She dialed Eliot's home number, but he did not pick up; she hung up.

Despite a late start the next day, Daphne charged up her iPad and began an online search for guesthouse rentals in the Five Cities vicinity. Looking around the spartan confines in which she had lived for the last eighteen months, she figured a two-room accommodation with a kitchenette and a shed in which to set up a makeshift studio would suffice. For the first time, she did not have to fret over the cost—of most anything.

But she did have to eat. With nothing in the fridge and now only a half-full box of stale crackers, Daphne jumped in the pick-up and drove to Trader Joe's. First, she sampled the coffee on offer, twice, and then filled her cart with everything that caught her eye. Including enough ground beef and focaccia bread to make sloppy Joes.

If all went well, she would take them over to Eliot's as soon as he was available.

Back in the trailer with her groceries, she stuck her store-bought sunflowers in her chipped vase and placed them on the windowsill. Then she mixed the ingredients for sloppy Joes in a large bowl and put it in the fridge next to the half-empty wine bottle. After another fruitless walkabout looking for Kahlo, she sat down and took a few deep breaths. If she had been overwhelmed by New York City—perfectly natural a reaction—she felt even more rattled in familiar surroundings. Despite the sunflowers, the trailer was depressing, her cat was missing, her relations with Arthur were strained, and those with everyone else were uncertain.

Within a few minutes, she got up the nerve to dial Eliot's cell. He picked up on the third ring.

"Daphne? Everything okay?"

"I'm back home and was hoping to see you. You know, catch up." She tried to make her voice light but without much success.

After a pause, he replied, "That would be lovely. When were you thinking?"

To her ear, he sounded distracted. She couldn't gauge his level of enthusiasm. "Am I disturbing you? We could speak another time."

"It's fine. I'm with Caroline. You remember my assistant from the firm—actually, she's now a bonafide lawyer herself."

"Yes, of course," she returned, not knowing what to make of that explanation.

"We're finishing up some paperwork."

"What about later, like this evening? I made something for us. You know, so you don't have to cook. We could eat in your kitchen and, you know, catch up. With things." She felt like her old inarticulate self, at risk of losing her thread.

Again there was a pause in which Caroline said something, but Daphne couldn't make it out.

"That would be doable. Around seven work for you?"

Arriving early, Daphne parked the truck down the street and waited for the Camry in front of the house to depart. For the first time, she noticed the iron-wrought sign in a curlicued script that spelled out *The Sorenson House* atop the mailbox. She wondered if Eliot would ever get around to changing it. Within a few minutes, a female figure appeared, shouldering a briefcase. Daphne ducked in her seat and waited until the Toyota pulled away.

After smoothing her hair in the rearview mirror and applying a trace of lipstick, she gathered up the bag with the covered glass bowl, the focaccia bread, and a plastic container of golden beets and goat cheese. Carefully, so as not to drop anything or twist her ankle in unaccustomed heels, she got out and headed for the house.

Eliot appeared agog when he opened the door.

"You look marvelous," he burbled, then amended himself. "Not that you didn't before but now so, uh, *à la mode*, your hair. Your outfit too."

She had chosen one of the jersey skirts she had bought at Bloomingdales and a cream-colored blouse from a shop in Soho, the combination she had worn for her gallery opening. Around her shoulders she had draped a black pashmina. The effect was far removed from the figure she cut with halter tops and torn shorts. She was still enjoying the novelty of it all, and that other people, especially men, looked at her differently, appreciative but less leering.

Over his initial shock, Eliot took the bag from Daphne's arms. She followed him into the kitchen where he slid the bowl of braised beef into the fridge along with the beet salad. He left the focaccia bread in its Trader Joe's wrapper on the counter.

"It's still early. How about I pour us a glass of wine. We can sit in the parlor and you can tell me all about New York."

Which, in a highly edited form, she did, going on about the gallery and the exhibition: "So many people had something nice to say about my style or wanted to know about my influences when I hardly knew myself, Eliot, and yet no one was rude. A number of them bought a canvas. More than I—"

Eliot nodded sympathetically, and as much as he might have liked to reach out and touch her arm, he limited himself to raising his glass in a silent toast.

She mirrored his gesture, took a sip, and recommenced her account: the days spent at the Metropolitan Museum, especially among the nineteenth-century European artists, (she still wasn't certain what the distinctions between Expressionists and Impressionists were), and at MoMA, which name she too now abbreviated, where she was entranced by Matisse, and the sculpture garden, and the crowds of visitors. "On my first visit there, can you believe, I sat on a bench and watched everyone come and go. A guard had to alert me to leave when it was closing time."

And not just museums. There was a play, on Broadway, she explained— "my first ever, anywhere, and we were so close to the stage"—without mentioning that it was Arthur who had paid for and escorted her to a performance of "Hamilton," or that two nights later he had propositioned her in his Soho loft. From there she could have gone on about Jared and how he had comforted her in the wake of the falling-out with Arthur. One weekend, the younger Etheridge took her along to a lecture at the 92nd St Y, (she couldn't now remember what it was about); on another, to a concert in a gigantic church in midtown (St Patrick's, but she did not remember that name either); yet another time, they went skating at Rockefeller Center, where he had to practically carry her around the ice. (She did not mention that either.)

Despite himself, Eliot could not help but recall how entertainingly Issie talked about everything going on in New York—she was amusing, and she was incisive. The woman sitting across from him now possessed none of that verbal dexterity. Whatever Daphne's inner life, too many things were communicated to others as simply *nice*.

It was an uncharitable comparison. He made an effort to sweep it aside.

"A lot of people live their entire lives in Manhattan and rarely notice all the wonderful things to do there, or they take them for granted," he responded. His tone reminded him of how he spoke to Eleanor when she was a teenager and came to him with some problem. Paternal in the former instance; arguably paternalistic in the latter.

"Yes, I get that," Daphne replied, vaguely irritated, "but I'd been deprived for so long, like not being nourished as a child. I'll probably always be—" Here, she broke off, fishing for a word.

Eliot raised his eyebrows but did not supply an adjective.

"You know, stunted, like a child starved for too long."

Looking off into the distance, Eliot let his gaze alight on the seascape on the far wall. For once, he thought, she had chosen an apt adjective. (How despicable to be so condescending, he chided himself.) Redoubling his efforts, he turned his head toward her. "Different people have different timing in life, Daphne. You were given a rare opportunity, and you seized it. You're not stunted: you had a lot to absorb in a very short time."

Momentarily consoled, Daphne blushed, not wanting to embarrass herself or, worse, tear up. And she did believe she owed it to Eliot to tell him that she had formed a bond with his son, a kind of bond she did not have with the father. And yet, with Eliot, she also had a bond, one she did not wish to jeopardize. Better to change the subject—and ask for his advice.

"Believe it or not, people liked my paintings enough to pay good money for them."

"As well they should."

"The gallery expects me to deliver more of them."

"Is Arthur Braunstein overseeing it all? You haven't mentioned him."

"Mr. Braunstein left New York shortly after the exhibition opened," she stated, quickly pivoting to say that his partner, a Mr. Dravidian, is handling her next phase. "I have a contract and everything." Eliot nodded approval but did not ask about financial details. "So, I'm looking to find a bigger place to live, and to paint."

"Oh?"

"You know, like an adjacency, as they call it, where I can set up and not have to worry about people trashing anything I leave outside."

"Makes eminent sense," he responded. In the pause that followed, he glanced at his Rolex. "Why don't we rustle up something to eat and you can tell me more."

"That's exactly what Jared says," she let out before catching herself.

"My Jared? Did you happen to see him?"

"Yes—once or twice. He used the same words, 'rustle up,' when he mentioned making dinner. If I remember rightly..." she trailed off, turning to put the wine glasses back on their tray and take them to the kitchen. There she concentrated on heating the beef and readying the focaccia.

Eliot doctored the salad and set out dinner plates on the table. He did not inquire further about his son. Rather: "If you let me know more precisely what you envision, I might be able to advise a place or two, presuming you want to stay in the area."

She did so readily, specifying that, ideally, her abode would be separate from the main house so she could have privacy and enough space to park the pick-up. Then they focused on the sloppy Joes, with the stereo on in the next room. String instruments, pieces she could not identify.

Finally, Eliot spoke again. "This may sound strange, but there's a possible lodging owned by someone you're acquainted with. He lives down the road, as it were, in Oceano, not far from the dunes."

Daphne looked puzzled.

"Seth. Silda's uncle with whom you sang sea chanties, Thanksgiving weekend."

"Of course. But I had no idea—"

"He rattles around in a ramshackle two-story, and there's a guesthouse and a shed in the back. Shade trees have been there forever. I haven't been inside the place in years, however. Might need fixing up."

"But does he want a tenant?"

"I believe he'd be tickled pink to have someone in that guesthouse, paying him a nominal sum, and looking in on him every so often."

From the context, Daphne assumed that *nominal* meant not too costly. The idea of a place to herself in a quiet neighborhood, with trees all around, was alluring. It would be so for her cat too, if Kahlo ever returned.

"By all means, ask him if he'd consider having me there," she said. "And if I can bring a pet."

Within ten days, arrangements had been made for Daphne to relocate. She managed to dispose of her trailer to one of the park attendants, an ill-tempered man named Perkins, for almost a grand. And although she barely knew them, several neighbors supplied her with cardboard boxes for her clothes, kitchenware and art supplies, and ordered their teenage sons to load her kitchen table and her easel into the back of the pick-up. The only thing still unaccounted for was Kahlo.

Meanwhile, Eliot had gathered up his toolbox, a shovel, rake and clippers and taken them over to Oceano. Early on a Saturday, the three convened on the old man's front porch for coffee and then spent the day spiffing up the guesthouse, replacing the dilapidated roof on the shed, and thinning out the jungle in the back yard.

"Been meaning to get around to this," Seth said, as they swept out the dust, cobwebs and wasp nests that had accumulated over what appeared to be decades of neglect. Yet, to Daphne's delight, the walls of the guesthouse were thick, the ceilings high, the windows functional. There was even a separate kitchen spacious enough for her table and two chairs and an entire wall of cabinets. Only the fixtures in the bathroom needed replacing, whereupon Eliot stepped in to say he knew a wholesaler in Santa Barbara who could install everything within two or three days.

"Only if you'll let me do what I'm good at," Daphne replied, turning from one to the other of the two men. Neither spoke. "Paint the place. And I do know the best store in the area for that!"

Seth beamed. "Seems like I've got the best of the bargain, so be my guest." Which made the other two laugh. The old man had ostensibly not had such fun in many a day.

To celebrate the transformation, both of Daphne's circumstances and to some degree of Seth's, Eliot took them out to dinner that Sunday evening. He reserved a table at the Lantana, where neither of his guests had ever set foot and where he had assumed Kathleen would not be present. He wanted to splurge, having orchestrated something to benefit others rather than himself. His back ached but he was bent on ignoring it.

Once they were seated on the balcony, it was Seth who spotted a woman across the dining room. She was holding a menu, speaking to a seated couple at another table. "Well, I'll be," he exclaimed, his eyes lighting up. "There's that pretty lady who came to Sorenson House and brought that pie."

Eliot and Daphne both turned their heads but only he blushed.

"Why is she standing up over there?" Seth went on, agitated.

"It's fine, Seth. She works here. She's the manager of the restaurant."

"Well I'll be. No telling what they'll be doing next." Eliot and Daphne exchanged a glance.

"She'll likely pass this way before long, and we can all say hello," Eliot continued, hoping to settle Seth down. He had forgotten how volatile the old man could be. "Why don't we go ahead and order," he added, picking up his menu and making a show of studying it. "The salmon and the sea bass are good here, if either of you is in the mood for seafood."

"Can't see a damn thing up close, Eliot. You do the ordering up. A fish would be fine. I like potatoes too."

"Not to worry. We do too," Eliot replied and motioned to the nearest waiter.

When Kathleen did make it out to the balcony, she hesitated before walking over, a fixed smile on her face.

"What a nice surprise to see you here," she began, acknowledging Eliot and then taking in his two guests. It wasn't clear if she zeroed in on who they were, Daphne having drastically altered her look and Seth having cleaned himself up.

"You'll remember Daphne and Seth Sorenson, who is—" (Here, Eliot fumbled for the correct designation, unsure if uncle-in-law was even a defined relationship.)

"I remember you both from that lovely holiday party," Kathleen responded. She stood holding the bills for a couple of other tables.

“We were saying what a delicious meal. The place improves by the month,” Eliot hastened to say.

“I appreciate that. So will the chef. Sad though, as it looks like the governor may move to lock us all down.” The three guests looked confused. “No more dining indoors as long as the pandemic is raging,” she confided.

“Here on the coast?” Eliot asked. “I wouldn’t have thought—”

“San Francisco is already reeling. Pierre had to let his staff go.”

“But the President says the virus will melt in warm weather,” Daphne interjected. “So here, where it’s already spring...” she stammered, seeing the flummoxed look on Kathleen’s face.

“You must keep me posted,” Eliot interposed, ignoring Daphne’s remark and looking directly at Kathleen. “Let me know if I can do anything.”

She nodded, a wan smile on her lips, and then reverted to her managerial role. “You might want to try the *tarte au citron*. It’s the most spring-like dessert on the menu,” she advised. Without lingering, she inclined her head toward the other two guests and then moved toward customers further along the balcony.

For an instant, none of the three spoke. Eliot studied the dessert menu intently, while Seth and Daphne watched Kathleen pause to chat with a table of four at the far end of the room.

“Tuned to the right pitch, that woman,” Seth commented, at which point Eliot eyed him across the table. “Not many of them as could steer a ship in a storm, and I’ve suffered my share of those who can’t.”

Amused by Seth’s unfiltered assessment, Eliot nodded but said nothing.

Daphne regretted her outburst about the president. People were so sensitive about Trump, one way or another, when she herself could care less. About the virus too, having paid it no heed other than being amused by Jared's mask-wearing everywhere he went. But New York City was one thing; California quite another. How could there be contagion here on the coast, where the breezes swept everything out to sea?

What bothered her more, however, was the figure that Kathleen so gracefully cut. Even Seth had recognized it. The woman was more self-possessed than she would ever be. And she imagined that Eliot saw it that way too, so she said nothing. And ordered, not the suggested lemon tart, but a double portion of chocolate ice cream.

CHAPTER TWENTY-FOUR

Caroline and Chloe

It's Not the Pale Moon

umbfounded though she was to realize that the Worthingtons might be culpable in a construction scandal, Caroline pushed the thought to the back of her mind. That her daughter had been entangled with the son would not likely come to light. As for her involvement in the probe Eliot was overseeing, it had never been spelled out, though her name appeared as a signatory on several interviews. Those were preliminary assessments, however, and she had yet to take the California bar. What she was doing could be construed as part of her routine duties for the firm. And be left at that. No conflict of interest would arise.

When she and Eliot had left Serena's place that afternoon in mid-February they had driven in silence. For whatever reason, he had felt the need to depart abruptly, his excuse an obvious fib. She could not define the attachment between the two—it appeared to have waxed and waned—but clearly Serena's mention of another dinner guest, the Russian neighbor, did not sit well with him.

Caroline pondered this mystery while Eliot drove, his face taut. As they passed by Eldwayen Park, several dogs were cavorting on the grass while their owners stood by, leashes in hand. An elderly couple huddled close together on a bench to soak up the last rays of the sun.

Only when he parked the car at Sorenson House did her boss speak. “Helpful to have had you along, Caroline, though I know it drags out your workday. Take the weekend to write up the notes. We’ll reconvene early next week.”

She nodded, opened the car door and accompanied him to the foyer to retrieve her briefcase. “By the way,” he added as she turned to leave, “How is Chloe? Has she heard back from Davis?”

“Not as yet. But I’ll keep you posted.”

It was not an exchange that easily allowed for a segue in which to confide that her daughter had gotten pregnant by the Worthington boy, had aborted the fetus, and yet still was subjected to unpleasant run-ins with the young man. As Ella had reported months ago, Ian Worthington had “blithely” shifted his attentions to the homecoming queen as soon as Chloe had dangled the word marriage in front of him.

In Central Coast High’s graduating class of three hundred students, it was hard to avoid crossing paths with the new couple and their ballooning entourage. Which now included Ella’s daughter Natalie. Sticky business, that. Chloe herself never brought up anything about these encounters. At home, she either buried her head in her books (which wasn’t all bad in her mother’s view) or pulled a long face and refused to converse.

High school could be a merciless minefield, her law school buddy Kevin had pointed out, suggesting that it was only natural that the girl’s ability to navigate it would be, as he put it, “daunting.”

So far, he was the only person Caroline had taken into her confidence regarding Chloe’s challenges. He was whip-smart—studying together had confirmed that assumption—and he was discreet. Plus, from the little he had let on about his upbringing, it had been hardscrabble, his father a groundskeeper at the local Earl Warren Fairgrounds, his mother an alcoholic who passed away when he was eleven. He had empathy.

And miraculously, Kevin had forged a relationship with Chloe, the two of them banging out tunes together on the piano or talking about soccer. On more than one occasion, he had stayed for dinner, chatting up a storm and eating, heartily, whatever Caroline served up.

Although she had known Eliot much longer, admired his talents and commiserated with his loss, Caroline woke up one morning to find she was no longer infatuated with him. Like learning to swim, one thrashed about for oh so long and then of a sudden found oneself zipping through the water like a fish. She felt relieved. Better this way, she told herself, especially since these other ladies—Daphne, Kathleen and Serena—were still vying for his attention. Which she surmised he might be ambivalent about but had not altogether discouraged.

And why should he? To find an appropriate companion for the remainder of one's life was a perfectly reasonable undertaking, though it did not pay to be too picky.

In Eliot's case, Caroline estimated, he had exercised considerable caution, though some moves he had apparently made in recent weeks. And not mentioned.

At the firm recently she had as usual sorted through her boss's mail, cramming everything of any importance into the pouch she took up to Shell Beach each week. Toward the end of January, she happened upon a postcard from Isabel Frankel. As a general rule, her cards featured a snapshot of whatever conference city they had recently met up in. Strange. No such out-of-town gathering had been on Eliot's schedule for months.

Shot on a starry night, this card showed quaint buildings along a deserted shore. From, of all places, Avila Beach. She and Mickey had visited it years ago when Chloe was little. They had built a sandcastle and the child had cried when the tide washed over it. He had fussed at her; they left soon after.

The postcard read: *"It's not the pale moon that excites me…'" You can supply the other lines of the verse, Eliot. I myself am still singing it. Yours, I.F.*

Caroline did not know the song but knew it intimated some shared experience. She stuck it in the pouch along with other correspondence.

The afternoon Eliot emptied the contents in front of her, he held the postcard in his hand, a puzzled look on his face, before turning it over to read the message. He made no comment.

Once back home that same evening, Kevin came over to study, California tax law on the agenda. When they finished going over their notes, they shared the leftover meatloaf in the fridge—Chloe at Gloria's to prepare for midterms—and she inquired if he knew the lyric. In response, he shifted over to the piano bench and humming softly, picked out the melody.

"That's lovely," she said. "And the words?"

He obliged, his voice not half-bad. He could carry the tune. When he finished the line, "It's just the nearness of you," he desisted, his face averted. Within a minute, a key turned in the front door lock. Kevin swiveled around.

Her backpack over her arm, Chloe, wearing leggings and a heavy sweater, entered and took in the scene.

"Doesn't look like studying to me," she said, her mouth curled in a "caught you" smile.

"We were winding up. There's meatloaf if you're hungry," Caroline declared, her expression quickly returning to normal.

"Dad dropped by earlier. He took me for pizza," she said.

Taken aback, Caroline countered. "I thought you were studying. At Gloria's."

"Did that too," Chloe retorted, irked by the cross-examination. "Getting some juice," she muttered, turning toward the kitchen.

Caroline closed her eyes briefly but let the incident pass. She could hear the fridge door open and the sound of a glass set down on the counter. Kevin stood to scoot the bench under the piano. Seconds passed in silence.

"Okay then," he said, as though some mood had been shattered. "I'll leave you two to it. Thanks for the meal and next week: the criminal code, right?"

"Sounds good, Kevin. We're on track, thanks to you."

He nodded, gathered up his folder and left the house.

Later that night, Caroline lay awake, going over the last few confusing weeks. She hummed the song Kevin had played.

"Everybody covered it," he had explained. "Ella Fitzgerald, Jo Stafford, Sinatra of course," he had gone on before Chloe interrupted them. And now here she was mouthing the words, realizing how much she looked forward to these sessions with her study partner. He had grown on her.

In the end, she concluded, love was nothing other than the desire for nearness, whatever that consisted of.

As for Eliot, it was his approbation she craved. She was determined to ace the bar exam and become a working lawyer—like her boss, and ideally at the same law firm. But as she had deduced that day at Serena's place, Eliot had his own demons to exorcise. He might well start by taking down that ornate Sorenson House sign and put up one that read The Etheridges. It was time.

Several days later, Ella rang the law firm to invite Caroline for a drink late in the day. "*Al fresco*, my dear. It might not be feasible for long. Will 6 p.m. work?"

The weather had turned warmer the second week of March. Everyone was eager to be out and about, despite news that the virus was worsening. Was that what Ella meant by claiming the respite might not last? Such an alarmist, her friend.

Before Caroline could properly take a seat at the cafe, Ella started in, commenting on her friend's "new look" and "highlights."

"Something's up with you, but you can tell me in good time. Meanwhile, if you ever do want to take David up and get a treatment,"—here Caroline looked blank—"book it soon. From what he says, businesses are going to be shut down all over the place. Frown lines will only worsen."

"Then we should drink wine, not coffee, don't you think?"

Which they did. Once into a second glass apiece, Ella broached a subject of more concern to her friend than the contagion. "Natalie no longer confides much, but she has mentioned that Chloe is being taunted. Unmercifully."

Caroline's face darkened. She took another swallow of the chardonnay and washed it down with a handful of nuts. "And who would be doing the taunting, did she say?"

"Seems Amy—you remember, the homecoming queen—has amassed a following, a few of whom are shaming your child online. Worse is that Worthington boy. Whenever he comes to pick up his new girlfriend, he goes out of his way, Nat says, to waylay Chloe. Calling her out publicly—a slut or whatever—when he should be the one hanging his head."

Swirling the rest of her drink in stony silence, Caroline watched the afternoon crowd saunter past, young couples holding hands, businessmen clutching briefcases, tourists gawking at the storefronts. Her daughter had never alluded to such harassment.

Steeling herself, she turned back to her friend.

"What would you suggest we do about this—I mean, what would you do if it were Natalie being bullied?" she asked, a note of challenge in her voice.

Ella made a face as if to say I'm only the messenger and by no means a gleeful one. "Since you put it that way," she retorted, "David and I would go to the principal and demand an accounting. If need be, an intervention involving Amy."

Caroline looked unconvinced.

"My dear, as I've said before, you are without a man to back you up, with things..." Caroline rolled her eyes, but Ella remained undeterred. "Mickey was a piece of work, but he could be, (here she gestured with her hand while searching for the right word), persuasive."

"Yes, brute force," Caroline returned drily.

"Then how about your boss. Couldn't he—"

"I should be able to handle what needs to be handled," she broke in curtly.

Rebuked, however mildly, Ella looked away, putting on a hurt look.

After their fraught exchange, a waiter timorously materialized, but Ella waved him off. The two friends defaulted to more pleasant topics, Caroline inquiring as to Natalie's college prospects (early acceptance at USC thanks to David's ability "to pull a few strings") and Ella asking after Chloe's prospects (UC-Davis, still up in the air).

They split the tab, which was less than what a sit-down with Ella usually ran.

"David says we should all cut back. It's not going to be pretty what this pandemic brings. There may not even be a prom. Our girls. Just think."

At the dining room table, Caroline and Kevin spread out their notes and study prompts for a final run-through before the bar exam. They alternated posing and answering the likely questions to be raised and the issues to be deconstructed. She had made a tuna casserole, and together they had drunk two pots of strong coffee, starting at 10 a.m. Chloe had gone out for soccer practice and to "hang" thereafter with Gloria, not likely to return, so she said, "until whenever, Mom."

Caroline shrugged but had let her leave unquestioned. Kevin trained his eyes on the pages in front of him.

At around 5 p.m. the two began to lose their focus.

"I think we're as on top of things as we can be, Caroline. Better to rest and clear our heads. What do you think?"

Before she could answer, the doorbell rang three times in quick succession. Looking puzzled, Caroline got up, her left foot half asleep. She limped her way to the door.

Two cops, both burly, stood with their legs slightly apart. Out on the street, a light on the top of their patrol car was flashing.

"Ma'am. Sorry to disturb you. Are you related to a Chloe Morris?"

"I'm her mother. What's going on?"

"An incident. Near Central Coast High. Your daughter threw a weapon."

"Threw or drew? Either way, not possible." Then turning her head, she called out, "Kevin, I need you."

In the car, they were given a summary account of the incident. Some students were milling about on the sidewalk after sports practice, several of them "horsing around." Names were called and Chloe shouted back at one young man—here one of the officers consulted his findings—an Ian Worthington and pulled a gun out of nowhere. Allegedly waved it, (unclear if pointed at anybody or at herself), and then hurled it at a red car parked at the curb. Which made the young man angry enough to grab her up and smack her across the jaw.

"They're both being interviewed, separately, to determine what charges will be filed," the cop at the steering wheel added.

"Yeah, and the Worthington kid was immediately on his cell to get his lawyers down to the station. A piece of work he is," the first officer volunteered.

"We haven't taken the bar," Kevin whispered. "You should ring your boss, Caroline. Get him on the case."

Reluctantly, she pulled out her cell. Eliot promised to get there within ninety minutes. They should instruct Chloe not to say anything more.

"So stupid of me. Mickey insisted we keep a gun around the house, can you believe." Kevin pursed his lips as though to indicate her husband had faults that were beyond their control. "But I had unloaded it, months ago, in front of Chloe."

"OK. Nothing illegal there. No intent on her part," Kevin whispered back. "I'll look it up to confirm tonight."

When they arrived at the precinct, several students from the school, a few of whom Caroline recognized, were huddled together. Amy sat alone, texting away on her phone and looking bored. Gloria and Natalie were seated along a bench murmuring to each other. "It was no big deal, Ms. Morris. He was asking for it, the creep," Gloria called out.

"That's enough, you two," one of the cops called out.

Caroline and Kevin were led down a hallway to a room above which a plaque read *Interrogation 2*. They waited there for thirty minutes, smoking the last of Kevin's Camels and flicking the ashes into a metal trash can.

Finally, they were escorted into another room where Chloe was seated on a metal chair across from a sergeant behind a scuffed desk. It was piled with folders. The girl turned to see who had come in. One cheek was red and swollen and her hair was a mess, but otherwise, she looked okay, sheepish her expression but okay.

"I couldn't take it anymore, Mom. I'm so, so sorry," she stammered, before bursting into tears. The desk cop, his pen poised in the air, rolled his eyes, a heard-it-all look on his face.

"We'll be waiting for her lawyer to get here, officer. Shouldn't be long," Kevin told the sergeant.

Shortly thereafter the cop left the room, whatever he had been told by Chloe not admissible in any case. She was still seventeen and no adult had been present for the initial interview.

Once Eliot arrived at the station house, things moved rapidly, just as they had for Ian Worthington when a phalanx of lawyers showed up to assist their charge. Chloe, Caroline and Kevin all heard the young man hiss as he passed the door where they were waiting.

"You'll pay for this, cunt. Totaled my car. You'll be sued for millions."

Chloe turned ashen; Caroline shook her head from side to side. Kevin got up to get them Diet Cokes and candy bars from a vending machine.

Once he had assisted Chloe in responding to more questions—yes, the boy had incessantly bullied her after their break-up, and yes, she knew the gun was unloaded but wanted to scare him somehow—Eliot accompanied the two women home. Having scribbled notes throughout, Kevin took his leave at the station, giving Chloe a hug and a thumbs-up. "I'm hoping to assist more properly after the exam—we're due to take it next week, Mr. Etheridge."

"It's Eliot, and yes, that will be helpful. Best of luck," he replied, reaching out to shake the young man's vigorous hand.

Intermittently during the weekend, Eliot and Caroline conferred as to the best tack to take.

First, they had to consider how serious a crime it was to pull out a gun near a school (though not on its property), and to what extent, if any, it was pointed at a person. Eyewitnesses, including Gloria and Natalie, would testify it was aimed at no one other than (mockingly?) Chloe herself. The gun was verified not to be loaded. As for the Maserati, the distraught girl had indeed thrown the weapon in its direction, immediately after the owner had called her some vulgarity. It had dented the driver-side door and shattered the window, but that was far from being "totaled."

Still.

"The aim will be for Chloe to avoid jail time and to demonstrate that she was acting out after a sustained period of verbal abuse," Eliot said. He did not sugarcoat things, however. "Nonetheless, what she did was unacceptable. She'll likely be obliged to do community service," he added, at which point Caroline's face fell.

"What about graduation? What about UC-Davis? What about her life?" she lamented, shaking her head in dismay.

Eliot sipped the coffee she had made and waited until she calmed down. "It could be worse. I'm sure the firm can handle things satisfactorily." She looked up, not comprehending. "I'll need to recuse myself, Caroline, because of the Worthington connection." He paused, allowing her to interject.

"I know, I know. I should have mentioned weeks ago that we had a history with the son, an unfortunate one, but I didn't want to muddy the waters. I never dreamed—"

"Don't berate yourself. However, we'll have to decline to affix your name to the notes we've compiled. So, essentially no credit, or additional compensation, will come your way on this property scam case. It's a shame but it obviates any suspicion of impropriety. You know how the firm operates."

"Yet another incentive for me to pass the bar as expeditiously as possible," Caroline replied as pluckily as she could.

"Hear, hear," he replied, reaching for an upbeat note. "And don't angst over that suit the kid threatened. Once the court hears how abominably young Mr. Worthington behaved—sex with a minor is a crime, and his egregious conduct thereafter, bullying her, punching her in the face—I doubt his family will wish to proceed."

"Again, I can't tell you how grateful I am for your taking charge. Chloe will be too. In good time."

"It's a blip, Caroline. Still, some support through this would be beneficial. You can't shoulder everything on your own." She smiled ruefully. "Kevin, for one. He seems eager, you know, to help."

After giving Keats his bi-weekly bath and downing the broccoli and cheese soup Caroline had insisted he take home with him, Eliot drove down that Monday straight to the firm. After a polite nod to the receptionist— "Nice to see you back, Mr. Etheridge. Been a while"—he headed, as requested, to the senior partners' private conference room. Coffee and doughnuts were on the table when he entered, several of his colleagues already partaking.

Two hours later, he retreated to the smaller office he had been allotted after his move up the coast, closed the door, and sat down at his desk, stunned. Five minutes later, he buzzed Caroline to join him.

As she had suspected after talking over the likely repercussions with Kevin that Sunday, the firm had declined to take on Chloe's case. Eliot appeared chagrined to have to tell her, insisting that the company had to avoid any whiff of conflict of interest involving the Worthingtons. She took all this in, using a Kleenex to hold back tears. Further, he explained, another local firm, Ridgeway and Madison, was recommended by the partners as "more suitable to defend against the charges, such as they are."

"And what do you think they will be, the charges?"

Eliot paused briefly, pensive. "At worst, reckless endangerment, but with mitigating circumstances."

A lump in her throat, Caroline found it difficult to swallow. Seeing her distress, Eliot retrieved a Ginger Ale from his mini-fridge and handed it over. She took a few gulps, placed the can on a coaster, and composed herself. She was not a person who believed in making a spectacle.

In the silence that followed, Eliot flipped through his notepad and underlined something with a pencil.

"What about the real-estate suit?" Caroline eventually asked. "Is there anything I can do or write up to make sure it stays on track?"

Flustered, Eliot kept his eyes trained on his notepad as though he was mystified by what he must have scribbled only minutes ago. She could hear the tick-tock of the grandfather clock in the corner, one of the few items of Sorenson family vintage that remained, somewhat out-of-place, in this nondescript office. Where he had been unjustly relegated, she thought.

"Actually, I've been taken off that project. It'll pass to Jacobson. I believe all the reports and depositions from homeowners are in order. No need for you—for us, really—to worry about it."

It didn't take long for Caroline to realize what a slap in the face this decision was. The investigation had been Eliot's baby all along, the only thing professionally (that she knew of) that had kept him energized over the last year. Altogether unfair, she thought, but that was not a sentiment that elicited much support in a law firm office.

"I'm so sorry, Eliot. It's my fault, well, Chloe's too, indirectly, but she isn't to be blamed, just me. I feel awful."

Thus rattled, she drank the rest of the soda and fell silent. Something about his quivering lips suggested the less said the better. Eliot was both proud and private, traits she was duty-bound to respect.

As soon as seemed proper, she rose to thank him for his help with Chloe's mishap. He, however, put up his hand, palm toward her, as though to indicate she should wait. Quickly, he jotted down something on a sheet of the firm's stationery. She stood as upright as she could. Within a minute, he handed over the piece of paper, which she took, inclining her head in thanks.

"Call Richard Hendricks at Ridgeway tomorrow. On his direct. He's an old family friend as well as a top-notch litigator. He'll have been apprised and will know how best to proceed."

"First thing tomorrow," she replied.

"And, Caroline, no need for you to drive up the coast for the next few weeks. You have enough on your plate. Do let me know how things are progressing though, the bar exam too, and if I can do anything further."

"I can't thank you enough. And again, I—"

"Please, no need."

CHAPTER TWENTY-FIVE

Daphne and Seth

An Unlikely Attachment

Eliot's loneliness felt both sharp and dull, like stepping out into unexpected winter wind. Throughout the rest of March, the weather was blustery, the sound of waves breaking on the rocks louder than usual. Sometimes he found himself sitting out on the upstairs terrace wrapped in a blanket, sipping hot coffee, watching the rise and fall of the swells. Alone and wishing he weren't. Especially now that work had come to a virtual standstill.

At the balustrade on a gloomy Wednesday afternoon, he looked out at the metal-gray sea. It was the time of day when he typically would be at his desk, pouring over the case files on which he was lead attorney. Or, if not that, placing phone calls to various clients to reassure them of the firm's attention. His voice, they always effused, was so soothing, his advice so sensible. But in that excruciating meeting at Bryson & Tillotson, he had been punched in the kisser, as it were, not K.O.'d, but forced to retire to his corner with little chance of getting back into the ring.

Tillotson had been smoking a smelly cigar, when, exhaling a bluish plume, he had turned to Bryson, for back-up. "We've been thinking, Eliot, you might want to throw in the towel. You know, take up something more enjoyable than the grudge matches we have to fight." The other attendees nodded in tacit agreement with this seemingly generous suggestion.

"Like all that dancing you and Silda used to do. Made all our wives jealous," Bryson offered up.

"And now this kerfuffle with Morris and her daughter. (She never does manage to shed the weight, does she?)," Tillotson kept on. "Anyway. Not worth our trouble and not a good fit with that property scam. We're going to relieve you of both problems and sic Jacobson on the Worthingtons."

Eliot had sat there benumbed, arms folded, his face all jagged lines. While they rattled on, he checked off in his mind the other cases he had been quietly relieved of during the last year, and how light the briefcase Caroline brought along with his weekly workload had become. The Worthington matter was the last major case he was overseeing—likely only because he had ferreted out the illegalities all on his own. And which, without so much as a thank you, was now being wrested from him, the incident involving Chloe affording the partners a plausible rationale for doing so.

Clever these gents, he thought now, but transparent in their conniving. He remembered the bewilderment on Caroline's face—her own boss brought low. And Tillotson's snide about her weight—in 2020! (Her daughter Chloe, on the other hand, so pencil-thin and unpredictable. Had Eleanor been as troublesome as a teenager? He doubted it, but then only Silda would have ever known.)

Uttering his wife's name, he wondered what she would have said to comfort him. Perhaps laughed it off, claiming he was too good for such a firm, or—.

He finished off the mug, lukewarm though it was, on the nearby table. Although only 4:30, the temperature was swiftly falling. Better to take Keats out now and enjoy the remains of the day. Might improve his mood.

The retriever had been napping but did not reject a walk along the waterfront. Having twirled a scarf about his neck and buttoned up his cardigan, Eliot set off down the boulevard at a clip, the dog keeping pace, then settled into a slower gait for the return leg. That's when Keats began pulling at the leash, barking non-stop. Eliot squinted into the setting sun and made out a woman with an imposing canine coming their way. She was wearing dark blue leggings, a light-blue pullover—and sunglasses. It was Serena.

"Keats is ever on the *qui vive* for his friends, but if this is Dog, he has undergone a dramatic makeover!"

Serena laughed, gave the animal more slack, and fell into step with Eliot. "This is Maks' Great Dane. Goes by Pushkin."

"Oh, I see," he said, as though to indicate he didn't at all see.

The two dogs slowed to sniff each other out, happy to have reconnected. Eliot likewise gave Keats more leash. He had no intention of inquiring as to why Serena was walking her Russian neighbor's pet.

"Since you didn't ask, I'm tending to the poor creature in Maks' absence. Despite everything happening in New York, he hopped on a plane to visit his daughter. Unclear when he'll make it back." Eliot nodded. Disinterested. Serena cast him a sideways glance. "So, are you well? You look overworked or overburdened."

"I'm all right. Tired perhaps. A lot going on."

"Indeed. However, if you need anything, I can come up with a casserole or something."

"Thanks, but it appears you have your hands full—the dog, and everything," he said, with an edge sharp enough to nick.

Serena winced. Tugging at Pushkin's leash, she quickened the pace of their walk.

Eliot followed along, disconcerted that his tone was more cutting than he intended. He didn't wish to come across as jealous of Maks. Nor was he the kind of man who would blurt out that Pushkin's master had been the lover of Keats' mistress. And thus, as a result, he didn't really like the guy or his dog, the two canines' affections for each other notwithstanding. He felt winded by his mental calisthenics.

"I sense you are preoccupied about something," Serena threw out as they approached her house. "No need to stand on ceremony. But I did volunteer. Don't forget."

"Very kind, Serena. Tricky times."

Coming to a halt, she added, "By the way, I'll be ordering face masks on Amazon. Looks like this thing will be with us for a while—even here in Paradise. Call me if and when you need one."

"Will do. Appreciate it. I just can't—"

"I understand," she said. "Such is life. Or rather, the lives of others: forever a mystery, aren't they?" Seeing his eyes liquid in the fading light, she declined to delve further.

He responded with the faintest of smiles, "I'm finding that out."

"Well, time marches on for us all."

Flummoxed by this remark, Eliot reached down to fuss with Keats' now tangled leash.

Serena stood by, but then on a lighter note added: "Of those movies I lent you, you could do worse than watch *The Apartment*. Cheer you up or your money back."

With that, she gave a tug to Pushkin's leash and steered him onto the pathway in front of her house. From the corner of his eye, Eliot saw Dog rouse himself to play with his new friend.

Over the next several weeks, Eliot redoubled his efforts to keep busy at home. With spring in the air, he set about to weed and fertilize the garden, clipping the unruly English ivy that had grown over the fence, pruning the plum trees, and whacking back the oleander bushes. After reattaching the long shoots of the climbing roses to their trellises, he watered the entire ensemble. From the back patio, Keats watched. Above-it-all.

In the evening, Eliot turned on the television to catch up with the news, most of it focused on the virus, none of it good. The havoc it was wreaking in New York City and even San Francisco appeared to have escalated overnight. Not entirely unlike bouts with the bubonic plague that had once decimated

Europe, killing millions. Must have been the fourteenth century or thereabouts. Issie would know. He must call her soon...

While he fooled around in the kitchen, settling for a ham and cheese sandwich and a beer, he heard pundits go on about the dangers of indoor exposure—in churches, offices and even restaurants. Covid-19 they were calling this thing. Surely, the country could get it under control, better than Europe, if not as expeditiously as China.

But Kathleen? She ran one of these places. Funny she had not bothered to pick up the phone—not after chauffeuring Issie all the way to the airport that new year's holiday. Then again, neither had he.

Around 8:30 p.m. he dialed her home number, but no one picked up. He left a short message, trying for a casual tone. He barely managed.

Still wide awake, Eliot decided to take Serena's advice, slipping *The Apartment* into the DVD player and sinking into the sofa. It occurred to him that he had never in his adult life watched a movie alone. That too saddened him, so it took a good half hour for Jack Lemmon and Shirley MacLaine to lighten his mood. Serena had not only excellent taste but pertinent recommendations. Once the philandering Fred McMurray received his comeuppance and the two stars "found" each other, Eliot went to bed with less of a heavy heart.

Early the next morning, the phone next to the bed rang.

"Kathleen?" he mumbled, still groggy, wiggling to sit up against the pillows.

"Eliot, it's me, Seth. Wondering if you got any bricks laying around. The old ones are best. Hard to find nowadays."

"What on earth. Are you okay?" He shook his head to clear the cobwebs. "What about Daphne?"

"Hold on, mate. We're both fine. Getting the yard in order. Thinking of a brick walkway and a patio area. Where she can paint." Seth sounded unusually peppy. In the background, another voice chimed in. "And where we can sit outside to eat." Daphne too sounded chipper.

Eliot thought for a moment they must be drinking, but at the crack of dawn? When had Seth demonstrated this much get-up-and-go, he couldn't recall. The man must be eighty-six if a day. As for Daphne, when had she shown such interest in anything beyond her easel? He reached for the water glass and took a few gulps.

Bricks? He had not checked behind the shed in the back yard for years, but if memory served, neat rows of old dominion bricks, the ones that made the façade of Sorenson House so striking, had been stacked there.

"I'll look around, Seth. Anything else you two might need?"

"Lend a hand when you can. Daphne's already turned the guest house into—what did you call it, dear?—yes, a *petite chateau,* like in those French paintings she goes on about."

Eliot could hear Daphne's laughter at the old man's attempt at Gallic pronunciation. "Ask him to come over around noon today. We'll have lunch outside," he heard her prompt Seth to add.

To Eliot's astonishment, these two opposites had clearly hit it off. He squelched a twinge of jealousy, considering such a reaction beneath him.

After a hot shower and a brisk round-the-block with Keats, he headed to Oceano with a box of saltines, several cheeses and a bottle of white wine. As far as he could surmise, Daphne had likely not gotten around to acquiring a stove or microwave—how had she ever concocted those seafood casseroles in that ill-equipped trailer?—so a snack and a toast to their renovation efforts might be in order.

In the back of the Escalade, he loaded a handful of old Roman bricks, each mottled distinctively. By his count, three or four hundred were stacked against the shed, more or less in decent condition. Conceivably, Seth had not forgotten all his masonry skills. He himself had never had any.

When he arrived at Seth's around noon, the first thing Eliot spotted was a pile of discolored rugs, broken tables and chairs, and tree limbs at the curb. Presumably for county haul-away.

Once to the front door, he could hear music, something classical coming from deep inside. Since no one responded when he knocked, he let himself in.

Seth's parlor was unrecognizable, its oak floors newly revealed and polished, the furniture re-arranged, with only the best pieces, of walnut or cherry mostly, remaining, and new lamps on the marble-top end tables. On the wall behind the sofa hung a seascape—unmistakably one of Daphne's. (Seth's ink drawings of Navy vessels were nowhere in sight.)

What Silda had once described (fondly, he was certain) as her uncle's aura of eccentric ineptitude had been dispelled in a frenzy of productivity.

Eliot wandered through the other rooms, also spruced up, following his nose.

In the kitchen at the rear of the house, Daphne was alternately stirring a huge pot on the stove and tending to a frying pan. With her back to him and the music blaring, she had not noticed his entry. He stood for an instant, taking in the scene, including her heart-shaped derrière clad in blue overalls.

Enough of that, he thought, though he could imagine what might have put such zip in Seth's step. He cleared his throat.

"Something smells delicious," he announced, feeling rather foolish for bringing crackers and cheese while she was cooking up something elaborate.

Daphne swiveled her head, her face flushed from the heat of the stove. She gave him a smile, put down her wooden spoon on the counter, and ran her arm across her glistening forehead. He stepped forward to give her a hug. Perfunctory.

"You did come. How nice. We're going to eat for the first time outside—in the sunshine—and get an idea of where to place the patio." She sounded child-like in her enthusiasm. "You can help." She held out her arms to take the bag from him, fished the wine bottle out and stuck it in the fridge.

"And where is Seth?"

She cast her eyes toward the door that led through a pantry to the backyard. "He's become maniacal, helping me fix up the guest house and now re-imagining the entire space in the back. Quite an eye he has," she exuded, as though they were birds of the same feather.

At the sound of garlic sizzling in the skillet, she turned around to drop several handfuls of okra into the pan. She sprinkled salt, pepper and unmarked spices on top and turned up the heat.

"That smells amazing, too," Eliot said. The compliment came out as lame; she barely reacted.

"You should see what he's up to, your uncle. We don't want him to overdo it."

To Eliot, she sounded almost proprietary of the old man. "No, of course not," he stammered.

Since she turned to set a timer for whatever was to be in the pot, he quietly headed out through the pantry.

Squinting in the sunlight, Eliot scanned the unrecognizable backyard. For one thing, it appeared larger: several nondescript or ill-placed shrubs had been removed, remaining ones trimmed, and the grass greened-up and freshly mowed. Looking down, he noticed rows of wooden pegs; they outlined a winding pathway toward a white oak tree. Seth, he eventually spotted on his haunches, measuring a small area underneath the branches, which presumably would be the patio they had envisioned.

He walked over. "Quite a transformation, Seth. Where is it you'll be laying bricks?" he asked, loud enough to herald his approach.

Seth spat on the ground, ran the back of his hand across his mouth and looked up. He was sweaty but beaming.

"Depends," he said. "I was thinking the pathway and the patio, but concrete might be better for the former. Bricks though would be nice right here." He patted the bare earth. "Plenty of shade and close to the guest house."

"That could work. I brought a few loose ones. You can see if they're what you're looking for."

Seth set his leveler and tape measure down and hoisted himself upright, one hand holding onto the tree trunk. "First things first. Daphne's rustling up some grub, and we'll have it over yonder at that table. Sound good?"

"Absolutely."

Over the shrimp creole and fried okra, Seth and Daphne chattered non-stop. At one point, Eliot calculated that he was hearing more from Silda's uncle than he had in all the years he had known him.

After they polished off the chardonnay he had brought along and before dessert was served, Daphne grabbed his hand and dragged him off to see the inside of the guest house. It had been notably gussied up. Colorful, in a discreet kind of way, and inviting, in a more overt way, he thought. The walls were painted pale apricot, the windows covered in beige bamboo shades, the furniture sparse but well-appointed, including a chaise lounge upholstered in dark red velvet which he wondered from whence it had come. (He even wondered, briefly, what Seth was charging his tenant, before, again, berating himself for wanting to know.)

Seth, she was busily explaining, had positioned three huge turquoise pots in front of each window with a fan palm in each. A burnished copper chandelier hung from the ceiling. Her kitchen appliances, as he had surmised, had not yet arrived, but Eliot glimpsed cans and jars on the countertops.

Following his eyes, she said, "In case you're curious, I'm not cooking up a storm every day in Seth's house. But today is so nice and we wanted to be outside, so..."

"You don't have to explain anything to me, Daphne. I'm glad it's worked out so well," he said adamantly.

She gave him a quizzical look.

Eliot turned away from her and looked the place over again. "What about your easel, your canvases?" Vaguely accusatory.

"They're stashed in the shed until things are completed," she replied quietly. Eliot managed a faint smile. She shifted gears. "Would you like to see the bedroom? I finally have a closet—and a shower that's large enough to turn around in."

"We should get back to Seth. Not leave him too long."

"Whatever you think, Eliot. But before..."

"Before what, Daphne?" he asked, his voice impatient.

"Nothing really. I wanted to thank you for helping me make these changes. All these changes. I couldn't have done so on my own and you—"

"As I said, you needn't thank me. I assumed, however, that..." (Here he hesitated, and while he fished for his assumption, Seth's voice rang out.)

"You two better come on out or this thing will melt."

Eliot looked at Daphne for a signal.

"Strawberry shortcake. He must have gone ahead and scooped the ice cream on top."

"Then we should not keep it waiting," he replied.

Upon leaving, Eliot retrieved the bricks from the trunk and stacked them on the front porch. Neither of his hosts came out to wave, Seth having returned to the backyard and Daphne to wash up in the kitchen.

On his drive back through the town to the freeway entrance, he had planned to ring Kathleen again, but he was too disoriented to do so. Not that he wasn't happy for Daphne's good fortune and for Seth's new lease on life, but he had been rattled.

Something as quotidian as how she stirred a stove pot dislodged something deep inside him, something he felt was fundamentally inappropriate in her regard. She was sexy in such a seemingly unconscious way—Lolita-like—that he had once again been aroused by her casual physicality. Perhaps Seth was too, he mused, though the old codger was presumably ignorant of what had hit him and too old to do anything about it. He himself was perhaps not too old, but old enough to know better.

It's not that Eliot didn't desire sex—even with his chum Issie, whom he had known for well-nigh fifty years, he could still become excited. (Alone in his car, it made him redden to recall their night at Avila Beach.)

But now he longed for something more than sex. What was that word Silda used to drop now and again? *Scintillating*. That's what he craved: scintillating conversation, perhaps more than scintillating sex.

Hence his verdict on Daphne. To hear the word *nice* in every other sentence from her would drive him to distraction. The wrong kind of distraction. He banged his hand on the steering wheel to reinforce his resolve. He would hire a truck to come over and haul off all the bricks to Seth's place.

As he maneuvered into the slow lane on the 101, he hit his speed dial, but to check in on Caroline, not Kathleen. Trying to ride herd on a wayward teenager. How did she manage without a man around the house? He really did want to be helpful.

On the third ring, Chloe picked up.

"This is Eliot. How are you feeling, Chloe?"

"Okay," she replied in a tone belying her answer. He waited for her to go on. "I've been suspended. Mom's talking to that new lawyer, and to Kevin, about the…the thing I did."

"Is your mother at home?"

"She's out. Taking that bar exam, Kevin too. I'm grounded and not supposed to see anyone. Not even Gloria, or my dad."

"My advice, Chloe. Continue to study, help your mother around the house, and let the lawyers sort this out." Silence on the other end. "Agreed?" he persisted.

"Yeah. Thank you, Mr. Etheridge."

"And tell your mother I rang. No need for her to call back. Unless she needs immediate advice."

"Got it."

CHAPTER TWENTY-SIX

Kathleen

Taking Charge in a Contagion

The home phone was ringing when Kathleen entered after work. It had been a trying week at the Lantana, with several of the employees anxious to know what was in store for them. She had put them off, not yet having spoken to the owners up in San Francisco and no official mandate from the governor. The news from New York City, however, had worsened by the day, with infections mounting and hospitals filling up with patients. Crowded places, she kept hearing, were hotbeds of contagion.

She dropped the container of leftover vegetables from the restaurant—the clientele had been on the thin side that evening—on the kitchen table. They would spice up her Sunday meals, though, as usual, too much for her to consume on her own. A persistent caller, it being almost 11 p.m. Rather than let it go to voicemail, she picked up the receiver.

"Kath? *C'est moi.*" It was Pierre's usual greeting to his stepmother, but tonight excitement tinged his voice.

"So glad you called. I had been meaning to, but with so much going on—"

"You won't believe what's happened. I flew to New York last week, took Eleanor to Nobu, proposed and *voilà*, she accepted!" He sounded like a schoolboy who had just been awarded the only gold star in the class.

"*C'est magnifique, mon cher,*" she mouthed, pulling out a chair to keep from fainting onto the floor. How long had these two young people known each other—a few months? Had he not heard a virus was running rampant? Love must still make people behave as though nothing else matters. "But so out of the blue, dear. Are you sure…?"

"Absolutely," he shot back forcefully. "Don't worry. We've agreed to wait a while, what with things so uncertain. Not just back East, here too," he said, a somber note creeping into his voice. "So, what do you think, Kath?"

"About waiting to get married or about the coronavirus?"

"Either, both."

"About marriage, it's usually a good idea to consider all the angles, get everyone on board." Silence from her stepson. "Has Eleanor told her father?" It occurred to Kathleen that Eliot's call to her days ago might have been to share 'the good news.'

"We tried him that very night, but he was out. Eleanor did not want to leave the news on his machine."

"I see."

"In fact, she suggested that it might be nice if you, Kath—how do you say?—'spilled some beans.'"

"Spilled *the* beans," she corrected him distractedly. "Sweet of her but I think not. Eliot and I haven't spoken for a while."

During the interval that followed, Kathleen removed her bottle of mineral water from the bag and took a swallow. She sensed her stepson weighing his response.

"*Pas de problème*, Kath. I'll let Eleanor know to call him, like pronto, if she hasn't already."

Quickly toggling to other things, the two talked over the likelihood that California's governor might take action to tamp down infections. Pierre felt Newsom wouldn't, in the end, do anything; Kathleen thought that he would. Neither wanted to say aloud what was troubling them both: among the list of activities and places that seemed to attract the virus, bars and restaurants were near the top.

They abandoned the debate after a few minutes, chatted about dishes he was introducing at *La Chanson,* and then hung up.

Afterward, Kathleen sat slumped with her head in her hands, mulling what most likely lay in store over the coming months. Big cities would seemingly bear the brunt of the outbreak; coastal enclaves and rural areas less so. But how long this virus would hang around and how many might contract it was anyone's guess. The White House insisted it would disappear as warm weather set in, she had heard; the country's top scientists cited no such evidence, warning things might get worse before they got better.

Still, this was America. How dreadful could things become?

Worst case scenario, she reckoned, Pierre might have to shutter *La Chanson* for a spell, but he was young and entrepreneurial—like his dad before him. And soon enough, he would have a supportive woman by his side.

As for herself, no denying she was getting older. Were she to lose her job—one she needed if she wished to maintain her reasonably comfortable lifestyle.

To take stock, Kathleen glanced around the kitchen, which she had had upgraded upon moving in. In retrospect, she probably didn't need the high-end convection oven or fancy glass cabinets. Of the traveling she had wanted to do, likely destinations—France, Italy, China—were rapidly becoming no-no's. And who, in any case, would rush to accompany her if she did venture abroad?

Shaking her head, she rose to put the container in the fridge, rummaged in a drawer for a bottle of melatonin, and made her way to bed.

The next day Kathleen spent the morning pouring over her finances, listing the expenditures she could cut back on—among them, weekly visits to the beauty salon, subscriptions to a half-dozen cooking magazines, a project to put in a sprinkler system for the back yard. Next, she took a hard look at her clothes closet, and despite how much she enjoyed the latest fashions, she nixed the online order for two outfits, one Max Mara, the other Hank Azaria. (Besides, eyeing them again, they appeared too young for her, and a size too small. She did need to walk more, and that cost nothing.) She made calculations. Altogether, the savings did not amount to anything instantly substantial, but over time, if she stuck to the plan, it very well might.

Feeling better, she made herself a lunch of the Lantana vegetables. She then read a few chapters of an espionage novel she had acquired, trying to keep her mind off niggling things, including whether to phone Eliot. In theory, she would be returning his call from a week ago, but in reality, it would demonstrate that she was, despite his aloofness, still pursuing him.

No, better to get on with the project that had been keeping her happily occupied and which might be appealing for others. Especially if, because of pandemic restrictions, people had to be cooped up at home doing their own cooking.

On the dining room table, she had already laid out three stacks of 3x5 cards and arrayed a half-dozen cookbooks alongside. As she had gotten into it, the thrust of her proposed cookbook had shifted. No longer strictly an homage to her late husband, it would now be a window into their world as married restaurateurs—how they adapted their eclectic culinary skills to spice up their mealtimes.

It had been Genevieve, one of her few remaining friends from the old days, who made the suggestion when last they got together.

“This may sound brutal, Kathleen, but cookbooks are a dime a dozen and François, rest his soul, is no longer with us. But *you're* here: and you and he were a team. People, I imagine, would be intrigued to know what you and he ate at home, how you made routine dishes come alive.”

Kathleen had been unpersuaded by this opinion at first, thinking her friend's idea unworkable (or dismissive of François), but it grew on her. She and her husband *had* had their most fun in the kitchen together throughout their married life. She would aim to capture that camaraderie at the same time she revealed the enhancements that could turn almost any dish into something delectable.

As Genevieve, a book editor herself, summed it up that night they had dinner at Pierre's restaurant, "The challenge, my dear, will be to find your own voice in this undertaking. If it works, you'll be sharing your secrets to a happy marriage as well as to a good dinner. And making money in the process."

By the end of the afternoon, Kathleen had settled on two-dozen recipes she would feature. That task completed, she scoured François' meticulous notes and her own jottings for tips to make these dishes more savory, or healthier, or otherwise appealing. The clock ticked on until 6 p.m. when she put her pencil down. She took a walk around the garden, clipped a few late-blooming roses for the parlor and refilled the hummingbird feeder. As shadows lengthened over the hilltop, she went back inside, poured herself a glass of wine, and stood out on the veranda to watch the sun slip into the sea. Albeit without someone to share the moment with, she felt more in control of things than she had for months.

If only that awful virus would somehow dissipate.

But it didn't.

Word came down from California's governor toward the end of March. To tamp down the spread of Covid-19, Newsom ordered the closure of all non-essential businesses as well as public schools, libraries, gyms, salons, gaming parlors, and churches. The shortlist of essential services remaining open included grocery stores, pharmacies and gas stations, but little else. That meant, as she had feared, restaurants and bars across the state were obliged to shutter. A few days later, New York's governor followed suit, his state reeling under an unremitting caseload and a hospital system struggling to care for the stricken.

Kathleen took the dreaded call from the owner of the Lantana soon after. The restaurant overlooking the ocean would close its doors three days hence and all Lantana staff would be furloughed.

Not an hour later, Pierre called to say he would close *La Chanson* by the weekend, laying off all of his employees.

"Anything I can do to help?" she asked, unable to disguise her dejection.

"I was going to ask you the same thing, Kath."

"What I want and need are the same as for you: the nightmare to end. And our lives to get back to normal."

CHAPTER TWENTY-SEVEN

Maks and Oksana

Father and Daughter Reunion

Excited though he was to be back in New York City, Maks was thrown for a loop. Everyone was jittery, everything felt jagged. *He* had not felt as unsettled since childhood in Moldova, when rumors of Stalin's pogroms sent shockwaves through the region. People in his village, his parents included, locked their doors, hunkered down for weeks on end, and prayed. "It is a plague over the land, Svetlana, but it will pass. If it doesn't, we will escape to America," he remembered his father whispering to his mother as they huddled in the bed across from his. And indeed, the ferreting out of Jews a never-ending blood sport, that is what the Mirovich family did, arriving in New York harbor when Maks was six. To his young eyes, the city dazzled and soon became less daunting a place for him than for his parents.

He thrived there.

Every time he had returned, that same feeling of promise reinvigorated him. But considerably older now and set in his West Coast ways, he had to strain. Especially with a daughter with whom he had only an intermittent acquaintance.

After settling into his Murray Hill hotel, he had walked up to Oksana's apartment on 44th St, a well-kept building with a polite doorman, and taken the elevator to the 19th floor. Father and daughter embraced tentatively. He then thrust a bouquet of roses at her and sheepishly followed her inside.

Their first exchanges over an *aperol* were in Russian, but once relaxed, they mixed in English and Italian, her grasp of all three impeccable. Maks had meant to take her out that evening, but she insisted upon cooking and having him stay the night. It was a two-bedroom with a view of the East River. He relented. She had made her paternal grandmother's Moldovian specialty, hearty beef and cabbage stew, which they washed down with a Georgian wine. It was tastier than his own version, if slightly more Americanized.

"I couldn't ignore my mother's side of the family," she called out from the kitchen, bringing out on a silver dish a tiramisu. "Grandma Novelli's recipe was a closely guarded secret, but eventually she shared it with me." Holding up the dessert platter, she added, "*Eccolà. Buon appetito,*" beaming at her father.

No exaggeration to say she was as beautiful as her Florentine mother had been, Maks thought—almond eyes, full mouth, coal-black hair.

As they chattered away—about the theater, concerts, movies, the ups and downs of work at the UN and teaching Russian (or was it Italian?) at Hunter College—he pondered what kind of social life such an accomplished and vibrant young woman had.

In short, was there a man in the picture?

But he dared not inquire so early on in their re-connection. Not only would he be presuming too much to be in her confidence, but if she turned the tables on him, he would be at a loss. Silda would be forever off-limits to discuss, but his thing with Serena? (If his affection for this woman were not serious enough to mention to his daughter, he did have every intention of ringing her—to check on Pushkin and to say that he missed her.)

However, after a glass or two of the wine, Oksana did ask questions. "I seem to remember you have a dog, Papà, with a poetic name. Who's looking after him in your absence?"

"Oh, just a neighbor," he burbled, and blushed. She raised an inquisitive eyebrow. "Serena's her name. She has a dog as well."

"Ah," she said, tilting her head to encourage elaboration.

He declined the opening, asking if she'd seen "Hamilton" or would like to go again. Yes, she had but no, they couldn't. Broadway had gone dark.

Thus occupied with dinner, father and daughter never got around to turning on the television, so it took a few days for Maks to register how rampant the spread of the virus had become. From what he intuited, everyone with money or connections or a house in the country had vacated the city. For the duration.

Only one of his contacts, a documentarian working on a project about endangered bird species, was available to meet up. They hit it off well enough to agree to a follow-up "as soon as this thing dies out," the producer had said. "In the meantime, Maks, keep in mind the series calls for somber notes. If there's any chirping, it'll come from the birds themselves."

While Oksana went to the UN each morning and taught her evening classes twice a week, Maks spent his days at the museums or at the few concerts still taking place around town. With eeriness all around him, he regretted being alone for these outings, especially since he had cavalierly relegated Serena to looking after his dog, never thinking she might have enjoyed the trip.

But one challenge at a time: becoming a bigger part of Oksana's life was his primary goal. As he walked to her apartment on his final evening in the city, he counted several storefronts along Second Avenue being boarded up, and the sound of sirens more persistent. Still, life had to go on, he repeated to himself. Determinedly. He would squire Oksana to a farewell dinner, at whatever restaurant she fancied.

They settled on one of her favorite places in the East Village, more authentically Italian, she insisted, than pricier ones uptown. "In fact, Papà, the food is so tasty you won't mind the guy who plays the accordion, though he will expect a tip," she had merrily warned him.

It was the very evening that Governor Cuomo declared drastic lockdowns. Folks would be asked to socially distance, wear face masks in public, and wash their hands frequently.

A musician passed by their table as Oksana was explaining that she, among countless others, would likely be let go. "Already, Papà, diplomats have headed for the exits, so it's only a matter of time before staff is placed on leave or required to work from home." He furrowed his brow. She hurried to amend her prediction: "But it shouldn't last long."

Maks looked skeptical but raised his glass in solidarity. The accordion player scurried over, winked at Oksana, and attacked a Neapolitan love song, likely assuming that the two were a couple. It seemed like a propitious moment for Maks to ask about her social life.

"I mean, you are so accomplished, and Manhattan is presumably full of smart, decent young men, right?"

She smiled, seemingly bemused. After he tipped the musician, lavishly enough to make him move along, Maks turned back toward his daughter.

"Not as easy as you think, Papà. Besides…"

"Besides what?"

Oksana took another sip of the wine he had ordered, a very dry burgundy. He had splurged. "It's that, well, for us—my generation, that is—friendships are a very big deal. More than marriage. As a general rule." It was her turn to blush.

"So, there's no one in particular?" he persisted, trying to strike a light-hearted note.

She puckered her lips to suggest the answer was complicated. Then: "There was a guy, but off and on. A magazine writer. They sometimes cover the UN."

"He sounds plausible; you have things in common."

She looked reluctant to elaborate.

Debating whether to pursue the subject further, Maks tried to calculate Oksana's age, concluding she must be thirty-four, with a birthday coming up in June. The fifteenth, to be precise.

The day of the month his wife had died, the newborn cradled in her arms for the briefest moment of shared love. He fought off the image—a blur of doctors, red blood, white sheets.

"Are you alright, Papà? You look pale," she asked, her black eyes anxious.

"A passing thing. Nothing really." He took a quick sip of the wine and wiped his lips with a napkin. "It's always more fun to enjoy the city with someone. Does your, uh, friend, like the theater and music as much as you?"

"I suppose. But he's extra busy, working on a novel." Maks smacked his lips to signal he was impressed. "He too has family in California. Spends holidays there." She said all this in a rush, as though to justify the fact that she and the young man did not see that much of each other.

"Come to think of it, I'm hoping that *you* might find the time to visit the other coast." Oksana looked down at her plate. "I mean, spend some time with me at Shell Beach. I don't know why I haven't..."

Gesticulating with his hand, Maks looked dismayed, unable to finish his sentence. Regrets. He had so many of them of late. He wondered how so many years could have passed without making more of an effort to get together with his only offspring. How absorbed he had become in his work, and then how obsessed with Silda. His eyes were suddenly brimming. He turned toward the other tables and gestured to a waiter.

Clearing his throat, he then asked, "What would you like, sweetheart? Coffee, dessert?"

To the waiter, Oksana replied in Italian, "*Per me, solo un espresso decaffeinato.*"

Recovering his composure, Maks mumbled, "The same. A decaf espresso. And the bill."

A raw wind had picked up by the time they left the restaurant, scattering dead leaves along the sidewalks. Rather than walk back uptown, they hailed a cab. The driver had the radio tuned to WNYC, where health care workers were complaining about the lack of protective equipment and ventilators for the ICU. When the driver swiveled his head to pull out into the traffic, they saw that he wore a mask, despite the glass partition.

To Maks' ear, the news reports sounded like dispatches from a war zone, Syria or some place. Unnerved, he reached over to pat his daughter's arm. "For one thing, if you came out west, you could get away from this. It's safer outside the big cities." Oksana nodded. Noncommittal. "Give it some thought?"

"Of course. I'd like to meet this Pushkin character. And perhaps even—"

"Even?"

Backing away from her thought, she generalized. "Oh, you know. Be in the warmth of the sun."

When the taxi turned onto 44th Street and pulled up to the apartment tower, she hugged her father, warmly, and got out, an alert doorman holding open the entrance against a sudden gust.

The first thing Maks did when he got home to Shell Beach was take a long shower during which he scrubbed every last inch of his body. After ten intense days on the East Coast and a crowded, nerve-racking flight back to LAX, he wanted nothing more than to wash away any trace of contagion, even if he had no clue how the virus managed to survive—on the skin, on his clothes, in the air, or inside a person. Unfortunately, he had no clue how to clear the distressing images he had seen in Manhattan out of his head.

Drink, he concluded, might help. In robe and slippers, he poured himself a glass of ice-cold vodka. Once the liquor took hold, he re-read the note that had been appended to his front door. *Welcome back. Pushkin has been staying over with Dog for the last few nights. They're both fit as fiddles. Hope you are too, but given what New York is going through…Come by when you're up to it. Serena*

He breathed a sigh of relief, glad that he had thought of buying his neighbor a gift—a water-proof Movado clock to append somewhere outside. She had complained about losing track of time whenever she entertained company on the veranda. Or perhaps he mistook her comment for a complaint when all she really meant that evening of the shish-kabob was that hours had flown by because she was having such a grand ole time.

What women say, and what they mean, don't necessarily coincide.

The timepiece, however, was a concrete thing that proved he had thought about the recipient, (though he had not rung her once during his trip). Moreover, it was a handsome ornament, something that had a purpose without being unduly personal.

But then again, why should he be concerned about being overly personal: they had fucked on her expensive Persian rug. If that wasn't personal, what was? Where this dalliance might lead, if anywhere, he had no inkling. Like the one his daughter had with that so-called writer: on-again, off-again. What had Oksana insisted? That friendship was more important to her generation than marriage, which sounded refreshingly liberated, but which might not reflect what she really wanted.

So many mind games women play.

Shaking his head in weary acceptance of these facts, Maks took another swig of the bracing vodka—(he ordered only the best, Beluga Gold straight from Moscow, but drank it sparingly)—and tried to settle on his next move. Too late to ring Serena, he would walk over the next morning, though not too early, exquisitely wrapped gift in hand, to relieve her of Pushkin. And propose they get together again in a day or two, as soon as he got his work schedule sorted out, his last commission, the bird series, needing immediate attention, and presuming she would still be interested in…He pictured how she might take all this, one corner of her mouth curled upwards in something of a skeptical smile. She would have a right to be.

He had no idea what he felt about her, or how strongly.

With Silda, Maks had never had to angst about how their relationship might evolve. She was married and that was that. Their times together were precious because they were deliciously rare. Only once did his lover, stretching out her limbs after a particularly inventive sex act, murmur something to the effect, “If I had only met you before, dear Maks, things would be different.” Which, however much he may have been flattered or aroused to hear at the time, was one of those wistfully vacuous pronouncements that a woman was wont to make after really good sex with someone other than her husband.

Serena, he believed, was not wistful or vacuous. She was purposeful, like a clock, and it appeared she liked what she saw in him, as much as, if not more than, what she saw in Eliot Etheridge. Was she playing the two men off against each other—making the same casseroles and pushing the same movies on them? Such an irony that would be.

Tomorrow he would assess the chessboard, as it were.

He finished off the vodka, checked to make sure the front and back doors were locked, and made his way, a little wobbly, to his bedroom. Once under the covers, Maks closed his eyes and tried to fall asleep. But not before he heard a beep on his cell phone. He reached an arm out for the device on his nightstand. *Hope your flight went well and you're safely back at Shell Beach. Been thinking about your invitation. It might work out if I'm allowed to teach my courses online and if the UN furloughs me. Will keep you posted. Oksana*

In Russian he typed back: *Can't think of anything better than having you here. As long as you like.*

Around 11 a.m. the next morning, Maks rang the doorbell but when there was no response, he circled to the backyard. Serena, in leggings, a red turtleneck sweater and sunglasses, was watering roses against the back fence. From a distance he could tell her hair had been bobbed. She did not see or hear him, but before long Pushkin and Dog came bounding off the veranda, barking, presumably in delight to see him. Serena turned to locate the commotion, twisted the nozzle off and then the faucet, and walked over, her gait slower than Maks remembered.

"You made it back," she declared, pleasantly enough. "As you can see, Pushkin is none the worse." She did not come close enough for an embrace. "Weeds never desist," she commented, upturning her dirty palms, "but take a seat on the veranda. I'll wash up and we'll have coffee and croissants."

Maks had meant to decline any invitation to linger but he was momentarily tongue-tied. Without waiting for a reply, Serena mounted the stone steps to the veranda and indicated the table where they had eaten weeks before. "Be back in a jiffy."

While he reconnected with the dogs, roughing the Great Dane's ears and rubbing Dog's proffered nose, he could hear cups and saucers being rattled in the kitchen. On the table in front of him, marigolds were blooming in a colorful pot. He placed the shopping bag with his gift next to the pot.

Within five minutes, Serena, without her sunglasses, reappeared with a tray, two mugs of strong black coffee—she remembered his preference, which matched her own—and two piping hot croissants, presumably picked up at the town's only open bakery. She must have guessed he'd show up sooner rather than later.

Once they took a few sips and nibbled at the pastries, they chatted amiably. "So how was your trip?"

"You know. New York rarely disappoints, but I'm sure you've been following the news. The city is reeling. Sirens all the time. Stores closing left and right. People eyeing one another suspiciously. My tickets to 'Hamilton' pointless, my contacts mostly out of town. My daughter, however, was a delight—the consummate New Yorker, a great job at the UN, did I say?"

After a pause it was Serena's turn. "Well, believe it or not, out here too we're beginning to feel the pall. Not like San

Francisco or Los Angeles but people are learning what an N95 mask is. Things like that."

They went on like this for a while, then paused to finish their coffee and croissants. Wiping her fingers on a napkin, Serena rested her eyes on the bag he had brought.

"It's for you," Maks said. "Something I saw at MoMA and thought—"

"You shouldn't have," she interrupted, allowing him to fish out the gift. "How exquisitely wrapped though. I hate to open it." But she did and appeared pleased.

"It's for out here—if you can figure out a place for it."

Serena looked around, spotted a hook that supported the awning, and rose to hang it.

"What do you think?" she asked, stepping back a few feet to make sure the clock was level.

"Perfect. Plus, I think it's time for me to let you get on with your day." Since she didn't object, he felt obliged to overcorrect. "Hopefully, we can get together on the weekend, if, that is, you don't have alternate plans. As for catching up with things, I received a new commission that I'll need to—that funny expression in English—'sink my teeth into,' but it shouldn't be that time-consuming."

She nodded. Inscrutable her expression.

In the silence, Maks got himself out of the lawn chair, the Great Dane immediately clambering to his own feet. Serena walked to a side table and retrieved the leash.

"It's been fun, hasn't it?" she said, leaning down to fasten the buckle to the Dane's collar. "Come visit us anytime, right, Dog?" Handing the leash to her guest, she added, her voice steely: "Call me when you come up for air. We'll figure out something."

For an instant, he started to inquire if everything were okay, but doing that to a woman often backfired or became time-consuming. Already off-balance, he was not up for either eventuality. Instead: "Oh, one thing I forgot: Oksana may come for a visit—depending on how much things worsen in

Manhattan, and what happens with her jobs. I hope you will get to meet her."

Again, Serena allowed a pause before what should have been the automatic "delighted" response.

"Only four houses separate us, last I noticed," she remarked, her eyes raised skywards as though to calculate the crow's distance between their respective places of residence. "I suspect it would be difficult not to meet her, what with our dogs so entwined."

Before Maks could decipher this as a signal of something amiss—how much she regretted their unfortunate intimacy or how much she resented that he hadn't bothered to call while away—she changed tone. "But yes, I'd be delighted to meet your daughter."

To Maks' delight, Oksana arrived unannounced on his doorstep, with two suitcases, her laptop, and a black face mask dangling from one ear on April 15, having been, as she had intimated, furloughed from her job at the United Nations and put on short-term leave by Hunter College. (The latter decision came with the proviso that she might be called upon to teach remotely if enough students signed up and paid their tuition fees.) On the plane out, she recalled the last time she had set foot in California, fifteen years earlier, during sophomore year at Middlebury College. One of her courses had organized a field trip to San Francisco, and finding herself with time to kill, she hopped on a shuttle to Los Angeles to surprise her father.

That visit had been unsatisfying. Most of the time was spent traipsing from studio to studio, where Maks hunkered down in editing rooms or on sound stages. From Oksana's perspective, he appeared much in demand but absorbed in his work. Throughout that visit, he made a point of charming everyone, but that was the problem: she did not feel special and never thereafter felt the urge to return. All their subsequent get-togethers, the few that there were, came at his behest and in New York, the last one, however, surprisingly pleasant. Her father had changed—more attentive, less judgmental.

After they hugged, he rushed to make her a cup of hot chamomile, it being midnight, and then showed her to the guest room in the back—: “It’s your *sancta sanctorum* for as long as you care to stay.”

He hoisted her heavier suitcase onto a chair; she placed the smaller one next to it. He then showed her the adjacent bathroom, hers alone, and further along the hall, a small study, with an antique desk and bookcases against the walls, which, he insisted, he never used, preferring to work in the parlor, close to the piano.

“Tell me you still play, my dear. You’ll love the touch of this instrument. The Germans do get some things right.” She had nodded, pleased by the enthusiasm in his voice.

That night Oksana slept soundly, awakened by the sun on her exposed arm and soon thereafter by the sound of scratching at her door. She waited until the noise ceased, figuring she’d best be introduced to a Great Dane only when wide awake. At around 8 a.m. she got up and looked out the window at a rock garden interspersed with cacti and aloes and other succulents she didn’t recognize. In the distance, birds of paradise preened against a wooden fence. She was charmed. More so, when she came downstairs and followed her nose to a well-appointed kitchen. A gray granite island dominated the center. Her father was hunched over on one of the stools sipping coffee and scrolling through his iPad.

He swirled around, eyeing her appreciatively. “I trust you slept well, but if not, the coffee will revive you. Probably a good idea to have a clear head before Pushkin bounds in.”

“Precisely why I came down,” she replied, scanning the counter for the pot and a mug. She gestured for him to remain seated and poured herself a cup. Drinking it black, the way he did.

Not five minutes later, paws could be heard padding across the parlor floor. Pushkin paused at the entrance to the kitchen, presumably awaiting a signal from Maks.

"Come on in, fella. There's someone you need to meet."

The rest of the morning Oksana spent unpacking and setting up her computer in the upstairs study. For lunch the two dined on clam chowder from one of the Pismo Beach restaurants set up for takeout and a rustic Italian loaf from the local bakery, one of the businesses still deemed an essential service. Warm enough to be outside, she spent her afternoon wandering around the garden. From there she could hear her father at the piano, improvising in different keys. After a while, she went inside and sat in one of the armchairs across from the Bösendorfer.

"Hope I haven't been bothering you, Oksana. Getting started on a score requires stops and starts. Wearying to anyone else."

"What is it you're working on? It sounds *drammatico*," she replied, gesticulating with her hand to accentuate the Italian.

"A documentary about vanishing species. Birds, to be precise. But the producer was adamant: nothing chirpy. it's for PBS."

Oksana laughed. "By the way, I will be glad to fill your bird feeders if you tell me where you keep the seeds. You wouldn't want them to go extinct too."

"As you will discover, I am neglectful of things, so by all means."

After they did the dishes, Oksana tended to the birds and watered the potted ferns hanging along the edge of the terrace. Maks plugged away until around 3 p.m., at which point he grabbed his car keys and took his daughter on a tour of the Five Cities. "Like in New York, things are slowing down here. One good thing: there isn't as much traffic to contend with."

On her seventh day in Shell Beach, Oksana felt she had gotten her bearings and worked out a routine.

After teaching her first class for Hunter College students online that morning and listening to a faculty conference call, she offered to take Pushkin for his afternoon walk. Maks was relieved to have more time to concentrate on work, the hiatus in New York having exacerbated his missed deadlines.

By 5 p.m. the air had turned crisp, but the sea still glistened in the fading sunlight, its hues purple and green in the distance. More accustomed to the gray skies of Manhattan's winter, Oksana was glad to wear sunglasses, and resigned to a mask around her neck, just in case.

An onshore breeze picked up on their return leg along the boulevard, waves breaking against the rocks audible as they skirted a grassy expanse called Eldwayen Park. She paused, took a few deep breaths, and stared out to sea. Several sailboats bobbed in the near distance; a large yacht floated past in the distance. Of a sudden, Pushkin tugged insistently at his leash, enough to force Oksana to follow his lead across the boulevard. Reluctantly, she acquiesced, not knowing if the dog ever got out of control and would try to bite her.

On the front porch of a two-story house, tall windows everywhere, sat a woman reading a book. When Pushkin started barking, she raised her head, one hand to her forehead to block the sun.

"I'm sorry, ma'am. The dog appears to think he lives here—and he is harder to control than I bargained on," Oksana called out.

"Not to worry. He simply wants to see Dog again."

Without hesitating, the woman rose from her chair, leaving the book in the seat. (She was tall, with the posture of a dancer, Oksana thought.) She moved along the wrap-around porch, her steps unhurried. "Dog, Dog. You're wanted out front. You have visitors," she called out, almost as though speaking to a human.

Oksana fidgeted on the woman's walkway, doing her best to keep the Great Dane from getting away from her. Soon, a strange-looking hound, low to the ground, materialized from around the side of the house. As soon as the creature saw

Pushkin, he bounded toward him. *Ruf, ruf, ruf* from both canines. The woman came down the pathway to oversee the reunion.

"You needn't worry about these two. They're well-acquainted. In fact," she added, noting Oksana's uncertain expression, "Pushkin had been staying with us recently."

A light suddenly went on in Oksana's head.

"You must be—" they both began at once and broke into laughter.

Serena held out her hand, Oksana responded with hers. And then fumbled to attach her mask.

"You needn't do that unless it makes you more comfortable," Serena said. "In the fresh air, we should be fine." Oksana nodded and desisted. Reaching down to undo Pushkin's leash, she added, "They can romp in the back yard, while we sit on the veranda—such glorious weather, despite everything going on. It so happens I've made lemonade—the fruit trees in the back do not know when to stop—and there are chocolate chip cookies, still warm from the oven. We need comfort food right now, wouldn't you agree?"

"Absolutely," Oksana replied.

And as though it were the most predictable thing in the world, the two women fell in love that afternoon.

CHAPTER TWENTY-EIGHT

Eliot

An Embrace Interrupted

When Eleanor connected with her father, he couldn't have been more gobsmacked. He fumbled for the nearest chair to collect his wits. He had just come in from a walk with Keats, a walk he cut short when he caught sight of a Great Dane in front of Serena's place. A striking young woman with black hair was struggling with the leash. The dog had to be Pushkin. Strange twosome, he thought.

Back in the house, he had poured a glass of Scotch and was headed to the study when the phone rang. He registered only the gist of what his daughter was going on about. Pierre had come to New York weeks earlier, proposed at a fancy restaurant and presented her with a diamond, which was gorgeous, though truly he didn't have to splurge. Naturally, they would delay an actual ceremony until this contagion had run its course. And on and on.

He had to cut into this recitation. "Does his stepmother yet know? Which coast do you plan to live on?"

"Funny. Kathleen asked the same things when Pierre managed to connect with her."

"Hmm…" followed by silence on Eliot's part.

"I take it you two have not seen each other. Restaurants are closing left and right."

"Yes, it's taking hold here. Some people are wearing masks, avoiding one another on the boulevard." Again, a pause.

"What about that place she runs, the Lantana?"

"I haven't noticed, dear, but I'll be asking her, now that we..." Eliot couldn't articulate how their relations would now change since he would be the father of the bride, and Kathleen, stepmother of the groom. Was there a name for that inter-relation? He would need to look it up.

"So, Dad, are you taking precautions? Still driving down to the office or have you discovered Zoom?"

He had heard the expression *to zoom* on some newscast but had no idea how to activate it. (Caroline likely had her hands full with Chloe but she was adept with computer technology. He needed to get her back up to Shell Beach. The firm couldn't begrudge him that.)

"Mostly, I'm working from home. What about Carlyle & Co?" he answered, then deflected.

"The partners haven't figured it out. I go in once a week if need be. However, working remotely means we can be anywhere. If, say, we settle on the West Coast."

"Well, if you're sure about this. He did seem, Pierre, that is... (Eliot's voice faltered as he fished for an apt description of his future son-in-law) charming," he uttered determinedly, "like his stepmother."

Why he hadn't made more of an effort to reconnect with Kathleen—or she with him—he could not say. Pride, a preoccupation with others, some deep-seated reluctance to commit himself. He pressed his thumb and index finger against his eyes, the receiver cradled against his ear. A headache was coming on.

"Dad, are you still there? I almost forgot—"

"Yes, what is it?" he blurted, straightening his back and blinking a few times. Keats, he noticed, had curled up on the floor, eyeing him anxiously.

"In case you haven't spoken to him—you know how erratic he is—Jared's had both good and bad news."

"As in?"

"He was let go from that magazine a couple of weeks ago. I can never remember the name, like *The Nation*, only not well-known."

"Because of the pandemic?"

"More or less. They upped some intern, a girl with whom he didn't get along. On the plus side, he finished that novel. In fact, it's out. He may not be Jonathan Franzen, but it got a few good reviews. So, there's that."

Thrown by the reference to this Jonathan somebody, Eliot hesitated before posing another question. "Will he make money off this book, or is he looking to get another job?"

"You know Jared. Not exactly forthcoming. And not a propitious period in the publishing business—and that was true before the pandemic."

They left that worrisome subject to fend for itself.

"Almost forgot," Eleanor tossed out, breaking the sudden silence. "I ran into your friend Isabel recently. At the 92nd St Y. She was coming out of a cooking class. She introduced me to a guy, also in your circle at Harvard, a Phil somebody. The two appeared quite chummy. Maybe learning to make dim sum does that to people."

Phil who? Eliot wondered. Surely not that architecture major who had a crush on Issie all those years ago.

"Dad? Everything okay? Remember, you really should wear a mask when you're out and about. At the firm too."

"I'll take precautions. Besides, I don't go out much."

Father and daughter chatted a few more minutes until it occurred to Eliot that she might ask him about the property scam case he had been building. The last thing he wanted was to go into detail about how he had been put out to pasture by the firm. Especially not to his newly engaged daughter.

Keats had begun to whimper, rubbing his nose up against his master's leg. Eliot broke into whatever Eleanor was going on about, something about how Zoom was changing workplace dynamics, making productivity both easier, and harder. Not having a clue how it worked, he voiced no opinion. However, some good things might come out of this global crisis, he suggested half-heartedly. And no matter what, they would speak again soon; about the engagement, he couldn't be happier—for them both. And he would forthwith reach out to Kathleen, though no, he wasn't sure what the status was with the Lantana or her cookbook project.

When he hung up, Eliot took deep breaths to soothe his now throbbing head. Surely there would still be a bottle of Excedrin in the medicine cabinet, though only Silda had ever had the foresight to keep it stocked. "Bad things can come out of nowhere," she used to say. "Best to have weapons on hand to vanquish them." The cruel irony being, he thought, that the worst of things had come out of nowhere for her—and all weapons were futile.

As for this latest scourge, this vividly named coronavirus, nobody seemed to know how to combat it. Letting out a sigh, he stood up, one hand reaching to clutch his lower back. It ached too; he couldn't have taken to the squash court even if the Pismo Beach gym were open. He ambled into the kitchen, Keats at his heels.

After filling a bowl with dog chow and a ham hock from the fridge that he doubted he'd ever put to use himself, Eliot rummaged through the freezer. He came up with a round Pyrex dish marked *Santa Fe Salad 2/28/20 S.S.*, which he remembered Serena had brought over to thank him for looking into the issues with her house. "So be it," he muttered, removing the foil and placing the container in the microwave for a couple of minutes. Adding a few shakes of sea salt and ground pepper—unlike Daphne, who never met a spice she didn't like, Serena left her dishes bland, "seasoning should be discretionary," she had once told him—he scooped out a portion onto a plate. The concoction of corn, peppers, purple onions, green olives, fennel, and a couple of things he couldn't identify came to life. Coupled with another Scotch, the food chased his headache into a far corner.

Back in the living room, Eliot switched on the television to catch the top of the 8 o'clock local news—he did not wish to appear as out of the loop on goings-on about town as he had been with Eleanor—and then he would place a call to Kathleen. Bound to be at home, he surmised, since the Lantana was likely as dark as every other eatery. He would invite her to do something, but where, if nothing were open? Everything around him had been turned upside-down.

Disconcerting.

After four rings, he would have hung up but Kathleen's machine came on. "It's Eliot. Wondering how you are and wanting to hear your thoughts on the happy news. Call when convenient. I'm usually up late." He sat down in the adjacent armchair, switched off the lamp and waited in the darkness. Ten minutes later, she rang back, having been, she explained, out on the veranda feeding two love birds in a cage. "They're gorgeous creatures but never stop cooing and whatever else they do, well, when we're not looking."

"I don't remember seeing them there."

"They're my stepson's. Romeo and Juliet, he calls them. But since all the closures, he's become peripatetic. Working with something called World Central Kitchen. Can you believe, hunger in our own country? He's asked me to take care of them—for the duration."

"Ah, the duration," Eliot sighed. "Can't come too soon."

"The French have a saying for such trying times, *il faut en finer*, which I needn't translate."

"Indeed," he replied, grasping the gist of the Gallic phrase, if not the precise meaning. She was going on, he thought, as pleasantly as if their relations had not been strained or negligible for the better part of three months. Prickly this woman was not, much to his relief. He relaxed into the armchair, the pain in his back subsiding.

"As for lovebirds, Kathleen, were you as dumbfounded as I to hear about our children's plans? Eleanor told me earlier today. I assume that you—"

"Pierre apprised me some days ago, but naturally it was up to Eleanor to let you know. She is lovely and Pierre is over the moon. However, they have more things to work out than couples typically do. I suspect you agree."

"Why I called. So that we can get together, go over things, see what can be done, to facilitate," he started. "But also, well, it's been too long. Been busy with this, that and the other. Work is complicated, and my assistant—you remember Caroline Morris—is having issues with her daughter. Among other things. Anyway, I don't know why but..."

Kathleen did not come to his rescue. Whatever he had to say in justification, he would have to bungle his way forward to get it out.

Sensing her tactic—(she might not be prickly but she had been snubbed)—he wiggled to straighten up in the chair.

"The thing is, it would be lovely to see you, and with so many places closed, a jaunt up in the hills—the fresh air, fewer people—might be doable. You know, if you enjoy that sort of thing. Sometime soon, I was thinking, like this weekend, if you're not—I don't know, the Lantana. I forgot to ask…"

"They've closed it. Indefinitely," she interrupted. Curt her tone.

"Oh, I'm sorry," he replied, taken aback.

"Anyway, I have written them a proposal to re-open, *al fresco*, putting up a tent in the parking lot, spacing the tables, rehiring as many of the staff as necessary."

"That sounds admirable. Very entrepreneurial of you," he rejoined, hoping he didn't sound paternalistic. He did not mean to be.

"As always, it's all about the numbers. But the place was doing so well I'd hate to see it go under. And then there's

Pierre's place in San Francisco. *La Chanson* may not survive, so he might relocate down this way. Did Eleanor intimate any of that?" There was a silence as Eliot took all of this in. "So much to juggle…" she trailed off.

"Or," he back-tracked, more decisively, "you could come over here, Saturday evening, and we can cook up something together, talk over their plans, and, you know, catch up." He paused to sum up. "I'd like to be of help. Plus—"

"Plus?"

"I've missed your company—a lot." He swallowed hard, glad that he had gotten that out.

For the rest of the week, Eliot wondered if Kathleen would wear a mask to his house, and if so, what should be his response. There were so many mixed messages, from the media, from the scientists, and from the president that he had been stymied. On the other hand, masquerades he had always found exciting—not only the Harvard Law Halloween party in which he and Issie both kept theirs on while they went at it in one of the building's unused classrooms but some ballroom dance in Santa Barbara when Silda had kept hers on in the car while they—. Their excuse: the children were four or five at the time and hard to get away from.

So long ago. He was a different person. How could he even begin to fantasize about such things? During a goddamn pandemic.

When he did get to the grocery store that Friday morning, he bought a packet of three face coverings, just in case. Meaning just in case his guest was wary of what the packet called "airborne viral transmission."

Right on time his doorbell rang. Eliot saw her through the smoked glass, dressed in a powder-blue dress, a flounce at the hem. Turned sideways, she appeared to be admiring the hanging ferns and wearing a face covering. He grabbed a mask off the rack and opened the door.

"Fancy meeting like this," she began, "as though we were on our way to a masquerade party."

Blushing, he fumbled to attach his own. "Not in a hundred years, right?" Lowering his eyes, he noticed the shopping bag she had set down. "Please, please come in. It looks like you went out of your way."

"The farmers market in San Luis Obispo. These days it's a much safer place to shop."

He carried the bags to the kitchen, placed them on the counter and turned to face her. "First things first. Does anything need the fridge? Unless you're starving, we could sit on the upstairs balcony and watch the sunset."

"Perfect," she responded, reaching into the bag and pulling out a small carton and something wrapped in aluminum foil. "The prosciutto and the cream we should chill, but the eggs, the mushrooms and the cherry tomatoes should be fine."

"You did go to a lot of trouble," he said, realizing she had brought along everything needed for a vegetable omelet other than a skillet.

"Don't feel guilty. I'll be putting you to work, chopping things, including the garlic, always tedious. Thought we'd try one of François's dishes—comfort food, really, for either the morning or the evening. Don't know about you, but I prefer such dishes late in the day. Sound reasonable?"

"Absolutely. We'll tackle it in an hour or so."

For a moment Eliot debated what was different about her, after so many months, but could not put his finger on it. As a rule, women did not like to be complimented about things that hadn't changed one iota, so he kept quiet. Instead, he searched around for crystal wine glasses and a corkscrew. "I found a Sancerre 2016 at that fancy wine store near you in Pismo proper. It goes down well when listening to Mozart—at least with someone else." Kathleen looked vaguely non-plussed. "And you do look so, so spring-like, and it is definitely spring, outside, I mean," he went on, acutely aware of the inanity of his chatter.

Inclining her head in acceptance of the compliment, Kathleen arranged the other items from her shopping spree on the kitchen table. "I don't recall being on your upstairs terrace but watching the sun dip into the sea never grows old. Shall we go upstairs?"

"By all means. And forgive me for not knowing the protocol, but if you're alright with it, we could dispense with the masks. For the interim."

Tilting her head to consider the idea, Kathleen then delicately removed her mask, letting it hang loose around her neck. Eliot followed suit.

While the sun, huge and purple, slipped beneath the waves, they sat in silence on the balcony. Eventually, once Eliot turned on the nearby space heater, they sipped the wine, listened to a Mozart horn concerto, and took turns petting Keats.

And they talked.

About the engagement between Eleanor and Pierre, they both professed misgivings, not only because of the pandemic and the precariousness of their respective jobs, but because, by any measure, the two barely knew each other. Did you intimate as much to them? It didn't seem appropriate. And where will they reside, and what will the one who has to relocate do and how resentful will that one be, and how anxious the other? And do they know about each other's previous attachments? Eleanor, you must know, was married for several years. Disastrous, in that her spouse constantly cheated on her. And Pierre was enamored of a lovely Parisian girl, but that never stopped him—he is French, after all—well, you know…

They both agreed the younger generation was clueless about pretty much everything. Still, a wedding is by definition an occasion to celebrate, even if a virus has not yet been vanquished. Surely, by the time of the ceremony though…

Later, while Kathleen doctored the eggs for the omelet, beating them, fluffing them, dripping in the cream and Eliot chopped the mushrooms and minced the garlic, they changed subjects. To François—masterful in the kitchen—and how she was coming to terms with his infidelity by turning her homage of a cookbook into a memoir of their shared delight in food. The draft was now in the hands of a publisher in San Francisco. And still later at the dinner table, Eliot lit two candles and dimmed the chandelier while they savored the omelet, perfectly paired with the tart, salty prosciutto and nicely washed down with the rest of the wine.

It became his turn to confide.

Silda? Such aplomb, and so sought after on the dance floor, on the charity dais and at the book club, and yet so vain about her svelte figure she declared cooking a chore. It's a wonder the children did not succumb to starvation—and then, stumbling over his words, he let out that sex too had become a chore for her, increasingly, until…As his account faltered, he feigned a cough and turned away to cover it up.

Not to let the opportunity slip away, Kathleen poured him some water. And coaxed what else was lodged inside out of him. How, to his unbeknownst and throughout her illness, his wife had carried on with a neighbor who still resides along the boulevard. He jerked his head to indicate the direction of Maks' place. Their dogs, fast friends.

Quietly, Kathleen rose and went to the kitchen to cut two slices of the *tarte aux pommes* she had made that morning. Within a minute she returned to see Eliot stroking the ears of the dog. "Not your fault at all, Keats. Poets have to stick together," he murmured. Whatever that meant.

They ate dessert in silence until Eliot recovered enough to say, "I did not mean to burden you. It's simply that—"

"*Pas de problème*, Eliot. It's good not to keep things bottled up." He nodded, a wan smile on his face. "But then…"

"Then?"

"It's equally good to move on from what can't be altered. That would be true in both our cases."

It was 11:30 p.m. when Eliot and Kathleen finished up in the kitchen, his last act preparing the coffee pot for the morning, hers, putting away the delicate wine glasses. Without any discussion as to what awaited, he took her hand in his and together they mounted the stairs for his bedroom. At the top, Eliot turned to dim the lights in the foyer below but was startled. The phone had begun to ring.

"What on earth," he mumbled, dropping Kathleen's hand and moving to the hall table. "Yes?" he snapped, none too pleased as he picked up.

"Eliot, It's me. Something's happened. Can you come over? Like now. I don't know what to do."

"Slow down, Daphne. What's the problem?" He glanced back at Kathleen, who remained at the top of the stairs. He shrugged his shoulders as though to indicate such a call from such a person was highly irregular. Gradually, as Daphne described the situation, Eliot's face clouded over. Soon, he interrupted her. "Slip a pillow under his head and offer him water. We'll be there in ten minutes."

"Whatever has happened, Eliot?"

"It's Seth. He's knocked out or fainted or something. Daphne is hysterical. She tried 911 and got no reply. I need to get down there."

"I'm coming with you." He did not argue.

When they arrived at Seth's place, lights were on only inside the guesthouse, the door ajar. Both the old man and Daphne were on the floor, his head cradled in her lap, his breathing irregular, eyes watery. He was clad in a bathrobe and slippers; she in a nightgown, her feet bare.

Eliot exchanged a glance with Kathleen, neither knowing what to make of the scene. Stooping down to feel his uncle's pulse, he got a whiff of both alcohol and perfume and was unsure what to make of those either.

He looked askance at Daphne's distraught face. "What exactly took place here?" he challenged her.

"I was asleep. Your uncle came in, calling my name. He came toward the bedroom but stumbled. And he's been coughing, like crazy."

"Like, before all this, before barging into your room? What the hell, Daphne."

So accused, the young woman could no longer hold back tears, a few of which streamed down her face. "Since yesterday. I heard him wheezing and then today I made him soup. But I didn't stay. And I didn't invite him over, if that's what you're implying," she hissed. Angrily.

"We should get him to the emergency room," Kathleen broke in, her voice hard to argue with. At that point, Seth struggled to raise his head, briefly opening his eyes. He muttered something incomprehensible but couldn't muster enough energy to sit up.

"Grab a blanket, Daphne, and a bottle of water. We'll put him in the back seat. San Luis Obispo will be open."

The three managed to get Seth upright and out the door to the car, where they lay him flat, except for his head in Kathleen's lap.

"You stay put here, Daphne," Eliot ordered. "We'll call when we know something." She did not object.

Once on the freeway, Eliot put on the emergency light and sped up. Kathleen whipped out her cell and got through to the hospital. Seth began to mutter, fragments that meant little to her. She stroked his forehead, hot to the touch. When, twenty minutes later, they pulled up to the emergency entrance, two medics in personal protective equipment met them outside and handed them masks and paperwork to fill out. Eliot scribbled answers, outside, under bright lights, while two orderlies lifted Seth onto a gurney and rolled him inside.

"May we come with him?" Kathleen asked.

"Only to the waiting area. You say he may be infected?"

Kathleen deferred to Eliot. "He's been wheezing and coughing. For days. Don't know about a fever. He's in his eighties, though, so…"

"Actually, he's at 102," one of the medics rejoined after pointing the thermometer at Seth's forehead. "We'll test for Covid as soon as the shift changes."

"When will we know what needs to be done—I mean, what he has, how serious it is?" Eliot asked.

"And if he has to be in the ICU," Kathleen interjected.

"In the morning. We'll have a better idea." The medic looked from one to the other. "If he is positive, you'll need to track down those he's been in contact with, isolate them, and quarantine yourselves. You know the routine."

They nodded their thanks, but no handshakes were exchanged. On the drive back to Shell Beach, Eliot asked Kathleen what she made of his uncle's condition. "Not just alcohol, in my opinion. He did keep murmuring in the car something about a desk. That you'd find it all spelled out there."

Eliot looked flummoxed. After a minute or two, Kathleen reminded him to ring Daphne. "This wasn't her fault, whatever the circumstances." He didn't contradict her.

"You're right. And I'm grateful you came along. Except that now you may have been exposed to this thing. I had no right..."

"Don't fret about it, Eliot. It is what it is."

"I don't know what I would have done without you there—she's so irritating."

Kathleen did not counter his opinion of the young woman. Instead, she dialed the number in Oceano, put the phone on speaker and placed it in the cup holder.

"Yes, he's been admitted, Daphne, and no, there's nothing we can do right now," Eliot told her, coldness in his tone. "However, you should stay indoors. If he does test positive, you'll need to keep your distance from others, and wear a mask."

"Daphne, it's Kathleen. If you haven't already, wipe down the surfaces Seth might have touched in your room. Use disinfectant and wash your hands, thoroughly. Little things like that help. Okay?"

"Well, that's done," Eliot sighed when they clicked off the call.

They drove the rest of the way to Shell Beach in silence, both lost in thought, but for different reasons. When they got to Sorenson House, Eliot pulled up behind Kathleen's Porsche, killed the engine and turned to face her. She managed a faint smile, her eyes searching out his.

"Timing is everything, don't you think?" she said quietly.

Nodding, he took her hand in his and carried it to his lips. Then he opened the car door, came around and helped her out and into the Porsche. "To be continued," he said, tapping the window to signal she could go, no reply necessary.

As he walked up the sidewalk toward the front door, he wondered why he hadn't gotten around to taking down and replacing the Sorenson House sign.

CHAPTER TWENTY-NINE

Caroline

Fired Up

On the day in late May Caroline found out she had passed the California bar via a terse form letter, Tillotson summoned her into his corner office, closed the door and cleared his throat. She had half-expected to be presented with a bouquet of roses but the old man, puffing away on a cigar, held out a pink slip with his free hand.

After twelve years at the firm, rarely missing a day and taking on whatever the partners threw at her, she was stunned. "I don't understand, Mr. Tillotson. I just passed the bar. I'm now legally able to practice."

"Then you should have no trouble finding yourself another position. Once the pandemic is under control," he had countered, beginning to rattle through a folder on his desk as though to signal the colloquy was over.

"But there's so much to do now, with the virus and everything. All the lawsuits to come."

"Nothing you need to worry yourself with," he shot back. Samantha Miles, he hurried on to say, would be calculating her severance and mailing out the necessary forms. "She'll be taking on your duties, such as they were," he further jabbed.

How demeaning, Caroline thought. Samantha, the ditzy blonde who couldn't tell a plaintiff from a plantain but pushed her perky breasts into all the men's faces, was being promoted. "I don't mean to be uncharitable but—"

"We've made a decision, the senior partners," he cut her off. "We're planning to streamline things, freshen the place up," he revealed, his filmy eyes raking her body disapprovingly, as though she were too rumpled for the sleek image the firm wished to project.

Ignoring protocol, she persisted. "What about Eliot, Mr. Etheridge? Who's going to look after him—commute back and forth, at their own expense, by the way—to assist with his schedule, his clients?"

"Again, Ms. Morris. Not an issue you need to concern yourself with. When required, he can access our Zoom sessions. His papers can easily be FedExed to Shell Beach as...Well, you get my drift."

Tillotson paused to let his decisions sink in and pulled his gold watch from his vest pocket, even though a perfectly reliable Timex ticked away on the wall opposite him. "Now, if you'll excuse me, I do have calls to return," he wound up, gesturing toward the door with one hand and pressing a button on the intercom to summons his assistant.

As she headed down the hall to her cubicle on the floor below, Caroline heard peals of laughter from the commons room, likely Samantha being entertained by one of the firm's up-and-comers. Over coffee and blueberry muffins, the latter that she herself had baked that very morning, leaving a couple for Chloe on the kitchen table and taking the rest along for her colleagues. To celebrate her achievement.

Heat rising in her chest and likely spoiling her new spring suit, Caroline ducked into the ladies and splashed cold water on her face. Next, she detoured into the supply room, another of her unheralded competencies that of stocking the office with everything from paper clips to desk fans. She retrieved two collapsible cardboard boxes from a pile, knocking over a stack of ledgers in the process. She left the mess on the floor.

Back in her office, Caroline closed the door, opened her desk drawers and piled whatever looked personal or useful into the boxes. Everything else she dumped into the trash can.

From her desktop she slipped into her briefcase the only two framed photos, one of Chloe dressed for the junior prom and another of the two of them in front of a Christmas tree, along with a folder marked *Etheridge-Current.*

Whatever would her boss say, or did he already know? She and Eliot had not spoken in weeks, he having insisted that he'd get down to the office whenever there was something of importance, so as not to have to bother her at such a difficult time. Only once, several weeks ago, when Chloe received an acceptance letter to UC-Davis, (his personal recommendation having doubtless made the difference), she had picked up the phone. Since there was no answer, she wrote him a thank-you note on her fanciest stationery.

But now? She would check on him that very evening, offer to drive up in the coming days.

For the remainder of the day, Caroline went through her calendar, methodically returning calls or setting up meetings between clients and relevant lawyers, and then typed up the notes Jacobson's assistant had left her regarding the property scam. The Worthingtons had not settled the suit for shoddy construction brought against them, but mercifully, they had backed off their threats related to the incident with Chloe.

Further, the team at the Ridgeway firm had maneuvered to have the worst charges against her daughter dropped, the judge handing down a sentence of three months of community service. As a result, the ever-resourceful Kevin had steered Chloe toward a stint at a half-way house for addicts and additional hours at the local women's shelter. "Volunteerism is something colleges look favorably on," he had told the girl. The man could finesse a trick with a teenager, where she herself only ever made a poor hand worse.

Bryson & Tillotson? There were other fish, and other firms in the sea, she told herself. When she clocked out early at 4:45 p.m., on her way to meet Ella for coffee, Caroline forced a smile and held her head high.

A number of shops along State Street were still boarded up, though a growing number had erected signs saying *Opening Again Soon*. Several outdoor cafes had, however, taken over the sidewalks, spreading their tables as far apart as regulations called for and requiring staff to wear masks. As usual, Ella had arrived early and secured a table at the end of a row. She was without a mask, her face meticulously made up, her bouffant do with not a curl out of place. Caroline plopped down opposite, keeping her covering on.

"I know what you're thinking," Ella began. "How is it I have the gall to keep up appearances," she went on, flicking her fingers to draw attention to her face. Caroline gave her a look to indicate she had no intention of passing judgment. Rather, she bent her head to study the menu.

"Okay, I can see you're not at all impressed that I had an injectable not two hours ago and *voilà*, no tell-tale sign. David is a magician, and by the way, his business is booming as never before."

A waiter approached, stood stone-faced, cell phone in hand to take their order. Pinot grigio, crudités to share. A bowl of nuts, too," Ella rattled off. Then under her breath, "To get it out of the way. Less contact, the better."

Caroline nodded, amused by her friend and still grateful that Natalie had proven more supportive of Chloe than she would have imagined, coming over to study with her and Gloria, the three of them finishing out the term with decent marks, doing it all online, notwithstanding. Ella was nothing if not persuasive, as a mother too—a good egg, despite Botox. With no one else nearby, Caroline removed her mask and slipped it into her purse.

"You, however, look as though you've been put through the wringer. Chloe again?" Ella started in.

"No, no. She's toeing the line. And thanks. Natalie helped, not making a big deal about the ceremony. 'It's just a stupid ole diploma, which as soon as we're in college no one will care about,'" she quoted the girl.

Ella rolled her eyes and lit a cigarette. "Down to one a day. I assume you don't mind."

Drinks having arrived, they toasted their daughters' graduation and the likely easing of restrictions for the summer.

"Can't come soon enough," Caroline said.

"So, beyond the trials of motherhood, what's up with you?"

"Good news and bad: I passed the bar, and I got fired. All within the last twenty-four hours."

"That counts as ironic, I believe. What did your boss say? I thought Eliot what's-his-name was something of a mentor or a..." Ella trailed off, drawing a circle with her arm to suggest whatever was in her head about him.

"Not sure if he knows. He's hunkered down at Shell Beach."

Ella looked skeptical. "I thought you two were—"

"Colleagues, Ella. Just colleagues."

"Whatever you say," she replied, not entirely convinced.

"Besides..."

Ella did have a way of getting under Caroline's skin, which meant that she dilly-dallied a couple of days before picking up the phone to call Eliot. For all she knew, he could have taken a trip—to New York City to see his children—but then flying did seem ill-advised. No one at the office had seen him, at least that's what the longtime receptionist had told her when she returned her severance forms on the Friday before Memorial Day. "It's outrageous, Caroline, they let you go. And for that sniveling nincompoop," the receptionist whispered.

"There are worse things," she replied, stoically. In truth, she had principally enjoyed working with Eliot, and that was no longer an option. She smiled, shook a few hands with junior lawyers and assistants on the ground floor, and left the building for the last time.

When she did gear herself up to ring the Sorenson home, the housekeeper answered briskly, as though she were now the office assistant.

"Mariella? It's me, Caroline."

But no, Mr. Etheridge was not at home, either he'd be with Daphne in Oceano or with Ms. Pavonine—somewhere.

Whatever did that mean? Caroline wondered, but adopting the same crisp tone, asked when he might return and be available to speak.

"Hard to say," the housekeeper continued, her tone now more confidential. "Might depend on the hospital."

"I'm lost. What does the hospital have to do with anything?"

"It's poor Mr. Seth. On a ventilator. They don't hold out much hope, says Mr. Etheridge."

Clearly, a lot had transpired in the last two months. Daphne was no longer living in a trailer, Kathleen was back in the picture, and the threesome was apparently trekking back and forth to San Luis Obispo to tend to the patient. She insisted that Mariella take down word-for-word a message for Eliot—: she wanted to be helpful and thus would stop by Sunday afternoon unless she heard differently.

Time to bake. From a pantry full of cookbooks, she pulled out a recipe for her favorite comfort food from childhood and spent her Saturday morning shopping for ingredients for her chocolate mint dessert. A special tip, in her mother's hand, was scribbled in the margin: *don't forget to add rum for flavor and shave chocolate on top*. It made her smile; she followed the advice.

That out of the way, she swung by the women's shelter, delivering a case of Lysol and one of the coffee cakes she had taken out of the freezer. Chloe was on her hands and knees, scrubbing out the commons room. A couple of the women residents, ones who had no other place to retreat to when the pandemic hit, were wiping down the chairs and re-arranging them at discrete distances along the walls. Several others, presumably volunteers like Chloe, were washing the windows.

A retired nurse who ran the place took the cleaning supplies from Caroline and motioned her to the adjacent kitchen to store the coffee cake. "If we had the funds, dear, we'd hire your daughter. A real sugar-pie."

Relieved and gratified, Caroline sliced the cake and slid pieces onto paper plates. "Whenever you want them to take a break, let them have at it. Unfortunately, I've still got errands to run."

On her way out, she stopped in front of Chloe, who quickly got up, wiped her hands on her overalls, and slid her mask down around her neck.

"I'd stay, sweetheart, but unexpected things came up. Think about what you'd like to do on Memorial Day."

"Kevin came by earlier, looking for you. Said we could go to an outdoor concert, up in the hills. Gloria too." Caroline nodded in assent. "Said to call him, about the bar thing. The scores are in."

"Yes, believe it or not, I passed."

"Way to go, Mom. We'll have to celebrate. Kevin too."

During her drive up to Shell Beach, the pie in a round Pyrex dish wedged between her handbag and the *Etheridge-Current* ledger, she tried to focus on what likely awaited. Kevin rang up just as she passed through the town of Santa Maria.

"Bad time?"

"No, no. I can't believe we missed each other earlier. So…?"

"I passed. As I know you did. Champagne is in order."

"Yeah. At some point." After a short pause, she added, striking less upbeat a note, "Anyway."

"Anyway, what?"

"I got fired." Silence. "From the firm, the same day I received my score."

"But I thought you were headed up to see Etheridge, to work on something."

"It's a long story, Kev. Essentially, Eliot got sidelined and I got shafted."

"From the Worthington suit? Because of Chloe?"

"Maybe. Partially."

"So, you're going up there now to…to do what?" he asked, to Caroline's ear in a failed attempt to be off-handed.

"A family issue. And because I haven't had the chance to update him." A pause followed as she pulled out into the fast lane to pass a tractor-trailer.

"Okay," he replied, signaling his reluctant acceptance. Then, regrouping, he went on. "Did Chloe tell you? There's a concert tomorrow that might be fun and not too crowded. If you're free."

"Of course. Call us late morning."

As she pulled up in front of Sorenson House, Caroline noted several cars parked at the curb, none of which she recognized. She tapped the doorbell once, but since the front door was cracked open, she let herself in, following the sound of voices to the side porch. Several guests were gathered around a buffet table, munching sandwiches and speaking in hushed tones. An older couple, both masked, were huddled off to the side with Eliot, who also wore a covering. Kathleen and Daphne were seated on a glider, their face coverings around their necks, sipping cokes, a plate of nuts in front of them.

Right then Mariella appeared, wearing an apron, and unceremoniously relieved Caroline of the Pyrex dish. "The fridge?"

"Ten minutes in the freezer should do it, thanks. Do you need help with anything?"

"Never you mind, Ms. Caroline," she replied. "Poor Mr. Seth is in a bad way, with the virus. Mr. Eliot will be glad to see you."

She spoke loud enough for her boss to hear, Eliot excusing himself from his guests and walking over. He looked fatigued, the lines on his forehead etched deeper, circles under his eyes.

"I apologize, Eliot. I had no idea—"

"It took us all by surprise."

Caroline lowered her gaze in sympathy, wondering how the old man, who rarely went out, caught the disease and whether other ailments made him more susceptible.

"A shame, really," Eliot went on, "since he had so enjoyed the last few months. Ever since Daphne moved into the guesthouse, he has been tireless in fixing up the place. These long-time neighbors of his—(he swerved his head to indicate a group over in the corner)—have been astonished by the transformation in him as well as in the property."

After a few more minutes in which Eliot asked after Chloe, she too having undergone a transformation, Caroline hastened to say. The Worthingtons' threats of a lawsuit, she added, had evaporated into thin air. At that moment Kathleen approached.

"I don't want to interrupt," she began, "but unless you need me tomorrow, Eliot, I'll be at the Lantana." She patted his arm in a gesture at once formal and intimate. Turning to Caroline, she added, "We're planning to open back up—outdoors. And Memorial Day seems a fitting time to start. You're all invited as my guests, your daughter too. Everything remaining status quo, that is," she murmured, glancing back at Eliot.

Once Kathleen moved on to say her goodbyes, Eliot and Caroline stood together stiffly, other conversations here and there filling in the silence. Then business-like, Caroline mentioned that she had the password for the firm's Zoom account, which she would be happy to install. It would allow him to attend meetings remotely. He looked at her quizzically.

"That would be splendid of you," he replied, "though I'm surprised they asked you to do so."

She reddened, not sure what to say. "Actually, they hadn't gotten around to it. I just thought—"

"Typical of Tillotson," he chuckled resignedly. Eliot, she quickly calculated, was indeed out of the loop. Which made it harder for her not to clue him in

"Though now isn't the appropriate moment, as I had not realized what was going on with you. Or with Daphne or Kathleen or your uncle..."

"What is it you're trying to say, Caroline? You're not one to mince words."

"Tillotson terminated me, the very day I came in, with blueberry muffins, to celebrate,"—she shook her head, exasperated for supplying such an irrelevant detail—"that I had passed the bar. And Kevin did too, by the way."

"Why, that's excellent, on both your parts and execrable on Tillotson's," he rejoined, raising his glass and tinkling hers. They both took sips. "And keep in mind," he continued, "I'm getting into the habit of writing recommendations, so if you need one for another law firm, I'd be delighted to assist."

After that exchange and a few more sips, Eliot introduced her around to Seth's neighbors in Oceano and then moved off to attend to the buffet. Caroline soon excused herself and sat down on the glider to eat something near Daphne.

"You don't mind, I hope?"

"Of course not. And this chocolate mint pie, yours? It's delicious. I don't often eat other people's cooking."

"One of my mother's recipes, quintessential comfort food, which, I guess, you need now."

"I adore Seth. He isn't the easiest person but he has a zest for things. And once he took on a project, nothing could stop him. I admire that. Tried to capture it."

"Capture it?"

"My paintings. I've done a series called *Youth and Age*. He is the central figure. Pretty much the only one. Except for my cat."

"So, is the cat *youth* or *age*?"

"Unfortunately, the cat disappeared from Paradise Park while I was in New York. I've had to re-imagine her. But in real life, she was barely more than a kitten when she showed up. Hadn't returned by the time I sold the trailer."

"I see," Caroline commiserated. "And her name?"

"Kahlo. As in Frida Kahlo. *You* would know the name. I didn't until Jared told me."

Puzzled by this last remark, Caroline simply nodded. A strange young woman, Daphne Dupree, though not unlikeable. She couldn't figure why she had previously been so critical.

They chatted for a few more minutes until the remaining visitors departed or went inside. Caroline took the opportunity to tiptoe into Eliot's study, where in ten minutes she installed the Zoom app on his MacBook, leaving him the password on a post-it note alongside the *Etheridge-Current* folder.

Word from the hospital in San Luis Obispo around 8 p.m. was "no change," at which point both Caroline and Daphne took their leave.

"If there's anything I can do, Daphne, you can call me," Caroline thought to say as the younger woman got into her pickup.

"Thanks, Caroline," she replied, turning back around. "It's not what I wanted for Seth. A good man he was. I never..." she trailed off, her lips beginning to quiver.

"He felt the same way, I'm sure. Drive carefully."

Daphne nodded, got in and started up the engine, from what Caroline could make out, wiping away tears before setting off.

Memorial Day dawned sunny and breezy but mother and daughter both slept late. Caroline made an extra-strong brew, sliced the last of the coffee cake for the two of them, and sat down to ruminate, Asta curled up at her feet. After a few sips, her head cleared. To lose a pet is distressing, she thought; to find one you had given up on can be life-affirming, especially if it helps to offset some other loss.

When Chloe came down, she poured another cup and slid the last piece of cake in her direction.

"Thanks, Mom," she murmured, eyeing her mother quizzically. "You look like you have something you want me to do, right?"

"Not a typical chore. I want you to come along to help me—it'll be a challenge."

Chloe looked alarmed. "What is it, Mom? Is it Dad? Or Kevin?"

"No, no. I want you to help me find a cat, if she's findable."

"I'm not even going to ask," Chloe said, rolling her eyes.

They found a carrier case up in the attic and took along a bowl for water and a bag of dry pet food. Despite the traffic, heavier than usual because of the holiday, Caroline made it to the entrance to Paradise Park in less than an hour. She pulled up in front of the office and knocked on the door. The manager regarded her askance.

"I'm a friend of the painter, Miss Dupree. I've come to make one last attempt to find her cat. Can you point me to what was her location?"

The woman, who appeared to be chewing tobacco, cast her eyes toward the Camry. "Dupree in the car with you?"

"That's my daughter. She came along to help."

"It's against the rules, but being as you is here, take a gander. Last trailer before them pine trees. Perkins lives there now. Ain't said nothing to me about no cat."

Before the woman could change her mind, Caroline drove down the dirt road to the end of the row of hitches, the last one being vaguely familiar to her, though the trailer looked more dilapidated, and tall weeds had sprung up around it.

She and Chloe, carrier in hand, got out, took a look around, and approached the door of the trailer. From inside, voices, raised in argument. Caroline knocked anyway. A worn-down woman in a grungy bathrobe soon pried the door open.

She glared at the two interlopers, her hand shading her eyes to block the noon-day sun. "Yeah. What is it?" she asked, none too cordial.

"We're looking for the previous owner's cat, an orange and black calico. We wonder if you've seen her around."

"That scrawny thing?" She jerked her head back around. "Hey, Leroy. People's here for that damn feline. Whatcha-wanna-do?"

After some cursing, a man lumbered up behind the woman in the bathrobe, he too not thrilled with the sun in his eyes. Or anything else seemingly.

"Mr. Perkins. We were hoping you might have seen Miss Dupree's cat. It sounds like you have," Caroline said, not wanting the conversation to devolve into a guessing game.

"And what if I have?" he snipped.

"If you produce her, we're ready to offer you two hundred dollars for your trouble."

The man ran his hand across his mouth, wiping away crumbs. "Don't sound like much to me, if you've come all this way for the thing."

Caroline stood there stone-faced, not budging.

"I'd say five would be more like it," he lobbed back.

Caroline purposefully turned her head to look out toward the sea. Seconds passed. "Well, if the cat means so much to you, so be it," she said in a tone resigned and sarcastic at once. She sighed audibly, smiled at her daughter, and slowly headed back to the car.

"God damn it, Leroy. Give her the cat and be done with it," the woman sputtered, pushing him out of the way and retreating into the trailer.

As she pressed the button to open the driver's side of the Camry, Caroline heard a cry, an animal cry. She turned to see the woman sidestep Perkins, Kahlo in her arms, and make her way toward them. Chloe opened the door of the carrier and set it on the ground next to the car.

"Two hundred bucks and she's yours. Nothing but a nuisance anyway," the woman said.

Reaching in her shoulder bag, Caroline pulled out two loose bills, what she had settled on spending to begin with, and thrust them at the woman. As if on cue, Chloe grabbed the cat by the scruff of the neck and deposited her in the carrier, slamming the cage door. The calico appeared too stunned to object.

Once out of the trailer park and at the first stoplight, Chloe gave her mother a high-five. “That was fun,” the girl declared. “Where to now?”

“We’re going to drop Kahlo off in Oceano. It’s not far and Daphne’s likely there. Then we’ll head home.”

“So, Mom, how did you know that two hundred would do it?”

“I didn’t, but when you were small, your dad and I played a lot of cards. I learned to keep a poker face.” Chloe looked impressed. “Anyway, it was worth it. Having that cat back will make Daphne’s day. Never hurts to do something nice for someone.”

That evening after the Memorial Day concert, the majority of young people mask-less and bunched together, Kevin took the three of them—Caroline, Chloe and Gloria—to dinner at the Fish Exchange in Santa Barbara where they sat outside with plates of fried calamari. He offered a toast to the two graduates (the ceremony held outdoors, though Chloe wasn’t allowed to attend) and to Caroline for orchestrating the capture of the calico. Plus, he wound up telling them, he’d pick up the tab, having just landed a job at a law firm in nearby Montecito.

Finally, a happy day amid so much uncertainty.

CHAPTER THIRTY

Eliot

The Solace of a Sympathetic Ear

That same holiday weekend, Eliot invited Daphne to dinner at the Lantana, but she declined, her voice breathless with excitement.

"You won't believe what has happened. Kahlo has returned! Thanks to Caroline, and her daughter. They convinced that creep to hand her over. She's scrawnier than ever, skittish too, so I can't leave her right now. I just hope Seth will be able—when he gets out—well, you know what I mean. See us all again." Her voice quavered.

"I do, Daphne. Keep the cat indoors for a few days until she's familiar with the place. Okay?"

Putting the phone down, he considered whether it made sense to phone the couple who had stopped by on Saturday to check on Seth's condition. Not only had they lived on the same street for the last forty years, but the husband, also an engineer, had worked with him on various projects, including a bridge over the Russian River. The two wives had been fast friends as well. However, they were elderly. Not likely to want to risk a restaurant, even if outdoors. It would be for another time, once the virus had let up or a vaccine became available.

Who would have ever predicted this scourge, he asked himself, as bewildered as everyone else. Though not Keats. The retriever had padded his way into the parlor. Time for a late-afternoon walk, holiday or not, contagion or not.

Once out on the boulevard, they set off at a brisk pace, Eliot, like the retriever, needing more exercise than he had been getting. Tennis with Bryson or Jacobson was out now that his position at the firm was so—he wasn't sure whether tenuous or nebulous better described it—but whatever it was, it wasn't conducive to a friendly game with either. As for the gym in Pismo Beach, that too was out—closed for the duration. The swimming and the exercise bike had done him good, as had racquetball against Serena.

But no, it wouldn't do to ring her out of the blue to dine out three hours hence. Not at the place that his other lady friend ran. He would make do with leftovers, sending Kathleen a text to wish her luck on the outdoor opening.

On their return leg, Keats spotted another of his friends up ahead. Not Dog but the Great Dane. He tugged on the leash, obliging Eliot to move faster. Fortunately, it was not the Russian walking Pushkin, but a young woman. Unless he erred, the same one he had noticed a month or so ago. The dogs jumped at each other in greeting. The young woman, with short black hair and almond eyes, shrugged as if to suggest she could do little to prevent her charge from expressing himself.

Eliot took a deep breath. "Don't worry. They are acquainted but don't get together as often. As before," he heard himself say. The woman looked at him curiously.

"Well, it's always good to have friends, as many as possible," she replied.

"Are you the dog walker or…" he asked, though not able to pronounce the name that he wished to banish from his memory.

"Not exactly," she said with a laugh. "Especially since he more or less walks me! My father lives down the street. I'm Oksana Mirovich. I live in New York, but things have changed. I guess I don't need to elaborate on that."

"No, you don't," he returned, his mind doing somersaults. *A grown daughter—what did that indicate*?

"And you are…?"

"Eliot. I live over yonder. The Sorenson House, the oldest on the boulevard." He had no idea why he had volunteered that last fact. "Anyway, this is Keats. Two poets—rivals but friends," he added, indicating the two canines, who were now nipping at each other's ears.

"Meaning the actual poets or our two charges?"

"Good question," Eliot replied, narrowing his eyes. "I believe the poets lived at the same time but never met. Keats died tragically young."

"So did Pushkin. A shame, in both cases." Now Oksana tilted her head. "But your name. I've heard it. You know my friend Serena. And thus, Keats would also be acquainted with Dog, right?"

"You have excellent deductive powers," he added, charmed. Despite himself.

Oksana's cheeks flushed at the compliment, such as it was. She gave a tug to Pushkin's leash to signal time was up for the outing. "I must be getting back. Serena is making something special for this evening. I'll tell her I ran into you."

"Please do. I've meant to call, but things have gotten away from me…"

Oksana scrutinized him more closely, the edges of her lips outlining a faint smile. "That's what my dad says when he doesn't get around to phoning me." Eliot nodded but said nothing. "Anyway, nice to meet you. It's a small world out here. Already you look familiar to me."

With that, Oksana turned heel and headed toward Serena's house, Eliot toward his, turning over a lot of different things.

Two weeks later, as coronavirus cases began to creep up again in the wake of crowd-filled Memorial Day celebrations, Seth Sorenson passed away, never having come off a ventilator. Eliot and Kathleen had driven up to the hospital in

San Luis Obispo early that morning, fearing the end was nigh. Not allowed into the ICU, Eliot spoke to him, as soothingly as he could, on the cell phone the nurses had placed next to the patient's ear.

"He might have heard your voice but was too weak to respond," the doctor explained when she came out to inform them. After making arrangements for the transport of the body to the mortuary in Arroyo Grande—Seth would be interred in the family plot, next to his long-dead wife and right behind Silda—they drove back to Shell Beach. To keep busy, they hammered out details for a graveside service during a pandemic.

For a late lunch, Kathleen ladled out some of the chicken casserole she had made the day before, enhanced with green chiles and wild rice, and put the remainder back in her tote to take to Daphne.

Seth's newly installed front door, of sturdy oak, was locked so they walked around to the back yard. On the patio that the old man had built with the old bricks stood Daphne, in front of her easel, a brush in one hand. Concentrated on her canvas. Eliot cleared his throat, loudly.

When she turned, Daphne saw the bad news in their faces. Without a word, she scooped up the sleeping cat and scurried into the guesthouse. Eliot and Kathleen put the paint brushes to soak, moved the easel under the nearby awning, and went inside to see what they could do. Since the bedroom door was shut, Kathleen repaired to the kitchen, heated up the chicken, sliced a loaf of freshly baked bread they had picked up, and made coffee. Eventually, she knocked on Daphne's bedroom door, went in and sat on the bed. The two women talked, Eliot unable to make much out other than a few snatches about how important it was to focus on the positive: Seth's long life and his final months with his newfound friend.

Later, in the kitchen, with all new appliances and a charcoal sketch of the guesthouse hanging on the wall, the three broke bread together, dipping pieces into the stew and toasting Seth with a bottle of chianti.

"However short a time we had, he made me feel special," Daphne said, the food and wine having helped restore her faculties. "I know I don't often make sense, but he didn't mind," she went on. For an instant, Eliot looked flustered, wondering if she meant that as a criticism of him. "The best thing is, he only wanted to spend time with me. Nothing more nor less than that," she added. Purposefully.

They finished the rest of the wine in silence.

Finally, sensing that they had come full circle in their immediate sorrow, Eliot said, "I was thinking we might have '...down to the sea again,' inscribed on his tombstone. I believe John Masefield was his favorite poet."

After a minute or two, Daphne responded, "I think he would like that."

Around 8:30 p.m. after rinsing the dishes and feeding the cat, Eliot and Kathleen encouraged Daphne to take a shower while they went into the main house to retrieve funeral clothes for Seth, along with several Navy medals from his dresser. Not long after, they said their goodbyes, leaving Daphne curled up in bed, Kahlo in her arms, purring.

"Again, I don't know what I would have done without you," Eliot said once back in Pismo, coming around to help Kathleen out of the car. She placed a soft kiss on his forehead and went inside her house at the top of the hill.

CHAPTER THIRTY-ONE

Serena

Out of Sync

The pall did not lift over the summer, the virus having stuck around. Despite the wishful thinking of most everyone.

Ever practical, and now bent on doing whatever to please her unexpected lover, Serena spent inordinate hours online trying to find places that she and Oksana could still visit and activities that they could still enjoy. The dogs helped. Often, they would load up the Infiniti with a picnic basket and the two canines and spend the day on deserted stretches of beach between the Five Cities and Santa Barbara to the south or between the Five Cities and Monterey to the north. Other times, the two would pack boots and head inland to hike and horseback ride.

For Serena, Oksana was a tonic—eager to experience more but without any competitive streak. That Serena could detect. For Oksana, Serena was both the older sister and the mother that she never had—her affection freely bestowed, her generosity unlimited. Nothing withheld that she could discern.

Not that the two women talked much about their mutual attraction, how instantaneous it was, less fraught than their relationships with men.

That she could recall, Serena had only ever had a flirtation with one other female, a fellow lacrosse player at Duke, with whom one night after a tournament and much drink to celebrate, their sweaty bodies had ended up in the same bunk bed. She could not now recall the girl's name, but she could pinpoint her in the photo the year they won the pennant. She had gone into the library one evening and lifted it off the wall to refresh her memory.

Regarding the current liaison, Serena first slept with Oksana on the younger woman's birthday, after an elaborate meal of sea bass, fresh asparagus and arugula salad. (With racquetball on hold, Serena had redoubled efforts to eat healthily, and now had to offset Oksana's predilection for beef stews and creamy pastas.) Still, she compromised, baking a red velvet cake to celebrate the occasion.

Maks had walked over for the meal, a bottle of Georgian wine in hand and a gift in a tiny box for his daughter. At first, he appeared discomfited by the unabashed pleasure the two women took in each other, gaily interrupting each other, but eventually—perhaps it was the wine—he sank his large frame into a chair and relaxed.

After the cake, they removed to the parlor, where Oksana opened her father's gift—an antique locket of rose gold, it having been, he was eager to explain, his own mother's. Inside, blurry photos of the dark-haired, high cheek-boned Russian grandparents she had known as a child. She insisted on putting it on, turning to her father to fasten the clasp.

Stunning, Serena thought, nodding appreciatively. Her gift was a CD of tangos, she deciding not to go overboard and make the young woman feel beholden by any lavishness. Oksana insisted on playing the disc. And they danced, the three of them, in different iterations of twosomes until Maks confessed he had no more moves at his command and looked around for his cell phone.

"I've got to finish up a score. Deadlines, you know. You two…well: continue to enjoy this special evening."

Said, to Serena's ear, without any obvious note of sarcasm, or censure. Oksana nonetheless blushed. She may have had a finer ear.

In any case, it was the first night she did not return to her father's home.

Eventually, the two women fell into a routine, though, as with most couples, one that weighed more heavily on the one rather than the other.

Serena began to devote time to learning Italian and tackling the fancier pasta dishes Oksana favored; the younger woman took to walking the dogs, watering the garden and shopping for herself online, using her friend's password, and occasionally her credit card. Twice a week she conducted her Russian classes at Hunter College via Zoom, for which she presumably was paid. Neither spoke much about the pandemic or what might change when it abated. In the evening, Oksana would often run down to see her father, or take him something they, meaning chiefly Serena, had cooked up.

In those instances, Serena would switch on the news. Some places around the country were enjoying a respite while others were rattled by a surge in infections and deaths. Younger people continued to congregate, without masks, without distancing themselves one from another; millions of workers were laid off or furloughed or required to work from home. Older folks, those most vulnerable to contracting Covid-19, took the most precautions. Hunkering down at home, rarely venturing out except to walk their dogs or risk the grocery store.

As much as she hated to admit it, Serena, now fifty-nine, was on the cusp of the so-called older set, her asthma making her exposure to the virus problematic. At thirty-five, and perfectly healthy, Oksana, she reckoned, would likely be asymptomatic, if she were to catch it. And she very well might. The young woman had become cavalier about the risks, not donning a mask unless prompted, talking right up into people's faces, complete strangers too.

From what Serena could ascertain from these news snippets, the Central Coast was managing better than many regions, worse than others. The usual deluge of tourists had dried up. Lodgings, from Shell Beach at the north end of the Five Cities to Oceano at the southern end, struggled with reduced occupancy; some restaurants called it quits while others converted their operations to curb service or outdoor dining. At one point, Serena caught a glimpse of Kathleen on the TV, going on about the precautions taken to guarantee "a delightful dining experience *al fresco*" at the Lantana.

Despite the sunshine and palm trees, there was an eerie sense of dislocation across the Golden State.

At home too. The affair with Oksana was becoming more ticklish than she had bargained on, the pandemic adding its own complications. The disparity in their ages had never explicitly come up between them, not even the night of Oksana's birthday when such a question might have popped up. Such a gap wouldn't have made Serena bat an eye years ago, but now, the higher slopes of the Sierra Madre made her calves ache, and it was harder to catch her breath.

More often than not, people living in close proximity day in and day out got on each other's nerves, she told herself.

After one tense evening—Serena peeved that Oksana had not touched the fruit salad with gooseberry dressing she had labored over, preferring to fry a steak, divide it into three parts, and share it with the two dogs—they agreed to confer ahead of time if meals were to be shared. Otherwise, their shopping lists would be kept separate.

"It might do us both good," Serena suggested as tactfully as she could, "if we spent less time in the kitchen and more time letting others do the cooking. There's a place called the Lantana. They're seating people outside. It might make a nice change."

When they finally made arrangements to go out for dinner, Serena checked the weather, specifically the direction and intensity of the winds. To make a bad situation worse, fires had broken out across the state and sent smoke, ash and soot first in one direction and then another. It wasn't until the last week of August that their sliver of the coast enjoyed enough of a respite to spend a few hours out-of-doors.

Serena called ahead to book a table for two on a weeknight, though at the last minute Oksana invited her father to come along. The three of them were escorted to a table at the far end of the Lantana's parking lot, about half of the tables already occupied. Once they had ordered—broiled salmon for the ladies, a grilled swordfish for Oksana's father—Serena spotted Eliot coming in with a younger couple.

While Maks talked on about birds that were dying out and how many other species would be lost if we did not do something, her eyes wandered. She saw Kathleen, in a dark suit and lacy black mask, walk over to Eliot's table. There was something intimate about how she positioned her hand along the back of his chair and bent in to hear what he was talking about. After a minute or two, she straightened up, patted Eliot's arm and headed back inside to the kitchen. And still, Maks, undeterred, was going on about hummingbirds and their loss of habitat and how the fires were endangering countless other avians, not to mention—

"So, Papà, do you think we will be next? Sooner or later made extinct, whether we wear a mask or not?" Oksana asked, making a gesture of poof with her fingers.

Maks gave his daughter an indulgent look. "It's her Italian side, Serena, so dramatic, not her no-nonsense Russian side."

"Well, we don't want to end up like the ivory-billed woodpecker, do we?" Serena returned drily. "Shall we drink to the discovery of a vaccine so we can all get back to normal?"

"Excellent," Maks enthused. "And to controlling climate change." He swiveled around to call for more wine.

Their second bottle, an expensive Syrah from nearby Edna Valley, was accompanied by a plate of cheeses and another peroration by Maks on the merits of the Paris Climate Accord. When he paused to try the stilton, Serena motioned for the bill.

"We should split this," he ventured but made no move to do so. She wondered if his latest music commissions were paying off, the going rate not a part of the business she was familiar with.

On their way out, Serena stopped to greet Eliot and his companions. Ever the gentleman lawyer, he scrambled to his feet, blood rushing to his cheeks as he realized who *her* companions were.

"You're looking well, Eliot. You'll remember our neighbor, Maks Mirovich. And this is his daughter, Oksana."

"Yes, we've met. All of us," he stammered, turning then to his own guests. "My daughter, Eleanor Etheridge, and Pierre Pavonine, from San Francisco."

"Lovely to see you both again," Serena replied. "All the way from Manhattan, Eleanor?"

"It couldn't wait, her trip," Pierre stepped in to say. "We're soon to get married. Trying to figure out where to live."

Taken aback, Serena inclined her head. "I had no idea. Congratulations. And have you decided?"

Eleanor and Pierre glanced at each other. "Out here," Eleanor announced. "We're working out the details. My childhood home in Santa Barbara to begin with."

Eliot turned back to Serena. "Pierre is working with an international food program. Eleanor is looking into local law firms."

"You must tell me more at some point." She turned to her companions to signal they should move on. "Enjoy your meal. Ours was excellent. You must let Kathleen know," she added.

"Nearly forgot, Serena," Eliot stopped her. "I had been meaning—I have something to run by you, something you might be interested in doing. May I phone you during the week?"

"Or drop by. Late mornings are good."

In the car for the five-minute ride back to Ocean Boulevard, all three were silent until Oksana piped up. "I thought Eliot's last name was Sorenson, but his daughter's is Etheridge. I know an Etheridge in New York, about her age. A guy. It's not a common name, is it?"

Serena, who was driving, pulled up in front of Maks' house before responding. "The brick house up the street belonged to the family of Eliot's wife, the Sorensons. Most people around here call it that, especially since he never took the sign down."

Oksana still looked puzzled. "What happened to his wife?"

"She passed away. Some eighteen months ago," Maks interjected, sounding as though he wished to curtail the discussion. He worked the handle of the door to extricate himself from the back seat. "Great to get out of the house—with you two. And thank you for treating, Serena. We'll do it again soon—on me," he said, his tone brisk. Without waiting for any response, he banged the car door and walked up the flagstone path to the house.

Both women watched him until he flicked on a light inside.

"My father can be moody. Didn't seem to like Eliot either," Oksana remarked. "They must know each other from the neighborhood, the dogs and all."

Serena hesitated but then declared, with some force, "Your dad knew Eliot's wife, Silda. She had cancer."

In the dim car light, Serena could see a twitch in Oksana's face.

"Explains a lot," the younger woman replied as the engine started up.

CHAPTER THIRTY-TWO

Eliot

Where There's a Will

Shortly before the Labor Day weekend, Eliot arranged a bowl of fresh fruit acquired at the farmers market and set out for Serena's house. There was a whiff of smoke in the air but not enough to impede a brisk outing. Oksana came to the door when he tapped the bell.

"Ah, you did come over. We had wondered if you would. Serena's in the garden and I was about to go online for a Zoom class I teach. Come in, come in."

"Sorry to interrupt. I'll put this bowl in the kitchen and leave you to it," Eliot said.

But instead of stepping to one side, she remained firmly in front of him, a curious look on her face. "Ever since I heard your name, your last name, that is, I've been trying to piece something together."

"I have no idea what you mean…"

"I know a Jared Etheridge in New York. He and I—well, he is a writer and we had lost contact, but I'm sure he had family out this way. He had said as much, more than once."

"Well, I'll be," Eliot murmured, trying to calculate the odds of this connection, she 'the daughter of who she was the daughter of.' So impeccably polished, she was presumably fastidious about her friendships; and his son was nothing if not finicky about the people he frequented.

"Yes, Jared the writer would be my son. You must let him know of the coincidence when you return," he suggested, smiling at her.

"So glad this happened," she responded, gracefully letting him pass to the kitchen, bowl still in hand.

Once outside, Eliot scoured the garden until he spotted Serena, pruning shears in hand, whacking unruly branches from the fruit trees along the back fence. He walked over, clearing his throat a couple of times so as not to startle her. She was wearing a mask, despite no one else being about. He hurried to secure his around his mouth and nose.

"Wish we didn't have to go through this ritual but better safe than sorry," he began. "And I don't want to disturb you except to fill you in on what I mentioned the other night."

"You didn't disturb me, Eliot. I was pondering the imponderable. Like, how there are times when life seems impossibly easy, and others when it seems impossibly hard," she said, standing there, surveying her gardening efforts.

"I couldn't have stated it better," he replied, noting all the branches on the ground, the fruit trees still looking more overgrown than not.

"Enough philosophizing. You're a good reason to take a break," she said, placing the shears in a nearby wheelbarrow and motioning him to follow her. "We could have orange juice or even a screwdriver, if you're so inclined."

"Fruit juice would be fine," he said. "I came to relay a proposal. That you would be perfect for."

"Oh?"

"As you may recall, I teach a course on legal ethics down at UC-Santa Barbara, and with all the upheavals of late—anyway, I noticed an opening on the bulletin board, and a couple of faculty confirmed it. They're in need of an instructor for an introductory film course. On Zoom or in person or both."

Serena gestured toward the large round table with four metal chairs arrayed around it. "I'll only be a minute and you can tell me more."

While waiting, he noticed the familiar inhaler that Serena kept within easy reach. It was propped up against the flowerpot in the center of the table. Nearby was a slender volume, cream-colored and seemingly new. He leaned forward to read the title: *Twenty-One Love Poems* by Adrienne Rich. He had never heard of her.

Within five minutes, Serena returned with a pitcher of orange juice, crackers, a jigger and a bottle of vodka. She lowered her mask, revealing marks across her cheeks and the tip of her nose. He followed her lead. "We don't do this every day, but this is excellent vodka—Maks has it imported from the motherland—you know…they're Russian," she stage-whispered conspiratorially, her eyes shifting back toward the house, presumably to indicate Oksana. "We'll add a tincture. That work?"

"Far be it from me to object." He bided his time until she had doctored the drinks and handed his over. "I did not want to presume, but I did mention to the powers-that-be that I knew someone with extensive Hollywood experience, not to mention an encyclopedic knowledge of movies. They seemed intrigued."

Serena looked both embarrassed and flattered. She took a sip of the juice and bit into a cracker.

"In short, if you are interested, I could email you the application or the names of the department heads," he added.

Serena cocked her head. "My first question would be to ask if *you* enjoy teaching the course you were hired for. Especially now, with all the mixed signals and students who flaunt the rules."

"Actually, the kids have been pretty good at complying with whatever the university requires. Besides, my course was online during the summer. Soon, it'll be back to the classroom. However, I can't speak for you, Serena, but unless something is more amusing than it is onerous, I've been telling myself that it's not worth doing."

"Sage advice," she responded, holding up her drink to mime a toast. He lifted his. "*Zazdarovye*," she said, attempting a Slavic accent.

"Then I will leave it to you to follow up, or not. I have no doubt you would be a great addition to the place."

For a few more minutes, they chatted about the logistics of a socially distanced wedding ceremony and the likelihood that the newlyweds would both be able to find suitable work on the Central Coast. Then, eyeing her new clock, Serena thanked him for the job proposal and accompanied him to the front door. He could hear her breathing, more labored than he remembered.

"Until next time," she said wistfully, holding out her hand. Eliot held it a couple of seconds, the thought crossing his mind that he might never place another kiss on her forehead. Let alone on her lips. He walked home slowly, wondering what the fall would bring. Surely better days.

Since Eleanor changed her mind about traveling back across the country during the Labor Day weekend, Eliot seized the opportunity to have Seth's will read in her presence as well as Daphne's. Three months had passed since the old man's death and no creditors had come out of the woodwork; rather, a few neighbors of Seth's surfaced to say they had received the occasional loan from the deceased over the years. "He might have looked like an old coot, but he was a right generous gentleman, that's the truth," one of them averred, insisting that in Seth's memory he would forthwith write out a check for the outstanding amount of three thousand dollars. Eliot wouldn't hear of it.

On a muggy afternoon in mid-September, he and Eleanor picked up Kathleen atop the hill in Pismo Beach and then swung by Oceano to fetch Daphne. She was in the backyard, holding fourth to a trio of kids seated on stools, distanced from one another, her easel off to one side. They each had a sketchbook in front of them. When she saw the new arrivals, she paused, pen in hand, and waved them forward. "OK, kids.

We'll finish up our picture next Tuesday—and start another. That good?" The children murmured, reluctant to leave. "Now, now. Terry, you walk Caitlin and Allie home. I'll see you again on Tuesday. Don't forget."

The youngsters washed their hands in a sink that Seth must have installed outside the tool shed. Terry then dutifully took the hand of the younger girl, the older one gave Daphne a hug, and the three passed through the yard on the brick pavers and out to the sidewalk.

"We didn't mean to interrupt—nor did we know you were giving art lessons," Eliot began.

"It was their mothers' idea. Sometimes I have six or eight, depending. It gives them something to do besides staring at computer screens all day. For me as well," she said, beaming. Taking off her paint-stained smock, she added, "I'll only be a minute," and headed into the guesthouse. Soon they heard a tap turned on.

Meantime, Eleanor glanced around, taking in the newly spruced up back yard, the renovated guesthouse and the patio area. "I don't recall any of this. But Seth seems to have gone out of his way," she said.

"Something of a collaboration between the two," Eliot explained. "Why don't you take the key and look around the main house. You'll be stunned. Just lock the front door behind you. We'll be out in the car."

Eleanor went in the back way and through the pantry. By the time she came out onto the front porch, Daphne, in a seersucker suit, her hair neatly pinned up, had joined them. Under her arm, she was carrying a rectangular package tied with string.

"Hard to believe. The place has been transformed. It's charming. In New York, it would be—" Eleanor cut herself off, waving her arm.

"Seth had an eye for spatial arrangements," Daphne said, "as well as boundless energy. It's too bad..." she sighed, shaking her head.

Once they pulled up into the parking lot of Madison & Ridgeway in Santa Barbara, all four fumbled around to put on a mask, three of them donning black ones, Kathleen attaching a pale green one that complemented her dress.

"You're too elegant to be taken for one of us,' Eleanor said. "We three look like ghost riders in the sky." They all laughed.

In the conference room, they were joined by Richard Hendricks and a junior partner named Sullivan, in charge of setting up the video call with Jared in New York. "On Face Time, if everything works out," the young man said, fiddling with the pod in the center of the table.

"Before we proceed, I did want to offer my condolences again. Seth was one-of-a-kind. Of the old-school but a good heart and a sharp mind. A Sorenson through and through," Hendricks began.

Eliot sighed, not of a mind to dispute this appraisal. Daphne wiped away a tear. Eleanor and Kathleen inclined their heads in assent.

Leaving aside the legalese, the will boiled down to three items, each surprising.

The property in Oceano, including the main structure in which Seth had lived for sixty-odd years, as well as the guesthouse and all other fixtures on the grounds, were to be deeded to Daphne Dupree. The bulk of the liquid assets, in two separate bank accounts and a few mutual fund investments, were to be equally divided between his great-niece and nephew, Eleanor and Jared Etheridge. When last valued, the total amounted to almost three million dollars, the junior partner chimed in, reading from a separate financial appraisal.

"Did I hear that correctly?" Jared broke in, his face on the screen suggesting disbelief. "We only ever saw him in that navy blue jacket circa 1972," he blurted out. The others exchanged polite smiles.

"There are a few minor cash dispersals to be made," Hendricks specified, "but yes, the money involved is not insubstantial. He did earmark, for example, in item three"—

here the lawyer returned his bespectacled gaze to the document in front of him—"the sum of five thousand dollars to the Veterans of Foreign Wars and a similar amount to the Naval War College in Rhode Island as well as his military paraphernalia, including his Korean War journal."

"A Navy man to the end," Eliot murmured.

"Just two caveats," Hendricks continued, rattling the last page. One, that if Daphne were ever of a mind to sell the house, Eleanor and Jared would have the option to buy her out at list price. And secondly, as he put it in his recent revision, (at this juncture, Hendricks cleared his throat to conjure the voice of the deceased), "If, as seems likely, I don't get around to doing it myself, I implore my executor and any other friends or family to clean up the graves, repair the iron fence around the Sorenson lot, and replace the broken lock on the entrance to the cemetery."

"All things that should have been our doing long ago," Eliot responded.

And finally, the lawyer wound up, again approximating the deceased's voice, "Lest I forget, flowers on the ladies' graves would not be amiss from time to time, I only having ever seen a stranger there, placing birds of paradise around Silda's tombstone."

Silence around the table. No one budged except for Hendricks, who pushed his glasses up and looked from one to the other of his clients. None returned his gaze, so he passed a copy of the will and a fancy ball-point pen over to Eliot for his signature.

While he was so occupied, Kathleen reached for the bottle of mineral water on the tray and poured water into three of the glasses. Eleanor exchanged a look of sibling solidarity with her brother on the video screen but did not speak.

Daphne gulped her entire glass and replaced it on the tray. "I don't know about any of you, but that reading was a roller-coaster—kinda like Seth himself," she said, staring down at the table.

"Intense," Jared added, "even from across the country." After a pause, he added, "And nice to see you, Daphne. You too, Kathleen. I gather there's a wedding in the works out there, virus or no virus."

The tension having begun to dissipate, the lawyer shook everyone's hands and ushered them out. "You know how this works, Eliot. There'll be a few more papers to sign, after which everything should proceed like clockwork."

"Much obliged, Richard. Glad you and Seth remained in contact all these years. And I appreciate your efforts in helping my assistant and her daughter. You'll remember the Morrises?"

"Not only do I remember them: we've hired Caroline. She'll be coming on board at the end of the month."

"Why, why that's splendid."

Back in Eliot's Escalade, Daphne waited until they crossed State Street before speaking. "Since we're here, I wondered, Eliot, if you would stop for a minute at Caroline's place. If it's not out of the way." She picked up her wrapped package and held it in her lap. "To thank her and Chloe for rescuing my cat, I painted a picture of Kahlo in my arms. Something of a self-portrait."

"Why that's lovely of you, Daphne," Kathleen said. "Fine with me if we stop by. How about you two?"

"Not a problem," Eliot said. "Why don't you alert her on my cell, Eleanor?"

When they got there, the first thing they noticed was the aroma of freshly baked bread and the scent of apple in the air.

Coming to the door, Chloe was all smiles. To Eliot, she looked less fragile and more poised. "Mom's baking something new," she said, inviting the three into the hallway. "There may be enough for you to take some, she said."

"We'll only stay a minute. Daphne has something for you—both of you," he said.

"Mom. They need you out here," Chloe called out.

Caroline soon came bursting in, wiping her hands on her apron. The others stepped back toward the front door and let

Daphne hand the package to Chloe. "I did it to thank you for saving my cat. And in a way, saving me. How you managed to wrest her away from that awful man, I'll never know." While she spoke, Chloe untied the string, carefully pulled off the paper, and held up the canvas.

"It's beautiful, Daphne. A marvelous portrait of both of you."

"Cool," said Chloe. "That creep did not deserve to have a pet, that's for sure."

They all laughed, while Caroline hastened back to the kitchen and returned with a loaf of hot bread wrapped in aluminum foil. "To my mind, bread is always best straight out of the oven, and you have a ride to make. So here are napkins and a knife to slice it with in the car."

"Smells like apples," Kathleen said.

"It's apple cider sourdough something or other. Kevin's mother gave me the recipe. He'll be over later if you all can wait. He wanted to tell Chloe goodbye. She'll be headed up to Davis on Sunday."

"So proud of you, Chloe. Coming through everything," Eliot said.

"Thanks again for helping me, Mr. Etheridge. I mean Eliot."

"And we're proud of you too, Caroline. Richard told us about your joining his firm."

"It came as a shock to me—but also a godsend," Caroline replied. "And you were right. Ridgeway is a welcome change from Bryson & Tillotson."

"Mom?" Chloe interjected, dragging out the syllable to indicate there was more for her mother to say. Caroline looked flustered. "Tell 'em all now or I will."

Color rising in her already rosy cheeks, Caroline took a deep breath. "It happened the other day. Kevin and I—we're engaged. Don't know when we'll manage to tie the knot, but hopefully, people will be able to come."

"How serendipitous," Eleanor broke in. "Pierre and I are too. We're planning on a ceremony sooner rather than later."

"That's fabulous," Caroline responded. "Nice to be hearing more good news."

"Amen to that," Kathleen and Eliot both said, in perfect sync.

Back out on the freeway, they drove in silence through the thickening Friday evening traffic.

"I have an idea," Eliot eventually said, slowing to pull into the rest area thirty miles north of Santa Barbara.

Inside the tourist office, they helped themselves to coffee and sat outside on a bench where they divvied up the warm bread and watched the sun go down. Each guarded his or her thoughts, neither Eleanor nor Daphne yet fully realizing how life-changing Seth's will might be, Eliot and Kathleen simply reveling in the September sunset, and the reassuring company of each other.

CHAPTER THIRTY-THREE

Eleanor and Jared

Tying Knots, Undoing Others

Jared had not picked anyone up from the airport since Silda visited seven years earlier when he had dutifully driven out to LaGuardia to meet her in his Pontiac, (which even back then he had secretly hoped someone would steal and he'd receive insurance money to buy something more reliable). Still, the car worked, it was a cinch to park, and the Delta flight was right on time. When Eleanor emerged, she was wearing a black suit with matching mask and Audrey Hepburn sunglasses—so like her, he thought—and pulling a roll-on with computer case atop.

She spotted the car instantly. "You still drive this beat-up thing? I'm doubly impressed you made the trek."

"How was it, El, the flight?"

"Not bad. The middle seats were blocked off, so I propped my head against the window and dozed off," she said, removing her mask and fumbling to turn her phone back on. She stared at the screen, swiped this way and that, and tapped a few keys. Jared pulled out into the fast lane leading toward the 59th St. bridge and shot her a glance. "Pierre, checking to make sure I arrived. And Dad, texting to see if you and I managed to connect."

"So, how did it go? Are you two still going to get married—or are you going to traipse off to Tahiti with your million dollars?"

"I thought I'd leave the traipsing to you, dear brother. So yes, we are planning to do this—outside in the garden, barring the unforeseen. Just the family, such as it is, and a few friends of Pierre's and Kathleen's. Oh, Dad's assistant Caroline and her daughter, Serena, a few neighbors—and even Daphne. After all, Seth found her likable enough to—"

"You don't have to say. An original, if ever there was one."

"Seth or Daphne?"

"Both, now that I think about it."

"Surely, you don't begrudge her the house. I can't imagine she was expecting anything like that. Even we had no idea Seth had more than a nickel to his name."

"Fair enough. My memory of Uncle Seth's was that it was a shambles, quirky like him, with little to recommend it other than the size of the lot."

"That was then. He and Daphne worked their magic and the town, like all the others, has become a destination. It's not Carmel or Newport Beach but prices are way up."

Once he found a parking space on 67th Street, Jared insisted on coming up, bringing along a shopping bag from Zabar's with wine, cheeses and crackers. "Don't get your hopes up, Sis. I'm not setting a precedent, but we did pass go and collect two hundred dollars, metaphorically speaking."

She laughed and led the way inside and up to the 17th floor. While Jared unwrapped the snacks, Eleanor jumped into the shower, soon reappearing in a blue terrycloth robe and matching slippers, her hair pinned high on her head, a few wisps left to dangle.

After uncorking the wine, he looked up and over at his sister. "You look more like mother with every year, and that's a compliment. She'd be happy to see you so."

"Certainly more promising than the last go-round," she retorted, sardonic as ever about her previous marriage. They toasted her engagement and chatted about the logistics, the precise date yet to be determined.

"And what about Dad: has he moved on? I mean, with all those women hovering, I would think..."

Eleanor shrugged. "Hard to say, though I think we can rule out Caroline—however proprietary of him she had seemed, always baking something or other."

"Wouldn't have bothered me," Jared quipped. He had put on a few pounds with so much time spent indoors. She made no comment.

"Point is, she's getting married herself. To that guy who outdid us at charades. Kevin somebody."

"So that leaves...?"

"Not sure, but Dad's keeping busy. Been sidelined, I intuited, by the firm, but he has latched on to consulting work, representing small businesses suffering in the downturn. Not for the money but because it's something worthwhile, and something to enjoy."

"Makes sense. What about Serena? He seemed to be following her lead on things."

"Funny, I ran into her on the boulevard the other day," she replied, something odd in her voice. "She was with another woman—: very Louise Brooks, if you know what I mean."

Jared looked perplexed. "For a lawyer, you do jump to conclusions."

"Well, her hair was severely bobbed and very black. Anyway, it came up about the wedding. Serena stood there expressionless. I'm thinking things have curdled between her and Dad."

They drank most of the bottle of pinot noir, chatting about Jared's intention to spend a couple of months in Shell Beach, "until this plague is over, and we can get back to normal."

"It's never going back to normal, but it is less sad out on the coast, especially during the winter," Eleanor replied. "And you and Dad. It would be good for him, possibly for you too."

"And guess what? I have a small advance to write another book. I may not even have to get a job again—for a while."

"One last toast then: to your literary career, and to poor Uncle Seth. How about it?"

"*Salut.*"

Through October, Eleanor and Kathleen spoke regularly about the wedding preparations, both agreeing that a low-key affair at the Sorenson House was an ideal arrangement. Caught up with managing the distribution of food to community shelters, Pierre acquiesced to whatever the two women came up with. (Like most men, he considered wedding ceremonies a colossal waste of money—like his father, he had catered enough of them—but for the all-important cake, he promptly tasked a fellow chef who had recently been laid off to do the honors.)

Left to make most all the other decisions, Kathleen and Eleanor settled on a Sunday afternoon, Nov. 15, for the ceremony, wedging the happy occasion on the only conceivable weekend between the 2020 presidential election, which would be good and over by then, and people's travel plans for Thanksgiving.

They were wrong on both counts.

The aftermath of the balloting became an ongoing crisis, with President Trump refusing to concede, and the pandemic, far from receding, worsened, with a surge in virus cases and predictions of a dark winter. Scientists and some state officials began calling for more restrictions and pleaded with people not to travel far from home for the holidays. Eleanor's two closest girlfriends in New York both sent regrets; Pierre's best friend in the restaurant business was holed up in Paris, trying to keep his bistro there afloat.

In the end, the only two having to travel any distance for the wedding were the bride and her brother.

Meantime, on the West Coast, Kathleen worked on the niggling details, handling the invitations and the ordering of food and drink, some of which from the Lantana, a few other items from San Francisco. She made a point of keeping Eliot in the loop and involved: "We're leaving it to you to have the garden trimmed up and to line up a minister. And I need your opinion about something else. What do you think about a string quartet?"

"Great idea," he agreed and got on the phone to a company that fielded musicians at ballroom dance events.

Hearing Kathleen's rundown of items ticked off, Eleanor broke in more than once during their calls to apologize.

"This has been fun for me," the older woman countered. "Oh, and one final thing. I spoke to Pierre, and though a proper honeymoon is out of the question, he thought you might like to spend a few days at the Bacara. The bridal suite is available. It's close by and the beaches are deserted. A nice place to...well, you know, be together and alone, at the same time."

"How lovely. We'll let you know as soon as I speak again to Pierre. Jared and I will be flying out on Sunday."

When she hung up, Eleanor made a cup of tea and sat at the kitchen table with her list of things to do, perturbed. The mention of the Bacara had done it. After all, she barely knew the man she was about to marry and could count the occasions they had slept together on one, well, on two hands, depending on how one counted.

Point was, the newlyweds would be discovering from scratch each other's predilections, pet peeves, politics, and everything else. Admittedly, she had known and lived with her first husband for two years before they got married, and a lot of good that did. And it was probably Kathleen's idea, not Pierre's, to spend a few days hidden away in a luxury resort, with little to do but sit in a jacuzzi, walk on the beach and...

She took another sip of the tea and shook her head. Okay, she reasoned to herself: Pierre could make a soufflé rise like no one she knew and he could carry a tune better than most. Was there more to him?

Dismayed that she had no firm answer, Eleanor emptied her cup and glanced at the to-do list. Too long to deal with at such a late hour.

Despite predictions of rain, that third Sunday in November at Sorenson House unfolded in an afternoon of red-gold sumptuousness. The exchange of vows and rings went off without a hitch, food and drink were plentiful, the music inspirational, the flowers on the tables perfectly arranged. Everyone seemed elated to be dressed up and in company. Kathleen had seen fit to supply all the ladies with lacy, cream-colored masks, which complimented Eleanor's gown and did not unduly hinder small talk. A few longtime neighbors of the Sorensons, who insisted on recounting the antics of Eleanor and Jared as youngsters, came over for refreshments, staying, blessedly, only a few minutes. Caroline and Chloe came in their Sunday best and brought along assorted sweets for the newlyweds to take on their honeymoon.

"Restaurants may be closed at that spa. They can't live on love alone," Caroline told Mariella, who discreetly put the tote in the backseat of the limo.

As for Eliot, ramrod-straight in a three-piece suit, he appeared pleased enough to be escorting his daughter yet again to the altar and even more pleased to be seated next to Kathleen during the ritual. Both Jared and Eleanor observed him take her arm when they walked to the buffet table or motion to her to join him in this or that group, including with Dr. Angus Martin, who had long ministered to the Sorenson family.

Within earshot, Eleanor heard the preacher say in his jovial yet barbed way, "My dear Madame Pavonine, you must prevail upon our Eliot to make it to church one of these days. Keep Christmas in mind. Even with the pandemic, we will have music and good cheer afterward. And my sermon will be shorter."

"It is hard to imagine doing anything more enriching, Reverend Martin, especially during a year like this." He had patted her hand as though she were a member of the family, Eleanor thought.

As for Jared, he was stunned when he first spotted Daphne, attired in a flowered dress with long sleeves and a flounce for a hem, something vaguely Spanish about it, her hair in a twist secured with two pink berets.

"I hope you like the dress," she ventured, forestalling any compliment, "since I thought of you in having it made. The blossoms are right out of a painting by Frida Kahlo, one that hangs on the second floor at MoMA. I took pictures of it and had it made here. You don't think it's too loud, do you?" she then asked, shifting tone, back to her uncertain self.

"It becomes you. The new you."

She smiled bashfully and switched gears. "So, your book. It came out. Are you happy about it?"

"They've advanced me to do another one. In fact, I'm likely to stick around here and work on it for a few months."

"Since you brought it up, you can always stay in the guesthouse. It's quiet there. You ought to see the place. Seth did miracles with it."

"I would like that." He took her hand and raised her fingers to his lips.

After the bride and groom were waved off to spend a few days at the Bacara, Eliot, Kathleen and Jared retired to the living room, while Mariella handled the clean-up outside in the garden. They could hear the clatter of chairs being folded and silverware being gathered up. Eliot poured them Cointreau and put on organ music, sonorous and soaring.

"I don't know about you two, but to my mind, this was a lovely affair. At home, elegant but understated, in the company of those that matter most," Eliot declared. "Thanks mostly to you, Kath, things went so smoothly. I don't know what I'd do..." he trailed off, embarrassed in front of his son.

Kathleen nodded sweetly. Eventually, in her gently persuasive voice, she said, "Most importantly, the bride looked radiant, the groom excited. That is all one can hope for on such an occasion, don't you think?"

"Indeed," Jared interposed. "They did seem that." In the dying light from the tall windows, he raised his glass. "A toast to love—however and whenever it befalls us," he declaimed, more exuberantly than necessary.

A couple of days later, Eliot and Kathleen drove to Santa Barbara to inspect the clean-up of the Etheridge home for Eleanor and Pierre, leaving Jared to his own devices. He donned a mask, whistled for Keats and undertook a walkabout. He headed first up to Shell Beach Road, where several shops he had known as a child were now shuttered.

Fortunately, a bakery was open. He bought croissants, one of which he ate on the next leg, which led him and the retriever back down to the far end of Ocean Boulevard. Along the route, other walkers were about, it being another balmy November day. Only masks betrayed any hint of what was going on across the country. "Okay Keats. We can still enjoy the simple pleasures. What do you say?" Jared intoned aloud and picked up his pace.

By the time they neared Eldwayen Park, they were both winded. Jared looked around for an empty bench but saw none. However, just one person, a young woman, occupied the one closest to the cliff, a funny-looking dog at her feet. He led Keats over.

"If I didn't know better, I'd say these two know each other," he commented, seating himself at the other end, not quite six feet away. The young woman looked up from her book. It was a slender volume, like poetry or something, Jared surmised.

Hearing his voice, she did a double-take. Despite the masks, the intruder upon her space was recognizable.

"Jared? Jared Etheridge? I never dreamed this would happen."

He looked her way, befuddled. "I'm sorry. Do I know you?"

"Yes, it's me. Oksana Mirovich, from New York." To prove it, she put her book down and stood up, unlatching her mask.

Dumbfounded, he lowered his mask as well. But still couldn't speak.

"I found out that your family lived here. And there was to be a wedding. But I never—"

"How is that possible? I don't think we ever—"

Then he heard her laugh, infectious. She was a lovely girl—complicated but lovely. Even now, with the marks of the face mask across the bridge of her nose and no make-up.

"I'm visiting my father—he lives across the street," she pointed down the boulevard. "But I'm actually staying with—well, a friend of his. A neighbor. They cook together sometimes. So do I in fact, with him, and with her."

From there the two went on for a good thirty minutes about where their lives had led them. "Wow. That you actually finished writing that book. That's marvelous. Topsy-turvy for me, though. Because of the virus, turmoil at the U.N. Since all the bigwigs scurried home to their countries, I got furloughed. But teaching at Hunter, and doing it remotely, so that when my father invited me out, I thought why not. Oh, and I forgot: turns out the neighbor I mentioned, Serena Samuels, also knows your dad."

Jared appeared newly flabbergasted, shaking his head in disbelief.

"You're right," Oksana went on. "If this were a novel, no one would believe it. All the ironies."

"*All* the ironies?" he lobbed back.

She closed her eyes to distill her reply. "My father, it turns out, knew your mother."

He looked dubious. "Why do you say that?"

"For one thing, she played his Bösendorfer, not something he'd allow just anyone to do."

"That sounds...ominous, or illicit."

She laughed again, not at him, but at his confusion. She was an effortlessly engaging person. How was it that things with her petered out without so much as a fare-the-well?

"His piano, silly. I was flipping through some music. Mozart. He had scrawled across the top of the "Fantasy in C Minor": *Silda plays this divinely, hardly tapping the pedal.*"

At this revelation, Jared stared out to sea in consternation, the veins in his forehead prominent. Oksana's eyes followed his. A flock of seagulls was making loops in the sky, a few peeling off to alight on the craggy outcroppings offshore. She waited a few moments and changed the key. "Anyway, you and I are New Yorkers. Things are different here. Sooner or later, people know one another. And I gather the Sorensons have been here for eons."

Jared slowly mulled all this over, his gaze still fixed on the horizon. "My great grandfather built the house not long after the gold rush. So, yeah, they've been here quite a spell."

The two then moved on to other topics, like where they'd want to travel once the pandemic was over. And so forth. More gaily. Without taking heed of anything around them. The sound of the waves lapping against the rocks provided a perfect backdrop.

Until they heard the screech of tires. And then car doors slamming, voices crying out. A few passers-by or dog walkers rushing out to the street. The creature at Oksana's feet no longer there.

Of a sudden, she bolted, her book abandoned on the bench. Jared followed.

The driver and a passenger were huddled over the poor animal, bloodied and inert. Oksana bent down, wailing in dismay. Several bystanders offered to help but there was none to give. The dazed driver of the SUV searched in the back for a blanket and came back around with a beach towel. He wrapped the dog in it and asked where he should take the crushed body.

Sobbing now, Oksana pointed across and down the street. "The third house. The one with the rocks in the front. Just put him on the ground next to the stone bench."

"Why don't I carry him, Oksana," Jared offered. It was not a question.

"Yes, yes. You do it. She'll be furious with me."

"We're so sorry," the driver said, wringing his hands. "We were backing up to park, didn't see him. He didn't move out of the way."

Oksana did not seem to hear or care.

When they got to Serena's front yard, Jared laid the dog down carefully, covered except for his head. Agitated, Keats began to whimper over the body and had to be pulled away.

"I know Serena too, Oksana. We'll simply have to explain what happened."

"You don't understand, Jared." She looked distraught, sufficient to deter him.

"I'll wait out here. Go inside if you think best."

A few minutes later, he heard raised voices, one of them angry. Shortly thereafter, Serena, her face taut, and mask-less, came out of the house and strode toward the heap on the ground. She stared and bit her lip. Not knowing what to say, Jared waited for her to speak. "She let this happen?" she asked between clenched teeth.

"I am so sorry, Serena. We were talking and did not notice that the dog had wandered away. It must have been instantaneous, the wheels backing over him. At least that…" he trailed off.

If Serena took all this in, it didn't calm her. She began to cough and rummaged in her pocket for a handkerchief. Jared remained frozen in place, relieved to have his mask on. Oksana meanwhile had crept out onto the front porch but did not venture further.

After a minute or two, Serena looked up and back at the house. She glared at Oksana, shaking her head from side to side.

Not likely an emotion caused by a mere neighbor, Jared thought. Serena, as well as Oksana, would seem to be a complicated person.

"If you don't mind, please carry Dog to the back yard and place him under the mimosa. His favorite tree. I'll bury him there," Serena said, and without waiting for a reaction, she headed back to the house, passing Oksana on the porch without a word.

Once Jared had placed the dog—Dog, yes, *that* was the name of the hound—he considered trying to referee between the two women but concluded he might make things worse. With no further sign of either woman, he took Keats home, gave him a handful of dog biscuits, and sat on the sofa stroking his back. He would wait for his father, and Kathleen, to figure out what to do. If anything.

Soon enough he fell asleep. So deeply, Eliot and Kathleen startled him upon re-entry, flicking on a light, not expecting to find him curled up with the dog. The two had decided to grab dinner in Santa Barbara before returning. "Are you alright, Jared? It's 9:00 at night."

"Dog is dead," the first thing out of his mouth.

"What dog?" Kathleen asked, noting it certainly wasn't the very much alive Keats.

"Serena's. Got run over. We were chatting in Eldwayen Park and didn't notice when he trotted out to the curb. An SUV backed over him."

"You and Serena?" Eliot asked. Surprised.

"No. no. That's the strangest part. Oksana Mirovich. She was sitting there reading and I sat down, with Keats, and—you're not going to believe this—but we know each other. From New York. She's the girl I had told you about—a translator, for the UN. I was doing a story during the General Assembly, and we met. Anyway," Jared went on, realizing the explanation was disjointed at best.

"What did you do with the poor dog?" Kathleen asked.

"We took it back to Serena's and she was—how can I put this?—livid. Mainly at Oksana."

Eliot sat down across from Jared. After a minute or two, Kathleen suggested tea for the three of them and a sandwich for Jared. While she was in the kitchen, Eliot attempted a recap. "Let me get this straight. This Oksana, whom I met not long ago, is the woman you were dating back in New York. Did she know you were here?"

"We had drifted apart. She came out here to visit her father when one of her jobs fell through. I think she found out inadvertently, from Serena or Mr. Mirovich, that you were an Etheridge and she put two and two together. But she didn't have a clue that I was out here at Shell Beach. Or that Eleanor's wedding had taken place."

Eliot shook his head, trying to absorb what his son was saying, as disconcerting as it was. "So then…" he continued, trying to recreate the scene. "You two were catching up and the dogs just—"

"Something like that, except that I was holding Keats' leash. Oksana had a book in her hand, and I think she had let the leash drop. I didn't focus on it—Dog mostly sleeps wherever he is, right? We didn't notice his absence until we heard the racket. Tourists, from Oregon. They too were upset. Wanted to pay Serena. But you can imagine. She was insulted as well as devastated."

Over cups of pomegranate tea and a few remaining wedding cookies, the three discussed what to do, a suggestion from Kathleen ultimately prevailing. They would the next afternoon take Serena some wedding cake and provided the print shop in Pismo Beach were open, purchase a plaque on which to have Dog's dates engraved. "Is that going overboard?" she asked the two of them. "Pets, you know, can mean a lot, especially if one lives on one's own."

If not enthusiastic (for their different reasons), neither Eliot nor Jared demurred.

Without calling ahead, the three, masked and somber-faced, rang Serena's doorbell around 5 p.m. the next afternoon, figuring it was too late to be gardening but too early to be dining. They were about to give up when the heavy door creaked open. Serena, all in black. Her face was made up but her eyes were puffy.

"Oh, I was expecting—" Serena let out but quickly regrouped. "Hello, Eliot. Jared, Kathleen." She sounded deflated.

"We wanted to say how sorry we are about Dog," Eliot rushed out, hoping to forestall anything unpleasant Serena might say. "And thought you might wish to put a plaque on his grave. Such a memorable dog and friend to Keats," he wound up, pulling an expensive-looking copper plate out of a bag. You just have to tell us what you want engraved thereon and it'll be done."

It was unclear if all this registered.

"There's a place in Pismo that does this work. Fortunately, they are open and can oblige within a day or so," Kathleen added.

Still holding onto the door frame with one hand, Serena reached out to run her other over the copper plate. "Thank you," she said, nodding her head. "I'll think it over—what I'd like it to say—and call you, Eliot. If that's all right."

"Of course. And if you need anything else, let us know."

"Also," Kathleen hastened to add, rummaging in her bag, "Eleanor and my stepson—you remember Pierre—did indeed get married the other day. They wanted you to have some wedding cake."

Serena looked discombobulated. "Yes, well, I wasn't feeling myself that day." She paused but then resumed. "So much easier when one is young," she volunteered, *à propos* of what exactly none of them was sure.

With that as enough of a cue, Jared spoke up in defense of the young, Oksana in particular. "I did want you to know, Serena, that we were so involved in catching up, we failed to notice—*I* failed to notice—that Dog had wandered off. I feel terrible about it. As, needless to say, does Oksana."

For a moment, Serena scrutinized his face, the part not covered by a mask. Then she bowed her head in weary resignation. “Well, it is what it is.” That settled, as banal as the phrase was, she reached out to relieve Kathleen of the cake. “Thank you for coming over, and for your thoughtfulness,” she wrapped up. She then stepped back into the house and closed the door.

The three stood there on the porch, no one speaking.

“If it had been Keats, I probably would have been similarly upset,” Eliot soon declared. “We did what we could.” The other two shook their heads in agreement. “Shall we go?”

As they exited Serena’s front gate, another person, his face ashy gray in the shadows, approached, carrying an outsize tote bag. Clearly heavy.

“Looks like Serena’s dog had quite a few friends,” the man ventured. “How is she feeling would you say?”

Kathleen sensed Eliot stiffen and immediately knew who the visitor was. “She’s broken up about it but managing. My name’s Kathleen and this is Jared, Eliot’s son.”

“Yes, I sense the resemblance, even under a streetlamp. But I can’t shake hands because of the soup.”

“That’s alright,” Jared said. “It smells good.”

“It was my wife’s family recipe—a hearty sausage and pasta concoction. My Italian in-laws swore no sorrow could endure if one spooned enough of it.”

“And were they right?” Eliot asked, a note of challenge in his voice.

Musician that he was, Maks likely picked up on the note. After a pause, he replied, his tone rueful. “No, they were not right. But if someone brings you soup, it usually helps. Perhaps it will her.” He then inclined his head and slipped past the threesome toward Serena’s front door.

On the way back to Sorenson House, Kathleen and Eliot walked slowly arm-in-arm, Jared at his father’s shoulder, silent, puzzling over things. Love, for example: how hard it is to ever know another’s heart but how important it is to try.

So much food for thought. To be shared though. That was the crucial thing.

EPILOGUE

Of the things that had stymied Eliot for so long, several had of their own accord worked themselves out by the beginning of the new year—one that the world augured would be less devastating than 2020.

To his astonishment, the idea of Maks Mirovich and Silda no longer made him bristle—their relationship, whatever it amounted to—did not involve him and had not noticeably impinged on his marriage. No more, say, than his sporadic encounters with Issie had done. (Thus he decided to believe.) Assigning blame was a game he had grown weary of.

As for his shabby treatment by the firm, he no longer lay in bed plotting to sue the partners or to badmouth them publicly. Once freed from their routines and their entitled clientele, he tentatively began to spread his wings. Ashamed though he was to admit it, he had heretofore never thought much about rolling up his sleeves to help those less fortunate.

Yet now, the opportunities to make a difference in the world appeared countless.

Shortly after Pierre and Eleanor settled into the house in Santa Barbara, his son-in-law rang up with a proposal.

Mightn't he, "with all due respect to your illustrious career, Eliot," consider lending his legal expertise to the disparate organizations which had banded together to feed the hungry? Mightn't he, even, take a look at a proposal to lobby incoming president Joe Biden to consider authorizing a cabinet-level secretary of food? "It's not that far-fetched an idea. We have to start somewhere," Pierre had argued.

Not long after, Kathleen described to Eliot the bars and restaurants that were bearing the brunt of pandemic restrictions and were suffering disproportionately. Mightn't he consider joining the team that would be representing their case to the powers-that-be in Sacramento?

In short, the Pavonines were eager to tap into his knowledge and have him play a key role in these undertakings.

"Yes and yes. Whatever I can do," he heard himself say.

If those new challenges weren't enough to re-energize him, Eliot now had his daughter and son-in-law in proximity, Eleanor soon announcing she was pregnant. He was over the moon. Jared too had delayed his return to New York, and once ensconced in the upstairs study of Sorenson House, set about drafting his next novel—at least when he wasn't taking walks with Oksana or having her over to cook up one of her specialties.

At first, Eliot steered clear of the two but the smells from the kitchen, not to mention their banter, soon broke down his defenses. The young woman was delightful, and Jared's perennial sourness had been replaced by enthusiasm for just about everything. He walked the dog, he puttered around in the garden, he recommended novels for his father to read.

With new professional challenges and expanded relationships with his two children, Eliot found himself with less time and energy to dwell on his own disappointments or to wallow in self-pity.

Now when he lay awake at night, he did not obsess about the slights he had endured or angst over his failings. Instead, in being no longer impervious to or oblivious of the needs of those close to him, he had taken up their aspirations and struggles as concerns of his own.

If it could be said he was now back in the circle of life, that recommitment had all to do with the women whom he had, at first tentatively but finally more whole-heartedly, let into his life. Just as Silda had wished for him.

In their attentions to him, most vividly the presentation of food to nourish body and soul, he had arguably been dissuaded of his worst impulses. He did not deserve the constancy of any of them, of that he was convinced.

But after what could only be described as an *annus horribilis*, they too needed to get on with their lives. No one needed to be kept dangling. They had all figured that out, the still-ongoing pandemic making the case more stark. Life was fragile, one had to seize one's opportunities where and when one could.

Not only did Eliot come to think that way, but so too had Serena, and Daphne, and Caroline, and Issie.

From their different perspectives, he could be judged as having been indecisive, or dithering, or dismissive of any notion of settling down again. And thus, one by one they had disengaged. With him, they each in their own way determined to remain friends, but no longer would they cook with any calculation, if ever they had.

So he came to believe. (After all, he was a man, by definition clueless as to what women want.)

In Daphne's case, it was Art with a capital *A* that mattered most to her. In creating it, she was her happiest and best self. If men had always, like bees, buzzed around her, they were always secondary, and often annoying. If Eliot had for a brief moment allowed himself to imagine her as a partner, he could now admit that that fantasy—of being younger and less intolerant—had vanished. "Into thin air," he murmured, wondering how he could have ever been so deluded as to think otherwise. But now, with an inviting place to live for as long as she cared to, she was turning the guesthouse into a proper studio, Kathleen having upturned several additional clients for her, well-heeled ones, up in San Francisco. She was painting and prospering from it.

However much Serena was his intellectual equal, she and Eliot had never managed to feel comfortable with each other, or to let down their guards one with the other. And that was without even considering the detour that she had taken with Oksana. Perhaps they would have gotten around to talking about it all, but in February 2021, after a trip to Los Angeles to visit friends, Serena contracted the virus, her case severe enough to require hospitalization, San Luis Obispo being the closest facility with ventilators and personnel to operate them.

Both Maks and Eliot did what they could for her. The former took hearty stews to the nurses on call, cajoling them to let him into the patient's room, ever so briefly, and even corralled a few colleagues to perform music outside the Covid-19 wing on weekends. The latter rode herd on her portion of the Worthington cash settlement and oversaw workmen around her house to repair the damaged foundations. The two men even managed to speak to each other on one occasion, each grateful that the other was doing what could be done to help their mutual friend.

Once recovered and back at home, Serena had called Eliot to say the long-delayed interview at UC-SB had gone "surprisingly well," so much so that she was hired to begin teaching in the late spring of 2021 when most pandemic restrictions would have lifted. And he came to find out, she had also rung Maks, not only to thank him but to relay a message to Oksana: *I have adopted a rescue, a terrier whom I've named Columbo. Dog rests in peace under the mimosa. No need for you to further fret about what happened.*

Others too that Eliot had in different ways taken for granted or ridden roughshod over found their footing in the new year.

However many things big and small Caroline had done for her boss outside her job description, and whatever her motives might earlier have been for so doing, she had righted herself and found new purpose. He could not but agree that the solid, solicitous Kevin would make an ideal "partner in crime" for his former assistant. He smiled to think of the two arguing points of law over her coffee cake or his buttermilk biscuits, Chloe deftly (but sweetly) playing them off against each other. Theirs was going to be a happy family.

All these women would remain in his thoughts, and presumably he in theirs—they might even occasionally come over with a casserole—but ulterior motives would no longer have spiced the dishes.

And then there was Issie. Of all his lady friends, she was arguably the most wronged, having been strung along for decades. Whenever they got together, Eliot assumed they were perfectly in sync, comfortable with each other, even in bed, even as they aged. But if he had spared a thought for Issie only from time to time, she had let on that night at Avila Beach that he had colored her thoughts on a daily basis. (Speechless at this admission, Eliot had poured her more wine and feigned interest in the tourist brochures on the hotel nightstand.) In that moment—noting that nothing, ironically, had shifted in their relations even though he was now *sans* Silda—she read the writing the wall. And eventually added a piquant coda to their affair.

An unexpected postcard in her unmistakable hand arrived in May of 2021, right as the vaccines began to make a dent in the contagion. It was addressed not to the law firm but to Sorenson House, the picture that of a Big Apple, but with a bite taken out of it.

"So Issie," he murmured aloud, before flipping it over to read what she had scribbled.

Eliot, the casseroles in your freezer inspired me to take a culinary course. On Zoom, of all things. Who else was in the class but someone I hadn't thought of in four decades until you mentioned him last New Year's. Philip Baxter did become a successful architect but is now divorced. And still needing to eat. We bonded over béchamel and will marry as soon as the cooking class, or the pandemic, ends: whichever comes first! Until, Issie

Poetic justice, he had to acknowledge.

That spring evening, Eliot stretched out his long legs until they touched the footboard and lengthened his arms directly over his head. For the first time in ages, he felt no aches, no pain and no anguish. A sliver of the moon cut across the bed and reflected his wedding band off the ceiling. "Silda," he whispered, trying to recall what she had said exactly—something about the lovely ladies who might come calling.

She was right about them, and he decided that she would be content that it were so. He twisted the ring off and placed it on the night table.

After flicking off the light, Eliot turned his thoughts to the one woman whom he could not categorize or pigeonhole. However circuitously it had come to be, it was Kathleen who made his heart leap up. He was reminded of the old song he and Silda had danced to, "The Very Thought of You," and to which he might do so again. The tune had been playing in his head for some time, though when he had started to parse the words, he could not say.

But he would hopefully see Kathleen in the morrow, and together they would move forward—Pierre and Eleanor were expecting, Jared and Oksana were engaged—so, as he planned to put it to her, "Whatever the current state of the world, why should we not emulate the young?"

Acknowledgements

With each successive novel I have more people to thank for their encouragement, expertise and/or insights. Whether at the planning stages, during the writing process, or in the editing phase, these folks weighed in on my progress. In this regard I owe gratitude to Kenith Trodd, Judi Dickerson, Giovanni Troianiello, Wendy Oberman, Patricia Frith, Marlene Edmunds, Gordon Cotton, Linda Parker, Pam Mayfield and Eileen Everage.

Likewise, family members and close friends—all accomplished cooks—kindly supplied me with recipes to spice up the dishes sprinkled throughout the chapters: my sisters Mary D. Corkern and Sally Gray, sisters-in-law Linda Higgins Guider, Beth Harris Guider and Bernadette Morgera Guider, childhood friend Dannie Compton and Los Angeles friend Neil Gader.

Also, because the setting became a character in its own right, I am indebted to acquaintances on the Central Coast of California. It was observing the rituals of daily life along Ocean Boulevard in Shell Beach and environs that helped structure the novel.

Finally, my heartfelt appreciation to my publisher, Foundations Books, my editor Steve Soderquist, and cover designer Dawné Dominique.

About the Author

Elizabeth Guider

Elizabeth Guider is a longtime entertainment journalist and more recently a novelist who has lived and worked in Rome, Paris, and London as well as in New York and Los Angeles. Born in the American South, she holds a doctorate in Renaissance Studies from New York University.

During the late 1970s she was based in Rome where she taught English and American literature at the university level and where much of the action of her first novel, T*he Passionate Palazzo*, takes place.

While in Europe she worked as an editor for the *International Daily News* in Rome, a freelancer for several magazines and as an entertainment reporter for the showbiz newspaper *Variety.*

She also traveled widely, reporting on the politics and technological changes affecting media from Eastern Europe to Hong Kong as well as covering film events and media trade shows in Cannes, Monte Carlo, Venice, Milan, Moscow, and Berlin. She also served on festival juries, the International Emmys judging committee in NYC, and the Peabody Board, based in Athens, GA. Over the years she has moderated a number of industry-sponsored panels with entertainment executives, both stateside and abroad, and won several media awards while working for the trade papers in Hollywood.

After moving back to the United States in the 1990s, she specialized on the burgeoning TV industry and eventually held top editor positions at *Variety* and latterly at *The Hollywood Reporter*, including executive editor at *Variety* and editor-in-chief at *THR*. Most recently, she has freelanced for the magazine *World Screen* as senior contributing editor.

Elizabeth divides her time between Los Angeles, where she freelances, and Vicksburg, Mississippi, where she grew up and where she focuses on her fiction. Her second novel, *Milk and Honey on the Other Side*, an inter-racial love story in the post-WWI period, is set largely in Vicksburg. Her third novel, *Connections*, a family saga that spans fifty years, takes the reader from Atlanta to New York City and Hollywood, and eventually to South America. Her fourth, *Our Long Love's Day*, is an unflinching yet sympathetic look at a divorce between two academics who struggle to pick up the pieces and find new meaning in their lives. *The Casserole Courtship* is her fifth novel.

Follow Me Here:
Facebook – www.facebook.com/elizabeth.guider.79
Twitter – @GuiderElizabeth

f

More from Elizabeth Guider
With Foundations

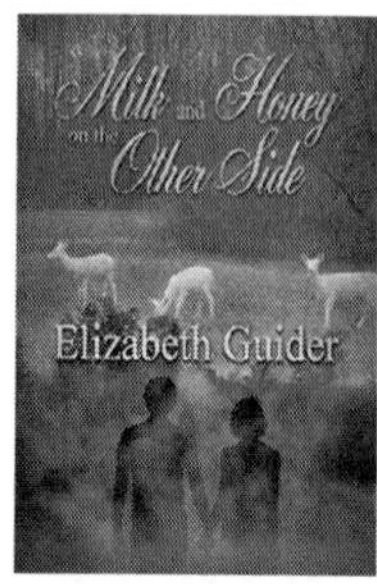

Milk and Honey on the Other Side

Connections

Our Long Love's Day

h

More from Foundations

www.FoundationsBooks.net

A Seaside Story by C.J. Foster

Love or money? Kate Toscano's life is upended when her sister Cassy is killed in a car accident. This jet-setting writer for a trendy Las Vegas magazine, is now the guardian of her five-year-old, autistic nephew, Jimmy. She's forced to move back home. Kate's mother, Lydia, is skeptical about bringing a young, special needs child into her well-structured and organized home in Avalon Bay. Sparks reignite for Kate when she runs into John Neal, her old high school flame. Is it too late for her? It appears John may already be in another relationship. Not everyone is accepting of Kate's new charge. Kate must make a decision: Choose security or take a bold chance on an uncertain future.

Marooned by Louise Jane Watson

A celebrity, a homely artist, and a cat are shipwrecked on a deserted island...what could go wrong?